CESARE

PRAISE FOR *CESARE*

'Charyn's blunt, brilliantly crafted prose bubbles with the pleasure of nailing life to the page in just the right words. Cesare is by no means lightweight fare, but it's provocative, stimulating and deeply satisfying' – *Washington Post*

'A breakneck adventure… it's a dark art to make a subject this grotesque quite this much fun' – *Wall Street Journal*

'Spectacular… this extraordinary tour de force showcases Charyn at the top of his game' – *Publishers Weekly* (**Starred review**)

'[An] edgy, hallucinatory, full-throttle fable' – *Kirkus* (**Starred review**)

'Darkly resonant… a convention-upturning tour de force' –*Washington Independent Review of Books*

'Charyn's taut story line is full of surreal visuals and elaborate illusions' – *Booklist*

'A complex and detailed story of the inner workings of the German Third Reich during World War II… Highly recommended' – *Library Journal*

'Charyn has created a terrific cast of original characters who speak in a language that reflects the selfish and predatory nature of that time… He tells a fascinating story of resistance against evil with a great deal of energy' – *Historical Novels Review*

Also by
Jerome Charyn
(most recent titles)

*The Perilous Adventures of the Cowboy King:
A Novel of Teddy Roosevelt and His Times*

In the Shadow of King Saul: Essays on Silence and Song

Jerzy: A Novel

A Loaded Gun: Emily Dickinson for the 21st Century

Bitter Bronx: Thirteen Stories

I Am Abraham: A Novel of Lincoln and the Civil War

Joe DiMaggio: The Long Vigil

The Secret Life of Emily Dickinson

Johnny One-Eye: A Tale of the American Revolution

CESARE

JEROME CHARYN

NO EXIT PRESS

First published in the UK in 2020 by No Exit Press,
an imprint of Oldcastle Books Ltd,
Harpenden, UK
noexit.co.uk

ISBN
978-0-85730-437-7 (print)
978-0-85730-438-4 (ebook)

2 4 6 8 10 9 7 5 3 1

Typeset in 11 on 15pt Adobe Garamond
by Avocet Typeset, Bideford, Devon, EX39 2BP
Printed and bound in Great Britain by Clays Ltd, Elcograf S.p.A.

For more information about Crime Fiction go to @crimetimeuk

It does not seem to me, Austerlitz added, that we understand the laws governing the return of the past, but I feel more and more as if time did not exist at all, only various spaces interlocking according to the rules of a higher form of stereometry, between which the living and the dead can move back and forth as they like, and the longer I think about it the more it seems to me that we who are still alive are unreal in the eyes of the dead, that only occasionally, in certain lights and atmospheric conditions, do we appear in their field of vision.

— W. G. Sebald, *Austerlitz*

Contents

Dramatis Personae

PRINCIPAL CHARACTERS

Erik Holdermann, a member of German military intelligence; he's also known as Cesare the somnambulist, or the magician

Admiral Wilhelm Canaris, chief of German military intelligence; he's also known as Uncle Willi, or the Old Man, and sometimes as Dr Caligari

Lisa Valentiner, the daughter of Baron von Hecht; she's also known as Lisalein and will later be known as the baroness, or the *Frau Kommandant*

SECONDARY CHARACTERS

Baron Wilfrid von Hecht, a German Jewish baron and industrialist

Emil von Hecht, the baron's nephew, also known as the little baron

Fanni Grünspan, a Jewish *Greifer*, or grabber, who works for the Gestapo

Colonel Joachim, a member of the Leibstandarte SS Adolf Hitler, the Führer's bodyguard corps, who will later be commandant of Theresienstadt ghetto and concentration camp

Commander Helmut Stolz, a member of German military intelligence who is the head of his own espionage group, Aktion

Franz Müller, a member of Stolz's Aktion group; he's also known as the acrobat

Fränze Müller, Franz's twin sister, also a member of Aktion

Benhard Beck, the cabaret king of Berlin, who ends up at Theresienstadt; he's also known as Mackie Messer, or Mack the Knife

Veronika, a little girl

Heinrich Percyval Albrecht, Erik's uncle, an aristocratic Bavarian farmer

Eva Canaris, Admiral Canaris' daughter

Werner Wolfe, a member of American naval intelligence

Tilli, a gun girl who is in charge of her own anti-aircraft battery

Josef Valentiner, Lisa's husband, a Nazi minister

Kapitän Peter Kleist, a submarine commander

Fräulein Sissi, a prostitute out of Erik's past

The Grand Mufti of Jerusalem

Frau Hedda Adlon, mistress of the Adlon Hotel

Pola Negri, a silent film star who once lived at the Adlon

Herr Winterdorf, known as Fritz, a Nazi barber at the Adlon

Little Sister, Colonel Joachim's adjutant at Theresienstadt

Ännchen, a retarded girl at Theresienstadt

Glossary of German Terms

Abwehr, German military intelligence

Aktion, an activity, or undertaking; Aktion is also the name of Erik's group within the Abwehr

Das Kabinett des Dr Caligari (1920), a German expressionist film about a mad magician, Caligari, and his somnambulist slave, Cesare (Conrad Veidt), who sleeps in a coffinlike *Kabinett* and murders people in a tiny mountain village while he's in a dream state

Das Schwarze Korps, *Black Corps*, the weekly journal of the SS

Die Blutige Rose, the Bloody Rose, in reference to Rosa Luxemburg, who helped lead the Spartakus Uprising in late December 1918, during which the Spartacists took over Berlin for several days

Dreckshunde, literally shit-hounds

Fabrikaktion, literally factory raid; Hitler and Goebbels were quite unhappy that there were still Jewish slave laborers in Berlin; the SS and the Gestapo organized a *Fabrikaktion* in February 1943 that would snatch Jews right out of their workplace and lock them up in various *Sammellager* throughout the city

Frauenprotest, women's protest; when the Nazis began putting half Jews in holding pens, their non-Jewish relatives staged a protest outside these *Sammellager* in March 1943

Fuchsbau, Fox's Lair, the code name of Admiral Canaris' headquarters

Greifer, or grabbers, Jews or half Jews who worked for the Gestapo and helped ferret out Jews who had gone underground in Berlin

Judenstern, the yellow star that all Jews in Germany had to wear from September 1941 to the end of the Third Reich

Jupo, Jewish auxiliary policemen who worked for the Gestapo

Krankenhaus, a hospital

Kriegsmarine, the German navy

Kripo, criminal police whose main headquarters was on Alexanderplatz in Berlin

Kristallnacht, Night of the Broken Glass, November 9, 1938, when Nazi goons and disgruntled Party members began attacking Jews throughout Germany; over a hundred synagogues were destroyed

Leibstandarte SS Adolf Hitler, a special unit within the SS that began as Hitler's bodyguards

Luftwaffe, the German air force

Milchkuh, or milk cow, an older submarine taken out of action and used to service other submarines

Mischling, a half Jew, someone with more than one Jewish parent or grandparent

Ritterkreuz, Knight's Cross, the highest award that a member of the German military could ever hope to achieve; it was worn from a ribbon around the neck

Sammellager, as used here, a holding pen for Jews waiting to be transported to a concentration camp

Schmiss, a dueling scar

Schwanz, a man's prick, used here as an expletive

Schweinerei, filth

Schwester, or sister, used here to describe a nurse or keeper at a hospital or asylum

Schwesternheim, the nurses' residence at the Jewish Hospital in Berlin

Spartakus Uprising, led by Karl Liebknecht and Rosa Luxemburg, who, in quixotic fashion, attempted to bring a socialist revolution to Germany in December 1918, with the help of an unruly band of radical workers and sailors; the uprising failed, and Liebknecht and Luxemburg were both murdered by right-wing military thugs in January 1919; Luxemburg's body was thrown into the Landwehrkanal

Spinnen, Spiders, high-priced whores who worked for the Abwehr

Spitzel, an informer or spy

Tipper, a stool pigeon

Totenkopf, death's-head, an insignia appropriated by the SS

U-boat, submariner, a Jew hiding from the Gestapo

V-Mann, a foreign informant or spy who serves as a go-between

Wehrmacht, the German military machine under Adolf Hitler

CESARE

February 11, 1943
From the desk of Admiral Wilhelm Canaris
72-76 Tirpitz-Ufer
Berlin

They did not want to hear anything but the latest news about Cesare. That's how bad the war was going. And the bombings over Berlin had started again after the quietus of a year. They were frightened, these wives of generals and diplomats. I shouldn't have been here. I ran a secret service, not a brothel for spies.

'Herr Admiral,' they said, 'is he phantom or flesh?'

And I had to reply, 'Gnädige Frau, I cannot discuss my agents.'

But it was the talk of Berlin. How Captain Erik Holdermann of the Abwehr had strangled a notorious traitor in a room full of Goyas at the Prado.

'And that swine had five bodyguards, did he not, Herr Admiral?'

They would embroider, multiply, manufacture, until I was their Caligari with his slave, Cesare, who strangled enemies of the Reich at will and then returned to his coffin at Tirpitz-Ufer. I have no coffins, I wanted to say. I didn't belong in Das Kabinett des Dr Caligari. I am not an ogre. I wanted to rid myself of their company and ride my Arabian mare, with her stunning white flanks. And I, who had always sought to be anonymous, a man of shadows, had become a hero in Berlin because of Cesare.

'Why do you not bring him to our luncheons, Herr Admiral?'

I would have strangled them all in the Beethoven Salon if Goebbels himself had not asked me to attend these affairs at the Adlon – it was necessary for our morale.

'But if you sat with him, gnädige Frau, what use would he have as a secret agent?'

They guzzled wine from the Adlon's cellars but still had to give up their ration stamps to the waiter, who cut out the stamps with a pair of scissors that hung on a silver chain at his side.

'But he's not a Jew, is he, Admiral?'

I had to answer, or they would complain to their husbands that Canaris was surly with them. How could I not be surly when I lived among sadists who butchered women and children in the streets?

'Herr Holdermann is not a Jew, but sometimes we employ Jews.'

And then Goebbels' own man, a clerk with bluish hair, intervened. 'The Führer permits Admiral Canaris to employ Jews for a reason – to trick the Jewish bandits in England and America.'

Thank God one of my own aides entered the salon. I had signaled to him from the door with a slight twist of my head. He handed me a blank slip of paper, which I began to peruse. I cupped my chin and then rose from my chair.

'You will have to forgive me,' I said with a bow. 'It's an urgent matter.'

They were thrilled.

'Does it have anything to do with Cesare?'

'Indeed,' I said, crumpling the slip of paper. They were gawking now. And I felt miserable. I shouldn't have talked about strangling them. I wasn't Berlin's Bluebeard. I had known some of them before this reign of terror began. I had gone riding with one or two of these wives in the Grunewald. But the war had turned them into petulant children, who had to be pampered and stuffed with foolishness. I went around the table, kissing their hands, the ever-gallant Canaris. But the moment I left the salon a sadness settled in. I grew morose. I couldn't return to the Tirpitz-Ufer. I longed to flee Berlin, and its cruel season – Jews were not allowed to enter the Adlon with their yellow stars. But *such badges were also my own badge of shame. I had suggested to the Führer, years ago, that German Jews wear a yellow star…*

Gott, I should have had Cesare cut my throat or strangle me. I was no less a monster than Goebbels and his men. I whistled for my driver. I tried to imagine Motte, my white mare, but another picture crept into my brain. I dreamt of my daughter locked away in an asylum as luxurious as the Adlon. I could not visit my poor little Eva. I did not have the courage. But she was twice as clever as her papa. Eva wrote to me from her mountain.

'Papa, my nurses insist that cowards make the very best managers of spies. But I tell them to be quiet. You have no time for one mad girl. You are much too busy with your spies.'

I didn't know where to turn. In another moment I would have wept in the arms of my aide.

'Herr Admiral,' he said, 'are you ill?'

'Don't be insolent, Hänschen – take me to the Lichtenstein Bridge.'

Hans was more confused than ever. 'Is it one of your private meetings, Herr Admiral? I neglected to bring my pistol.'

'The bridge, the bridge, before I pluck out your eyes.'

I had shaken the poor fellow. He'd never heard me shout. In order to compose himself, Hans shouted at my driver.

'The admiral has important business at the Lichtenstein Bridge. If you want to save your own skin, you'd better learn to fly.'

So we flew from Pariser Platz, but I didn't want to cross the Tiergarten.

'Tell him to take the longer route… I'd like to ride on the Budapester Strasse.'

Both of them must have thought their admiral had gone insane. We went down the Hermann-Göring-Strasse, which was blocked with every sort of construction and traffic – it looked like a war zone, with squads of SS men, and I wondered if Himmler's Einsatzgruppen were back from the front to haunt us all and make Berlin into their own killing field. But they didn't menace us when they peeked through the glass. In fact, they were very polite.

'Forgive us, Admiral, but there's a lunatic afoot — he has threatened to blow up Herr Goebbels. Would you like an escort?'

Before I could say yes or no, we were ushered through all the cordons on Hermann-Göring-Strasse. I was waiting for Wilhelm Canaris-Allee to appear on the map, or perhaps the gauleiter of Berlin would honor me with a portion of the zoo. The Cage of Dr Caligari.

My driver wound through the darkened, moonstruck streets and delivered us to the Budapester Strasse. He was flying much too fast.

'Slow down, damn you. I would like to breathe in the scenery.'

There was no scenery; the bars were closed in the middle of the afternoon. The shutters were painted black; I saw a crippled woman hobble along — I didn't believe in ghosts. I waved to her.

Hans was a suspicious little toad. He understood the route I was taking; I hadn't trained him for nothing.

'Herr Admiral,' he whispered, cupping one hand over his mouth.

'Isn't this where they took die Blutige Rose?'

I didn't answer him. We turned left on the embankment. I got out of the car. Hans was perplexed. He followed me to the bridge. I watched the water roil in that bloody Kanal. *Hans was frightened of the smile he saw on my face — not for himself. He was the most loyal aide I had ever had. We often joked that if I went to the gallows, Hans would want the same wire around his neck.*

'But this is where the Freikorps pitched Frau Doktor Luxemburg,' he said.

Hans was always a fine one for titles. Frau Doktor Luxemburg. I liked the ring of it. He'd heard the rumor; everybody at the Tirpitz-Ufer had. Their Old Man — when he was younger, of course — had helped the monarchists murder that bloody anarchist bitch, Rosa

Luxemburg, and dropped her in the Landwehrkanal, crippled leg and all. My coup de grâce, they said, had broken the Spartakusbund and put an end to the Berlin uprising. Did it matter that I wasn't even in Berlin? That I had gone to quiet down the mutinous sailors in Kiel? My minions had to shove their Old Man into the middle of history. In times of crisis, Dr Caligari was always there.

'Herr Admiral,' Hans said. 'You look pale. Should I find Cesare?'

I started to cackle. 'Do you want to rouse him from his slumber? He might murder us all.'

'God forbid, Herr Admiral.'

Hitler's reign began with the death of Rosa Luxemburg. Her disappearance had robbed the Weimar socialists of all their teeth. And the Reds never had another Rosa. I had once watched her stand on a table, under a circus tent, and harangue thousands with the voice of a bitter cherub. The women wept while the men shouted 'Long live Rosa,' until their voices broke.

I wasn't spying on her for my own silly pleasure. Die Blutige Rose was a danger to us all. She had to be stopped. But the Brownshirts appeared in her wake. Hitler climbed right out of the blood in the Kanal. The Spartakusbund had rebellious sailors who sang love songs while they occupied the royal stables, but not Einsatzgruppen, who create killing fields wherever they go. I should have joined those sailors, kissed their hands and feet.

There was no blood in the water now, nothing blutig *at all. And then I saw some creature bobbing in the* Kanal, *a woman, yes, but not with Rosa's dark brown hair. This creature was a blonde with broad shoulders. Was she practicing for some phantom Olympiad? Her strokes were perfect as she bit into the water. She was wearing goggles, I think – my winter mermaid.*

'Hänschen,' I said, 'do you see the Mädl *in the water?'*

'No, Herr Admiral.'

'But I insist. You must talk to her… She's a Jewish mermaid, hiding from Herr Himmler.'

Poor Hänschen started to cry. 'There are no Jewish mermaids, Admiral.'

I did not want him to cry. It irritated me.

'Ah, you're right,' I said. 'My mind is playing tricks. Jewesses are verboten in the Landwehrkanal.'

Hans was a magician. Suddenly he had a blanket in his arms. He unfurled it like a cape and let the blanket wind around my shoulders. I could have been a pensioner out on a stroll, or a madman with his keeper. We were all madmen at the Abwehr. We had to be. How else could we have survived the Führer's fiery wind day after day?

Lisalein

1

HE HADN'T ALWAYS SLEPT IN a coffin, hadn't always been Cesare. Erik was born in Berlin the same year Rosa Luxemburg was thrown into the Landwehrkanal like some fat mermaid, a mermaid who couldn't swim. His mother was a member of the Bavarian aristocracy who had fallen in love with a postman, Magnus Holdermann. The postman died when Erik was two, and his mother disappeared into Scheunenviertel, Berlin's Jewish slum. Erik grew up among the *Osten* Jews in their pointy hats and long cloaks. His playground had been the back alleys of Scheunenviertel. And then his mother died of tuberculosis a little after Erik's ninth birthday. It was 1928, and he roamed the streets like a wolf. It was the Jewish whores of Scheunenviertel who left their stations to feed him kuchen and coffee with hot milk. Erik was their spotter. He signaled whenever a policeman approached the Prenzlauer Allee, with its lane of cheap hotels. He lived at one of these hotels, the Kaiser's Hat, with its neon sign that hissed all night and blinked into Erik's eyes.

But the whores held their own council and decided Prenzlauer Allee wasn't the right place for their own little wolf. They sent him to the Jewish orphanage on the Rosenstrasse and subsidized his stay. He didn't live in any barracks. He had his own room, his own bed, his own pencil case.

Three years passed.

25

He wasn't apprenticed to some carpenter or sent to a trade school where he had to stitch leather aprons with a long needle. He attended the Jewish Gymnasium near Rosenthaler Platz. There wasn't much talk of religion at the Jewish Gymnasium. It was a German school that celebrated Mozart and Mendelssohn, Goethe and Heine, and every sort of foreign literature. Erik wasn't frightened to speak up in class.

'I do not understand Herr Hemingway. His men are all wounded and too sick to fall in love. It is like *amerikanische* jazz – much bumping of the body and a little music.'

The professor laughed and stroked his walrus mustache.

'Herr Holdermann, if you want to learn American, you must put your mind to baseball.'

The professor removed a baseball almanac from his desk, closed his eyes, and repeated the names of players as if he were reciting the profoundest poetry: *Baby Doll Jacobson, Jimmy Outlaw, Shoeless Joe Jackson…*

The baseballer, Herr Shoeless Joe, was an orphan, like Erik. He went from team to team, from the Cleveland Browns to the Chikago Black Stockings, but with his own *Wunderwaffe*, the Black Betsy, a bat that never split and could knock a ball out of the baseball park and into the cattle yards of Chikago. Herr Joe was declared a baseball *Krimineller* because he took groschen from gamblers and let the other team win the famous World Series of 1919. He became a wanderer, had to disguise himself with a false beard if he wanted to play for teams in the lesser baseball leagues. Herr Joe was still playing somewhere, in Alabama or the Tennessee.

Erik kept a memorial candle for Herr Joe near his bed. It was called a Yahrzeit candle, and Jews lit it once a year to remember the dead. But he did not think it unethical to light a Yahrzeit candle for Shoeless Joe, a living dead man, the zombie of baseball.

Erik also had to worry about his own fate at the orphanage. A bitter famine clung to the city. There was panic and unrest in the streets of Scheunenviertel. Berlin was a Red town, but that didn't stop the Brownshirts from coming into Scheunenviertel and pulling on the beards of old men. The Red Front had terrific battles with the Brownshirts. Professors at the orphanage predicted that Berlin would soon be run by gangsters of the Right and the Left.

The famine had come to Erik's orphanage. There was much less strudel and liverwurst. The whores at the Kaiser's Hat could no longer subsidize him. They couldn't even subsidize themselves. Overseers at the orphanage began to resign. Jewish children were turned away. Rosenstrasse couldn't feed another orphan, couldn't pay for its fuel. And then the orphanage found a savior in Baron Wilfrid von Hecht, Berlin's foremost philanthropist. The baron owned department stores and investment banks, manufactured chairs and table lamps. He'd been the first Jewish cavalry captain in the Great War and liked to wear his Iron Cross. He had the finest villa in the Grunewald, but he didn't forget the orphans of Scheunenviertel. Coal trucks returned to the Rosenstrasse. Strudel arrived from the bakery on Alexanderplatz. And the baron himself had come to the orphanage.

He was no taller than a twelve-year-old boy. He had wide nostrils and a broad nose. His eyebrows resembled an unruly forest. He wore a frock coat with a velvet collar and spats that glistened in the orphanage's weak light. The frock coat couldn't erase the slight hump on his back. The orphans stood in line to greet their benefactor, the tallest boys towering over him. He gave each orphan a Montblanc fountain pen to encourage all of them in such hard times. It was a *Meisterstück* – Masterpiece – with a gold nib and midnight black barrel, the exact pen that Greta Garbo used to scratch her initials in someone's souvenir book. And the baron had each orphan's name inscribed in silver on his very own pen. It was the gift of a lifetime.

The *Direktor* could have run Rosenstrasse for a year on the hard currency that such Montblanc Masterpieces could fetch. But his orphans were shrewder than he was. They grasped the baron's motives. He needed something outlandish in such difficult times. The *Direktor* was a compassionate accountant who lived with loaves of bread. But Herr Baron Wilfrid had to find the imprint of everything he touched.

He proceeded from boy to boy with each pen in its own velvet sack. He had studied every name and profile beforehand. And when he presented a boy with a pen, he could talk about the boy's dead parents and the district in Berlin where he was born. He had an assistant who helped him with the velvet sacks. It was his daughter, Lisa von Hecht, who was fifteen and seemed very bored. She was a head taller than the baron in her velvet shoes. She scowled at the boys, and Erik was frightened to look into her eyes. He had never seen a girl who could create such a storm and still be so beautiful. She had clipped blond hair like the ticket-takers on the tram, but none of them had azure eyes that softened the angrier she got. She was much more spectacular than a fountain pen.

'*Vati*,' she said, stifling a yawn, 'how much longer must I remain with your children? I have tennis class this afternoon with a divine boy who has dueling scars.'

The baron began to groan. 'Lisa, *Lisalein,* you're spoiling the presentation. I will bring you another boy with dueling scars.'

She pouted, and the long crease at both sides of her mouth made her twice as adorable. She clutched the baron's list of orphans and read Erik's name aloud. Lisa was near-sighted and had a terrible squint. But she wouldn't wear spectacles on her nose.

'Ah,' the baron said, 'Erik Holdermann. But your mother's maiden name is Albrecht, Heidi Albrecht... Isn't she the brother of my good friend Heinrich Percyval Albrecht?'

'I believe so, Herr Baron.'

'But this is astonishing!' said the baron, growing very agitated. 'Lisalein, make him give us back the pen. The boy is an impostor.'

Erik wouldn't cry in front of the baron and his beautiful daughter, even though the baron's accusation bit him to pieces. But it was Lisa who saw the dread and indignation in his eyes.

'Father, you must question the boy.'

'I will not.'

'Then I will.'

And she scrutinized Erik with the full force of her myopia.

'*Junge*, why are you here?'

'I am not certain, Fräulein. My mother died three years ago and I was brought to Rosenstrasse. It has a much better reputation than the other Berlin orphanages.'

'But your uncle is alive. Heinz Albrecht. I have visited him many times. Why are you not with him?'

'He would not have me, Fräulein, because my mother married a postman, and Uncle Heinrich said it was a stain on the family – a blotch.'

'Blotch,' the baron repeated, the word hovering on his tongue. He took out a silk handkerchief, which was as long as a man's shirt, and started to sniffle.

Lisa had to reprimand him. '*Vati*, behave yourself. You are embarrassing me in front of all the boys.'

'I can't help it,' he said. 'I remember now. The Rotten Sister – he spoke of Heidi several times. But I did not know there was a little boy... Erik, you must forgive my rude language. Come with me.'

'But where are we going, *Vati*?'

'To the Adlon. That is our Percyval's hotel. I spoke to him yesterday. He has some business in Berlin.'

'But you cannot steal the boy from Rosenstrasse.'

'Why not?' said the baron. 'I am his benefactor. And I can do with him whatever I wish.'

Erik couldn't understand the ferocious turmoil of the baron and his Lisalein. They propelled him out onto the Rosenstrasse like one of their own toys; a limousine was waiting, a black Mercedes with a sunroof. Children from all over Scheunenviertel surrounded the car, which had a chauffeur in a uniform that drowned in silver and gold. The chauffeur stood with one of his polished boots on the running board. He was the most insolent man Erik had ever seen. He looked at Lisalein with such lechery that even the boy blushed. His name was Karl-Oskar, and the baron had to slap his boot off the running board before the chauffeur would budge.

'Will I be driving you, Herr Baron?'

'Of course not,' the baron growled. 'Get in the back.'

Karl-Oskar ruffled his nose. 'With the little orphan?'

'*Dummkopf*, he is the nephew of one of the most distinguished men in Bavaria. Be grateful that I have not yet asked you to shine his shoes.'

'Then I would leave your employ, Herr Baron. And you will never find another chauffeur who is as cultivated as I am.'

'You are mistaken, Karl. Berlin is cluttered with unemployed lawyers and tax accountants. I could also replace you with a Lithuanian prince.'

Karl-Oskar smirked. 'There aren't many princes in Lithuania, Herr Baron, only Jews such as yourself and Lisalein.'

'Do not mention my daughter, Karl. And if you keep ogling her, I will have the pleasure of plucking out your eyes. Get into the car – and be quick!'

The chauffeur retired to the rear of the Mercedes, while the baron, Lisa, and Erik sat up front. The baron had to plop himself onto two cushions, or his eyes wouldn't have been level with the windshield. There was plenty of room for the boy to have his own seat, but the baron insisted that Erik sit on Lisa's lap. The boy turned crimson.

'Herr Baron, I am the man. Shouldn't Lisalein sit on my lap?'

'No,' said the baron. 'You are my guest.'

And so they bumped their way out of the Rosenstrasse, the baron driving in random jerks, and Erik couldn't even concentrate on the little shops and alleys he loved – the shoemaker at the corner of Neue Friedrichstrasse, the candy stalls in the courtyard nearby, the little store that sold model airplanes and tanks. It wasn't the baron's peculiar driving habits that bothered him. It was the fantastic engine of Lisa's body engulfing him with its heat and aromas. He began to shiver all at once, and Lisa wrapped her arms around him as if she were calming a dazed turtle, not a little man with his own desires.

They left the crooked alleys of Scheunenviertel and bumped onto Unter den Linden with its wide carriageway that was meant for a baron's limousine or the cavalcade of a king. The Jewish shopkeepers had told him about *their* Kaiser, who could be seen half an age ago riding with his honor guard along that line of trees. 'Kid,' the shopkeepers had said, 'Unter den Linden is the nearest we'll ever get to heaven.'

The Brandenburg Gate was a stone mirage at the very edge of Unter den Linden, but he couldn't enjoy a vista that was like a wicked dream while he rocked on Lisa's lap. The baron's Mercedes jolted to a halt in front of a sandstone castle with a mansard roof. It was the Adlon, where millionaires kept their mistresses in ten-room suites.

A doorman in derby and ducktail coat arrived out of nowhere, dusted off the baron and bowed to Lisa and the boy, who had begun to brood now that he'd had to climb off Lisa's lap. Then the baron and his little cortege, including Karl-Oskar, walked under a canopy and entered the Adlon, a wonderland the likes of which Erik had never seen. It had the mystifying light of a cathedral, but with carpets and red chairs, pillars with red veins. The baron could not take a step without a member of the staff saluting him and blinding himself to the hump on his back.

'Herr Baron, would you like your usual suite? It will only take a minute. We'll move out the admiral who has booked your rooms.'

'No, no,' the baron had to insist. 'Leave the poor admiral alone. I'm not staying, Fredi. It's just a visit. Please tell Herr Albrecht to come downstairs. Say it's urgent.'

The baron didn't even have to tread across a lobby that was larger than a *Fussball* field, filled with every sort of seeker – impoverished aristocrats, courtesan countesses, and bankrupt financiers who wanted some favor from the richest man in Berlin and would have loved to be caught chatting with him. But the baron was shown to a private salon hidden by a wall of mirrors. He stepped through the wall with Lisa, Erik, and Karl and disappeared from the turbulence of the lobby.

But then a very tall man in a silk dressing gown strode through the same wall – Heinrich Percyval Albrecht, a gentleman farmer with his own estate a hundred miles north of Munich. His family had held the land for five hundred years. He had been a member of the Kaiser's honor guard, had protected Wilhelm II all through the war, but had decided not to go into exile with him. Heinrich wasn't suited for exile. He hunted, shut his eyes to the intrigue around him, and waited for the monarchy to be restored.

He was irritated and didn't even say hello to Lisalein, who visited his estates twice a year and was like a goddaughter. He grimaced at the boy.

'Baron, what is the meaning of this? I don't like mysteries or intrusions. You could have sent your card up to my suite, or rung me from the front desk. I don't care to traipse around in my robe. *Come down immediately.* I didn't even have time to dress.'

'Ah,' said the baron. 'Heinzi, I know you too well. You would have kept us waiting for hours if I hadn't resorted to a trick. But don't you recognize the boy? I found him at the Jewish orphanage. He's your own kin.'

Heinrich Percyval drank his lager and came to Berlin twice a year, met with his bankers and a few friends, and couldn't forget that Berlin had almost become a Red republic – the rabble would have killed Kaiser Wilhelm had the Reds seized power. He wasn't in the mood to barter over the baron's boy.

'Wilfrid, have you come to blackmail me? I've fallen behind on our little loan. But I will pay you the next time.'

The baron's face was very raw. 'Damn you and your Junker ways. I'm not talking money or merchandise. Heinzi, you cannot disappear behind the Adlon's wonderful walls. And you cannot abandon this boy. *Gott*, he has your sister's face.'

'I have no sister,' said the Bavarian Junker.

And the baron began to cry into a handkerchief that was longer than a man's shirt. 'Heinzi, you have no heart.'

It was Lisa who continued her father's attack. 'Come, *Vati*. We'll adopt the boy ourselves. He will live with us in the Grunewald. I will become his aunt.'

Heinz Albrecht pursed his narrow lips, until he looked like a man with no mouth.

'Wilfrid, I could duel with you all day, but I cannot win against your daughter... I capitulate.'

'Then you agree that the little Herr Holdermann is your nephew?'

'I agree to nothing. I will take him off your hands and have my solicitor look into the matter. Meanwhile, he can stay with me.'

'But he is not your cattle,' said Lisalein, her eyes ablaze in the hotel's curtained salon. 'You must afford him some rights.'

'Lisa, be still,' said the baron. 'We've gotten this far with Heinz. He wouldn't deny his own flesh and blood.'

'*Vati*, don't gamble your life on that… but we have to allow the lion to get used to the cub that was thrown into his lap.'

She stood on her toes to kiss the tall farmer – 'Good-bye, *Onkel*' – and then she emerged from the deep shadows of the salon to touch Erik's crown, as if to anoint him.

'You must not shame us, little man. My father has vouched for you. You will have to obey your new uncle.'

He could not see much of her in the shadows. But the scent of her hair weakened his knees. Her blondness was like a visceral ghost in the salon.

Fräulein, he wanted to say, *please take me with you to the Grunewald, or drop me at the orphanage. I have to continue my studies.*

But the mirrored door of the salon shut on him and he was left with this tall stranger who might have been his uncle in another world, but his mother had barely mentioned her older brother, who lived in a castle, with a whole village at his beck and call. This ogre hadn't even entered the boy's dreams. Erik was a Berliner, not a Bavarian. Munich was the stronghold of Herr Hitler; Munich was where the Brownshirts marched with their swastikas and banners. Munich didn't have a workers' paradise like Wedding, with its Jewish Hospital and its Red Front that could swallow swastikas and massacre Brownshirts who strayed onto its streets. And Uncle

Heinrich didn't even take Erik's hand. The boy had to follow *Onkel* out of the salon, or be put on a shelf where the Adlon deposited orphans who were lost and never found.

Bavarian Nights

2

Tʜᴇ ᴡᴏʀsᴛ ᴏғ ɪᴛ ᴡᴀsɴ'ᴛ the farm boys who beat him up and tried to turn Erik into a slave. They kicked him without mercy, but they could not bend his will. He stole whatever scraps he could – a blackened carrot, a turnip, a stale piece of bread – and ate alone in the barn. He grew stronger within his isolation and learned to bite and kick. But what he couldn't bear was the lack of a book.

There was no schoolhouse in the tiny village attached to the castle. The loutish boys who belonged to Uncle Heinrich's manor couldn't even spell their names. They wore Nazi pins and practiced the Hitler salute among themselves. They copulated with their sisters and cousins, who at least went to sewing school and had grammar lessons from seamstresses and cooks at the castle. Some of these savage little girls were kind to Erik. They marveled at him because he came from a world of readers and could mouth entire sentences with his own peculiar melody.

'The master's nephew sings whatever it is he has to say.'

They undressed in front of Erik, let him watch while they went to pee. They fought over Erik, fed him, began to wash his clothes, and kept their brothers and brutal male cousins from harming him. He had to slave for his uncle, to feed the pigs in their mud piles, collect the hay, and milk the cows, but he soon realized that all the brutal children within a mile of the castle were related to him. Uncle Heinrich, who kept up the pretense of culture at his castle, who had a library of nine thousand volumes, with murals and tapestries on his walls, who invited string quartets to play for him, also slept with half the women in his service – seamstresses, pastry cooks, and chicken pluckers who warmed the master's bed. He sold his bastard sons off to the military or kept them in bondage on another farm.

His daughters were a dilemma. They could do little else but sew and copulate. They wandered into his bedroom in their nightgowns, their bellies outlined under the silk, their nipples almost as high as their necks, and he had to chase them with a stick.

He wished only to hoard them as he would a harem of racing horses he didn't intend to race. But Heinrich's daughters planned their revenge. They plotted his overthrow with nothing more substantial than a string of sentences. They had the orphan from Berlin give them lessons so that they could correspond with police chiefs and Nazi thugs in Munich when the time came to rid themselves of Heinrich. But he caught his nephew teaching the *Mädchen* how to write, and he scattered them all, ripped their notebooks apart, locked them in their rooms for a week, and made Erik live in the barn.

The *Mädchen* eased Erik's banishment. They shared his cot in the hayloft and sneaked him into the library while the master was away. But they were startled by the boy's reaction to this mortuary of leather tomes. He fondled the books, sniffed at the leather like some castle rodent.

'My darlings,' he said to the bewildered girls, 'you cannot imagine how happy I am.'

'But little Holdermann,' said Rose Marie, the brightest of Heinrich's daughters, 'you cannot go to bed with a book. A book cannot caress your tiny Berlin balls.'

They let Erik climb the ladder to all that musty leather, but it seemed like an unholy place, and they were much more content the moment they locked the library and returned the key to its corner behind the master's apothecary jars.

Once the Nazis toppled Weimar in '33, these same girls followed behind their brothers in the Hitler Youth and joined the League of German Maidens; they worked on farms in the countryside and slept with the farmers and their sons until the farmers' wives swept them back to the Maidens' barracks in Munich and Berlin. Erik missed these ferocious Nazi Maidens who had befriended him, missed their company. He was more stranded than ever in the barn, sleeping with horses and cows.

One night, his male cousins returned to the castle with members of the SS in long military coats. They weren't abusive. They bowed to Uncle Heinrich, marched up to the library, broke down the door, and flung every book out the castle window. Erik could witness those strange projectiles from the barn, Moroccan leather flying like colossal birds and crashing into Uncle's unkempt garden. The Hitler *Jugend* hurled the bruised and broken books onto the auto-da-fé in the garden and fed their little fire.

And then they were gone. Uncle Heinrich reached into the fire with his own hands and plucked out books shorn of their morocco covers and their spines, while Erik ran from the barn with a rake.

'*Onkel*, you'll burn your hands.'

And he poked at the charred remains in the fire.

'I feel like Saturn,' Heinrich said.

'But I don't understand, *Onkel*. Saturn ate his own sons. There is a painting on this subject at the Prado. I did not see it with my own eyes. But my professors at the gymnasium say that it exists.'

'You are mistaken, *Junge*. It was the sons who devoured Saturn.'

Heinrich did not take one book with him into the castle. He

strode within its walls, a slight tremor between his shoulders. The castle could have belonged to Saturn; its ramparts were ravaged; bits of stone crumbled from the walls.

Erik returned to the barn with his own prize – bits and pieces of burnt books. He devoured the pages under the wick of an oil lamp. The Jewish Gymnasium of Berlin had given Erik a ravenous appetite: He gorged on books the way Saturn had gorged on his sons, in spite of what Uncle Heinrich said.

But so occupied was he with the remains of Uncle's library that he had forgotten about the next winter storm, and he awoke one morning trapped within a wall of snow. Erik could not budge the barn door. And the snow that gleamed through the barn's one little window nearly blinded him. He had to stand on a ladder and block out the light with a horse blanket. He lit a fire near the feeding troughs and moved all the animals near the fire. The crumbs of cheese he had and a crust of bread lasted for two days, and then he had to live on whatever the animals ate. He could not milk the cows in such cold weather; their teats were hard as bone. The cows bellowed at him as if he were some kind of interloper. The horses did not make a sound; the bells tied to their ears didn't jiggle once. And the pigs couldn't root in mud that was as unbending as armor.

Erik's teeth rattled in his head. The noise exploded in his ears. He could no longer feel his fingers. And he had no more fuel to start a fire; the matchsticks he had were useless – their heads would fall off whenever he tried to strike one of them. The hay was hard as a knife. The whole barn was starving. And that's when he thought of Lisalein. She had stayed with him like a still wound. He hadn't seen her in four years.

It was his memory of Lisalein that fed sparks into him like some magic fuel. He had slept with six of Heinrich's daughters from the League of German Maidens – Rose Marie, Hildegarde, Helga,

Ursula, Ingeborge, and Blondi – and he wouldn't have been so startled by the baron's little blond Venus with her cropped hair and tall shoes if he were fortunate enough ever to find her in the flesh. In fact, he'd imagined himself hovering over Lisa's limbs while he rutted with Rose Marie – her nostrils flared under him like one of Heinrich's prize horses. He clutched her hands the way he always did with Ursula, but he wouldn't stifle her love cries. He'd let Lisa scream and scream.

But he couldn't hold on to her. The hunger pains seemed to split his skull. He lost the sea green of her eyes; the sockets stared back at him, mocking his own passion. He was making love to a skeleton, some bag of bones that wasn't Lisa. Herr Teufel had entered the barn, had poisoned Erik's mind. Heinrich's cows were lowing at him with the Devil's own music.

HIS EARS PRICKED. HE WAS lying on the barn's earthen floor. He could hear a slow, relentless gnawing on the other side of the door, as if a hundred rats were nibbling away at wood. Then the door began to splinter. A huge chunk of it exploded in front of his eyes. Uncle Heinrich stepped through the hole in the door, his face wrapped in scarves, like a Bedouin chief. He was wearing enormous fur mittens and clutching an ax.

'*Onkel*,' the boy whispered, his throat parched, 'we have to save the horses and cows.'

Heinrich wouldn't let him continue or drink from the canteen that was attached to his belt. He wet the boy's mouth with little pinches of water.

'Cows,' the boy repeated. 'Save the horses and cows.'

'We can't, *Junge*. It would take half a year to dig a tunnel tall enough to drag them out of the barn.'

'But I am in charge of all your animals. I will not leave without them.'

'*Junge,* they're all dead. You have been in the barn for two weeks.'

Erik closed his eyes. He could no longer listen. The words flew around into the rafters. Heinrich wrapped him in an old bearskin. He carried Erik out through the hole in the door. But they couldn't stand up. There was no sky, no clouds, no trees, nothing but the walls of a tunnel that was screwed into the snow by some whirling, implacable machine. That machine was Heinrich himself, who dug the tunnel with his own hands, picking at the snow with an ax – the handle had split halfway to the barn, and Heinrich had to clutch the head of the ax and burrow with it through barriers of ice.

It took him most of the morning to drag the boy from the barn to the castle door. He spat water into the boy's mouth and sucked on a few raisins and nuts. The boy was an icicle that could still breathe by the time Heinrich laid him out on the dining room table. He wouldn't bathe the boy. The shock of scalding water on his skin might have killed him. Working with his seamstress, who was as snowbound as he had been, he rubbed the boy in axle grease and machine oil, covered him with the bearskin, and rocked him in his arms. Erik was pampered for two weeks. He lived in the library, which had become a lit cave of ladders and shelves without books. He slept on a cot and ate with the servants. He was still a vagabond in his uncle's eyes.

The servants moved Erik back into the barn after his convalescence. He still had his treasure of burnt books. And with no chores to do, he read from morning to night.

And then, one afternoon, in the spring of '35, he was summoned out of the barn. There was a small gathering in Heinrich's wild garden. Laughter rang in his ear like a rifle shot. How could he fail to recognize Lisalein's robust voice? She was sitting on a chair in the garden, next to Uncle Heinrich and another man, who had thick eyeglasses and wore a Nazi Party pin in his lapel. His name was Josef Valentiner, and he was married to Lisalein. Erik could feel a wound in the walls of his chest. She couldn't have been more than nineteen – a *Mischling*, a half Jew, and the bride of a Party man. This Josef was one of Herr Hitler's economic advisers, and he wasn't that much older than Lisa. He was a wunderkind who had managed the baron's whole empire before he was twenty. He had pudgy fingers, and he sweated a lot under a weak sun.

But it was Lisalein who also irritated him. She'd changed her hair since he last saw her. It wasn't cropped like a cadet or a convict, but cascaded to her shoulders; she looked like one of his cousins in the League of German Maidens. And she glowered at him with her weak eyes. He wanted to strike her – out of jealousy, out of rage.

'Look at you,' she said. '*Onkel*, what have you done to the boy? He's all in tatters… and is he living in a barn?'

'Fräulein,' Erik insisted. 'It's the place I prefer. I am not comfortable in a castle, and Uncle Heinrich knows that.'

'But where are your schoolbooks?'

'In the barn,' he said. 'Uncle Heinrich does not believe in country schools. He is my tutor.'

The boy turned brazen, looked into Lisalein's eyes, not as a mendicant, or some petitioner from the Jewish orphanage, but as a lover might. He wasn't crude. He was declaring his own territory with a glance, as if he wore the special badge of a boy who had slept with the whole League of German Maidens and did not have to depend on a *Mischling* – a Jewess with some Christian blood – who was married to a man with a Nazi pin. Lisa had an attack of vertigo – the boy's boldness bothered her, but she recovered quickly enough.

'*Onkel,* shame on you. I believe you have mishandled my protégé. He is wild as a wolf. And a wolf with books is still a wolf.'

'Lisa darling,' said Uncle Heinrich, 'how can I make amends?'

'You can't,' she said. 'He is wasting away at your castle… and his education is already ruined. What gymnasium will have such a wolf? We must conspire to have him accepted as a cadet.'

Heinrich frowned at her. 'What kind of cadet?'

'At the naval college in Kiel,' she said, and nudged her husband, who had not said a word. 'Josef darling, you must have met an admiral or two at the Chancellery.'

Undersecretary Valentiner bit his fat lips and seemed stupefied. 'I cannot bother an admiral over some boy out of the blue.'

'He's not *some* boy,' Lisa had to insist. 'We found the Little One, *Vati* and I, and reunited him with his uncle. You must not demean our accomplishment, or you will have to face the divorce courts.'

The undersecretary may have once masterminded the baron's empire of department stores, but he'd never won an argument with his wife.

'Divorce?' he said. 'I have done nothing wrong.'

Heinrich intervened. 'Do not worry. I will have the *Junge* sent to Kiel. I do not require admirals from Berlin.'

Lisa grew tired of sitting in a country garden and wanted to be alone with the boy she hadn't seen in four years.

'Come, Little One, let's leave the two monsters. They can talk about the window dressing in Herr Hitler's own department store, how he's turning Deutschland into a democratic state for next summer's Olympics… but show me this classroom you have made inside a barn.'

She took Erik by the hand and led him across the garden. She wasn't shy. She squeezed Erik's hand with all her might. And he began to tremble.

They disappeared inside the barn, and Erik lost control in an instant. Lisalein seized upon his little empire of burnt books, fondling their shattered spines.

'You are the most unpredictable boy,' she said. 'It is a classroom, and I'll bet that Heinrich never tutored you once... Did you miss me?'

'No,' he said, determined not to reveal himself.

All his stratagems of wounding Lisa – showing off his manliness, pricking her – went awash in some foreign sea. What could it have meant to Lisalein that he'd suckled the breasts of Heinrich's Nazi Maidens, bastard daughters who were born in a crumbling castle? He had no ammunition, nothing to wound her with. He was the same orphan, even with his wealth of books.

It was Lisa who clutched his shirt of hairy wool. He froze like a rabbit encountering a pair of human eyes. He was taller than Lisalein, despite the alligator pumps she wore from one of the 'international' shops on Unter den Linden, a shop the baron himself might have owned. She never asked the boy's permission as she dug half her face into his mouth. It wasn't like kissing a Nazi *Mädchen*. Her tongue didn't leap. It was the brutal kiss of a blond executioner. Then she took her own mouth away from Erik, and he was utterly forlorn.

'Is that what you wanted? You obscene child. How dare you look at me with such lust and contempt in your eyes. *Gott*, you can't be a day older than fifteen. Did Heinrich raise you as a stud horse in his barn?'

'I raised myself,' he said. He was trembling, and Lisa took him in her arms.

'Fräulein,' he blubbered, 'why did you not visit me once in four years?'

'Darling,' she said. 'I'm a selfish pig. If I had known... *Vati*

44

should have realized that Heinrich would take his anger for his own sister out on you. He has revenge written all over him. I can't imagine why he detests you so much.'

'But he saved my life,' the boy said.

'It doesn't matter. You still can't stay here. You must be around children your own age.'

'But I'm not a child. And you are only a few years older than I am.'

She scowled at him. And her azure eyes glowed in the shadows of the barn. She was still clutching his hairy wool coat.

'I'm a married woman, you dolt.'

'Yes, you're married to a Nazi pin.'

She slapped his face. And it wasn't some polite love tap. His ears rang with the force of her perfectly shaped hand.

'You're twice a dolt,' she said. 'That Nazi pin is keeping us alive.'

'But the baron has millions. Why don't you quit Germany with him? You can have a château in a Swiss forest, or half a fortress on Lake Geneva.'

'How can Papa leave, my pretty little boy? Hitler is in power because of him. He and other Jewish financiers were more frightened of the Reds than of a lunatic with foam in his mouth. They considered him a marionette that could be dismantled and thrown in a box. But they did not take the measure of such a man, how he would be worshipped as the god of peace and war.'

'Fräulein Lisa, I'll take you to Switzerland if your father won't.'

'What would I do in a Swiss chalet? Wait for the next electrical storm? Row in the moonlight and read a book? I'm a Berliner. Let the Führer ride his bulletproof train to Munich and leave us alone… and you're going to Kiel.'

He could feel her drift away from him, and he started to sniffle.

'Stop crying,' she said. 'What a pest! You're just like my father. You cry over the tiniest thing.'

'But you won't forget me?'

She smiled and pinched his earlobes. 'Darling, how could I forget a boy in a wolf's hairy coat?'

She pranced out of the barn in her satin cape that she furled around her shoulders like some sleeping bat. And all Erik could do was follow her footsteps with his brown eyes, dreading a future without Lisalein.

Kiel

3

H E WASN'T EVEN A CADET, but a subcadet, a toady attached to the old Warrant Officers' School in the Mühlenstrasse, where all the cadets trained, not far from the Kiel Kanal. Heinrich sold him into an elaborate form of slavery. He lived in a shack with other subcadets behind the training school. He never got near a submarine, hardly even stepped onto the seawall. He went from Heinrich's barn to a cave near the sea.

The cadets, with their enamel swastikas pinned to the pockets of their middy blouses, expected the subcadets to be their toads. Erik had to bring them blood sausages and beer, shine their shoes, and wash their underwear, but when the first cadet tried to kiss him, Erik broke his nose. He could have been tossed out of this lowly subcadet corps and sent back to Heinrich, but the cadets voted to keep him. They still thought to conquer the subcadet from Berlin and make him their whore. But they hadn't counted on the *Teufel* inside him. Erik had fought Heinrich's bastard sons, who were far crueler than these cadets; he'd had a training they never had. It didn't matter how often they pummeled him or pissed in his locker. He could wield a 'cheese knife' as well as any of the cadets. And he kept that dirk with him whenever he was in the shower stall, or when he was in his little cave behind the cadets' own barrack – he slept like a wolf, always half awake, one eye open, the dirk under his pillow. And when the cadets attacked in the middle of the night, he would lunge with his dirk an inch from their eyes. They'd hiss and call him a devil-boy, but they always scattered.

So it went on for more than a year, this game of cat and mouse, where the mouse was even fiercer than the cat-cadets. But they had other diversions, their cadet balls and their very own nightclub, Trocadero, on the Kaiserstrasse, while Erik had little else but the seawall and patches of sky when he wasn't doing their chores.

And on a windy night he happened to be near the seawall when a little gang of drunken louts attacked a man in civilian clothes. The boy was seventeen, and his time in Kiel had toughened him. These louts couldn't have been cadets; they reminded him of the Red thugs who would wander through Scheunenviertel when he was a child, stealing apples and pieces of cloth from the peddlers, fondling women who had strayed onto the streets without their kerchiefs. But these weren't Reds. They were louts from the local beer hall. And the man they were kicking had gray hair and a knob of a nose. His suit had an aristocratic cut, but it was all crumpled and slightly worn, as if he were an elegant tramp.

The louts sneered at Erik and his uniform of a subcadet, which marked him as a kitchen slave. Their leader called him a little boy.

'*Knabe,* mind your business before we break your head.'

Erik flicked the dirk out of his sleeve and ripped a line of blood across the leader's face. The other louts rushed at him, and Erik tore their winter coats to shreds, like a master undressing his own pupils. They had an insane energy that propelled them beyond their own fear. Erik kicked them in the shins; they fell and rose again and stumbled away from the elegant tramp.

Erik picked up the man's homburg and dusted it off. '*Alte,*' he said, even though the tramp really wasn't that old. 'What the hell are you doing near the seawall at this hour? They could have cracked your skull.'

The tramp laughed. 'But I had you to protect me, *Männe,* my little man. Are you a cadet at the naval college?'

'*Nein, Alte.* I'm the toad who shines their shoes, a subcadet.'

'I never heard of such a thing, a subcadet,' said the tramp.

The boy grew irritated. 'What the hell would you know?'

That great knob of a nose began to twitch. '*Männe,* I was once also a cadet, and we had kitchen slaves, but not with the diabolic category of subcadet.'

Erik scrutinized the tramp a little closer. 'You must have fallen on hard times. Do you need a little pocket money? I could lend you a few marks. That's all I have.'

'Yes, they took my purse. What's your name? I'll send you a postal check.'

'It's a gift, *Alte.* I have no place to spend my money. The cadets have their Trocadero, and we have sour wine.'

The tramp smiled to himself. 'Is the Troc still open, *Männe?* It was a high-class whorehouse in my day. I married nine or ten of the *Mädchen* within its walls – for one night. The whores were given veils and everything, and there was even a minister, who was a client at the Troc. What's your name?'

Erik told him. He was still confused. 'I would walk you to the train station, *Alte,* but we're not allowed to leave the base.'

The tramp put on his homburg and bowed to Erik. '*Auf Wiedersehen.*'

And *Alte* disappeared into the fog that rose off the Baltic and flooded the seawall. Erik returned to his cave and wouldn't give the tramp another thought. He didn't expect a postal check and never received one. He went on shining the cadets' shoes. And then two members of the Kiel patrol appeared at his bedside and shone a light in his eyes. Erik assumed he was going to be court-martialed for having roughed up several citizens of Kiel. But he suddenly remembered that he couldn't be court-martialed. A subcadet had no real contract with the German navy, and didn't even have the right to exist. But to his great surprise, he was escorted to the cadets' barrack and given his own bunk.

As a cadet, he was free to wander through Kiel. He went to the Kaiserstrasse, strolled into the Troc, which wasn't much of a whorehouse in 1937, but a club for cadets. He danced with the *Mädchen*, but their lips were too red, and none of them had Lisa's perfume. They smelled of soap. He wouldn't even fumble with them in a dark corner behind the curtains.

He had little taste for this town. It didn't have its own Scheunenviertel, with courtyards full of peddlers, poets, and men in pointy hats. It was a sailors' paradise that came alive for one little moment in June, *Kieler Woche,* when yacht clubs from all over the world descended upon Kiel for a week of races. Hitler's Kriegsmarine presided over the regatta, with Kiel's naval base as its headquarters and the Kaiser's former yacht club as its host. Admirals strolled along the seawall, flags flying in their wake like war banners. Cadets and midshipmen served as messengers and pages, drinking schnapps with senior officers and their wives when they weren't dancing with the most marriageable daughters of Schleswig-Holstein. These were educated girls with magnificent flanks and without the smear of lipstick. They wore white gloves and carried little spangled bags attached to their wrists. They wanted to be the wives of navy men, but when they giggled at him, he wouldn't giggle back.

And while he brooded in the great hall of the Reichsmarine's own regatta, his eyes fell upon the tramp he had rescued from the seawall. The tramp was wearing an admiral's uniform, which was very rumpled. Erik didn't dare approach until the admiral-tramp beckoned to him.

'Herr Admiral,' the boy said, clicking his heels. *'Heil Hitler!'*

But the admiral did not return Erik's Hitler salute. He seemed apart from the other admirals, outside the ken of Kiel Week.

'Männe, do you remember me?'

'Yes, Herr Admiral, we met on the seawall.'

'And what did you call me then?'

'Alte – but I can assure you that you are the youngest admiral here.'

'Ah, you've grown into a flatterer since you've become a cadet. That admiral near the window with the *Schmiss* on his cheek is much, much younger than I.'

Erik saw an admiral in orange epaulets, with a dueling scar under one eye; the admiral could have been Serbian or Lithuanian, God knows, but he had the rough hands of a laborer.

'What if I told you he's an impostor,' said the admiral-tramp, 'an impostor who has come here to harm me?'

'Then we should arrest him on the spot, Herr Admiral.'

'Suppose we couldn't arrest him. Suppose it would cause a scandal. What would you do, *Männe?'*

'Make sure he doesn't harm you, Herr Admiral.'

Erik wasn't sure what hold this admiral-tramp had on him, but he wouldn't hesitate. *Alte*'s eyes weren't harsh and remote, like the other officers in Kiel. Such a mysterious tramp had to be crucial to the Kriegsmarine, or else a false Lithuanian admiral with a dueling scar wouldn't have risked breaking into Kiel Week to kill him.

'Alte, what if you are wrong about the Lithuanian?'

'Then follow me to the *Toilette* and we will find out.'

It troubled Erik and intrigued him. It was like stepping into *Alice im Wunderland;* suddenly he had become part of a strange book, where murderers followed admirals into toilets. The Kiel club had enormous windows, and he could catch the panoply of sails in the harbor, like sheets of a hundred colors in the pale sky. And with this admiral out of *Alice,* he began to feel his own place in the regatta.

Down they went into the rabbit hole, the winding stairs that led to the basement, the admiral never once looking behind him. It had been the Kaiser's own club, and the walls had silvered wainscoting; the banisters were embossed in gold. Erik heard footsteps behind him, but the admiral signaled that he shouldn't turn around.

There was a valet outside the toilet who handed both of them a towel. They went through a chrome door. The Kaiser's old *Toilette* was a festival of mirrors, where Erik could view himself from every angle; he and the admiral were multiplied so many times that it was like conjuring up an army. The tiles on the floor did not have a single chip. They might have been polished with a magic stone; he had to keep from sliding.

He heard a grunt outside the door. The Lithuanian must have knocked the valet over the head. *Alte* pretended to have heard nothing. He stopped in front of a urinal, undid his fly, and began to piss like a horse.

That's when the Lithuanian broke into the toilet clutching a kind of blackjack that telescoped into a long and thin metal club. He bowed to the admiral and the boy.

'Congratulations, Uncle Willi. I'm so glad I caught you with your *Schwanz* in your hand.'

The admiral continued to piss with great éclat, while the Lithuanian pointed to Erik.

'What is this child in the sailor suit doing here? Is he your protector, Willi?'

Erik couldn't have lunged with his dirk. The Lithuanian would have cracked *Alte*'s skull with that sharp metal stick before the knife ever landed. Erik would never get near enough, not while the Lithuanian controlled the perimeter with the long stick. But the boy didn't waver for a moment. He tossed his towel at the Lithuanian, who took his eyes off Erik long enough to flick at the towel like a fencing master. Erik ducked under the path of that murderous metal, dove into the Lithuanian, knocked him to the floor of immaculate tiles, and hit him between the eyes with his knuckles. The Lithuanian's throat began to rattle.

'*Männe*,' the admiral said, buttoning his fly. 'That's enough. Put him in a stall, *bitte*. And prop him up. When the porters find him, they will sing to themselves that one more admiral got lost in the *Toilette*.'

And while Erik dragged the Lithuanian to a stall and plunked him down on the toilet seat, the admiral stood near the mirrored sink and scrubbed his fingernails with a tiny brush as if nothing untoward had ever happened.

'*Alte*, who is this man, and why would he dare attack a German admiral?'

'He's nothing,' the admiral said, staring at his own imperfect teeth in the mirror. 'A delivery boy. Tell me, *Männe*, what is it you want most in the world? Make one wish.'

Wunderland

4

A MONTH PASSED, AND NOTHING happened. *Kieler Woche* was a dead dream that wouldn't be revived until next year. The base fell asleep again, though Kiel seemed all aclutter over its submarine fleet. There were bits of noise about driving the British sea lions from the North Atlantic. But the admiral-tramp made no more appearances. Erik assumed the Old Man was lost in *Wunderland*. But he began to make inquiries; he discovered that this white-haired admiral did have a name, and it was Wilhelm Canaris, but the name itself was surrounded by mirrors, like the ones inside the *Toilette* at the Kaiser's old yacht club. Canaris wasn't with the Kriegsmarine. He was attached to the Wehrmacht in some mysterious way. But whoever heard of a lone admiral huddling with generals at the war ministry? And then there was talk that Canaris had a ministry all his own, but not even the base commander at Kiel knew where it was. *Wunderland*, Erik muttered to himself. The admiral with the white hair had his ministry inside a rabbit hole.

But the wily illusionist couldn't even grant Erik his wish. The boy had asked for Berlin. 'Old Man,' he had said, while the Lithuanian sat in the toilet, more dead than alive, 'I miss the streets of Scheunenviertel. Bring me back to Berlin.'

And still nothing happened. He'd become a kind of royalty among his fellow cadets, a loner who had been seen talking to an admiral other admirals feared. The days dragged on. He had bad dreams about Scheunenviertel, where the streets collapsed like rotten teeth and he was caught in the maelstrom. He woke up with his own teeth chattering – a man of ice – while Kiel was in the middle of a heat wave.

And that July, after his instructors had fêted him on his eighteenth birthday with glasses of champagne, members of the Kiel patrol entered the barrack and ordered him to pack his belongings. He was delivered to a pair of SS men who stood outside the base with their death's-head insignias and polished black boots. He had to greet them with a Hitler salute. He couldn't read their blond, imperturbable faces. They both carried pistols and kid gloves under their belts, and Erik had to wonder if they meant to escort him to the nearest forest and put a bullet in his head. They did stop in a tiny wood, where submarine commanders stationed at Kiel liked to hunt and fish at the end of a long tour. Erik was bewildered when the SS men passed around a bottle of liebfraumilch and asked him to cut the sausages they had kept in the glove compartment with his dirk. Was it their own unkind ritual before a kill? He was preparing to puncture their throats when they placed the empty bottle on the stump of a tree, and took some target practice. In their drunken stupor, they didn't hit the bottle once. They started to dance and imitate the sound of a tuba. He put his dirk away.

These SS men had a little caravan attached to their Mercedes; it contained a guillotine. Their job was to deliver the guillotine to towns in the north that didn't have one and had to carry out a death sentence handed down by the People's Court. And they were squiring Erik to Berlin as a favor to Uncle Willi.

He couldn't help but like such gruesome companions. They both had been kindergarten teachers who were swept away by the Nazi regalia – the promise of black uniforms and a thousand-year Reich.

They had never heard of Rilke or Brecht and Rosa Luxemburg, but could recite tales of Hansel and Gretel for half an hour, and soon Erik began to think of them as Hansel and Gretel. They had both participated in book burnings but couldn't recollect which books they had burnt or why. They hated whatever they had been told to hate, and dragged this guillotine of theirs from town to town.

Hansel and Gretel were treated like visiting royalty in backwater provinces, where they would park outside the heavily guarded gate of some resurrected castle on Königstrasse or Königsallee, with bloodred Nazi banners riding up its front wall. The castle never varied – it served as a prison, a hotel, and local Gestapo headquarters. Erik would march into the main hall with Hansel and Gretel. A contingent of secretaries, SS officers, and Gestapo agents would swarm around them, excited by the delivery of a death machine and by the deliverers themselves. Erik had to mask his own rage and pretend that he, too, belonged with the guillotine. He had to take part in a banquet that often preceded the execution, and then watch the condemned man enter the castle's rear courtyard in a cloth hood, his hands tied behind his back, and proceed with the local pastor to this traveling guillotine, where Hansel or Gretel sat him down in its wooden cradle with a curious tenderness, whispered in his ear as they would have done to a high-strung horse, and dispatched him in the Führer's name.

The people of the town were often invited to the beheadings, which might even have a drummer boy to beat out the calvary of the condemned man. Erik's knees always jerked when the blade fell. He had to smile and smile even as he grew ill. Sometimes he vomited into a handkerchief that he hid.

He endured six beheadings on the road from Kiel to Berlin, having slept as a guest of the Gestapo in castles that were also killing grounds. The two executioners, Hansel and Gretel, had grown attached to him and insisted that he accept their last bits of sausage. They dropped him off at a nondescript gray building at the Tirpitz embankment, on the north side of the Landwehrkanal. He recalled his history lessons at the Jewish Gymnasium. Rosa Luxemburg's body had been found floating in the *Kanal* in the summer of 1919, after sailors in Kiel revolted against their own admirals, and Rosa Luxemburg's band of Spartakus radicals seized Berlin for five days and dreamt of a workers' paradise. But the Prussian police and a ragged army of irregulars broke the rebellion, and Rosa Luxemburg ended up in the Landwehrkanal.

A doorman in a sailor's uniform stood in front of the building on the Tirpitz embankment. Hansel and Gretel had already abandoned him, and the boy didn't quite know what magic formula would get him inside the building. He clicked his heels and said, 'Admiral Canaris, *bitte.*'

The sailor scowled at him. 'Can I say who is calling?'

'His Little Man.'

It must have been the right formula, because suddenly the sailor shifted his tone. 'Come with me, *mein Herr.*'

They entered the building, which was far removed from the castles that Erik had visited with Hansel and Gretel. It had no great hall. It could have been a spider's web with its warren of little rooms and dark passageways cluttered with admirals and generals who looked past Erik as if he had no right to exist. They followed one of the poorly lit passages until they arrived at a lone elevator cage in the middle of nowhere. They climbed to the fourth floor in this cage that rocked at every landing and seemed to scratch against some wall. The boy was terrified. He suffered a deeper vertigo than he had ever had aboard one of the training ships in the harbor at Kiel.

They got out of the car, passed through a metal gate that was like the ribs of an accordion, and arrived in a new kind of *Wunderland*, with a maze of tiny offices on both sides of a long hall that basked in a blinding light. And this *Wunderland* was peopled with rabbis, Gestapo agents, local gauleiters, department store managers, and diplomats – or at least men dressed to look like rabbis and diplomats. The sailor left him there and returned to the other side of the gate.

Erik advanced to the far end of the hall, entered an outer office, and introduced himself to a secretary named Wera, whose own assistant was also named Wera. The two Weras knocked on a door and guided Erik into an inner office with a balcony overlooking the Landwehrkanal. The office had a camp bed, a worn sofa, a safe, and several chairs. Admiral Canaris was standing near the balcony in the same rumpled uniform, speckled with cigar ashes. Erik noticed his pale blue eyes for the first time, in the piercing light off the balcony. But it wasn't the admiral-tramp who had startled him. It was the agent standing next to *Alte*. How could Erik have forgotten the man with the *Schmiss* under one eye, that false Lithuanian admiral from the yacht club in Kiel, who seemed to have recovered from the beating Erik had given him.

'*Alte,* you shouldn't have tricked me. I was trying to save your life in the toilet.'

Canaris began to purr like a delighted cat. '*Männe,* can you ever forgive me? Meet Commander Helmut Stolz.'

The Sheriff of Scheunenviertel

5

IT WAS AN ASYLUM CALLED the Abwehr, filled with cipher clerks, lab technicians, spies and counterspies, commandos and saboteurs. It had outstations, a *Hauskapelle* (or private orchestra) in every country under the sun, with its own *Kapellmeister*. Canaris' deepest pleasure was to visit these outstations, whether they were in Cairo or Seville. Thus he wandered from *Hauskapelle* to *Hauskapelle*, and was seldom in Berlin, where he had a wife and two daughters tucked away in a house on Dollestrasse, with its own private garden. He took his two wirehaired dachshunds, Seppel and Sabine, wherever he went, and if he had to leave them behind, he would telephone from Cairo or Baghdad six times a day to find out if Sabine still had an eye infection or if Seppel had had a walk on the *Kanal*.

Uncle Willi, as Commander Stolz called him, seemed to encourage chaos. He had little sense of order. His best agents intrigued around him. Yet he always uncovered their schemes. No one, not even Canaris, knew how the Abwehr worked. It had its own brigade, the Brandenbergers, who were soldiers and saboteurs. They were the finest military unit in Berlin and could have staged a coup d'état, locked up Hitler, Goebbels, the Gestapo, and the SS, had Uncle Willi snapped his fingers. But he wouldn't move against Hitler and Himmler's gang, wouldn't arrest Herr Goebbels. He was ashamed of Hitler's campaign against the Jews, though it was Uncle Willi himself who had suggested in 1935 that every Jew in Germany wear a Star of David as an identifying mark. He was fraught with contradictions, running to the Chancellery twice a month to meet with Herr Hitler. The little admiral had mystified half the Third Reich.

He didn't bother outflanking the SS as Hitler's generals had tried to do. He knew that the SS, which was encroaching upon his territories, hid microphones in his office and listened to most of his conversations. Uncle Willi learned to live with the SS, a state unto itself, blond men in black, the Party's own militia.

He hadn't brought *Männe* into the Abwehr to mind his dachshunds. He had Erik become the Abwehr's liaison with the Gestapo and the SS. The boy spent several weekends a month at the SS *Junkerschule* in Bad Tölz, where he learned to lie and cheat and handle firearms with blond brutes, men who had never gone to Erik's Jewish Gymnasium, whose sense of history came from *Mein Kampf,* who were oddly sentimental priests of the Third Reich, willing to die for their mothers, sisters, and the Fatherland. These officer candidates were all curious about the cadet from Kiel who had been kidnapped by Admiral Canaris and sent to their own training school. He did not talk of Scheunenviertel with them. And when they rasped about *Rassenschande*, the shame of pure blooded Germans who had defiled their race by marrying Jewish mongrels, he nodded and pretended to listen. He realized soon enough that these SS trainees would have kissed every rabbi in Berlin had Hitler told them to do so.

But the Gestapo wasn't made of bumpkins and priests. Its men were much more cultivated. And when he visited Gestapo headquarters at Prinz-Albrecht-Strasse, he was always on his guard. The Gestapo knew right away where he lived. He had returned to Scheunenviertel, had moved into his mother's old flat, and the commandant at Prinz-Albrecht-Strasse had remarked to him, 'How clever of you, Herr Holdermann. A spy in the house of the Jews.'

The Gestapo didn't dare spy on him; he was practically one of their own. Uncle Willi had signed a concordat with the Gestapo and the SS. They worked out a list of ten commandments. The Abwehr wouldn't enter into domestic espionage, and the SS wouldn't interfere with the Abwehr's outstations in other countries. Of course, the SS was always meddling and interfering in the Abwehr's business. But Canaris' *Tipper*, his stool pigeons, were usually half a leap ahead of the Gestapo and the SS. The agents of the Tirpitz embankment were living on borrowed time. One day the Gestapo would arrive at Uncle Willi's metal gate, eat right through it with gigantic clippers, and arrest the whole lot of them, including Canaris. But until then, they plotted and schemed, brought as many Jews as they could under their own secret veil, since the Abwehr could still keep Jews on its payroll. The admiral-tramp had reasoned to Himmler himself that an international network of spies couldn't operate without a token number of Jews. And Himmler had left Uncle Willi alone.

The Abwehr had tentacles everywhere. It had found each stick of furniture that the Jews of Scheunenviertel had put in storage after Erik's mother had died. And so when Erik first appeared at his old flat on the Dragonerstrasse, it was almost exactly as he had left it. There were the same mirrors, the same carved bed, the same armoire, and Erik thought he could sniff the wonderful musk of his mother's shoes. But not even the Abwehr could locate her dresses or shoes, her garter belts and stockings. And he hardly had a moment to contemplate his childhood.

He was always on some mission when he wasn't trying to please the SS or placate Prinz-Albrecht-Strasse. He belonged to Commander Stolz's *Aktionen*. That false Lithuanian had once been

Rosa Luxemburg's bodyguard and confidant and had taken part in the Spartakus rebellion. He was rounded up by the Prussian police after the rebellion failed and sat in Moabit prison. His 'dueling scars' had come from the batons of the Prussian police. It was Uncle Willi who had rescued him in 1925. Canaris was close to naval intelligence at the time and was looking for *Tipper* among the Reds. Helmut Stolz once had his own theater in the workingman's district of Wedding. The theater was called Aktion. Canaris persuaded him to reopen Aktion and put on propaganda plays. Helmut was one of the first to discover Brecht. He called himself the 'Red Commandant.' He took part in brawls. He attacked Hitler's Brownshirts. But he kept elaborate notebooks for naval intelligence. He betrayed no one. He just scribbled notes and kept track of every sailor who wandered through Wedding.

When the Nazis seized power, Stolz melted into the countryside, and Aktion became one more deserted warehouse. But after Uncle Willi was named head of the Abwehr, he brought Helmut back from obscurity and had him resurrect Aktion within its walls. It was a theater group, but not for Red propaganda. Helmut's *Aktionen* were intrigues with elaborate plots – a dozen actors among the Abwehr elite. He recruited Erik on the spot, turned him into the Abwehr's greatest actor-spy. Anyone who threatened the Abwehr's sanctuaries might be frightened into silence, kidnapped, or disposed of by *Aktion*. The Abwehr had no mandate to murder anyone, but its enemies still disappeared. And that's how the myth of Cesare was born.

Erik never varied his role. He played himself, though the Abwehr's Jewish tailors might fit him with an SS officer's uniform or a Gestapo agent's leather overcoat. But it wasn't much of a disguise, since the SS and the Gestapo assumed that Erik had some sort of dual appointment with the Abwehr and Hitler's political police. He could march into any Gestapo substation, and officers and secretaries would stand at attention. Hadn't he gone to Prague and gotten rid of a Moldavian agent who was selling the Wehrmacht's secret war plans to the British? He walked in and out of Czechoslovakia. But the SS never realized that this Moldavian agent was one of Uncle Willi's best *Tipper,* and the Abwehr's magicians had spirited him away to a remote island in Greece.

He began to brood when he got back from a mission in Belgrade, where he had to rip off the clothes of Canaris' *Kappelmeister,* who was selling Abwehr secrets to the Poles. It was a week after *Kristallnacht* – the Night of the Broken Glass – when Nazi goons all over the Fatherland destroyed the property and sanctuaries of the Jews. Erik witnessed the traces of this destruction in Scheunenviertel. The windows of Jewish shops had been shattered. The synagogue near Rosenthaler Platz had been burnt to the ground. He stood beside the ruins, remembering the gilded roof and the ornate dome and spires he had loved, and now the synagogue sat in a tiny sea of smoke and glass; the fire, he had been told, had raged for two nights, without a single fireman to save any of its relics.

A little girl crept out from a nearby door, stared at Erik's leather coat, began to howl, and ran back inside. He had become the sheriff of Scheunenviertel, who lived on the Dragonerstrasse, and seemed to watch over the district. The shopkeepers started to trust the man in the Gestapo coat who loved their strudel and almond bread, never spat curses at them, or sang obscene songs to their daughters.

A month after Erik had come to Scheunenviertel from Kiel, Nazi hoodlums had stopped crashing through the streets. There were few Gestapo raids in the middle of the night. The commandant of the local headquarters on the Französische Strasse knew where Erik lived, and it was out of respect to him and the Abwehr that the commandant decided to 'forget' the Jews near Hackescher Markt.

But nothing could have stopped the fury of *Kristallnacht,* and the commandant had reined in none of the hoodlums, none of his own men.

One of the district's 'gauleiters,' a printer who happened to have a shop at the very edge of Scheunenviertel, had been particularly violent during *Kristallnacht,* had kicked an old man to death and smashed the face of a Jewish housewife. It took Erik a week to track the printer down. He followed this gauleiter to a beer hall on the Prenzlauer Allee, in Alexanderplatz's own little red-light district, sat over a 'white' beer, and intended to murder the man once he went to piss in the toilet.

But someone familiar sat down next to Cesare. It was his own commandant, Helmut Stolz.

'*Männe,* do you want to have a second night of broken glass in Scheunenviertel? If you harm this *Schwanz,* all the Yids will suffer.'

'Then what should I do, Herr Commandant? I will smolder like that beautiful lost synagogue if I let him walk out of here alive.'

'But smoldering won't set your hair on fire. You'll survive, and you won't end up in a Gestapo cellar. Leave it to us. Let him walk around for another few months. And when he disappears, it won't be connected to *Kristallnacht.*'

Erik wasn't allowed to take part in this *Aktion.* A little after the new year, in the midst of a snowstorm, the gauleiter was shoved into an Abwehr ambulance parked in front of his printing shop, driven to a forest outside Berlin, and buried there. The Gestapo hardly even noticed. But Scheunenviertel must have had a *Tipper* of its own. In some mysterious fashion its inhabitants discovered that the gauleiter had disappeared for good. Children began to come out of their hiding places, and shopkeepers smiled at the sheriff of Scheunenviertel and begged him to taste their almond bread.

'Herr Cesare,' they said, kissing his hands. How could they have known that he was a secret agent? They must have assumed that their savior slept in a coffin. And sometimes he did feel like a ghoul, with his own Caligari, Admiral Canaris. When he walked with the admiral on the Tirpitz embankment, a dachshund under each of the admiral's arms, men and women did stare at them, as if they had already become an infernal couple – Canaris and his own walking nightmare, Cesare. Erik's sunken cheeks and gloomy look must have added to the legend.

And now that same legend had wandered through the alleys of Scheunenviertel. The ghetto had its own golem, not twisted out of clay, but a man of bone, blood, and gristle, born in Berlin. This golem had never harmed a single Jew. He often traveled about in the boots and silver sleeves of an SS captain. How wily their golem was. He mimicked their enemies, and could make a gauleiter disappear. And if their savior was a somnambulist beholden to a white-haired German admiral, what could it matter to them? The coffin Herr Cesare slept in was secreted somewhere in Scheunenviertel. And woe to any man who rocked that coffin and interfered with Cesare's sleep.

The Little Baron

6

T HE ADMIRAL HAD LITTLE TIME to play Caligari. He was involved
in a war he couldn't avoid. He had to lend his saboteurs to
the Wehrmacht. The Brandenbergers stole across the borders a
few nights before the Germans invaded Poland, half their bodies
painted black, cut the Polish lines of communication, dispatched
border guards and border patrols, and the Wehrmacht rushed in
and broke the siege of Warsaw within a month. It was the very first
blitzkrieg, perfected by Hitler and his generals, with the help of
Admiral Canaris. But the nightmare began once the Germans sat
in Warsaw. The SS arrived in their armored cars; they had become
the new commissars – it was in late September of 1939. They
rounded up rabbis and priests, university professors, Gypsies, and
journalists. They shot Jewish children in the streets. It was their
form of recreation.

And when Uncle Willi appeared in Warsaw, all his euphoria,
his pride in the Brandenberg Brigade, was gone. He discovered
a bombed-out and broken city ruled by SS assassination squads.
The Gestapo fanned into Warsaw, starved half the population, and
turned the other half into slaves. Uncle Willi flew back to Berlin
with the chalk-white face of a dead man. He withdrew into his
Fuchsbau, his Fox's Lair, that labyrinth of rooms above the *Kanal*,
and would see no one. The old fox had run himself into the ground.

He emerged from his lair with the same chalk-white complexion. He had Seppel under one arm and Sabine under the other. He was gruff with the two Weras, when he had always been polite with them. He had his chauffeur take him to the Tiergarten. And thus he blocked out Warsaw for half an hour as he rode Motte, his splendid Arabian mare, in the woods. When he returned to the *Fuchsbau*, most of his sallowness was gone. His *Hauskapelle* in Warsaw was still functioning amid all the ruins, and he had his agents rescue as many Jews and Polish aristocrats as they could. His tailors had sewn SS uniforms for the aristocrats; Abwehr trucks drove them out of Warsaw, with a visiting choir that had come to entertain the Wehrmacht during the misery of war. But this choir couldn't sing – it consisted of Jewish children dressed in angelic coats.

Uncle Willi had come alive again. He smoked his little cigars while the Wehrmacht had victory after victory, with the slight inconvenience of a world war. It was Hitler who seemed like the magician, not the little admiral in his Fox's Lair. Canaris could drape his overcoat over the telephone in his office, tap his walls for hidden microphones, and whisper to his subordinates that the Führer's mad, insatiable hunger would cost him the war. But who would listen other than Erik, Commander Stolz, some technicians and tailors, and a few forgers? Half of Canaris' agents, including women and men the SS had planted within the Fox's Lair, were convinced that no one could ever stop the Wehrmacht.

Hitler's own generals realized that the tanks had gone too far, that the supply lines were stretched too thin, but they had inherited their Führer's fever for war. And there were distractions in Berlin; cabarets and 'boy clubs' could be found five minutes from Gestapo headquarters; Brecht was performed right under the Nazis' noses. An SS officer appeared in *Mahagonny*; the gangsters in the play looked like Gestapo agents. Tickets were impossible to get; even majors in the Wehrmacht didn't have enough pull to worm their way in. And so what if a few British Mosquitoes bombed Berlin? So far, there had been little damage. *Mädschen* in the anti-aircraft auxiliary corps who happened to sit in the raised seats of ack-ack guns might soon be sending Mosquitoes to hell. These gun girls had become the pride of Berlin. Yes, butter was rationed, and real coffee was reserved for generals. But there was another great diversion – the Jews.

Hitler wanted to see a Berlin that was *judenrein,* and Herr Goebbels had decided to grant him his wish. Jews were plucked off the streets, and there was little that the sheriff of Scheunenviertel could do about it. Starting in September of '41, all Jews in Germany had to wear a yellow star over their hearts; the star cost ten pfennigs at special shops; every Jew had to buy six, and the Jews of Berlin couldn't be seen without a star sewn to their chests, or they would end up in a cell on Alexanderplatz. They had their own ration cards, which granted them very little to eat. They'd been thrown out of their jobs and had to live in *Judenhauser,* luckless apartment houses where only Jews could dwell. Jewish women had to have the name Sarah tacked onto their identity papers, and men had to use Israel as their middle name. Shopkeepers painted their own signs: JEWS NOT WELCOME HERE. Little by little, Jews were denied every scrap of Berlin life. They could only sit on park benches that were painted yellow, and then weren't even allowed to enter the parks or movie palaces and concert halls. They were forbidden to have bicycles or radios or typewriters. They couldn't use ordinary bomb shelters, but had to have shelters of their own, usually cellars filled with rats. They couldn't ride on buses without a pass and their yellow stars. Jewish children were pinched in the street; shopkeepers hissed at old men in caftans. Jews had to abide by special curfews, had to be home before eight.

Erik went on fewer missions. He'd walk the streets at night in his black leather coat, but he could not save the Jews of his own district. They were rounded up in taxis, Black Marias, and trucks, while the Gestapo sat and yawned and did not have to scream at the Jews. The Gestapo had their own assistants, Judenpolizei, or Jupo, Jewish auxiliary policemen, ex-schoolteachers who had lost their schools and their students and were now fed by their Nazi handlers. The Jupo did not carry whips or strike children and confused old men. They helped them with their bundles and other belongings. They whispered, soothed, stroked some wizened grandmother, and didn't even have to coerce her onto a truck. They bribed with bits of honey cake and brown rock candy. They wore mouse-colored velvet gloves and steered the Jews of Scheunenviertel into the collection camp at Erik's old orphanage on the Rosenstrasse. Some of the Jews would be sent to the ghetto in Lodz, others to labor camps, with their suitcases; it tore at Erik to see the little Jewish girls with their dolls. He could not rescue a single one.

He raced across Berlin from the Rosenstrasse to the Landwehrkanal and went up to the little admiral and his Fox's Lair. But the admiral wasn't alone. A strange little man sat in Canaris' chair, resembling one of Rouault's dwarfish emperors and Christ clowns. Erik's art teacher at the Jewish Gymnasium had loved Rouault, had talked about the images of Christ in a red beard that wandered like an apparition through Rouault's work. This little man also had a red beard. He wasn't exactly a dwarf, but his legs didn't touch the ground; he wore slippers instead of shoes; his soft shirt and silk tie must have been bought ages ago at Berlin's best department store, Die Drei Krokodile (once owned by Baron von Hecht), when silk ties could still be found. He was, in fact, a nephew of the baron, a certain Emil von Hecht, who was thirty-nine years old and had lived at a sanitarium in the Black Forest until Uncle

Willi whisked him away to Berlin. Emil wasn't insane; nor was he feebleminded, but he was slow of speech. Sentences wouldn't form. He lisped. Veins exploded on his forehead. He would scribble a note on a pad attached to his vest by a silver string, memorize the words, and chant them like some forlorn opera singer who had lost her melodic line.

The Gestapo didn't appreciate the peculiarities of such a male diva and convinced the doctors at the sanitarium to sterilize Emil. The game had begun. The SS would kidnap Emil and hide him in a factory that manufactured cuckoo clocks until Baron von Hecht paid their ridiculous ransom. It was a way of keeping Emil alive. But Uncle Willi knew it wouldn't last. Other patients at the sanitarium had fallen heir to *Aktion T4,* Hitler's mad scheme to rid the Reich of mental misfits, and one afternoon Emil would be led deep into the woods and shot in the neck. And so Canaris kidnapped him permanently from the SS.

'Herr Admiral,' Erik said, 'I am happy for Emil, but I must speak to you in private.'

'*Männe,* we have nothing to hide. Emil is one of us. I have brought him into the Abwehr.'

'Good, but what will we do about the Rosenstrasse? The *Dreckshunde* are rounding up Jews block by block. And the Jupo help them make their lists. Can't we borrow your Brandenbergers and have them march in front of the SS and their trucks?'

'And tomorrow the Brandenbergers will be locked out of their barracks and sent to guard Polish prisoners.'

'But it will give me time to mount my own *Aktion.* We'll send in our trucks, with our own forged documents, and empty out the Rosenstrasse.'

'And where will you put a whole *Sammellager* of Jews?' Uncle Willi begged with his pale blue eyes. 'You'll get them all killed.'

That's when Emil von Hecht, the little baron, decided to open his mouth. He didn't have to scratch on his pad. His cheeks puffed out perfect syllables. 'They'll die anyway, Uncle Willi... They'll go right from Lodz to the labor camps. And what magnificent labor! They'll all be starved to death or gassed.'

'Silence,' said the admiral. 'You're an agent of the Abwehr. I didn't bring you out of the Black Forest to speculate on the Führer's policies. There are no gas chambers at Auschwitz. There are no trucks filled with Zyklon B, no ovens that burn day and night... They are someone's feeble imaginings. We are spies, not philosophers and moralists. And if you utter another word about gas chambers, Emil, I'll sell you back to the Gestapo.'

The little baron sat with his velvet slippers dangling above a carpet that had been soiled and torn by Seppel and Sabine, while the admiral himself fell into silence. He leaned forward and put his hands over his eyes. His white hair shone in the weak light. He started to tremble.

'*Männe*, I will not tolerate civil war. You will not harm one hair of the Führer's *Polizei*. You will not involve our tailors in your schemes. They already have one foot on the other side of eternity. You will not use Abwehr real estate. We cannot hide Jews in our safe houses. You will draw whatever funds you need. And you must be discreet with our forgers. They have their own style. And it can easily be unmasked. So you must save only one Jew at a time.'

Erik coughed into his fist. '*Alte*, they murder wholesale, and we are pathetic retailers who have to dance on the head of a pin.'

'One Jew at a time. And no more than two in every trainload of a thousand, or they'll catch on to you in a minute.'

'Two in a thousand,' Erik whispered. 'That's unkind. And what team will I have? May I include Commander Stolz?'

'And compromise us all? I will allow you one man. Emil.'

71

Erik stared at the little baron with the red beard who was both a Christ and a wily cretin.

'*Gott*, he's been living in an asylum. And when the Nazis kidnapped him, he had to listen to the sound of cuckoo clocks.'

'*Männe*, that sound might save your skin.'

IT WAS A SERIES OF night moves. Erik had to wander into the local Gestapo headquarters, where the list of Jews was assembled, and pore over the list with the Jupo and whatever Gestapo agent or SS captain was in charge of that night's roundup. He would smoke a Roth-Händle with the Jewish auxiliaries, offering them cigarettes out of his silvered pack. The Roth-Händles came from the Abwehr's own stores and were worth a fortune on the black market.

It was while smoking with the Jupo that Erik realized which ones were truly 'tainted' and which ones he could trust. It was not a matter of soundings. He looked into their eyes, and sometimes he saw the mad gleam of a Jewish Gestapo agent, a convert who fed off the little power he had. Or else Erik saw the sad, conflicted eyes of a man lost in his own bewilderment. These were the Jupo he had to avoid. They were like children who might howl and run into the arms of their Nazi handlers, or jump onto a deportation truck. The others were zealots who were looking to survive. And Erik worked out business deals with them. He pretended to be a profiteer. It was like buying and selling cigarettes.

'*Mensch*, this one on Oranienburger, he's rich as Moses. His grandparents paid for half the gold on the roof of the Neue Synagoge. We'll squeeze them dry. Ten thousand marks if we scratch him off the list.'

'Herr Holdermann, anything can be done. We'll swear he had a heart attack on the way to the Rosenstrasse. But we'll have to pull another Yid off the street.'

Erik had to harden himself to their gambits, their promiscuity with people's lives. But he also realized that he was no less promiscuous. He'd turned the nightly roundup into a roulette wheel. He couldn't snatch children, because they didn't know how to play roulette. And he couldn't separate a parent from a child, or a husband from a wife, because the rescued one might rebel and want to climb back onto the truck. He had to pick men or women who lived alone, who wouldn't be missed. They were already half-dead in Erik's eyes, husks who had so little connection to other humans that there was no memory in their limbs. That's what he wanted to believe.

He'd kill himself, fall under a moving truck, if he had to follow the admiral's prescriptions. He'd save entire families, or no one at all. But he was far more quixotic than the families themselves, who recognized the terror of their own existence – whole families could not be saved, but a daughter could, or a son who had been thrown out of the gymnasium.

A father with tears in his eyes would touch Erik's shoulder. 'Take my daughter, Excellency. We will think of her and it will give us courage.'

The daughter would cackle like a lunatic and begin to cry. '*Papi*, I will not hide without you. Please don't abandon me to this hell.'

Erik would have a tantrum while pitying her. 'No, no, no! I'll save you all from the *Sammellager*.'

It was the little baron who had to take him aside. 'It's impossible. We would need an army to provide for them all. And an army leaves its own slugs, like a snail. The Gestapo will shut us down, Excellency.'

Erik had to whisper. 'Emil, why do you call me "Excellency"? I never even graduated from Kiel.'

But Emil's speech was whimsical. It came and went. He had to scribble on his pad. The sounds still wouldn't come. He was frantic. Erik had to stroke Emil's red beard.

'You're my field man, Emil. Don't fail me now.'

'Yes, Excellency. Our lives are in your hands.'

Erik took the lone daughters and sons and condemned their families to the Rosenstrasse. He had to find cellars where the submariners could hide, or lodge them with couples who were themselves Abwehr subagents. It was an elaborate subterfuge, where the 'U-boats' had to exist without the least commotion, with footless footsteps not even an angel could hear. But sometimes these submariners took risks. They could not bear to be cooped up and they'd wander into the streets with their false papers that wouldn't have fooled any of the Jew-hunters, and Erik himself would have to recapture these submariners and return them to their roosts.

It was like being the master of a band of brilliant, unruly children. He wouldn't have succeeded without the little baron. Protected by the Abwehr, Emil could move unmolested about Berlin, clutching a briefcase full of encrypted notes. He was the go-between who behaved like the U-boats' private counselor. They would present Emil with their own little list of needs: a chess set, a bar of rationed soap, winter underwear, a certain book. And Erik would have to supply the U-boats from the Abwehr's own stores. The Abwehr had the largest library of forbidden books in Berlin. Erik had improved his English by reading American authors whose books had been banned in Germany. He could not have comprehended America without *The Great Gatsby* or *Moby-Dick*. His favorite American author was Herman Melville, another submariner who had spent half his life under the surface of society, who had stopped writing books by the time he was forty and wandered around in the brittle and barren landscape of his own mind, a landscape that was not unlike Berlin.

So he assembled a little library for the submariners on his own watch. There was a certain danger, since each book carried the Abwehr's stamp inside the front cover. But it seemed worth the risk because of the pleasure it gave Erik to be the submariners' librarian. He felt as if he were back at school, prowling through the great Babel of books at the Jewish Gymnasium. He considered his own work at the Abwehr trivial compared to his manhunts across the pages of *Moby-Dick*. Hitler's mad dominions meant nothing to Erik. He was loyal to Uncle Willi and played Cesare for him. He would have gladly murdered Herr Goebbels, the gauleiter of Berlin, who had a villa on Hermann-Göring-Strasse, at the eastern edge of the Tiergarten; the somnambulist could have strangled Goebbels in bed without harming his six little children – Hildegard, Helga, Helmut, Hedwig, Heidrun, and Holdine, whose sonorous names were like chords plucked out of a dream.

An assault on Hermann-Göring-Strasse would have compromised Uncle Willi and destroyed the Abwehr in one blow, but it still tempted Cesare. So what if he'd have to lie down in the cradle of Hansel and Gretel's traveling guillotine? He'd refuse to wear a hood. He'd face the Nazi banners and go to the guillotine with a look of bliss. But nowhere in his cosmology could he ever have imagined slaughtering Herr Goebbels' six children. Ah, but he couldn't leave this world now that he had a new friend and fellow agent. What would happen to Emil? The little baron thrived on his descent into the cellars with a satchelful of forbidden books. He was a perfect *porte-parole*. He could maneuver like no other dwarfish man with a red beard. He hadn't always been locked away in a sanitarium. He had once been the heir to Baron von Hecht's fortune at Die Drei Krokodile. He'd managed that magnificent department store on Alexanderplatz, with its walls of steel and glass. He had looked like a diplomat in his striped trousers, spats, and swallowtail coat. He terrorized the baron's personnel. But he lusted after the salesgirls and the mannequins in the women's fine-wear department. He made a mess of things, fell in love with a mannequin, who laughed in his face. He had her fired. But her brutish fiancé, a Brownshirt, arrived at Die Drei Krokodile with five other Brownshirts, broke into the little baron's office, and hurled him headlong across counters of merchandise, as if Emil were a professional midget who made a living at country fairs being hurled by strongmen from Bavaria.

The little baron's swift decline began after this invasion of Brownshirts at Die Drei Krokodile. It was in the spring of 1934, and the Brownshirts still ruled Berlin. Emil lost the will to speak. He remained as manager, but his eyes were listless. He couldn't remember the simplest detail. He wore the same trousers for a month. The baron had to come in his limousine from the Grunewald and have Emil removed from the glass and steel wonderland of Die Drei Krokodile. He kept Emil at his villa, fed him soup with his own hand, but he couldn't cure the despair and humiliation of a man who had been hurled across a department store. He had Emil sent to the sanitarium in the Black Forest, which had been a refuge for the richest Jews of Berlin, where catatonic nephews and daughters and wives who had lost their minds could live in a kind of regal prison-hotel. The little baron might have remained there in perpetuity if Hitler hadn't decided to cleanse the Reich of 'degenerates and dwarfs.' He had to thank the Führer for his sudden freedom. How else could he have gone from a palatial room with bars on the window to the Abwehr?

He began wearing striped trousers again as the submariners' *porte-parole*. His speech wasn't as slow. He did look like one of Rouault's suffering emperors, but he suffered less. He entered the strange, fluid world of wartime Berlin.

One freezing afternoon in '42, he stood on his toes and tapped Erik on the shoulder with a ferocious growl.

'*Männe*, we're invited to a soiree.'

'Who invited us, Emil? We're much too busy with our submariners.'

'Then we'll have a holiday. It's my little cousin, Frau Valentiner. She hasn't forgotten her protégé.'

Erik was bewildered for a moment. And then he began to shiver under his long leather coat.

Lisalein.

He'd been having a sort of quick romance with a gun girl whose station was the roof of the IG Farben offices across from the Hotel Adlon. He'd met her in the bar of the Adlon, where ack-ack auxiliaries had their own little roost. Her name was Tilli. He never brought her to the Dragonerstrasse. He either went to her tiny apartment near the Charlottenburger Chaussee or made love to her in the suite that the Abwehr kept at the Adlon to recruit some *V-Mann* (a foreigner who served as an informant and go-between). The *V-Mann* might have been a minor diplomat from a neutral country. He would be trapped into a liaison with one of the Abwehr's 'Spiders,' high-priced whores who were paid to catch some poor soul in the Abwehr's own web. At first, Erik thought that Tilli herself was a Spider. But she was a patriotic gun girl. And when he pinned her arms to the bedpost at the Adlon and listened to her deafening love screams, he could luxuriate for a moment in the delicious perfume of her armpits. He dreamt of little else than to empty out the *Sammellager* on Rosenstrasse and to possess enough magic to have Jews melt back into Scheunenviertel, a hundred at a time.

And now this blond witch from his own past would wreck whatever little peace he had!

Die Drei Krokodile

7

H E COULD HAVE WORN HIS captain's uniform, with its epaulets and buttons made of pure bone. But he didn't want to come swaggering into Lisa's foyer as a military man. So he arrived on the Hermann-Göring-Strasse in a worsted suit that he had inherited from an Abwehr agent who died of a heart attack while on active duty. It was his 'Cesare' suit, which he would wear on missions abroad. Its cuffs were slightly frayed, but he liked to think that the simple elegance of its worsted wool had brought him luck. It was an assassin's suit.

Emil was much more diplomatic. He'd come in spats and a swallowtail coat from his days at Die Drei Krokodile, bearing Belgian chocolates in a heart-shaped box. Erik could have found some exotic gift in the Abwehr's stores, but he would have felt foolish with a stuffed panda in his arms.

Lisa lived a few doors down from Herr Goebbels in a classic Nazi Alpine cottage with a gabled roof. Goebbels' street was always guarded, but the SS men on duty recognized Erik and didn't bother much with the little baron. A maid in blue mascara met them at the door. Erik had to blink. The maid reminded him of a notorious Jewish streetwalker named Sissi who had patrolled Alexanderplatz while he was still at the orphanage. Sissi had been kind to him, had given Erik bonbons and cigarettes, and had even allowed him to touch her breast. And if it was Sissi, he didn't want to embarrass her, but he couldn't help kissing her hand.

She had a mole painted on her cheek, like Madame de Pompadour.

'Fräulein Sissi,' he said, 'do you remember me?'

She laughed in the doorway with all her robustness, and it nearly split the seams of her white blouse. 'My orphan with the big eyes,' she said, nuzzling him without shame. 'You mustn't spill my secret to Herr Valentiner. He'll ship me to a Farben factory, and the petrochemicals will kill my complexion... Who is your handsome friend?'

'I'm Emil,' said the little baron, who barely reached the black lace bands of her apron.

'Frau Valentiner's cousin, who was the little führer of Die Drei Krokodile?'

She nuzzled him, too; Emil was already smitten. And then Erik heard a thick, melodious call from inside the chalet.

'Sissi, how many times do I have to tell you not to flirt with my guests? They'll think I run a bordello.'

Lisalein appeared in a gown of spun silver, clutching a goblet filled with pink champagne. She'd startled the life out of poor Erik, who'd expected to see a beautiful dragoness on this Nazi street. Marriage must have agreed with her. She'd grown an inch. She was taller than Erik as she swayed on her heels. But female dragons weren't usually nearsighted. And Lisalein stumbled around like a half-blind girl. She was twenty-six. And he'd never seen her as a woman, only as a child bride, seven or eight years ago. She was much fleshier now, with a gorgeous rump. She squinted at Erik and gave the little baron her hand to kiss.

'Emil darling, whom have you brought here? One of your comrades from the secret service? A gigolo who preys on married women with weak eyes.'

'Ach, Lisa,' said Emil. 'You ordered me to bring Herr Holdermann. You said your father had found him in an orphanage. He's a captain now.'

'Oh,' she said, shaking Erik's hand. 'Captain, how nice to see you again. You were living in a barn when I saw you last.'

'I still live in a barn, Frau Valentiner. Scheunenviertel was once a district of barns and a great cow pasture. But how is your father?'

'Please don't stand at the door, Captain. We are not barbarians... Sissi, take their coats.'

Sissi carried the coats to a closet and then followed Lisalein and her two guests through a long, dark corridor and into a dining room that was as grandiose as a castle's main hall. It was lit with several torches that reached right to the ceiling. There were tapestries on the walls that depicted hunting scenes: aurochs with terrible teeth devouring hunters and their horses; hunters piercing the aurochs' eyes with javelins; other hunters bleeding to death.

Beneath the tapestries were benches with leather seats and a rough table that belonged in a hunting lodge. Erik wondered if the paraphernalia had come from Hermann Göring, who loved to dress up as Robin Hood in leather jerkin, high boots, and a feathered hat. But the man who stood beside the table wasn't Robin Hood. It was Lisa's husband, Josef Valentiner, who was no longer a Nazi wunderkind. As economic führer of the conquered territories, he was responsible for milking whatever wealth there was in Holland, Belgium, and France. He was also a colonel in the SS, and he wore a black uniform with a silver *Totenkopf* ring. He still had a boy's fat cheeks and fat hands and was as nearsighted as Lisa herself. He didn't like Emil, whom he had tangled with many times at Die Drei Krokodile when he worked for Baron von Hecht.

He poured champagne and sat down at the table with his guests.

'Captain Erik, how is Canaris? He used to be cozy with my

wife… They conspired to bring Cousin Emil back from the dead. I was in Brussels, at the Metropole, dining with Belgian diplomats who swore that King Leopold did not have an ounce of silver or gold. I would have torn the gold from their mouths. War is a hungry animal, Captain. I will have every barrel of oil in Bessarabia before I am through with the Russians, and I will visit Leopold's castle at Lacken and flay him alive. I do not like barons and kings – do you?'

'I have only met one baron, Frau Valentiner's father, and he was quite kind to me.'

'Ja, ja,' said Valentiner, growing impatient, 'but a Jewish baron doesn't count. I am talking about meddlers like Leopold – Leopold is one of our subjects now. I would starve him to death. But how is Canaris? Is he still creating make-believe captains like yourself?'

Valentiner smiled and turned to his wife. 'Darling, didn't you know that your Erik couldn't even survive his training as a cadet?'

Lisalein stood near her husband like a silver sheath, her eyes glistening under the fickle torchlight as she smiled back at him.

'Josef, if you insult all our guests, we'll have to move into the Tiergarten and dine with the zebras.'

Erik closed his eyes and imagined what it would be like to have Herr Valentiner swallow his own death's-head ring. He had dueled with much better men than a civilian colonel who picked the bones of defeated countries.

'It wasn't an insult, Frau Valentiner. We are magicians at the Abwehr – we produce captains and corpses.'

'And many of your corpses come back to life,' said Valentiner. 'Dr Caligari can't even hold on to the dead. A rogue Bulgarian diplomat in Portugal was selling our secrets. The Abwehr silenced him. But he went from the morgue to the island of Corfu, where he lives like a king on an Abwehr pension, with two mistresses and three wives.'

Erik created his own mask of a smile. 'That was the admiral's greatest coup. The Bulgarian was one of ours. He compromised half the British agents in Lisbon with the lies he spread. And we pulled him after someone in the SS blundered into Portugal and bribed the Lisbon police to have him killed... but I'm afraid we're boring you, Frau Valentiner, with these fairy tales of ours.'

Valentiner brooded for a moment, his piggish eyes darting behind thick glasses, while the maid went into the kitchen and returned with a silver tray of asparagus in white wine; the asparagus stalks were arranged like pieces of art against the silver, in their own perfect design. Valentiner maneuvered with his knife and fork, but his head was whistling and he couldn't shut up, even with bits of asparagus in his mouth.

'It's Heydrich who's keeping you all afloat,' Valentiner said. 'He would have squashed the Abwehr years ago if he hadn't served as a cadet under Canaris. He's fond of Uncle Willi, and blind to his faults.'

Reinhard Heydrich was chief of the Gestapo and the SS, second only to Himmler himself. Known as 'Hangman Heydrich,' he was the most cunning and cruel of Hitler's apparatchiks. He was tall, blond, with a long, crooked nose and effeminate hands. His classmates had called him 'Ziege,' the goat, on account of his high voice. He'd had no friends at school. He practiced fencing, played the violin, and decided on a career in the Reichsmarine. The cadets at Kiel made fun of him and his fiddler's hands. But he happened to train on one of Canaris' ships, and Uncle Willi, who was also shy, took a liking to him and kept the other cadets at bay. Heydrich was cashiered out of the Reichsmarine after he broke his promise to marry the daughter of a powerful industrialist. He met Himmler in '31, was welcomed into the Gestapo, and turned the SS into the Party's own great spy machine. He was a major in the SS before he was twenty-seven. Heydrich didn't run to Berlin, the Red Beast. He concealed himself at Party headquarters, the Brown House, a palace on Brienner Strasse in Munich. It was Heydrich who had convinced Hitler and the Party to appoint Canaris as head of the Abwehr in '35. He came to Berlin with the Führer and followed Canaris around like an acolyte; he would move wherever Canaris moved, first to the Dollestrasse, and then to the Schlachtensee, where Heydrich and Canaris had adjacent villas. He went riding with Uncle Willi in the Tiergarten, and played duets on the violin with Canaris' wife. But he still watched the Abwehr like a menacing hawk with a long nose. It was a curious game of hide-and-seek. Heydrich kept Uncle Willi from falling, but he maneuvered him closer and closer to that fall.

Erik knew that his own mortality, and that of the Fox's Lair, depended on how long the Hangman himself survived. Heydrich was reckless with his own life. He went about in an open car, standing defiant on the front seat, whether he was in Berlin or in the Low Countries, where some madman or member of the British secret service could blow his head off.

'We owe everything to Heydrich,' Valentiner said. 'His *Nacht und Nebel* is a stunning success. He has broken the resistance everywhere in the Reich's new territories.'

'And murdered thousands of innocent people with his nighttime tactics,' said Lisalein.

'Darling, it can't be helped. How could we police Paris without *Nacht und Nebel*? A German soldier wouldn't be able to stroll Montmartre, or sit in a café without a bomb going off. Paris has become our playground. It purrs at our feet.'

'We had *Nacht und Nebel* in Berlin,' Lisa said, 'before German soldiers ever climbed the hills of Montmartre.'

'Berlin? Never! *Nacht und Nebel* is for foreigners. The Führer would never allow it in Berlin.'

Nacht und Nebel, Night and Fog, was a decree dreamt up by Heydrich to rid Paris and Amsterdam and Prague of saboteurs and other troublemakers without interfering with the rhythm of everyday life. Lists were made up with the help of the local Gestapo, and potential saboteurs would vanish in the middle of the night and never be heard from again. Thousands disappeared, some of them with only the merest whisper of suspicion; there were 'saboteurs' with one eye or one leg, 'saboteurs' who couldn't read or write, 'saboteurs' who belonged in an asylum.

'Darling,' Valentiner persisted, 'just ask your make-believe captain if the Abwehr doesn't have its own *Nacht und Nebel.*'

Erik growled under his breath. 'Ah, your husband has unmasked us, Frau Valentiner. We spies couldn't live without Night and Fog.'

But he knew that Lisalein was right. There had been Night and Fog in Berlin long before Heydrich's men began to depopulate Paris. And it wasn't only Gypsies who had disappeared, with their caravans at the edge of Berlin, or transvestites and Jews, or pastors and lawyers who were a little too loud or too public in their displeasure with the Reich's racial laws and euthanasia programs. Some were warned, some were punished, and some vanished without a clue in *Nacht und Nebel* before it had a name.

Emil didn't like the warfare at the table and decided to play the diplomat. 'I'm starving,' he said. 'Cousin, I cannot appease my appetite with asparagus stalks.'

The maid had wheeled a trolley out of the kitchen filled with butter, pickles, Viennese bread, glazed carrots, a rack of lamb, and an enormous trout cooked in paper, which cost a fortune in ration stamps.

Erik barely nibbled on his lamb; he had no appetite in this Nazi chalet next door to Goebbels' villa. He couldn't even say if it was because of Valentiner or Lisalein. What was she doing in this Night and Fog? Had she closed her eyes to the troglodytes around her, these *Übermenschen* who broke the backs of little children and planned to turn entire countries into concentration camps? But he was a fool to consider such questions. He was also a troglodyte, part of the same regime.

'Herr Kapitän,' Valentiner said with a mouthful of glazed carrots, 'did you ever see my wife dance? She does a marvelous duet with the maid – a Jewish tango. Our Sissi's a whore. I pretend not to notice. They dance at all the forbidden clubs, where we poor Party men have to go down on our hands and knees to get in. Berlin has always been a Jewish town, and it will always be, no matter how many *Sammellager* we set up, or how many midnight raids we plan – we're infested with Jews.'

Lisa tore the paper from her trout. 'Josef, you should have married some Brunhilde or another blond Valkyrie.'

'God forbid. Our Brunhildes die on the limb. They aren't cultivated flowers. Jewish women make the best wives, provided they have enough German blood. I didn't marry you because of your father's fortune – it belongs to the Reich. And what other wife would have brought such interesting men to the table? An overripe cadet and a mad dwarf who escaped his own death sentence.'

Lisa was trembling. She stood up, reached across the table, and slapped Valentiner's face. His jaw twitched, but he continued to eat.

'Darling, the lamb is delicious… Perhaps I ought to thank Sissi. She has the whore's touch. But don't think you can save Sissi by sneaking her into our home. She'll end up in a *Sammellager* when I'm tired of looking at her tits. And after our guests leave, I'll drag you across the floor until you're black and blue – don't think your cadet can save you from a beating.'

And when Valentiner saw the fury in Erik's eyes, he began to laugh. 'Lisa, you've brought an assassin into the house. Look, he's going to cut me from ear to ear with his navy knife.'

'And bleed you like a pig,' Erik told him.

Valentiner sniffed his own triumph. 'Darling, your cadet will murder both of us in his sleep. He's Caligari's puppet, Cesare.'

Erik was prepared to mount his own *Aktion*, when the little baron touched his knee under the table.

'Cousin Josef,' Emil said.

'I'm not your cousin,' Valentiner said. 'You come from a family of depraved little men. I once worked for you, remember? I started as your slave at Die Drei Krokodile. You were a tyrant who seduced hysterical salesgirls. They cried on my shoulder.'

Emil smiled like a despotic angel. 'Did you ever tell Lisalein how I hired you?'

'Dwarf, shut your mouth, or I'll have the Gestapo return you to your room in the Black Forest.'

'Excellent. And I'll have them give you the room next to mine. You snake, you hypocrite. You were a little thief… and a wizard.'

'I'm warning you, Emil.'

'I caught the thief myself with flasks of perfume in his pockets. I could have sent him to the police barracks across the *platz*, had him sit in a detention cell, but I realized in a minute how smart he was. He'd made a fortune stealing from the department store and selling his contraband to the shylocks in Scheunenviertel. And what did he do with his bundle of marks? He didn't buy silk scarves. He bought books. He lived in an attic, and his own little library had displaced him.'

'Dwarf,' said Valentiner, 'you're signing your own death certificate.'

'I hired him as my stooge, had him tell me all the plots of the books he had read. But he was a cannibal. He learned all my tricks as a retailer. I introduced him to Baron von Hecht. That was my big mistake. The baron was overwhelmed that one of my lowly clerks could recite whole chapters from *The Magic Mountain*. He took him into his own service, and within eighteen months Cousin Josef sat in my chair.'

THE FIGHT HAD GONE OUT of Valentiner. He sucked on his champagne like the little thief of Die Drei Krokodile. Then he got up from the table, excused himself, and disappeared into some hidden alcove of the chalet. It was Lisa who broke through that pall of silence in his wake.

'Captain, you must forgive my husband. He wasn't always this way. It was my father who converted him into a Nazi. Papa and his little band of Jewish bankers thought they could tame the beast, have the Nazis drive the Communists out of Red Berlin. But Hitler took Berlin and the bankers, too. And *Vati* never quite recovered from the shock.'

'But where is your father, Frau Valentiner?'

'You must call me Lisa, Captain. You have known me long enough.'

She got up from the table and shook Erik's hand. The stark formality of that gesture rippled through Erik, made him feel like a little boy; he was that orphan again on the Rosenstrasse, running after Lisalein, who reigned beside the baron.

'Lisa,' he blurted, 'I still have the fountain pen your father gave me, a Montblanc *Meisterstück,* with my name inscribed in silver. The cadet who tried to steal it paid a pretty price. I scarred him for life.'

But Lisa wasn't listening. She removed her hand from Erik's.

'Please excuse me, Captain. Sissi will look after you. I must attend to my husband.'

She fluttered past Erik, stooped over the little baron, kissed him on the cheek, and climbed some dark staircase. Erik shouted after her, into some invisible void.

'You still haven't told me about your father.'

Nacht und Nebel

8

WHAT THE ABWEHR FEARED MOST finally happened in May of '42. Hangman Heydrich was ambushed in Bohemia; carried from his wrecked car to a hospital in Prague, he played the violin and lived for another week. It wasn't absolutely clear who the assassins were. Some said it was a splinter group within the Abwehr itself that had plotted the assassination as a favor to Admiral Canaris. What sort of favor could it have been? The admiral mourned Heydrich's death, even if his underlings had conspired behind his back. Canaris was estranged from his own family. As the war darkened and bombs began to fall over Berlin, he sent his wife and younger daughter to live on a lake in Bavaria. His elder daughter, Eva, a complicated creature, had run away from school. She grew more and more morose, and Canaris had to put her in an asylum near Munich. He adored Eva, wrote her long letters, but no one at the Fox's Lair could quite remember if he'd visited her even once.

And so Reinhard Heydrich, the Hangman, was his lost son, the cadet who had become an intelligence man, like the admiral. The Abwehr had commandos and sabotage teams, but it never served the Party. When Hitler asked Canaris to kidnap the Pope, or poison some bothersome Dutch diplomat, the admiral procrastinated. He drew up elaborate plans that were never delivered to the Führer and his band of wolves.

Without Heydrich, the other wolves prepared to strike. The Gestapo and the SS sat on Uncle Willi's doorstep, waiting for him to fall, and he had to smile and deflect their most sinister moves. He could no longer afford to have Erik devote all his time to submariners in Scheunenviertel. These submariners were putting the Abwehr at great risk. Jews were disappearing from transport trucks, marching right through *Sammellager* searchlights, even coming back from the dead. It was as if Cesare the somnambulist had used Heydrich's *Nacht und Nebel* in reverse, shielding Jews from the Germans in a fog of his own. And Canaris couldn't sit idle while the Gestapo broke through this fog and uncovered all of Cesare's night moves. The Abwehr was already rife with informers, *Tipper* who reported back to Prinz-Albrecht Strasse; every third agent at the Fox's Lair was probably some SS captain in disguise. Canaris trusted no one but his dachshunds and his own inner circle.

His male dachshund, Seppel, had died, and Canaris replaced him with another wirehaired male, Kasper, but the admiral couldn't rid himself of Seppel's ghost. Poor Kasper peed on the carpets and wouldn't swallow his food until the admiral relented and began to fondle him. The admiral took long naps on his camp bed and locked himself inside his office with his dachshunds, sometimes with Erik and sometimes with Emil.

The Abwehr's own networks discovered that the Gestapo in Munich had arrested Erik's uncle, Heinrich Percyval Albrecht, the gentleman farmer who had no love for the Nazis; he'd insulted an SS officer in the bar at the Hotel Marienbad, where he'd gone to get away from the gloom of his own castle.

'*Männe*,' the admiral said, 'you must go to him and come right back... I cannot spare you.'

Erik couldn't leave his uncle to rot in a Gestapo cellar; the People's Court might ship him to Dachau, or sentence him to sit out the war in a Wehrmacht prison. The admiral had another motive for sending Erik to Munich, and it had nothing to do with a lost uncle. Erik could become his go-between, his *V-Mann*, who'd carry lavish gifts to his daughter at her insane asylum in the Bavarian Alps.

And so the *V-Mann* decked himself in an SS captain's uniform, with its silvered collars and sleeves, took an overnight transport train to Munich, and was met by a local Abwehr agent, who delivered him to Gestapo headquarters near Maximilian Strasse, in a former palace that mad King Ludwig had built for one of his male companions. Ludwig had drowned almost sixty years ago, right beside the castle where his own ministers had held him captive, but Bavarians believed that his ghost could be spotted riding over Munich in a silver carriage.

Erik was startled by the town, which seemed to reside in its own fairy tale of red roofs and pink and tan façades. It hadn't endured a single air raid. The British hadn't scoured Munich with their low-flying Mosquitoes, hadn't dropped a bomb. And the town was drenched in sunlight during these first sultry days of July. It didn't have Berlin's constant smell of machine oil.

Erik didn't have to use much persuasion with the local commandant.

'We had no idea that he was your uncle, Captain. But he was very abusive, calling us swine.'

'I would be delighted if the People's Court sentenced him to the guillotine. I will guillotine him myself.'

A look of terror sprouted like some carbuncle across the commandant's face. 'Not your uncle, Herr Holdermann. What will people think of us? We aren't blind to your accomplishments. You have destroyed countless enemies of the Reich.'

The commandant would have lent him his own office, but Erik insisted on meeting his uncle inside the cellar. The Gestapo spent half an hour cleaning up Heinrich. Erik waited and went down into the dungeon.

Uncle Heinrich sat in an ancient armchair in one of the interrogation rooms. There were whips hanging from the wall. Heinrich seemed scrawny in an agent's spotless white shirt. He had bruises under his eye and tiny clots of blood on the wings of his nose. His hair had gone white. It pained Erik to look at him, not because of the bruises, but because he reminded Erik of his own mother. They had the same disturbingly blue eyes.

The Gestapo had given Erik half a pail of beer and two gigantic schooners from the Black Boar, Munich's most celebrated beer hall. Heinrich growled his hello.

'I'm not impressed with you, Little Holdermann. How can we have a secret service if all its exploits are known?'

'But they aren't known, *Onkel*. We reveal what we want to reveal.'

'Like that vile uniform you're wearing?' said Heinrich.

'Uniforms are misleading. Mine is a cosmetic to get you out of jail.'

'But I didn't ask you to come for me.'

'And I might not have come,' said Erik. 'But my admiral told me it's bad business to have the uncle of an Abwehr officer sitting in a Gestapo cellar.'

'Then I accept this courtesy of Admiral Canaris… Look what's become of you.'

Heinrich started to cry. His shoulders heaved, and his crying came in long, relentless gasps.

'I loved your mother,' he said.

'If you mention my mother's name, *Onkel*, I'll strangle you in your chair, and the Gestapo will give me a medal.'

'She was my sister,' Heinrich rasped, 'my favorite little sister. *Heidi, Heidi, Heidi.*'

Erik couldn't harm this miserable man. He poured from the pail.

'Drink. Your throat must be dry.'

The cellar had the foul taste of prisoners' sweat and blood, and the two of them finished a whole schooner in four or five gulps, the foam remaining on their lips. Even the Hotel Adlon began watering its beer by 1942, but this beer came unwatered from the Black Boar's own cellars.

'She shouldn't have married that damn postman with his devil's dark looks, a postman who painted and scribbled poems.'

'*Mutti* never told me that. She hardly ever talked about him. He died before I was two.'

'What talent! A consumptive postman who painted landscapes, like Herr Hitler… can't you understand? Or are you a devil like him? I was jealous to the point of distraction. Our own parents were dead. I wasn't trying to keep her for myself. I would have found a husband for her, from an old Junker line. Not a postman who was little better than a vagabond… and a thief.'

'*Onkel,* you're speaking about my father. And why didn't you help her after he died?'

'I was a stubborn, imbecilic fool,' Heinrich said; he'd tipped the schooner so high that the beer had washed the clots of blood away from the wings of his nose. 'I waited, waited for her to come back… and I resented you as much as the postman who had spawned you. When the baron brought you to me at the Adlon, I couldn't bear to look at your face. You had the postman's devil eyes.'

'Then you should have left me to die in your barn, Uncle Heinrich.'

'But I did leave you to die,' said Heinrich with a madman's grin. 'It was another Heinrich who dug through the ice and snow for a week to save you, a much younger fellow who worked in a feverish dream, with the memory of his sister's hair in his eyes, the memory of her skin. That's what drove me on. I was digging for Heidi, for her.'

THE *V-Mann* COULD HAVE TAKEN Heinrich out of the cellar with him, but he decided to have Heinrich held as a captive for another four days. It wasn't deviltry. The moment Erik left, the commandant would move Uncle Heinrich upstairs, and Gestapo headquarters would become his private luxury hotel. Heinrich would heal much better on Maximilian Strasse than in his own castle.

The *V-Mann* went into the Bavarian Alps to visit Uncle Willi's elder daughter at an asylum that was a mile from Schloss Neuschwanstein, one of the castles Ludwig the Mad had built. The temperature dropped ten degrees, and Erik began to shiver as he sat next to his driver. He had a terrifying sense of vertigo in this tall forest. But when he saw Schloss Neuschwanstein on its own little mountain, his vertigo was gone. Ludwig's castles had bankrupted Bavaria, and perhaps that was the real reason why his ministers got rid of him, and not because of the midnight bacchanalia with his bodyguards and grooms, or the pathological shyness that sometimes didn't allow him to greet his own courtiers. He was king and castle builder. Neuschwanstein rose out of a wall of trees like some flying circus, bone white in the sun. Erik couldn't get close to the castle, not even in his SS uniform. It had become a fortress filled with gold. Nazi bankers hid their gold in Schloss Neuschwanstein, like the wicked dwarfs of the Nibelungen.

But Erik had other things on his mind than Nazi storage bins. He couldn't stop thinking of his mother. She had her own blond mystery. Who paid for his clothes? She would take Erik to Die Drei Krokodile, where she splurged on him with coats, hats, school supplies, and a child's painting set, with its own wooden case and easel. Erik could recall the colors – burnt sienna, cobalt blue. He would paint by the window, wash his brushes in turpentine, while his mother sewed...

The asylum that held the admiral's daughter was also a castle. It was run by a little band of Lutheran nurses with long noses. He couldn't tell these *Schwestern* apart. They dressed in gray and had their hair swept back. He didn't see any patients on the front lawn, nothing but a few chairs, a volleyball court, and a bridle path.

A nurse asked him to wait for Eva Canaris on the castle's rear porch, which had an untrammeled view of the Alps, with their crippling beauty. He'd been to Munich before on a mission to silence one of the Abwehr's own *Tipper,* who was a little too free with his tongue.

Erik had no choice. It was at the very beginning of the war, and Munich was in the midst of a murder epidemic. All the victims were men. The Abwehr found the strangler through its own elaborate file of index cards. He was a former Brownshirt who had been banished from the Party and preyed on homosexuals. Abwehr commandos buried him in the Englischer Garten, his favorite stalking ground. And then Erik lured the *Tipper* into the gardens and copied the strangler's style. It was cold-blooded and cruel. And Erik had to cleanse himself. He went up into the mountains, which were cobalt blue in the summer mist, like the color Erik had squeezed out of his paint tubes when he was a child. Those blue mountains robbed Erik of his whimsical command over life and death.

'Lord God,' Erik had mumbled, 'forgive my sins. The *Tipper* would have given our secrets away to the Gestapo and neutralized half our index cards. Lives would have been lost, networks compromised. And we would have had to begin from scratch.'

And here he was hypnotized by the same mountain mist.

Eva Canaris arrived in a blue sleeveless gown, wearing mascara and a light smear of lipstick, like a whore from Scheunenviertel. She couldn't have been more than nineteen. She was short and pudgy, with the admiral's pale blue eyes and knob of a nose.

Erik was laden with gifts – a bracelet from Brussels, Swiss chocolates, perfume from the conquered city of Paris, a silk scarf from Italy, and a primitive carving of a cat that the Brandenbergers had brought back from Bulgaria for Eva Canaris, who worshipped creatures with whiskers. She opened her gifts like some precision jeweler while she sat with Erik on the porch. She had him clasp the bracelet around her neck, which was covered with beauty marks. She pondered the carved cat, tested the perfume on her own cheek, and wore the scarf like a turban, which only brutalized the plain features that she herself glanced at in her pocket mirror.

'Captain, did Papa send you here as my suitor?'

'I don't think so, Fräulein Eva.'

She licked her lips in the mirror. 'Do you have a fiancée?'

He had to lie. 'Yes.'

'Then I shouldn't be here without a chaperone. *Schwester,* you must come at once. I'm with a dangerous man. He has a fiancée. And he might be unfaithful to her.'

One of the Lutheran nurses arrived and calmed her down by holding the pocket mirror while Eva combed her hair.

'*Schwester,* you may go now. I'm perfectly safe with this man.'

The nurse left and came back with a pitcher of lemonade. Eva dismissed her again. She poured the lemonade.

'Captain, what if we captured you? We have the means, you know. The *Schwestern* are members of a secret society. They like to kidnap Berliners.'

'Fräulein Eva, it would be a delight.'

Erik laughed to himself. He wouldn't mind sitting for seven years on this Zauberberg. His teachers at the Jewish Gymnasium had all talked of spending seven years on their own magic mountain, away from the Brownshirts and the Bolsheviks.

'And would you strangle all of us, Captain? I've been told that you are my father's best strangler.'

Erik wanted to shrink into his own skin. Who could have told her about the inner workings of the Fox's Lair?

'Captain Erik, you shouldn't be frightened. I wouldn't dare seduce you. I have my own fiancé. He's serving on the eastern front with the Waffen-SS. But please don't tell Papa. He wouldn't approve.'

Erik couldn't imagine a more fanciful tale. The admiral's daughter on her Zauberberg with the Waffen-SS. But she showed him snapshots of herself and a young German officer, with the walls of Schloss Neuschwanstein in the distance. And the tale didn't seem so fanciful. Her Hans had wandered onto the lawn of the asylum, and Eva had fed him a cup of cold water. She played chess with him, even though the nurses didn't encourage it. He was from a family of peasants in Lower Silesia and had been sent to the Zauberberg to guard the gold of the Nibelungen dwarfs. He'd done nothing more than kiss Eva's hand and kidnap her queen on the chessboard. But the *Schwestern* had informed on him to his superiors, and he was banished to the eastern front, with all its bedlam and daily massacre. Or perhaps it was Canaris who had gotten wind of Eva's sweetheart and had Himmler pull him off the mountain.

'Do you think my father loves me, Captain Erik?'

'Yes, very much.'

'Then he should not interfere in my life. I do not need French perfume and wooden cats from Bulgaria. I need my Hans.'

He finished his lemonade and had to lie to her again, promise that he'd talk to Canaris about her sweetheart, or she wouldn't have stopped crying. He kissed her hand, whistled for his driver, and rode down off the Zauberberg.

Baron von Hecht

9

HE RETURNED TO THE DRAGONERSTRASSE in the middle of the night, longing for the sleep of the dead. Eva Canaris didn't need informers and spies to uncover his work at the Abwehr. He had the look of an executioner, that remote, distant stare of a man who was adrift, tied to nothing but a world of secret agents. He could catch the flick of a shadow in the dim light outside his door. Was it someone from another secret service?

Erik took out his dirk. He wasn't in the mood to cut some enemy from ear to ear, but he couldn't have people dogging him like that.

'*Mensch*,' he said, 'step out with your hands behind your neck, or you won't make it to the morning.'

A voice shot back at him from the shadows without the least tremor.

'Captain, you might be doing me a favor.'

He recognized that melodic growl and put his dirk away. He unlocked his door and let Lisalein into his flat. She was wearing a light summer cape, and before he had a chance to accustom himself to her own particular climate, she ventured forth from inside the wings of her cape and kissed Erik on the mouth with a hunger he could never have imagined. But something wasn't right. It was a kiss close to hysteria, and it crushed Erik once he realized that she was bargaining with him, and this was the beginning of the bargain. She could have been a fellow Abwehr agent.

The blood beat like a hammer over his eyes. His head hurt. But he moved out of Lisa's embrace and returned with some cognac in a pair of whiskey glasses.

She tasted the cognac and growled at him, 'Hypocrite, you were dying to kiss me.'

The hammer still beat inside his head. He had to brace himself against his mother's armoire.

'Is that why you invited me to dinner with Emil? To show off one of your conquests to your husband?'

'I didn't have to show off,' she said. 'Your tongue was hanging out at the dinner table. If Josef hadn't gone upstairs, he would have had to duel with you on our lawn.'

She turned away from Erik and began to prowl the apartment like a pantheress, brushing against the furniture. 'Since when does an orphan acquire Queen Anne sofas and chairs?'

'These are my mother's heirlooms, the little she had. I haven't changed a thing. Why have you come here? What could be so urgent that you had to stand in the dark?'

'It's my father,' she said.

Erik didn't soften to Lisa, but he grew alarmed. 'Has the baron been arrested?'

'Yes – no. Who can tell in their little game of *Nacht und Nebel*? He's being held at the Jewish Hospital.'

'But can't your husband help him?'

'It's Josef who had him put in the *Extrastation* at the Jewish Hospital. He says it's better than any hotel, that Father will be safe there, but I'm not so sure. He can't make up his mind whether he loves Father or hates him. But my husband is so devious, it comes to the same thing. I thought of hiring someone to poison him, but that won't get Father out of the *Extrastation*.'

'And so you counted on your protégé. But why did you come as Mata Hari in a cape?'

'I thought that's what you would want,' she said.

He tumbled into a blinding rage. His trip to Munich had unsettled him – an uncle who had denied Erik's existence for so long and sat in a Gestapo cellar like a demented man, and a pudgy, plain-looking girl in a madhouse on a mountain, waiting for a soldier who had already been sent to his death. He would have liked to rescue Eva from her retreat, take her past the nurses with their long noses.

The admiral shouldn't have sent him on a mission to his own daughter. Even stranglers had half a heart. And he couldn't say why, but he struck Lisa with a softened, unclenched fist. He was the one who belonged in a madhouse.

There was blood at the edge of her mouth. She wasn't startled. She smiled and wouldn't wipe the blood away.

'Liebchen, now I see what it is you like.'

He struck her again with the same soft fist. It frightened him. He must have wanted to squeeze the life out of Lisa all this time, he realized.

He undressed her with the murderous precision of a matador, licked the blood off her cheek, sucked in the perfume of her naked flanks. He hadn't imagined that her hip bones would be so sharp. She had little blond hairs around her nipples. He had her lie down on his mother's sofa like some magical mermaid, with her face dug into the cushions; he touched the delicious fluting of her back and proceeded to bite every portion of her body, leaving blue marks on her milky skin. And the very act of biting aroused him in a terrifying way. He was vanquished by Lisa all over again. He lay beside her, and his moaning was as guttural and deep as hers.

THE JEWISH HOSPITAL OF WEDDING was once the best *Krankenhaus* in Berlin; doctors had come from all over Germany to practice there; patients were willing to wait months for a free bed; ministers, bankers, and industrial barons were once faithful to its clinics. There had also been a Jewish Hospital in Munich, but the Nazis shut it down and turned its little community of buildings into a barrack and police station, where Jews were flogged and beaten to death. But neither Hitler nor his SS seemed able to close the Jewish Hospital in Berlin. Its nursing school was still flooded with applicants, even after Jewish nurses had to wear yellow stars on their uniforms. The *Judenstern* didn't seem to matter much. For some mysterious reason, the Reich continued to grant Jewish nurses a State certificate. Perhaps it wasn't even a mystery. There was a terrible shortage of nurses, and the Führer must have calculated that he might have to count on nurses with a yellow star as a last resort. And so the *Schwesternheim*, or nurses' residence, at Iranische Strasse continued to flourish. And Hitler's own ministers, who could have gone to the Charité or another Berlin hospital, would sneak into the main building with its mansard roof and walls of blackened stone and visit a Jewish urologist who no longer had the right to practice in Germany.

That was the strange aura of Iranische Strasse. The hospital consisted of seven pavilions, with an immense private garden and an underground passageway that connected all the buildings. But the Reich had eaten into its territories. Three of the pavilions had been taken over by the Wehrmacht as a military hospital, a *Lazarett*. And the Gestapo seized the former pathology pavilion and turned it into a *Sammellager,* the very last collection camp for Jews in Berlin; in the basement of this pavilion was the *Polizeistation,* or prison ward, where Jewish 'criminals' were kept, those who had dared escape from the Gestapo's clutches and had been found again.

Doctors wandered through the other three pavilions like ghosts without a license, the pharmacist sold narcotics on the side, black marketers had their stashes of cigarettes and stolen ration stamps, and Jewish auxiliaries helped police Iranische Strasse for their Nazi masters. The Gestapo ran their own factory in one of the wards, where Jews stitched together children's clothes and manufactured toys; the foreman of this factory, who might be sent to Auschwitz next week, was earning a fortune meanwhile. He picked the women who sat behind the sewing machines and slaved without respite seven days a week; the Gestapo was reluctant to part with these sorceresses of the sewing needle and put them on a transport truck, while the wizards who could design a toy for children in Munich and Frankfurt were pampered and stuffed with real marmalade and the whitest bread; a miniature fire engine or a hand-carved battleship, reproduced a hundredfold, fattened the Gestapo's pockets and delighted the manufacturers of Nuremberg who no longer had the material to make toys.

It wasn't all business and calculation; the doctors from the Wehrmacht *Lazarett* brought their wounded soldiers to the main pavilion and had them treated by specialists who had been stripped of all their titles and couldn't even be called Herr Professor. Such wounded members of the Wehrmacht filled the corridors with crutches and bandaged limbs and would flirt with hospital sisters wearing yellow stars.

'*Schwester*, you haven't looked at the marks on my legs.'

And so romances spread like wildfire between the Wehrmacht and nurses of Iranische Strasse. In warm weather, they would climb up to the sundeck on the roof of the main building, or stand in the corridors and kiss. But not even soldiers with Iron

Crosses could protect their sweethearts from a transport truck. The Gestapo would pluck a nurse at random right off the stairs if they hadn't been able to fill their quota of a thousand Jewish souls for the next transport. No one was safe from this sudden kidnapping; no one was immune, except perhaps those privileged Jews of the *Extrastation*.

It was a secret ward hidden from the other wards in the main building, and it resembled a hotel rather than a hospital clinic. It had its own porter, like the Adlon, its own registration desk, even its own Gestapo guard; and the *Schwestern* who served in this hidden ward were seldom put onto a transport truck. One of the hotel's current guests was a Rothschild waiting to be ransomed; another was the widow of a banker who had fallen into a coma and couldn't be moved; there was also an economist who worked on the budget of Bulgaria from his bed; but the star of the *Extrastation* was Baron von Hecht, who had his own furniture, his own butler, and his own sitting room. His meals didn't come from the hospital's kitchen, but from the chef and the sommelier at the Adlon, where the baron still had his own suite. His suite here wasn't so different, except for the Gestapo guard who smirked a lot and the *Schwestern* who smoked the baron's Roth-Händle cigarettes while they massaged his legs. He missed the page boys at the Adlon in their white gloves and pale blue caps, who carried messages to the baron, whether he was in the basement barbershop or sunning himself in the Goethe Garden.

There were no page boys in this glorified prison right under the roof. But he did have a telephone, even if the Gestapo listened to every word, and a stenographer from Prinz-Albrecht-Strasse who could decrypt all the baron's codes. He held conferences in his sitting room, met with bankers, nursed whatever holdings he had left. The Gestapo protected the baron from blackmailers and other plunderers, and took half of what he still owned. He couldn't even see how sallow he was in his silken robe. His blue eyes had lost their fevered light. He was languishing on Iranische Strasse.

He had even more of a hump on his back than his nephew, Emil. His dark, unruly eyebrows had turned white. Erik wanted to hold the baron in his arms and run out of the Jewish Hospital with him, race to the end of the world.

He had come to Iranische Strasse in the black-and-silver uniform of the SS and marched into the *Extrastation* without a pass from the Gestapo. The baron was confused.

'Are you the *Teufel, mein Herr,* or a messenger from one of the little führers who owes me a million marks?'

Erik took out his Montblanc Masterpiece, and the baron started to cry.

'I know you from somewhere? Were you once my chauffeur? They're all with the SS. Or were you ever a floor boy at Die Drei Krokodile? I know you.'

'Baron, I'm an orphan from Scheunenviertel. You gave me this pen, with my name inscribed in silver.'

The baron's crying grew twice as fierce.

'I'd rather you were the Devil – a Jewish SS man!'

Erik had to explain that he was the nephew of Heinrich Percyval Albrecht, and that the baron and his own daughter had kidnapped him from the Jewish orphanage and condemned him to a barn in Bavaria.

'So you're here to punish me for having abandoned you with a Montblanc.'

'No, Baron. You shouldn't mind this uniform. I'm with the Abwehr. I'm going to free you from the *Extrastation.*'

'Free me?' the baron said, growing agitated; his chest swelled inside his narrow little world of silk. 'Are you insane? I'm the master here. I drink Hedda Adlon's best wine. I have caviar right off the cuff.'

'And when the Gestapo tires of you and sucks out all your money, they'll send you to the camps with your caviar.'

'Of course,' the baron said. 'I'll go to Theresienstadt. It's already been arranged. I'll sponsor a theater company and a choir. I'll have my own suite overlooking the walls of the town.'

Theresienstadt was a fortress town in Bohemia. The Nazis had turned it into a showcase to convince the International Red Cross that Herr Hitler was relocating Jews to luxurious settlements; Jews had even been filmed working and playing inside the fortress of Theresienstadt. It was supposed to be a haven for prominent Jewish actors, novelists, scientists, and stockbrokers. But Theresienstadt could have been created by the Abwehr itself. It was one more illusion, a fortress prison dressed up as a playground.

'Baron, who told you about Theresienstadt?'

'My son-in-law. He swears that Einstein would have been sent there had he not run to America.'

Erik could no longer control himself. He clutched the baron's lapels and swayed him like a doll until the baron's ears turned blue.

'Theresienstadt's not a Jewish postcard, Baron. It's a way station to Auschwitz. The Nazis treat it like a movie set at Babelsberg. They have their own cameramen, with miraculous images of the children's orchestra. And after the film has been shot, the same smiling children are marched off to the camps in their new clothes.'

'Who sent you here with such lies?' the baron rasped.

'Your daughter – Lisalein.'

The baron had such venom sitting under his eyebrows that Erik had to release him. But he couldn't stop thinking of Theresienstadt and orchestras that melted away into nothingness.

'Baron, I could carry you out of here on my back, and who would ever notice? You're one more refugee in a hospital of refugees.'

'Everybody would notice. I could buy and sell this hospital. I'm Baron von Hecht. Tell me, did my daughter seduce you? Husbands mean nothing to her. She's a heartbreaker. I embarrass my little Lisa and her fashionable girlfriends. She's ashamed of a father who has to wear the *Judenstern*.' And he ruffled the yellow star on his robe. 'She has to find a different black knight every week to do her dirty work. She wears them out. But if you lay a finger on me again, I'll have you arrested. And *you* can test the waters for me at Theresienstadt.'

'There are no waters,' Erik told him. 'It's a fortress, a city of walls.'

And there was no point in planning an *Aktion*. He could have had the baron commandeered to Berne in six hours and left him to bask in 'neutral waters,' but the baron would only have returned to his bed on Iranische Strasse.

This hospital had its own curious sirens – sisters in long white stockings who visited every ward and had to comfort patients who were as precarious as the sirens themselves, all of them a whisk away from transport trucks and a fortress in Bohemia, where each gesture, each breath of air, was like a cruel, relentless *Aktion*.

Wolfie

10

IT HAD ONCE BEEN THE Kaiser's hotel. Wilhelm II would walk down Unter den Linden from his own dismal palace and have a pilsner in one of the Adlon's private rooms near the chandeliers and clouded yellow marble pillars and stone fireplaces of the reception hall. He paid the Adlon a yearly stipend to house his own guests, and took his dinners with them at the hotel. But a world war and the Spartakus uprising ruined the Kaiser's hold on the Adlon. Wilhelm fled Berlin and crossed into Holland, while mutinous sailors barricaded themselves in the Café Viktoria or behind the Brandenburger Tor and fired upon the hotel from across Pariser Platz; there were still pockmarks in the outer walls twenty-five years later; the mutinous sailors swept through the Adlon's revolving doors wearing red armbands, announced their own workers' paradise, stole whatever food they could find, and ran out the rear of the hotel with candelabras and damask tablecloths from the dining room.

The Adlon had never belonged to the Reds, nor was it really a part of the Weimar Republic; ministers dined there, but they couldn't captivate the Adlon, not the way Kaiser Wilhelm had done. It catered to visiting royalty and the business elite. Millionaires brought their mistresses; dukes stayed in the Adlon's ducal suites. To those who cherished it, the Adlon had become the finest address in the world – Number One, Unter den Linden. Some permanent guests never even bothered to venture beyond its doors. The barreled ceiling in the lobby and the sweeping marble staircases provided an enchantment and a vista that turned mountains, lakes, and monuments mundane.

Then Hitler arrived with his torchlight parades through the Tiergarten. He shunned the Adlon, called it 'a Jewish snake pit.' The Kaiserhof had always been his hotel in Berlin; he'd taken up the entire top floor, along with his SS bodyguards. But a mystery began to prevail: There was a tunnel under the Chancellery that led right to the Adlon, and the Führer could be seen there with his bodyguards once or twice a week. Was he having a liaison with some diva who lived at the Adlon? Who would have dared ask? But he always returned from the Adlon with his mustache trimmed and his hair slightly clipped. He was visiting the barbers' salon in the basement of the Adlon, with its little nest of Nazi barbers. He brought his own Bavarian chef into the glassed-in cage of the Adlon's kitchen, and began to dine on soufflés and carrot concoctions in the little alcove off the Goethe Garden, while a certain barber was summoned from the basement. And the boldest of the Nazis soon abandoned the bar at the Kaiserhof and flocked to the Adlon. Field marshals sat on its plum-colored armchairs; SS officers congregated in their own corner of the bar, while the Gestapo agents, who monitored the Adlon's phones and had planted hidden wires and microphones everywhere, were mainly curious about the filing system that the hotel had for all its guests.

Erik wasn't troubled by the Adlon's new reputation as Hitler's hotel. He would sit at one of the bar's low tables, with submarine commanders and secret agents, and sip on a pilsner or some champagne. Sometimes the gun girls from an anti-aircraft crew would join them, but there were no gun girls this afternoon with their shapely calves and soft blond swagger. Erik suddenly found himself on the same leather settee with Werner Wolfe, a merchant from a neutral country, who lived at the hotel and conducted all his business at the bar. Wolfe was a Berliner who had gone to the United States as a child and had later settled in Sweden, where he sold electrical supplies. He wasn't much older than Erik; tall and blond, with a delicate mustache, he also worked for U.S. naval intelligence; he was some kind of strange conduit between the Germans and the Allies. He never spied at the Adlon, never served as much of a secret agent, never hid who he was. The lieutenant would often tease Erik about Conrad Veidt's role as Cesare in *Dr Caligari.*

'Did you know that our Conrad was the handsomest transvestite on Unter den Linden before he became a big hit in the movies? He was the rage of every boy bar. The rouge he wore could be seen for miles.'

'You couldn't have been one of his customers, Wolfie. You were much too young.'

'But I saw him on the Linden, saw him with my own eyes. He stuck out his tongue at me. It was indecent.'

'Yes,' said Erik, 'he must have been dreaming of Cesare long before he met Caligari.'

'And how is your own Caligari?' the lieutenant asked, fingering the microphone that bulged right out of his leather seat.

'Ah, perhaps you'll invite us both to America one of these days, after the Wehrmacht rides into Manhattan.'

'With the Wehrmacht in Manhattan, you won't need me.' Their little duet for the Gestapo was over now. The lieutenant did have one role at the Adlon that the Nazis were unable to unmask. He helped smuggle Jews out of Germany. It had nothing to do with naval intelligence. His government wasn't partial to Berlin Jews.

And so smuggling had become a secretive sideline. He did expect a high fee, but that was for bribing border guards and corrupt officials, who were far too compromised to inform on the American Berliner at the Adlon. One false step and the lieutenant would have become an instant casualty of war. He also risked the wrath of his own government. He had become a 'spotter,' a listening device, planted like a chess piece in the heart of Berlin to feel out the Nazi war machine as it gathered at Hitler's hotel. The Gestapo didn't care whether he passed this information on to some *V-Mann* stationed in Geneva. They were delighted that America's naval intelligence had sent a Berlin Jew as their secret agent. It supported their own image of a mongrel America rampant with Jews.

Submarine commanders saluted Wolfe and talked to him about naval strategy. Captains and majors in the SS had schnapps with him and reminisced about all the beautiful women at the Adlon. The barman fed him. He'd become the hotel's mascot. He could have slept with half the women who strolled into the bar and bumped into him, pretending to be blind. But they stank of the Gestapo, with their ivory cigarette holders and bloodred nail polish.

The lieutenant liked to sit alone; he had slept with one or two of the gun girls who would come down from their batteries on the roof of IG Farben to visit with him; even if they were Gestapo plants, they never pumped him for information. And he shared one of the girls with Cesare, a sergeant with her own ack-ack gun, a certain Tilli, who left bite marks on his back and complained that Erik had lost interest in her. She had Betty Grable's million-dollar legs, and he couldn't understand why Erik would give her up. He meant to ask, but he couldn't afford to sit too long with an Abwehr agent.

Their bargaining had to be brief. He couldn't smuggle anyone from Berlin without false papers from the Abwehr's passport and visa division. And he couldn't supply the Abwehr with pictures of the Jewish souls he meant to save, or fool around with microdot images in a matchbox, or the Gestapo would have been all over him. And so they sculpted a primitive sign language that served as a sketchbook. But it was done in an instant, with their own lightning war; six or seven signs, when doubled, composed a complete vocabulary; a tipping of the lieutenant's champagne glass in one direction might mean blond or brunette; male and female were another set of signs; an unexpected smile stood for tall – and Erik would have the portrait he needed for the Abwehr's wizards.

It didn't matter that there wasn't a perfect match; the passport photographs would be retouched from another face, and a new creature would emerge from the Abwehr's Night and Fog. Then the passport was smuggled out of the Fox's Lair in a pouch that ended up in the pocket of a page boy at Hitler's hotel; these page boys were the lieutenant's most trusted couriers. They wore the Adlon's pale blue cap, could enter any room with a message on a silver tray, and could even carry messages out onto the street. And thus the American Berliner had his Pony Express. He took a big chance. But the page boys weren't marked with any evidence. There was nothing to incriminate them. The passports they carried had the authentic stamp of the Third Reich ('borrowed' by the Abwehr itself from the Interior Ministry). The stamp was as good as Nibelungen gold. And what if a page boy got greedy and threatened to squeal? There was always the specter of Cesare, the somnambulist who could walk through walls and strangle a reckless page boy while he hid in a closet or sat huddled on the throne of his toilet seat.

It wasn't his page boys he had to fear, not even the Gestapo, or a *Spitzel* in the Abwehr itself, but naval intelligence; if his own admirals ever discovered that he had spent precious hours saving Jewish souls rather than gathering information on Hitler's madmen, they would abandon Wolfe, let him sit forever, or hire some Swede to assassinate him. But he couldn't sit idle while ghoulish bureaucrats in the Adlon's bar talked about the fortune they had earned selling the property of Jews thrown into the camps, or while Gestapo agents sang obscene songs about the stench of Jewish children in Scheunenviertel. He would have run howling through the hotel if he couldn't have helped some of these children.

He grew reckless. He had his own military uniform sent from Sweden. It hung in his closet at the Adlon; the page boys had it cleaned; the porter polished his insignias and his black regulation shoes. The hotel's female house detectives, who were Gestapo spies, searched his quarters routinely, once or twice a week. But nothing was ever said about his uniform; it even disappeared for a few days, and suddenly was back again, in its leather bag. What could the Gestapo expect from a mongrel nation that chose a Jewish intelligence man to sit in Berlin with all his insignias in the closet?

But the presence of that uniform kept him sane. And Wolfe couldn't have known that the staff at the Adlon, its front line, didn't see him as a lunatic American Berliner, but as a prince-in-waiting who might redeem them at war's end. So it guarded the Adlon's future prince and his uniform. And smiling all of a sudden, he sang to Erik, who was still sitting on the settee.

'Cesare, Tilli the Toiler says you've dropped her for some other damsel. She's mad as hell. Says she might shoot out the window of your suite from her perch on the Farben's roof. Of course, I'm forever grateful. She's fallen into my arms. I cherish her love bites.'

But Cesare wasn't listening. And the lieutenant understood why. He was staring at a blond apparition who'd wandered into the bar with a whole company of colonels from the Wehrmacht and the Waffen-SS. He'd seen that apparition before. She was wearing a backless gown of silver sequins. He could follow the apparition's shoulder blades and the delightful bumps of her spine. He remembered now. She'd had a fight with Baron von Hecht in this very bar before the Gestapo kidnapped him and held the baron in the *Sammellager* on Iranische Strasse. But she hadn't been in silver sequins. She was the baron's only daughter, Lisalein, married to an SS colonel who once ran a department store.

She was also a *Mischling*, a half Jewess with a Nazi husband. The Fürher didn't seem to know what to do with his *Mischlinge* – wipe them out like cockroaches or let them live under the Nazis' bloodred banner. His racial laws were stuck in their own Night and Fog. His Office of Racial Purity could measure Jewish noses, trace back lineage a thousand years, drag 'contaminated' grandparents out of the closet, but it couldn't seem to calculate the innocence or the guilt of a Jewish baron's daughter who could have leapt from the League of German Maidens, whose nose and ears and sea green eyes mocked Hitler's racial laws and lent her all the seductive mystery of the Lorelei.

This Lorelei of Unter den Linden must have had a little too much to drink. She moved among her company of colonels with a crooked swagger and had to keep from tripping over their polished boots. It took the lieutenant another moment to recall that Lisa-Lorelei was nearsighted and could barely see what was in front of her face. But that didn't prevent her from showing a gruff affection to her colonels. She went from one to the other, fondling ears and noses. A Wehrmacht colonel with very large ears tried to reach for her rump, but she swatted his hand away.

'Darling,' she growled, 'I'm not a piece of *Fleisch*. The Wehrmacht must have its own butcher shops. That's where you'll find your rump steak.'

But she'd ventured too far along her line of colonels, tripped over a bar stool, and fell into Cesare's lap. She stared into his dark eyes with the same truculence. But she wasn't enough of an actress to mask her own deep surprise.

'What are you doing here, Captain? Did you follow me into the Adlon? Are you spying on me for Admiral Canaris and his monsters at the Abwehr?'

The lieutenant was even blinder than Lisa-Lorelei. He should have sensed that Erik was in love with the blond apparition, that her spectacle had pained him: Erik was about to throw her off his lap. But a *Berlinisch* American agent who had squatted in Hitler's hotel for two years couldn't have survived without a touch of clairvoyance: he imagined all the carnage inside the Adlon, imagined Erik's demise at the hands of the colonels. And so he played the buffoon. He bumped into Lisa-Lorelei, swept her off Erik's lap, and broke her fall as she landed in the Adlon's little sea of carpets.

'*Gnädige Frau,*' he said, 'can you ever forgive me?'

She slapped his face, but she was looking at Erik, not at him; he didn't even exist. 'Werewolf,' she said, still looking at Erik. 'One of these days I'll rip out your rotten heart.'

Then she rose off the carpets like some miraculous flying fish with silver scales and disappeared into the soft tundra at the edge of the bar.

The Grand Mufti of Jerusalem

11

THE LIGHT FROM THE MAGNIFICENT dome in the main hall left spangled lines that could cut into the Adlon's enormous square pillars and bleach the color of their burnt yellow marble. And for a moment Erik thought how the Kaiser must have felt when he marched through the revolving doors into *his* cathedral for the first time. This was the Kaiser's home, not the dusty palace ten doors away. And Wilhelm must have danced in the Adlon's ballroom under its own spangled light, with two orchestras on silvered bandstands that had to compete for a Kaiser's love.

The more he could reminisce about a Kaiser he had never met, the less he had to think about Lisalein. The page boys pawed at him near the elevator bank.

'Herr Kapitän, how can we help? Are you looking for the Frau in the silver dress? She went upstairs.'

'Where?' he had to wheedle like a little lost boy. 'To the baron's old suite?'

'No, *mein Herr*. That's impossible. Herr Adlon could not have an idle suite on the first floor. It's wartime. Rooms are also rationed. The Grand Mufti of Jerusalem now sits in the baron's suite. He never leaves the hotel. The *Engländers* call him a gangster and a pirate. But he is the Führer's friend. He treats us well, *mein Herr*. He lines our jacket pockets with gold coins from Jerusalem. The coins are heavy, but we are still obliged to the Mufti and his men. It is most unusual to see Arabs in a German uniform, *mein Herr*. But we aren't sure where the Frau with the *Silber* went. She took the stairs. She is very beautiful, no? And even more beautiful when she cries. Then her eyes begin to glow under the lamps.'

Erik had to wonder if this page boy was the new Thomas Mann – he talked like a novelist, with all the colors of a chameleon and a novelist's love of detail. But Erik couldn't stop and chat about the robes and turbans the Mufti wore, or how the Mufti's cooks compared to the Adlon's own kitchen staff.

Erik strode up the marble staircase, decided he would search every floor. But he didn't have much maneuverability, even in an SS officer's uniform. He was stopped on the stairwells by the Mufti's own bodyguard of Arab Gestapo agents. They weren't unkind, only distrustful, since the *Engländers* had put a price on the Mufti's head and might have a hired killer in the main hall of the Adlon. But how could Erik prove he was with the secret service? Abwehr agents had no identity card, not even a proper bank account. They were the victims of the very masks they had to wear, and all their multiple legends. Few civilians had ever heard of Admiral Canaris and the Abwehr. And most members of the Wehrmacht couldn't have said that the Fox's Lair was on the Tirpitz embankment. It was Uncle Willi's secret cove.

Erik would have had to strangle every Arab Gestapo agent on every stairwell if he meant to track Lisalein to *her* secret cove at the Adlon, but he did find a way out of his dilemma. He happened to have a green Gestapo card in his vest pocket with his photograph and the Gestapo's own seal. It satisfied the Arab agents that Erik was not an *Engländer* and could wander wherever he wished. But his wanderings brought him nowhere. He searched the maids' closets, went up and down the fire stairs, hoping to hear the noise of Lisa's heels on the carpets; Erik even unlocked the bathrooms in the attic with a skeleton key, but couldn't find a whiff of Lisa's perfume or a trace of her silky blond hair.

His trek had exhausted him. He decided to take a nap in the Abwehr's suite on the third floor. It looked out upon Pariser Platz and the great green expanse of the Tiergarten; he liked to boast that he could hear the tigers prowl in their cages, but it was a lie. The tigers had been removed from the zoo, not because of the constant threat of Allied bombings, but because it had become too expensive to feed them. Berlin's tigers didn't have ration stamps. But no one could tell him where the tigers had gone and when they would be back.

He opened the outer door of his room, and standing there in that dark well between the outer and inner door was Lisalein.

'Darling,' she growled, 'aren't you going to invite me in? How long does a *Mädschen* have to wait for her lover in an SS uniform? It becomes you, darling. You look divine in black.'

'Frau Valentiner, it's the exact same uniform your husband wears.'

'Shut up and open the door,' she said. 'I didn't come here to talk about my husband.'

Erik unlocked the inner door and Lisa leapt past him like some rapid-fire machine while she shucked off her silver sequins and scrutinized the Empire mirrors, the Chippendale chests, and the Abwehr's hammered bronze bed.

'They've cheated you, darling. This isn't Frau Adlon's very best stuff. It must have all gone to the Grand Mufti. Did you know that Father met him once – in Jerusalem? He was most gracious to a Jewish baron, offered to make him an honorary consul, or close to that. Papa could have been a little pasha... What's taking you so long? Why haven't you undressed?'

'I want my uniform to glide against your naked body,' he growled like a ventriloquist in Lisa's throaty voice. He had never been so perverse, not even with the high-priced prostitutes whom he himself handled for the Abwehr, Spiders who could trap almost any man. He slept with these *Spinnen,* and sometimes they brought out an incredible cruelty in Cesare, encouraged it even, relished it, but he'd never slapped a Spider, and he longed to slap Lisa again and again. He stared at the blondness between her legs, at the rise and fall of her navel, at the soft blond silk of her arms.

'I'll make you my Spider,' he said. 'You'll work for me. I'll find all your clients.'

'And how much will I be paid? It's wartime, darling. There's a terrible inflation.'

'I'll pay you nothing, not a pfennig.'

'Ah,' she said, 'that's the kind of job I like.'

He shook her shoulders. 'No more grand entrances with the Waffen-SS.'

'Darling, I did it for Papa. I need all the colonels and generals on my side. Someone has to get him out of that infernal hotel on Iranische Strasse. I sent you to him. What happened? He's still there.'

'Ask him. He wasn't so anxious to leave. I offered to carry him out on my back. He wouldn't go.'

'But you were supposed to charm him, darling. You're the magician. You turn all your enemies into dung beetles and flies. Couldn't you have spared a minor miracle for Papa?'

He didn't believe her, not a word of it. She had always been able to weave a spell around him from the moment they had met. He'd become her private page with a fountain pen. He'd never understand why she and the baron hadn't ransomed themselves and bought their way out of Germany. The Nazis had seized Die

Drei Krokodile, and still the baron stayed. He'd lost his villa in the Grunewald to a German general, and the Grand Mufti now occupied his suite at the Adlon, where some barber with a Nazi pin in his lapel had fawned on him and spat behind his back. There were Party pins all over the Adlon, and yet the baron, who could have bought half the Pariser Platz, bumped into a multitude of pins like a blind man. It left a metallic taste on Erik's tongue; it was one more legend, a mask the baron had decided to wear. And Lisalein crept right under that mask.

He tied her arms to the bedpost with the strings from one of the Adlon's white robes, pushed into her chest with the buttons of his uniform, but the more he tried to humiliate her, the more he humiliated himself. And his anger turned to tenderness. He kissed the marks on her breasts that his buttons had made. He didn't even have to confess his love. She could read the turmoil in his dark eyes, the terror that love could bring.

She couldn't clutch his ears while her hands were tied.

'Darling,' she said, 'kill me now, before I kill you.'

But she was also crying. And she fell asleep in Erik's arms, with her hot breath on his shoulder.

When he woke up with his own yawning face in the mirror, she wasn't there. Had she untied herself with the help of some local Houdini? He had to console himself with the Adlon's bathroom, which was like a battleship, with its own heated towel rack and a marble tub that could have accommodated a team of polar bears.

He couldn't find his uniform, or his necktie and his shoes. He cursed and opened the inner door of his suite. The uniform hung on the doorknob from a golden hook. His clothes must have been pressed and cleaned by the Adlon's midnight tailors, his shoes shined by the barber's apprentice. His black tie gleamed. His shirt was crackling white. He put it on with fumbling fingers. The collar was like a silk napkin against the hairs on his neck.

He went downstairs to the Adlon's inner court, which had its own fountain with the luscious whish of a waterfall. This inner court and garden often served as a breakfast room, summer and winter. Most of the Adlon's clientele had breakfast in bed, with or without their mistresses. But Erik hated to eat alone in a little world of brutal red drapes.

And so he sat in this garden with its potted plants, the sound of water in his ears. He wasn't the only guest this morning. The Grand Mufti of Jerusalem arrived in his robes and tall white fez, surrounded by his bodyguard of Arab Gestapo agents. He was close to fifty, with a graying beard and large round ears, but he looked much younger, almost like an inquisitive boy. It was the Mufti himself who beckoned Erik to his table.

And Erik was bewildered by the Mufti's mysterious cuisine. What could his cooks from Jerusalem have prepared in the Adlon's kitchen? The waiters served him shirred eggs in a gold chafing dish, a rack of rye toast, and peppermint tea. Not wanting to offend the Mufti, Erik asked for the same thing. And the two of them sat with chafing dishes and racks of toast that resembled the torture machine at Prinz-Albrecht-Strasse, which could squeeze a man's knuckles until nothing was left.

'You must give my regards to Uncle Willi. I helped him establish his outpost in Jerusalem, but he has not been so kind to me.'

'I don't understand, Holiness. How did the Abwehr fail you?'

The Mufti rubbed his beard. '*Holiness*. I like that. But I am not Pope Pius, with his long, long nose. I am a much simpler man.'

'Then what should I call you?'

'Excellency will be enough – I preferred Rome. The climate

suited me, and the red sky. I could dream I was still in Africa. Have you ever been to Rome, Herr Cesare?'

'No, Excellency. I have not been granted that privilege.'

'Then you must believe me. Rome has an African sky, red in the morning, like the stone of a succulent peach. But Herr Hitler said that he could not protect me in Rome. The British had spies everywhere and a hundred paid assassins. I was told that I wouldn't have lasted another month. And the Führer flew me to Berlin on his private plane. I would be safe at the Adlon, he said, safe in the heart of Germany, far from Il Duce's corrupt and incompetent secret service. Then why can't the Abwehr, with all its agents, protect me? Why has Uncle Willi allowed an assassin inside this hotel?'

'You must not believe every word of the Gestapo.'

The Grand Mufti patted his lips with one of the Adlon's enormous napkins. He was still smiling, but it wasn't meant as a slight to Erik himself, since his own secret service had told him stories of the Abwehr's magician, who could murder a man without even entering a room.

'If I had confidence in the Gestapo, Herr Cesare, I would not be sitting here with you. There's a mole at the Bulgarian embassy who is in touch with British intelligence. He is very loyal to my people. The mole assures me that the *Engländers* have penetrated the lobby of this hotel. They have an assassin inside the Adlon.'

'Excellency, I wonder if this mole was paid by the *Engländers* to misinform you. They are marvels at misinformation. We're amateurs compared to them.'

'At first, I thought this assassin might be you,' said the Mufti, with a bit of shirred egg in his mouth. 'I hope you will forgive me – one of my men was in your room all night, behind the drapes. We had to be certain that you weren't plotting with the Jewess.'

Erik's mouth turned bitter and dry, and the Grand Mufti seemed to have a moment of alarm. 'The baron's daughter,' he said, 'Frau Valentiner. We did not intend to pry. And we were the ones who collected your uniform and had it cleaned.' He thrust his knife and fork away. 'I cannot eat such tasteless food.'

Erik could feel his temples pound. He was no longer listening to the Adlon's waterfall. He had to live and die according to the Abwehr's alliances, but in another world he would have knocked off the Mufti's tall white hat.

'Excellency, you brought your own cook from Jerusalem. You didn't have to eat baked eggs in a pot.'

'Ah, but I am enough of an oddity at Berlin's best hotel. And when I sit down to breakfast with a Berliner, I must pluck at the Adlon's menu like a falcon in captivity. You will help us, won't you, Herr Cesare?'

Erik stood up and bowed to the Grand Mufti while the Mufti's men formed a shield around him.

'I will not fail you, Excellency. You were under the Abwehr's protection from the moment you stepped inside this hotel. On Admiral Canaris' behalf, I beg you to return to your suite and sit there for one hour. Please let no one into your rooms, neither a waiter nor Frau Adlon herself. I promise you. I will have an answer to your riddle.'

And Erik left the inner garden, walked under the dazzling light of the Adlon's gold-ribbed dome, and exited the hotel with his uniform still ablaze.

Zorro

12

CESARE WENT THROUGH THE SLIDING metal gate, but it was like a ghost town at the Abwehr. The section chiefs were in the screening room with half their men. They were all watching whatever Hollywood production could be smuggled out of Istanbul. Erik rounded up half a dozen agents who weren't in the screening room, and together they rummaged through the Abwehr's little mountain of index cards and the floor plans of the Hotel Adlon; he memorized every light well, every socket, every fixture at the Adlon, every double door, every landing, and the number of steps – sixteen – from the lobby to the basement barbershop. He had files on the Adlon's celebrated Nazi barber, Fritz, and the prominent people who sat in his chair and preferred him to every other barber in Berlin; even in wartime a chair at the Adlon was worth a fortune; among his list of clients were Adolf Hitler, Hermann Göring, and Baron von Hecht. The barber couldn't have been a double agent; he may have loved reichsmarks, but he wouldn't have risked his chair to become a *V-Mann* for the British secret service.

The Adlon itself was divided between Gestapo and Abwehr *Tipper*. Uncle Willi understood how important the Adlon was as a listening post; the barman belonged to him, the cashier, the captain of the desk clerks, the maids' own female führer, and not one of them had hinted at a British hireling, an assassin in the halls. Yet Erik still believed in the Grand Mufti's reports.

He went to Commander Stolz, who wanted to mount an *Aktion* in the lobby of the Adlon, flood it with Abwehr agents.

'That won't draw him out,' Erik muttered. 'He'll spot us in a second.'

'Then we'll have to go to Uncle Willi.'

'No, it will upset *Alte*. He'll brood over how he's disappointed the Grand Mufti. *Kinder,* we'll have to solve it ourselves.'

But Admiral Canaris had come out of the screening room with the little baron, Emil von Hecht, trailing behind him. The little baron followed *Alte* everywhere now that he was forbidden to pluck Jews from the transport trucks and form new networks of submariners; he formed them anyway, behind the admiral's back. Canaris knew about these dealings but said nothing to Emil. The little baron was one more delinquent, like his dachshunds.

Crumbs fell from the admiral's uniform; he had pee stains on his trouser cuffs from Kasper, his dachshund with bladder problems. He was scowling. His own *Tipper* must have told him that Erik had been ransacking the admiral's prize index cards.

'*Männe,*' he said, 'you missed your *chou-chou,* Tyrone Power – Emil, tell him what we were watching.'

'*Crash Dive,* Herr Admiral.'

'A submarine picture that knows nothing about submarines – Hollywood should have borrowed one of our ace U-boat commanders, like Joachim Fischer, who tossed his *Ritterkreuz* and all his ribbons into the toilet bowl at Kiel. And he wouldn't allow the Gestapo on board his boat. But he would have taught those dunces at MGM how a man's face begins to swell when he's locked inside a submarine, and he could have given Tyrone Power a few lessons in crash diving.'

Emil clutched at Canaris' rumpled sleeve. 'Fischer is dead, Herr Admiral.'

'Not dead, Emil, missing at sea – and there's another missing man, eh? An assassin whom my little Erik cannot find. But you are looking in the wrong place. You will not find him in the index cards. We've mapped that hotel from top to bottom. And don't interfere with the barbershop, please, or I'll never be able to get a shave at the Adlon again. It's not the unknown that haunts us, *Männe*, but the known. You've already met this assassin.'

ERIK RETURNED TO THE ADLON like a somnambulist dispatched by Caligari himself. Canaris had a clarity that no field man ever had. He could lie down on his camp bed with Sabine and Kasper, or sit in a darkened room, watching Technicolor ghosts on the screen, and have a sudden illumination. The Grand Mufti had spoken to Canaris through the medium of his somnambulist. Mohammed Amin al-Husseini was a fearless man. He wasn't looking for protection from the Abwehr. He would have stayed in Italy, under the African sun, with his own Arab Gestapo agents, if Hitler himself hadn't needed the illusion that Amin al-Husseini was his own exalted prisoner – so he came to Berlin with his entourage, and lived in this curious palace of a hotel that had more prayer rugs and jeweled light than a mosque. And now he was giving Admiral Canaris, the one friend he had here in the West, a master of espionage and *quaa'id* of the most secret of secret services, the chance to redeem himself.

Erik walked out from under the maddening light of the main hall, ducked into the bar, and whispered to Günter, the barman, who was practically an Abwehr agent. Günter went from client to client, telling them all that the bar would be closed the next half hour for a private party.

One of the regulars complained. She was the wife of a submarine commander, waiting for her husband to return from the North Sea. 'Günter, don't be foolish. There is no private party.'

The barman pointed to Erik, whose eyes were raw and unruly, and the woman disappeared with the wife of another submarine commander. Only Lt. Werner Wolfe remained on his leather settee, where he always sat sipping champagne. He smiled when Günter bolted Erik and him inside the bar.

'Sounds like fun,' the lieutenant said. 'I think Admiral Canaris has suddenly entered the picture.'

The somnambulist sat down on the settee. 'You shouldn't have suckered me like some fat trout, Wolfie. Berlin isn't your private stream. How much are the *Engländers* paying you to finish off the Grand Mufti?'

'Does it matter? It's not about money. And you'll have to cooperate. If the Gestapo ever finds out that I've been plotting with the Abwehr to help rescue Jews from the trucks, Uncle Willi will fall, and so will you. Let's make a deal.'

Erick saw blood in front of his eyes. He had to keep from pounding the Adlon's American Berliner into his own grave.

'Wolfie, I'll give you two hours to flee Berlin. That's the kindest offer you'll ever have. You shouldn't have used Berlin Jews as your cover. I was born in Scheunenviertel. I still live there. I don't belong to the *Engländers* and I don't belong to you.'

The lieutenant had a sudden laughing fit that sounded like the bark of a seal. Erik knew it was a diversion. He could feel a pocket pistol pressed against his cheek. It was a Sauer 6.35 mm, made in Berlin. It would have blown bits and pieces of Erik into the chandelier and splattered the mirrors with his blood.

'Congratulations, Wolfie. That's very sporting of you. Is this the gun you would have used against the Grand Mufti?'

The barking had stopped and was replaced by a grin. 'I'm not Jesse James. This gun is just for you, Cesare. I knew the admiral would figure it all out. It was a matter of time, and I wasn't taking any chances.'

'Enlighten us before you pull the trigger. How were you going to checkmate the Mufti? Put a bomb under his pillow? Poison his lentil soup? You don't have a plan, do you? You've been playing your British masters like you've been playing me. You're stalling, Wolfie, hoping the *Engländers* will parachute into Berlin one day, land on the Adlon's balcony, and you can run through the hotel with your pocket pistol and arrest everyone in sight, including dachshunds and the Nazi barbers downstairs.'

'*Richtig*,' said the lieutenant, digging the Sauer's blue nose deeper into Erik's cheek, until it left a sucking hole. 'But you won't live to see it.'

He'd expected Erik to beg for his life, but the somnambulist didn't even blink.

'Go on, pull the trigger. Günter won't mind. He'll just wait until the Gestapo crashes through the door. Have you ever been to Prinz-Albrecht-Strasse, Wolfie? They have a wonderful iron grip that will remove the knuckles from your hand.'

The Sauer 6.35 began to shake. Erik slapped it away and let it fall. He clutched the lieutenant by the collar, dragged him across the pale carpet, and hurled him over the Adlon's mahogany bar, into that little wet world of floorboards that was as mysterious to him as a submarine commander's bridge. It was wiped clean morning and night, but it was always wet with beer drippings and seltzer water from the siphons that Günter kept on a shelf behind the bar. Erik had never been here before, but he had to hide Wolfie in case Frau Adlon had to feed one of her twenty-eight dachshunds and demanded to be let in (Günter kept the dog biscuits in a special jar near the seltzer siphons).

Erik straddled the lieutenant, who lay on the wet wood, his face recast with a blue tint in the bar's many mirrors, his hands clasped like a mendicant.

'Cesare, I had to deal with the *Engländers*. They would have betrayed all our submariners and sold me to the Gestapo.'

Erik took out his dirk and cut the lieutenant's cheek. He had to leave his mark on Wolfie, not a full *Z*, like Zorro, just a line an inch long on the lieutenant's cheekbone, a little deeper than a scratch.

Wolfie didn't howl once. He was petrified. Erik took a wet towel and placed it over the wound as a kind of camouflage. Then he handed him over to Günter.

'You'll take the lieutenant through the Rembrandt Room and out the service entrance. A delivery truck will be waiting. It's one of ours. Ride with him to Tempelhof. An Abwehr plane will return him to Sweden… Wolfie, if I ever see you in Berlin, even after Winston Churchill wins the war, I'll slice you from your nose to your balls, I swear to God.'

Günter picked up the lieutenant and rushed him out of the bar, shielding the wound with that wet towel, while Erik poured himself a glass of pilsner from the Adlon's weakened tap; he could hear a gurgling sound. He knew that the beer had been watered down – another casualty of Winston Churchill's war. His hand was shaking. He'd never cut a man before with such cold deliberation. He could have gutted Wolfie, skinned him alive. The Abwehr had made Erik into a monster with an SS man's silvered sleeves. No wonder Lisalein copulated with him like a wild animal and ran away into the night. What could she have found when she looked into his eyes? A zombie who couldn't even see his own reflection in the mirror. She must have been drawn to dead men with dark eyes.

It was Berlin, with its furor to rid itself of Jews, while it remained a Jewish town even after all the roundups and the *Sammellager*, and the paper stars that the Gestapo put on every door where a Jew still dwelled; children who had been snatched away still haunted Scheunenviertel, rode above the rooftops like lost angels looking for a home; the steel and glass skeleton of Die Drei Krokodile seemed to rock and sway on Alexanderplatz; the Café Kranzler, which had once reigned over that magnificent crossroad at Unter den Linden and Friedrichstrasse with its Jewish clientele, was now a pretty morgue where men and women drank ersatz coffee in tin cups and had to feast on kuchen made of sawdust and paste – the Jewish fiddler was gone, the Jewish gamblers and chess players, the Jewish prostitutes who picked up customers in the café's ice cream parlor. The Kranzler was filled with Gestapo agents in felt hats and Gestapo spies, landladies who watched out for Jewish submariners.

Gott, he was living in a morgue and a madhouse. He picked up the lieutenant's Sauer 6.35, dismantled it, and tossed the pieces into Günter's garbage barrel. Then he sat down again and had another glass of watered beer.

BERLIN MITTE

BERLIN MITTE

From the desk of Admiral Wilhelm Canaris
72-76 Tirpitz-Ufer
Berlin

Why, why did I have to see her on the street? I wasn't in the Jewish quarter.
I was several blocks from the Chancellery, on the Wilhelmstrasse, in the
heart of Hitler's Berlin. And what was she doing all alone, wearing a
yellow star in front of the Führer's own bodyguards? She couldn't have
been more than six or seven, and as blond as any Brunhilde, her hair
braided in a magnificent bun.

I had my driver stop the car. Thank God I wasn't with my little
aide. Hänschen was half a Nazi, and he would have had a fit. I had to
jiggle like a madman to open the door.

'Well,' I said, 'climb aboard.'

She hadn't even stopped strolling to have a look at me. But I was far
more stubborn than a six-year-old girl.

'Get in!'

Ah, now I'd caught her eye. She hopped with one foot in the air.
'Mutti says I shouldn't get into cars with strangers.'

'And where is your Mutti now?'

'I have no idea. Men in long coats knocked on our door. They took
her away. Nurse hid me in the closet. And then they took Nurse and
kept calling out to me. "Come, come, little cuckoo." But I didn't answer.'

She climbed into the car. 'If you have kidnapped me, mein Herr,
then you are also obligated to feed me, or I will report you to the police.'

I didn't want her to see my tears. She reminded me of my Eva, with
her imperious manner. But Eva wasn't beautiful and never had blond

hair. I had my driver stop at the Kranzler. I gave him my special ration book and he returned with a glass of milk and a little mountain of Black Forest cake on a silver platter.

'Fräulein, what is your name, bitte?*'*

She kept looking at the cake. 'Veronika,' she said, and she started picking off the maraschino cherries with her gorgeous little hands. She gobbled them all in half a minute.

'Fräulein Veronika, they are not barbarians at the Kranzler. They have given us napkins and forks. And you were meant to share that cake with me — it's a mountain!'

'I am so, so sorry, Grossvater,*' she said, and she fed me a sliver of cake with one of the Kranzler's silver forks, patted my chin with a napkin, and shared her own glass of milk.*

I was in love with this little Jewess, deeply in love, and she saw the tears in my eyes.

'Don't cry, Grossvater. *I won't let any harm come to you.'*

I wanted to knock Hitler's teeth out, poison his dog, piss on Goebbels, shit on Göring's carpets at Carinhall, but it was the posturings of an old man whose officers were members of the Wehrmacht and had helped murder Jews. Fräulein Veronika saw right through my fit.

*'*Grossvater, *you are a naughty man.'*

'And why is that?'

'You have captured me in your car, and after you have finished your cake, you will chew on my arms — as your second dessert.'

'But I am stuffed,' I had to insist.

And now she started to giggle. 'But if you do not eat one of my fingers, I will vanish, and you will not have such a pleasure again.'

She teased me with two hands that were as lyrical as little animals. I was powerless. I pretended to bite off her fingers, one by one. She laughed with such complete abandon, I forgot the war. But my good humor didn't last. I imagined her on a transport truck, with other Jews.

I knocked on the glass wall between the driver and myself.

'Dragonerstrasse, bitte.'

Erik wasn't home. I couldn't take her to Tirpitz-Ufer. There were too many spies in my own lair. We went to the Adlon. My driver found him reconnoitering in the bar. Erik was puzzled when he saw us.

'For God's sake,' I said, 'don't stand there and make a spectacle of yourself. Get in!'

She abandoned me and jumped on Erik's lap. I was heartsore, sick unto death.

'Männe,' I said, 'we have to hide this little girl.'

He started to scold me. I have no loyalty among my own men. They are all scoundrels, all Cesares.

'Stop panicking,' he said.

'But she's a Jewess.'

He took out his dirk, and with delicate strokes, he removed the yellow star from her coat; not a stitch could be seen; there wasn't the slightest wrinkle in the fabric.

'Alte, what is she now?'

And then he ignored his own chief. I was the extra party, the outsider. She told him her name and repeated the story about the men in long coats. And suddenly he insisted that Fräulein Veronika take my hand, and we went into the Adlon like three revelers. The bar was cluttered with SS officers and Gestapo commandants. Erik introduced her as his own niece, who had gone riding with us in the Grunewald. I don't think Erik had ever been on a horse in his life. And how dare he expose her to such danger! What if they asked her questions about the stables?

'Fräulein Veronika, how do you like to sit on a pony?' asked one of the commandants.

I searched for my pistol. I would have to shoot the entire bar.

She smiled at the commandant. 'Pony is too small.'

Then I guided her to our own table.

'Erik,' I hissed, 'I'll send you back to Kiel as a subcadet.'

'Herr Admiral, if you get excited, people will come over to pay their respects, and how will I ever find a home for Veronika?'

I panicked. 'Home? Will I ever see her again?'

'You'll ruin her cover. We will find a family of Lutherans, farmers who are beholden to us. But we cannot interfere, or see her again. You must say good-bye.'

I kissed her on the forehead. She followed the line of my tears with a finger, as if my skin were tracing paper.

'Good-bye, Grossvater. *And don't be naughty.'*

I didn't want to leave, but if I sat there, every SS officer would come over to ask a favor from Admiral Canaris: Moroccan plums for a pregnant wife, or some other miracle they imagined I might accomplish for them.

And as I marched out, I realized that Erik got along with Veronika because both of them were orphans — and I was excluded from their little orphans' club.

I went back to my car, and we rode without a destination, nothing to guide us — no wind, no black burning sun. My blood froze without that mysterious little girl, and soon my heart would pump nothing but piss water.

Veronika

13

CESARE LEFT VERONIKA WITH A woman in Charlottenburg who hid several submariners while he arranged to deliver her to Lutheran farmers in the Black Forest. But he didn't want to give up the little girl. He would swipe her from Charlottenburg, where Jewish doctors, lawyers, and dentists had once lived.

'*Mein Herr*,' she'd say, 'where's my pony?'

And he'd answer, 'Right here, Princess Veronika.'

He'd ride her on his shoulders through the Tiergarten, policemen saluting the little girl while they hid their own envy: They, too, wanted Veronika.

She'd call down to Erik from the heights of her own head. 'Herr Pony, you're much too slow. If you can't improve, I'll have to trade you in.'

He'd gallop with her across the gardens and right into Gestapo headquarters on Prinz-Albrecht-Strasse, because it was the last place in Berlin where one could still get decent ice cream. The Kranzler served sweetened sawdust. He'd sit with Veronika in the officers' canteen without a bit of fear. The little girl was a born actress. And who would have dreamt to ask her about a yellow star in this lions' den?

It tore at him whenever he had to return Veronika to Charlottenburg. The little girl was never sentimental. She would kiss him repeatedly and sing, 'I will give my horse a rest. But I will expect you very soon, Herr Pony.'

And he would tell the woman who watched over Veronika to guard her with her own life. But the woman grew careless; she let Veronika play with a submariner, who abandoned his hideout one winter afternoon and strolled with Veronika on the Palace Bridge. He shouldn't have gone out with the little girl into the streets of Berlin. A pair of drunken detectives from Kripo, the criminal police, found him on the bridge, asked him for his papers. The submariner tried to flee with Veronika in his arms. The detectives caught up with him. He struggled, bit one of the detectives. They beat him senseless and tossed him into the Landwehrkanal with Veronika still in his arms. Both of them drowned.

Erik could imagine her shaping a scream as her body hurtled over the bridge. He could see her arms flail but couldn't hear the scream. And whenever he dreamt of the little drowned goddess, it was Erik who woke up with a scream, his voice mottled and raw.

He closed down the woman in Charlottenburg, moved the rest of her submariners to another location. Erik couldn't stop mourning. He blamed himself. He should have sent Veronika to the Black Forest and not interfered in her life. He had his own informers find the names of the two drunken detectives. He waited two weeks, lured one of the detectives to the Palace Bridge with a fake call to headquarters, cut him from ear to ear, and threw his corpse into the *Kanal*. He plotted a more elaborate revenge for the second detective, who had a daughter of his own, exactly Veronika's age. Erik's mind moved in diabolic twists and turns, but he couldn't bring himself to harm the little girl. He finished off this detective while he was out walking his dog in Friedrichshain. The dog cowered in the grass even as its master lay dying.

The papers talked of a Berlin Werewolf – no, Jewish Werewolves in a Jewish cabal. Suddenly a little band of Jewish Reds was unleashing havoc on Berlin. Kripo began gathering evidence. It had to find this Jewish underground that had savagely murdered its own men.

Erik laughed to himself. It was a bitter laugh. *Jewish cabal*. But he didn't laugh very long. Commander Stolz broke down his door on the Dragonerstrasse.

'Cesare, do you want us all to suffer? I'm putting you under quarantine.'

Stolz had arrived with two of his assassins from Aktion. But Erik was in no mood to be trifled with. He was still mourning Veronika.

'And what will you do, Commander? Exile me to Holland, like the Kaiser?'

'I could break your neck. We're in danger because of you. They're not idiots at Kripo. If you can't promise to sit here for a month, I will break your neck. And don't you dare run to Admiral Canaris. Not even Canaris can save you.'

Yes, he can!

The admiral had arrived with his two dachshunds, pee stains on his cuffs.

'Helmut, I'd like to be alone with the Berlin Werewolf.'

The commander left with his two assassins. Canaris looked like a wild man. His face was ravaged.

'You promised to get my Veronika out of Berlin.'

'I was selfish,' Erik said. '*Alte*, I couldn't bear to part with her. I took her on tiny trips.'

The admiral perused him with the saddest eyes in Berlin.

'And where did you go with Veronika? I want all the details.'

'To the Tiergarten,' Erik said. 'I was her pony. And to Prinz-Albrecht-Strasse.'

A deep furrow appeared in the admiral's forehead.

'Uncle Willi, where else could I get her ice cream?'

'And if those butchers had asked her questions, or seen the outline of a yellow star on her coat?'

'There was no outline, and even if there had been, she would have talked her way out of it. She was my protector.'

'*Männe,*' the admiral said. 'I spent two hours with little Veronika, and I think of her night and day. Did you curse them for me when you tossed those two Kripo bastards into the *Kanal*?'

'Herr Admiral, I only tossed the first *Kripo*. I let the other one die on the dead grass in Friedrichshain.'

'One or two,' the admiral said. 'It makes no difference to me.'

And he stood there while Kasper and Sabine nibbled at his trouser cuffs.

Fräulein Fanni

14

BERLIN WAS STILL FLOODED WITH Jews. Goebbels blamed it on the *Mischlinge*. It was difficult to round them up, protected as they often were by Junkers and other pure-blooded Germans in their family. They could go into hiding, sink into Berlin's tumultuous sea. But the Gestapo had its own weapon to assist Herr Goebbels, informers among these half Jews themselves, *Greifer,* or grabbers, who could lure other half Jews from their hiding places. And Erik had come to the Mexiko, a whores' bar near the Alex, to meet the most successful and diabolic of all the *Greifer,* Fanni Grünspan.

Fräulein Fanni had lured eighteen mongrels, men and women alike, to the *Sammellager* at the Jewish Hospital, or to the Rosenstrasse, where another reception center was situated in an old Jewish orphanage – Erik's orphanage.

So he had a colossal rage against Fanni Grünspan, the Gestapo's little siren, who enticed half Jews into *his* orphanage, now a holding pen for the living dead. What Fräulein Fanni couldn't have known was that he trained with the SS and sat in on interrogations in the cellars of Gestapo headquarters. He often did favors for the local commander at Französische Strasse. He'd stumbled upon Fanni Grünspan after one such favor.

He intended to break her neck.

He wore a wax rose in his lapel – it was the recognition sign for her Gestapo handlers. She wandered into the Mexiko wearing a beret and a silver fox coat. She sniffed about with her nostrils and spotted Erik's wax flower. He could already feel his fingers on her throat. And then she dug the beret into her pocket and he caught the thickness of her blond hair. Becoming a *Greifer* hadn't hardened Fanni Grünspan. She had the green eyes of a startled lady deer.

'*Mensch*,' she said in that practiced gruffness of the Gestapo, 'will you buy me a beer? I'm parched. I've been running down *Mischlinge* all afternoon, and I'd like a whiskey chaser. I deserve it.'

'Fräulein, the whiskey is made of fermented sawdust and the beer is nothing but piss.'

She stared at his long, gloomy face and must have sensed that he couldn't have been her new Gestapo contact. It was much too complicated a face, with sunken cheeks and the sensual mouth of some dreamer, not a hangman or handler of *Greifer*.

'I'll have what you're having,' she said.

He took out his flask and poured some cognac into a teacup. She drank the cognac in one long gulp, her nostrils quivering with all the aristocratic mien of an Arabian mare.

'*Mensch*, would you like to dance? It's dark, and no one will notice us in here. I'll be your slave if you let me go. You're not my handler… you and your ersatz rose. It's ridiculous. You're some gigolo paid by my enemies to ruin me with a kiss. I won't listen to you. I'll close my eyes like a good little girl and you'll go away. You'll tell your masters that you never saw Fanni at the Mexiko. Poor Fanni's a wisp of smoke.'

He had to calm her down, or she would be worthless to him, and he'd have to bury her right under the bar. He touched her blond hair and whispered, 'Who am I?'

She didn't waver or blink.

'Cesare,' she said. 'You're a magician. Tell me, darling, do you really sleep in a coffin, or is it just a rumor that the Gestapo likes to spread about its biggest rival? What do you want?'

This *Greifer* reminded him of Lisalein, with her wild talk and wilderness of blond hair. She must have been born into that tiny breed of Jews that had once ruled Berlin.

He poured brandy from his flask. 'Fräulein, I will ask the questions. Where did you grow up?'

She rolled her eyes, as if the Abwehr's prize magician had turned into a dolt.

'In the Grunewald, Herr Cesare. We had our own villa. And I had two nurses, a nanny, and a tutor. I loved living in a forest. I could dream of wild boars.'

He should have remembered. Grünspan & Co. was once the biggest shoe manufacturer in Berlin, second only to Salamander Shoes. Its flagship store on Alexanderplatz lit up half of Scheunenviertel day and night. The huge dolls in Grünspan's window would beckon customers with a lewd smile; Grünspan's mannequins had Fanni's green eyes, and skin that seemed to undulate in the window like some marvelous human serpent.

'Fräulein Fanni, did you ever meet the Jewish baron on your walks through the Grunewald?'

She was irritated with her new handler. 'You're not listening to me, Herr Magician. I dreamt of wild boars. They would eat me alive, and I could watch my own bloody fingers disappear into their mouths. What Jewish baron?'

'Baron von Hecht.'

'Oh, him,' she said. 'His grandfather bribed Bismarck's ministers and sank millions into the treasury. Bismarck cursed and had him made a baron, or he couldn't go to war. And the current baron is no better. He financed the whole Nazi putsch. He has a daughter who married the Nazis.' She stared into Cesare's gloomy eyes. 'But you didn't bring me here to talk about Lisalein, or did you? She was our captain at summer camp, a million years ago on the Wannsee. It was the most exclusive camp in the world, Herr Magician, composed of *Mischlinge* heiresses. Our fathers paid the Berlin police a fortune to protect us. We weren't frightened of the Nazis, but of the Reds. They liked to kidnap rich Jewesses and hold them for ransom. And our captain was kidnapped right out of the water. Her father, the baron, went around like a crazy man until his Lisalein was returned. I hear he paid those Red gangsters half a million marks. But it stank of rotten fish. The Reds returned her after sixteen hours with scratches and bruises all over her body. I tell you, the Reds had touched her up, had modeled her –'

'Like the mannequins in your father's window.'

'Yes, but those mannequins couldn't breathe. And they weren't accomplices in any Red plot. Comrade Lisa was more than an accomplice. I'd swear she planned the whole thing to help finance the Red Front behind her father's back. He was frightened of the Reds. That's why the baron backed Herr Hitler. He must have hoped that the thugs on both sides would beat one another's brains out. You're in love with Lisalein.'

His face fell in and out of the dimmed light. It was impossible to see much with blackout curtains in the windows of the bar.

Fanni smiled, her green eyes on fire.

'Cesare, before you fuck me or kill me, tell the truth. You're in love with the baron's little bitch.'

She felt like his accomplice now, his mother confessor. She would do anything for the magician.

'*Mensch*, what is it you want me to do?'

'Stop feeding half Jews to Französische Strasse.'

'But there's not much future for a retired *Greifer*. They'll ship me off to one of the women's camps. I won't survive a week. The guards are all bull dykes. I'd rather die in Berlin. Make love to me. I mean it. We might not survive another week. You can strangle me while I'm coming… and then I can lie down in your coffin, Cesare.'

She'd aroused him with her banter. He pressed up against her in a bar of zombies and somnambulists. Berlin had become a city of sleepwalkers, except for the Nazis, who pranced about and tried to pull some order from the disorder they alone had spun. This very month, General Paulus had surrendered the remains of his army inside the tomb the Germans had created for themselves in Stalingrad – the Wehrmacht had lost over 100,000 men in the blink of an eye. And still the Nazis busied themselves building more and more bunkers in Fortress Berlin, an underground city where the Führer intended to roam with his secretaries and his maps. He dreamt of tearing down Mitte – central Berlin – the oldest part of the city, where the Polish Jews had lived in their ghetto without walls, and creating a new Berlin, 'Germania.' The war had interrupted his plans. Himmler kept rounding up the Jews, but the ghetto streets still existed with their ghosts. And some of these ghosts were in the Mexiko, *Mischlinge* who had become whores to pay their bills. The only clients they had were policemen and officers of the Reich – there were no Nazis at the bar tonight, just *Mädschen* who sat on their stools and drank warm beer out of teacups, since Berlin was short of glassware, and the Mexiko had run out of schooners months ago. The *Mädschen* never moved. They were half mad with hunger. Erik would raid the Abwehr's storerooms tomorrow and have a small mountain of marmalade delivered to the Mexiko, if he could ever unglue himself from Fräulein Fanni.

He was caught in her trance – she was the magician, with her own labyrinth of garter belts and stockings. Then the air raid sirens wailed, and Erik could feel the shiver in his spine, as if the sound had crept into him like some dybbuk from Scheunenviertel. He had to shout at all the *Mädschen* who sat with their teacups.

'Children, you'll have to go into the shelter – now!'

None of them moved, and he appealed to Fräulein Fanni.

'Help me, please. We can't leave them here. They'll all be buried in the rubble if there's a direct hit.'

Fanni traveled from stool to stool and pulled on the left ear of each prostitute. Her body shone in the blinking light. She went down into the cellar with all the Mexiko's girls. But Erik remained aloft.

'Cesare, where the hell are you?' Fanni growled.

Erik was already gone. He'd vowed never to climb down into a shelter. He wasn't frightened of the dark – it was the closeness of unwashed bodies mingled with the strange perfume of fear. He went out onto Alexanderplatz. An air raid warden screamed at him.

'*Scheisse,* get the fuck out of here, or I'll have you locked up.'

But the warden must have recognized the outline of Erik's sleek leather coat and assumed he was shouting at the SS or a Party man. The Party ruled Berlin. A gold Party pin was greater capital than Himmler's death's-head insignias. Erik had never joined the Party, but even Gestapo commandants believed that Cesare the somnambulist could pull a gold Party pin out of the air.

Searchlights swept the sky. It was the only light in Berlin. Every window had been blacked out. And the sky itself had a sweetness that Erik had never seen until now. The cluster of stars overwhelmed him – a bitter February wind had washed away the yellow smoke of military vehicles. And there was so little coal left in Berlin that citizens had to live with the cold or burn their own debris.

The sirens continued to wail. There wasn't a soul out on the Alex except for the wardens and a few stragglers rushing toward the bunkers at the U-Bahn station. So he had the Alex all to himself, like some reborn Kaiser. The line of roofs was already ragged from the bombs that the British Mosquitoes had dropped on Berlin. War or no war, he admired the Mosquitoes and their wooden hulls that were like galleons in the black skies, beautiful floating pirate ships.

He couldn't hear the grind of motors. The Mosquito was practically a silent plane. Its engines didn't bark like the heavy bombers that flew right over the flak. There were three enormous anti-aircraft bunkers in the heart of Berlin – one near the zoo, another in the north, and a third east of Alexanderplatz – but the gun girls who were amount these deadly batteries couldn't seem to solve the riddle of a low-flying plane that had all the pestilence of a glider with bombs and machine guns.

A Mosquito glided over the Alex and headed toward the Tiergarten. Last month, another lone Mosquito had bombed the zoo, and now tigers suddenly roamed the streets. Hungry as they were, they didn't bother Berliners. One had wandered onto the Alex with glassy eyes; it was the tamest tiger Berlin had ever seen. It nuzzled air raid wardens and allowed women and children to feed it ersatz tapioca pudding. The police lured it into a Black Maria and returned it to a barren zoo.

Erik heard the muffled sound of flak and that curious, teasing whistle of a bomb that fell somewhere in the factory land of north Berlin. These British 'air gangsters,' as the Luftwaffe called them, seldom found their targets. Wehrmacht engineers had built decoy factories with the help of movie sets from the studios in Babelsberg. The decoys were marvels of construction that managed to fool these air gangsters, but streets still burned, rubble began to collect, and tigers were still missing from the zoo.

Erik wandered into Scheunenviertel while flak continued to explode and create orange gashes in the northern sky. It was the only part of town that comforted him. Himmler's secret police couldn't have known the back alleys of Scheunenviertel. They might venture onto the Oranienburger Strasse with their own Black Marias and pluck Jews from some apartment that faced the street, but they couldn't have penetrated Scheunenviertel without a *Greifer* such as Fanni Grünspan. And like a fool, Erik almost rutted with Fanni near the Mexiko's zinc bar and hadn't even bothered to strangle the life out of her. The Gestapo strangled men and women with piano wire. Erik had been taught to do so at the SS officers' training school, but he couldn't have wrapped wire around Fanni's beautiful throbbing throat. It would have been like strangling Lisalein.

It was only in Scheunenviertel that he had a few moments of peace. As he walked through the measured alleys of Hackescher Markt, with its glass roofs, its pink columns, its cluster of glazed tiles, he recollected the alley's former occupants – the tradesmen, the carpenters, the Lithuanian poets' society, the ballet school, the tiny guild of leatherworkers that made and repaired the Kaiser's boots and hunting clothes, the bund of Jewish girls that could argue into the night about the latest German or Czech *Literatur*, the juggler who gave classes under his own skylight – all gone. Goebbels, the gauleiter of Berlin, hoped to replace them with loyal Nazis, but no one wanted to move into Scheunenviertel, because they might be mistaken for Jews, plucked into a Black Maria, and taken to a holding pen, even with their Party pins. Herr Goebbels knew how clever these Jewish devils were at impersonating Christians.

So Scheunenviertel was strewn with bits of tile and stucco and colored glass. Erik lived in a red stucco apartment house that had been put up at the end of the nineteenth century. It had its own patchwork of painted tiles that looked like a canopy of stars in some lost Jewish heaven.

He didn't even have to bother with the rent. He hardly had any groschen in his pocket. There was always some Abwehr clerk around to pay his bills. And what bartender in all of Berlin would ever have asked Cesare to take care of the tab? But the somnambulist preferred to drink at home. He took out his flask and cursed Fanni Grünspan while he sipped cognac. Cesare fell asleep in his own coffin on the Dragonerstrasse with the flask still in his hand.

Jewish Jazz

15

THE CONE-SHAPED FLARES THAT the Mosquitoes dropped were called 'Christmas trees,' because they were suspended from parachutes that lit the sky like huge red and yellow bulbs. Children loved to follow these falling parachute flares, but mothers and air raid wardens had to drag them into the nearest shelter. The Mosquitoes, which were mostly made of wood and could fly very low, were both bombers and spotter planes. They didn't make that grinding noise of Britain's heavy bombers. And thus the Mosquitoes gave very little warning. Suddenly, they were there, gliding right over your head, under the flak of anti-aircraft guns. Mosquitoes were almost impossible to chase from the sky. But Tilli, the gun girl on top of IG Farben, had managed her own miracle. She captured two in one night. The first Mosquito exploded in midair, and its crew fell like tattered pieces of shrapnel into the Tiergarten; the second Mosquito landed in a potato field north of Berlin; none of its 'air pirates' left the plane alive.

Tilli was on the cover of *Berliner Illustrirte*; she posed in an airman's scarf and her worn leather flak jacket, sitting in the saddle of her own anti-aircraft battery on Farben's roof. She looked like Betty Grable going to war, but the Reich's Betty Grable, in a gun girl's peaked cap. Plucked from her anonymous life on the roof, she was suddenly as popular as a movie star. Half of Germany and the whole of Berlin had seen her picture in the *Illustrirte*. She was offered the chance to play herself in a Babelsberg production, but Tilli declined. She would rather shoot real Mosquitoes out of the sky than attack cardboard planes at the Babelsberg studios.

A general, a banker, and a U-boat ace with the *Ritterkreuz* hanging from a ribbon around his neck offered to marry her. And that malevolent dwarf, Herr Goebbels, wanted to make her his mistress. But she was in love with the somnambulist and would be fondled by no other man. She waited for him at the Adlon, surrounded by her admirers. The bar was packed with SS colonels and Gestapo agents, who kissed her hand, with film producers and opera stars, who dreamt of Tilli naked in her saddle. Party officials might have proposed to her, but they didn't like the Adlon and its Jewish *Kultur* – Chaplin had stayed there, and Pola Negri – and so they kept to the Kaiserhof Hotel. Tilli had once belonged to the League of German Maidens and had slept with many soldier boys before she met the somnambulist. But she shed all her fiancés, and was as pious as a nun in her saddle, waiting for Erik.

He arrived in his leather coat, with that long, lugubrious face, his eyes like amber buttons that glowed in the dark. Under the spell of blackout curtains, the Adlon bar was a study in scarlet, with red tapestries on the walls, red carpets, red velvet cushions, and only a hint of light coming from the main hall. Tilli was wearing a black dress with a décolletage that could have turned generals into shivering swine. Her nipples were taut as pinpricks against the black silk. She had to prevent an SS colonel from falling at her feet. But Erik hadn't even glanced at her, hadn't eaten her alive with his amber buttons. She had to shove along the bar to him, weave in and out of all that company of men.

'My little secret agent,' she said, 'are you the only one who hasn't seen me in the *Illustrirte*? I was thinking of you when I shot down the Mosquitoes. The Führer sends me notes. I cannot read his scrawl. Herr Himmler wants to climb into my pants. I'm everyone's sweetheart except Cesare's.'

She started to cry among all her admirers. Erik was forlorn. She was lovelier than she had ever been; it wasn't her black sheath that excited him. It was her shyness. He might have married her in another lifetime, even with her devotion to the Nazis; she had a purity in her saddle that was far from the SS and its assassination squads. She didn't want to enslave the world, only to stop the Mosquitoes from ravaging Berlin. But he was addicted to Lisalein, and he didn't have the heart to tell Tilli.

'It's your other blonde,' she muttered, 'isn't it? The little Jewess with her Nazi husband. I could report her to the police.'

She saw the ripple in his forehead, under the trace of scarlet light.

'Don't worry. I wouldn't compromise my darling's darling. I couldn't have you walk around with a broken heart.'

'Tilli, what are you talking about?'

'Frau Valentiner. She's the brains behind the new Spartakus.' Spartakus was the code name of a mythical Jewish underground in Berlin. It had resurrected the Spartakusbund of 1918, but without Rosa Luxemburg. This new bund hadn't exploded a single bomb, hadn't shot holes into the Adlon's walls, hadn't harmed one German soldier. It couldn't have finished off the two detectives from Kripo, since Erik, the Berlin Werewolf, had acted alone. It didn't send out manifestos, or drop leaflets from the roofs. It had no signature. Spartakus was supposed to rescue Jews from the transport trucks, but not one truck had been diverted, or Erik would have been told about it at Gestapo headquarters. Did it have a secret list of submariners? Was it sheltering runaways, providing Jews with false *Papiere*? Did it have its own passport and visa division, like the Abwehr, its own forgers? Spartakus couldn't have kept such a secret from Erik's bloodhounds at the Abwehr. And wouldn't it have bumped into the little baron, who had his own network of submariners? No, it was a fairy tale meant to soothe a frightened horde of men, women, and children who vanished day by day with their yellow stars. Ah, went the tale, Hitler had his SS, and the Jews of Berlin had Spartakus.

'Tilli, you've been on your saddle too long. Spartakus doesn't exist.'

She wasn't crying now. She had Erik's attention.

'Ask Frau Valentiner and Fräulein Fanni Grünspan. They're the ringleaders.'

'That's crazy,' he said. 'Fanni's a *Greifer*. She snatches submariners who come out of hiding, hands them to the Gestapo.'

'That's her cover,' Tilli said with a wanton smile. 'She sacrifices a few submariners, and saves a hundred. She went to school with your Lisalein. They both lived in the Grunewald, with all the Jewish barons… Darling, take me to the White Mouse. I want to hear Jewish Jazz.'

The White Mouse had been a notorious cabaret during the Weimar years, with transvestites, boy prostitutes, society women who slummed as whores, dwarfs, Jewish jugglers, and jazz musicians. The Nazis had closed it down, sending the transvestites and Jewish jugglers to a concentration camp. But the war had lent a terrible nostalgia to Berlin, a longing not for Weimar itself, but for its powerful aromas and stinks. The Party members who descended upon Berlin with the Führer had nothing to do with the town or its ancient musk, but there was among the elite of the Wehrmacht, the Gestapo, and the SS, a secret wish for the White Mouse. And so it reopened in a tiny cellar a few doors from Gestapo headquarters on

Prinz-Albrecht-Strasse. The Gestapo considered it their own spider house, a trap that might lure submariners and other riffraff looking for Jewish Jazz.

It had a lone clarinetist, who had once played with an orchestra at the Adlon, during the reign of afternoon tea dances, when the hotel hired gigolos – cultivated young men – to rumba with the bored society women of Berlin. This clarinetist, who had both Gypsy and Jewish blood, and was seventy years old, lived inside the Gestapo prison at the Jewish Hospital. He was waiting for his own ticket to Auschwitz. But his Gestapo handlers made a fortune letting him sneak into the White Mouse. The Gestapo could have assembled an entire band, could have recreated the aura of the tea dances and the cabarets, but that would have meant a constant deluge of customers. And so this clarinetist, who might find himself on the next transport truck, had to offer the Gestapo and the SS a whiff of the old White Mouse.

Erik couldn't remember his name – Isaak or Diego. He seemed in a permanent state of palsy when his hands weren't on the keys of his clarinet. His tunes often made no sense. But they had a marvelously sad wail. He was the White Mouse.

ERIK SAT WITH TILLI ON his lap in a field car filled with SS officers and female Gestapo agents. The female agents were in love with Tilli but felt she was a little coarse, showing her cleavage to half the men at the Adlon. They wore daggers at their belts, like submarine commanders, and must have contemplated cutting Erik to pieces in this twilight world of a blacked-out Berlin; he'd nuzzled their sweetheart, had licked her from head to toe, but he also carried a dirk, and he might rip their throats with that cheese knife of his while all of them had one eye on Tilli. And he was enough of a magician to make sure they arrived at the White Mouse as a bundle of corpses.

So they left Herr Cesare alone. And he looked out upon the desolate streets. Few people wandered after dark. A streetcar still ran here and there with its blue windows, like landmarks out of Hell. For some reason it was always followed by a caravan of rats. Perhaps the caravan was intoxicated by the traveling wedges of blue paint. But he could have been wrong. The field car had its own caravan.

They were all going to the Pied Piper of Prinz-Albrecht-Strasse, Berlin's own Benny Goodman. The White Mouse had a tattered blue awning above its cellar door. There was no other sign that it was a Nazi cabaret. It did have a doorman, an SS guard with a bull's neck, but he was crouched under the awning.

Tilli approached him first, wearing an SS colonel's cap tilted over one eye.

'Permission to enter Die Weisse Maus.'

'*Jawohl, meine Prinzessin,*' he said, recognizing Tilli under her hat. He also recognized Erik, who liked to come to the White Mouse when he couldn't sleep.

Erik climbed down six steep steps and ducked into the cabaret. He caught the usual crowd – SS officers wearing lipstick, Gestapo agents with boas wrapped around their necks, cigarette girls with their cardboard displays cupped under their breasts, sailor boys with codpieces pinned to their trousers, whores from Alexanderplatz without a tooth in their heads, the wives of Wehrmacht officers searching every corner of the cabaret for vials of morphine. All were packed into a room that wasn't a whole lot bigger than the barbershop in the basement of the Adlon, and with a dance floor that could have fit inside a sofa. There was no space for a bandstand. The Jewish Gypsy had to climb onto a chair, which tottered while he played but never seemed to topple over. He was held up by his own raucous melody, a series of wild, irregular bleats that thrilled the regulars at the cabaret.

That staccato wail had become Jewish Jazz, and Berliners at the White Mouse loved to lean back and listen, tapping their feet to Don Diego's time, or dancing with whoever was near: men danced with men, women danced with boys or movie stars, but no one dared approach the princess of IG Farben's roof, not even the Gestapo's female agents. Tilli was untouchable after she appeared in the *Illustrirte*.

She had to pull on Erik's sleeve. '*Mein Engel*,' she growled like her own clarinet, 'dance with me.'

But he wasn't her angel or her deliverer. He was much too absorbed in Lisalein. He couldn't believe that she was part of some Jewish underground, and certainly not with a *Greifer* like Fanni Grünspan. He had warned Fanni, threatened her, and still she snatched submariners who had been lured out of their lair as if by a siren's call and were captured by this brazen blond Lorelei at the Café Kranzler or a movie palace. She would hold a pistol on her victims and lead them to the little Gestapo jail at the Jewish Hospital. The somnambulist would have to come out of his Berlin dream long enough to strangle Fanni. But he dreaded it. He knew he would see Lisa's smile on Fanni's face the instant he was at her throat.

So he let Tilli entice him onto the tiny dance floor. He clasped her hands and did a version of the boogie-woogie that he had once seen in a newsreel about Harlem's cabarets. He paddled to Don Diego's music like a spastic bear and spun Tilli around. It was as much as she could ever want, dancing with her fiancé at the White Mouse while Berlin was about to burn.

She knew that everyone was staring at her, and she could afford to close her eyes and move to Erik's touch like a blind mouse. But then that Jewish wailing multiplied, and she could hear a strange murmur in the room. She opened her eyes and saw not one but two blond *Mischlinge*, Frau Valentiner and Fräulein Fanni. They'd come into the cabaret in identical dark cloaks, looking at no one but themselves; each helped the other unfasten her cloak and hurl it into the air. They wore black silk sheaths, with a finer cut than Tilli's and just as much décolletage. They talked to no one, acknowledged no one, while the female Gestapo agents gawked at them like hungry children.

The clarinetist had stopped playing; he, too, was bound to them, had become their slave. Then Frau Valentiner smiled and the clarinetist started to wail. The two *Mischlinge* stood still, their heels clamped to the floor while their bodies undulated under the silk sheaths. This, Tilli realized, had to be Jewish Jazz – motion without motion, wild Jewish abandonment without lifting your foot.

She turned to look at Erik; the button eyes were gone, replaced by hot amber holes. Her fiancé was on fire. He ran out of the room, leaving her with a pair of blond witches who had broken the equilibrium of the White Mouse. It didn't matter that she wore an airman's scarf on the cover of the *Illustrirte,* that men chased her everywhere, that housewives pointed to her while they clutched their ration booklets. She was only safe in her saddle on top of IG Farben. But she could have shot every Mosquito out of the Berlin sky and still not have been able to solve the riddle of Jewish Jazz.

Fabrikaktion and Frauenprotest

16

Spartakus. NOW IT MADE SENSE. He remembered the tale Fanni had told him at the Mexiko bar. Lisalein and Fanni had both been to the same summer camp on the Wannsee. Lisalein was kidnapped right out of the water by an unruly band of Reds. A ransom was delivered, and Lisalein returned with cuts and bruises on her arms and legs. Fanni hinted that the kidnapping had been staged by Lisalein herself. Why had she told him all this? Was it to mock Erik, flaunt her own secret pact with Lisa?

Comrade Lisalein, commandant of Berlin's Red underground. The Nazis had broken the Reds, hung them from hooks, shot multitudes of them in the forests outside Berlin, tortured them in their cellars, kicked them to death, arranged mock trials so that their commissars could be guillotined. And now the Reds had resurfaced as a Jewish underground so clandestine that it did not leave a trace. Nothing but a whisper: Spartakus.

Erik had seen all the lists prepared by the Gestapo and their own Jewish police. He had bribed the Jupo, had gotten them to erase or juggle certain names so that he could pull submariners out of the air. And if there was a rival group, with rival submariners, how could it have flourished right under Erik's nose?

An SS captain was waiting for him outside the White Mouse.

'It's urgent, Herr Kapitän. Come with me.'

Gestapo headquarters was only three doors away. It was an old art school that had been turned into a dungeon, a dormitory, and a field office. Bloodred Nazi banners ran from the roof to the ground floor and decorated half the front wall. The same banners emblazoned the Adlon's front wall but couldn't overwhelm the hotel's façade. Still, Herr Hitler was everywhere.

Erik had to click his heels and give the Hitler salute again and again until he arrived at the Gestapo command center on the second floor. A new reign of terror was about to begin. The Gestapo and SS were bunched around a table. But these were no ordinary SS men. They were members of the Leibstandarte division, Hitler's personal bodyguards – the Death's-Heads, the elite of the elite. They wouldn't have descended upon Gestapo headquarters for some ordinary roundup. These were birds of prey – *Raubvögel*.

What Erik feared had happened, or Hitler's birds of prey wouldn't have hovered over Gestapo headquarters. There would be a new roundup, much more thorough than the last, when Jews were plucked out of their apartments or picked off the streets. Jews and half Jews who survived the Nazi dragnets had become slave laborers in the Third Reich; they toiled in factories, swept the streets, picked up broken glass after the bombings while they starved to death. Farben and other factories depended on this slave labor; bankers wanted these Jews in place. Air Marshal Göring relied on Jewish expertise at his own aircraft factories. Jews seemed to have a magical hand in the manufacture of ball bearings. The Wehrmacht's Jewish tailors were the only ones who could stitch a proper uniform. Berlin thrived on this free labor force. But the Party wanted the Jews of Berlin out of the way, and it overruled the Wehrmacht and IG Farben.

The Death's-Heads had devised the diabolic plan of capturing Jews at their workplaces and would coordinate this *Fabrikaktion* –

factory raids and roundups. Every inch of Berlin was accounted for on the Gestapo's roundtable. The Leibstandarte had prepared its own illustrated map. But Erik still didn't understand why the hell he had been summoned here. The Abwehr consisted of ciphers and secret agents, not policemen.

The Leibstandarte commandant smiled at him across the table. 'Herr Kapitän, we are counting on you. We do not have our own experts on Scheunenviertel. And if the Jews escape our dragnets and try to return to their nests, we expect you to be there with our very best detail. Should these vermin resist, you have my permission to shoot them on the spot. You will have ten marksmen at your disposal. Will that be enough, Herr Cesare?'

'More than enough,' Erik rasped, though he could barely control his panic. He had to warn the Jews before they went to work, had to hide them in the back alleys of Scheunenviertel until the *Fabrikaktion* was over. But how could he escape these Death's Heads, the Leibstandarte SS Adolf Hitler? They recognized him as some kind of magician. But Erik couldn't fly out of Gestapo headquarters like a bird of prey.

He couldn't warn the Jews. He'd have had to cut the throats of ten Leibstandarte marksmen and arrive at the factories before the Jews and the SS. But these sharpshooters couldn't have understood the contours of Scheunenviertel. He would lead them awry, have them sink into the most desolate alleys, where they could do little harm.

He spent half the night in the company of these men. They were all curious about the captain who slept in a coffin at the Fox's Lair. He didn't try to discourage their sense of him as a zombie and a magician. He passed around his own flask of schnapps. They sipped from it with suspicion, worried that Cesare's schnapps might turn them into zombies.

He sat with them long after sunrise. They had breakfast in the officers' commissary. They were served by Jewish waiters and Jewish cooks who wore the yellow star. A Jewish valet appeared and began to polish their boots. They bantered with Erik, never once looking into the valet's eyes. The kuchen at the table had come from the Gestapo's Jewish pastry chef. The coffee was from Arabia. Erik cursed his own appetite. He should have fasted before the *Fabrikaktion*. But he gobbled almond cakes that had begun to disappear from Berlin. He savored the coffee, drank it with his schnapps.

The Leibstandarte commandos left first, in their own trucks, with a handful of Gestapo agents and nurses from the Jewish Hospital to care for the old and the ill, who might be swept up in the factory raids. Then Erik left with the sharpshooters. They had their own field car, with a death's-head banner. It was almost noon.

The Gestapo must have killed most of the traffic to clear the lanes for Leibstandarte commandos and their trucks. Not one streetcar moved along its tracks. Shopkeepers hid behind their metal shutters. There were little fires in the rubble from the last Mosquito raid. But Erik couldn't hear a sound except for the bump of tires along the cobbles. He arrived in the crooked lanes of Scheunenviertel within ten minutes. Erik had to lead his sharpshooters on a phantom chase. He watched them climb out of the field car with rifles as tall as a man; they did not even bother to mount their telescopic sights. They could pick off Jews in this stinking hovel with their eyes closed.

'Herr Cesare,' said their sergeant, 'shall we wait for these vermin on the roofs?'

The slaughter would soon begin; those who had managed to dodge the raid would return to Scheunenviertel, one by one. So the sheriff of Scheunenviertel had to pluck something out of the air.

'Spartakus,' he said, and like a miracle the sharpshooters stopped looking for Jews.

All ten stared at Erik while they sniffed the Jewish streets. 'Herr Cesare,' said the sergeant, 'are you so clever that you can lead us to Spartakus?'

'I'm not sure. But I might know where they have their headquarters.'

'*Nartürlich*,' said the sergeant. 'Jewish spiders in a Jewish den. Will we require reinforcements?'

'For such spiders?' he said. Spartakus had no headquarters. But he led them to the Hackescher Markt. On the way, these men spotted a little Jewish girl with black hair who'd ventured out of a cellar to find her ball. They would have exploded her head like a pumpkin if Erik hadn't intervened.

'Fraülein,' he said, shoving her back into the cellar with her ball. 'The sun is still shining. You mustn't play in the street.'

They passed abandoned shops and stalls, and Erik led them deeper into the labyrinth of Scheunenviertel. They entered an old building at the edge of a courtyard, went up a flight of winding wooden steps, and Erik knocked down the door of a photography studio; the photographer had died a few months ago, but no one had bothered to clear out the space; the landlord and his five sons were in the holding pen on the Rosenstrasse, and what Christian photographer was crazy enough to rent a studio in a district of Berlin that was raided every other week? The dead photographer had been a bit of a madman, and this is what had encouraged Erik. It would take the Death's-Heads two weeks to sift through the madman's work; Erik had known him as a boy. An older brother in Munich had supported this mad photographer, whose name was Johann. He liked to photograph snails and lines of mildew on a wall; he liked to photograph bits and pieces of Hebrew letters on a storefront, the interiors of hallways where no light ever lived, the strange beards of old women, the breasts of old men. Such were Johann's subjects. He never sold a photograph in his life, not that Erik could recall.

But Johann's photos would intrigue the sharpshooters, at least for a little while. They would interpret the Hebrew letters as signs and symbols of Berlin's Jewish underground.

'A treasure trove,' said the sergeant, 'what a bounty, Herr Cesare.'

Erik had to violate Johann's work in order to save some Jewish souls. And what would happen after the Leibstandarte packed all the photographs and had them cataloged by their own cipher clerks? They would discover Johann's chaotic mind, not a plan to launch and protect submariners. And then Hitler's elite would fall upon Cesare.

He could have walked home to the Dragonerstrasse after the lightning raids were over. But it spooked the sheriff to stay in Scheunenviertel. He could sense Johann's images in each cranny of the old Jewish quarter, in each veined wall. And so he crossed the Spree, marched past an air raid warden's hut and the dead lanes of Unter den Linden with their Nazi banners and flags, and arrived at the Adlon. He didn't wander into the bar with its red plush seats and watery beer. He was in no mood to chatter with submarine aces or gun girls. He went up to the Abwehr's suite, which was never occupied – it seemed like Erik's private *Pension*.

His leather coat was filled with dust from Scheunenviertel; his pants stank of plaster and rotting wood. He tore off his clothes and took a bath. There was never a problem with water at the Adlon, which had its own well. It also had its own generator; the lights never died, not even during an air raid. He sat in the marble tub, under the Adlon's mirrors and golden spigots, wishing he now had a glass of wine. He got out of the tub but couldn't find his robe. He wrapped himself in a towel that he plucked from the heated towel rack, put on his white slippers, and tread across the carpets to his bronze bed. And there was Lisalein sitting like a cat, wearing his robe, as if she were a hausfrau from the hotel.

'How long have you been here?' he muttered.

'Ages, darling. I can't even count.'

'I'm not your darling,' he said. 'You danced with that *Greifer*, Fanni Grünspan.'

She laughed in that gruff voice of hers, which was almost like a growl.

'Darling, I'm flattered that you're so jealous. But you had your own whore, who loves to shoot down Mosquitoes. Tilli the Toiler. I watched you after every step with Fanni.'

Erik leaned over and started to shake Lisalein, but it had no effect. Her growls came from some secret place in her throat.

'You went to summer camp with her,' he said. 'She's your own lieutenant – in Spartakus. How many trucks did you waylay during the *Fabrikaktion*?'

'Idiot, I've been here all night. A whole battery of SS men escorted me from the White Mouse to the hotel. I wouldn't even have a cognac with them. I was waiting here for you.'

'Like my little wife. You've been a Red ever since summer camp. And why didn't you trust me? Haven't Emil and I been helping submariners?'

'Submariners,' she said. 'Submariners. Fanni has her own Gestapo card and her own pistol. I had to court her, darling. Did I have a choice? I pay her a queen's ransom to help Papa.'

'I don't believe you. She belongs to Spartakus. She's part of your whores' brigade.'

Lisalein rose out of bed, with the white wings of Erik's robe fluttering around her, and scratched his face. The scratches went deep, but Erik didn't howl once. He didn't even grip her hands. She could have scratched him all over again. The pain seemed to rouse him from his slumber. He searched with his tongue but couldn't find a lick of blood.

He must have been born in some unholy cradle. Her violence had unleashed a tenderness in him. He touched her face. He didn't want to tie her arms to the bed, punish her with his own passion. He reached under her robe, fondled her, his hand gliding across the surface of her skin. He started to tremble. She didn't mock him now. Her green eyes glowed under him. He'd had to use all his cunning, all the guile of Cesare the somnambulist, to prevent the Leibstandarte from slaughtering Jews in Scheunenviertel. But his rage against the Death's-Heads didn't fall on Lisalein, couldn't fuel his love. He landed in a dream once their mouths met.

HE HAD WANTED TO WAKE with Lisa in his arms. He would have sat beside the bed like a pilgrim, begged her to leave Valentiner and live with him. With Lisa as his Frau, he could walk away from the war. Erik would sneak the baron out of the *Extrastation* at the Jewish Hospital, find Emil, the little baron, and cross into Switzerland. He would mount his own *Aktion*. Dr Caligari would help him. Erik could get whatever papers he needed from the passport and visa division and a bundle of cash from the admiral's own strongbox. He would work as a chauffeur in Basel or Zürich.

It was like a blitzkreig in his head, his own lightning war. But Lisa was gone, the bathrobe she had worn bundled at his feet – a little Swiss mountain. He looked into the Empire mirror near his bed, ignoring its gold filigree. He had blood lines on both cheeks, marks across his face that made him look like a vampire.

It didn't take him long to learn about the echo of the

Fabrikaktion. All he had to do was get dressed and go down to the bar, which was full of SS officers with red faces. The raid had been a roaring success. The Leibstandarte had marched into factories with their bullwhips and bayonets and rounded up Jews, while the Gestapo rode across Berlin and arrested anyone who was wearing a yellow star. The Jews were crammed into several *Sammellager* – an old riding stable, an abandoned Luftwaffe barracks, a shuttered nightclub called the Clou, two synagogues, an old-age home, Erik's own orphanage on the Rosenstrasse, and the Jewish Hospital. And then the complications began; with their own thirst for order, the Nazis had decided to separate half Jews and Jews who happened to have an Aryan spouse. These special cases were locked away in Rosenstrasse and the Jewish Hospital.

But not even Herr Hitler's wise men and ministers could have predicted what would happen next. The wives of Jewish husbands and the mothers of *Mischlinge* began to congregate outside Rosenstrasse and the Jewish Hospital. And they shouted in their own orderly fashion, 'Give us back our husbands and children.'

The Nazis couldn't use bayonets and bullwhips on these *Hausfrauen,* who were soon joined by the Aryan husbands of Jewish wives. There were no images of this revolt in the *Berliner Illustrirte*. But the crowd of protestors began to build. The SS arrived with machine guns and threatened to rip into the crowd. But they saw members of the Wehrmacht who were married to Jews. They saw movie stars, a famous acrobat from the circus, and they saw Cesare, who had joined the *Frauenprotest* outside the Jewish Hospital. They recognized the Abwehr's chief magician and regarded the scratches on his face as war wounds. Their own captain bowed to him.

'Touché, Herr Cesare. An excellent trick, attaching yourself to misguided *Hausfrauen*. But how long will it last?'

'Until you send your machine gunners away,' he said.

'And if we arrested you, Herr Cesare?'

Erik smiled at his executioner. '*Mensch*, I'm with the secret service. I don't exist.'

The Aryan husbands and housewives gathered behind Erik and shouted, 'Butchers, give us our children and go away.'

The SS captain signaled to his men, who carried their machine guns back to their car and drove off. The housewives wanted to kiss Erik's hand.

His mind had begun to drift. What if he wore a yellow star, like the king of Denmark, who defied the Gestapo and saved as many Jews as he could? The Gestapo would only laugh if they discovered a yellow star on Erik's leather coat. They'd see it as one more intrigue, one more disguise, and offer Cesare the somnambulist a glass of blond beer.

Under the Adlon

17

THE *Frauenprotest* CONTINUED THROUGH AIR raids and firestorms. The Party was petrified. No full-blooded Germans had ever sided with the Jews before. Finally, after more than a week of protests, Goebbels dismissed the machine gunners and freed all the *Mischlinge* and Jews with Aryan spouses.

Most of the *Sammellager* were emptied out, except for the Jewish Hospital, which had become one enormous collection camp, with its *Schwesternheim*, its *Extrastation*, its Gestapo jail, where Fanni Grünspan now lived, behind a green curtain, and its clinic, where the sick were taken in the Nazis' zeal to cure Jews before they could be killed.

It was the last outpost of Jews in Berlin, and because three of its pavilions belonged to the Wehrmacht as a hospital of its own, the SS and the Gestapo found it hard to raid the hospital grounds. It had its own vegetable garden and sundeck, even its own cows, which provided the hospital with milk. It might even have had a submariner or two in its cellars. But the main clinic itself had become a refuge for a certain kind of submariner, treated by nurses from the *Schwesternheim* on the hospital's grounds and by doctors who could no longer practice anywhere else. They kept patients out of Nazi hands as long as they could, even risked their own lives to do so. And Erik believed that the sisters themselves had to be hiding submariners. There was no other explanation. A transport truck packed with Jews from the *Fabrikaktion* had vanished from Berlin – fifty children. And there wasn't a single clue.

An alert was sent out for the fifty Jewish children and their phantom truck. The Gestapo chieftains whispered Spartakus. And Erik wondered when he himself would be caught in the dragnet, since he had led the Leibstandarte to Johann the photographer's lair. He began seeing Johann's photographs on the walls at Prinz-Albrecht-Strasse; they were the secret pockets of Scheunenviertel itself – mildewed doors, a dead mouse, an aleph lying on its back, like the contours of some profound lament.

But Erik knew where Scheunenviertel's lament had gone – to Iranische Strasse and the Jewish Hospital. It had to be Spartakus' lone warehouse and headquarters. There was no other location where the Jews of Berlin could meet. And the *Schwesternheim* must have been the nerve center of the Jewish underground. The Nazis hadn't stripped Jewish nurses of their licenses, had allowed them to flourish in their own school, even though some of them had ended up on the transport trucks. The SS wandered through the hospital and all its clinics but never went near the *Schwesternheim*.

Cesare followed Fanni like a hawk. He knew that the pavilions were all connected by underground passageways, which also served as a bomb shelter. Fanni could climb down to the cellar of the main pavilion and 'elope' into the *Schwesternheim,* but she never did. She kept to her room in the *Sammellager,* which was fenced off from the rest of the hospital and had its own attack dogs, or she roamed Berlin in a beret and silver fox coat, a pistol in her pocket.

What kind of *Greifer* could she have been? He followed her onto streetcars with their blue windows, followed her into cafés, had kuchen at the next table, and she never spotted him. He followed her into the *Sammellager* itself, keeping ten paces behind her and flashing his green Gestapo identity card, always the best cover for an Abwehr man.

Fanni was queen of this little camp. Most of the *Sammellager* had emptied out. There were twenty Jews, stragglers who had escaped the transport trucks for some reason, or submariners who had been caught by Fanni and hadn't been processed yet. She ruled over them.

He had an urge to break her neck, and then he discovered a different Fraülein Fanni. He'd forgotten that Fanni's mother and father were inside the same *Sammellager*. The Nazis had stolen Herr Grünspan's shoe store on the Alex, with all its mannequins, and all his cash. He was just another pauper in a Gestapo holding pen. Yet this *Greifer* didn't play Queen Fanni with him. Her mother and father had grown half-blind, and she spent the afternoon reading *Faust* to them. She took all the parts – Margarete or Mephisto and the Young Witch – and when she frightened her Papa as she spat out Mephisto's mockery of mankind, she plucked her father's chin and cried, '*Vati*, it's the Devil, not me.'

Erik grew ashamed of spying on her. But he followed Fanni one last time… to the Adlon Hotel. She sat at the bar, and all the savagery had returned to her face. Her eyes blazed in the bar's reddish light; her lipstick seemed to burn her own mouth. She was a Gestapo *Mädschen* with that pistol in her pocket. She puffed on a Roth-Händle, biting into the golden lip of her cigarette holder. And then she saw her prey. A submariner had come into the bar, a girl of seventeen or so, skittish, trying to have a whiff of freedom before she returned to some cupboard on a side street.

The *Greifer* grimaced, wearing her own raw mask. She clutched her pistol and was ready to pounce, when Erik grabbed her arm.

'*Mensch*,' she snarled, 'walk away. I'm with the Gestapo.'

'So am I,' he whispered. 'So am I.'

She looked up, terrorized for a moment, and then she smiled. 'Herr Magician, are you going to strangle me in the Adlon? I could pose for you. I'd love to see my picture in the *Illustrirte*.'

'Dancing with Frau Valentiner at the White Mouse?'

'Why not?' she said, shaking a bit of ash from her Roth-Händle. 'That lizard couldn't keep her hands off me. I was lucky to walk out of there with my own ass. I'm her little whore, did you know that? Does it excite you, Herr Magician? The White Mouse is a lesbian bar. That's where she goes to pick up other lizards when I won't sleep with her.'

The *Greifer* had outsmarted Erik, hurled him off the track. He kept seeing images of Lisa dancing with her lizard at the White Mouse. He didn't know what to think. Perhaps it did excite him, or made him angry enough to break her bones in bed. But he wasn't going to let this *Greifer* out of his grasp.

He had his own surge of cruelty. 'Shall I read *Faust* to your father? I can push him right out of that little collection camp. He won't survive on the streets of Berlin.'

He couldn't break into her smile. 'Herr Magician, was it Lisa who scratched your face? We're comrades, you and I. Shall I show you the love bites on my back?'

'Tell me where you and Lisa got that truck and SS uniforms with all the right patches.'

'From inside your own pocket, Herr Magician.'

Perhaps he was a magician, because he seemed to conjure up Dr Caligari out of his own thoughts.

Admiral Canaris had arrived at the Adlon bar with a dachshund under each arm, Kasper and Sabine. He couldn't bear to leave them alone on the embankment. And Erik had to let the *Greifer* escape. She fondled the scratches on his face and fled without her submariner, who sat hunched on a stool.

171

The admiral looked gray in the bar's dim light. His white hair was unruly; his hands were shaking.

'*Alte*, should I hold the dogs for you?'

And that's when the air raid sirens began to wail. The dachshunds shivered in the admiral's arms. But he wouldn't release the dogs, not even to his own somnambulist. They left the bar, went down the sixteen steps to the barbershop in the basement. This was the Adlon's most celebrated salon, with its black porcelain chairs, its network of marble sinks, its rows of pomades and hair tonics, its enormous brass holder for heated towels, its tile floor that was like a kingdom of checkerboards. The Adlon's barbers were all Party members. And it was the barber-in-chief, Herr Winterdorf, who trimmed the Führer's mustache, massaged his scalp, and pomaded him. The Führer would sit with a heated towel on his face, while Leibstandarte commandos stood around him in a perfect shield. These Nazi barbers were as good as secret agents. They spied on foreign diplomats and the hotel's Jewish guests long before Hitler came to power. And it was the one area of the Adlon that the Abwehr had been unable to penetrate. Admiral Canaris couldn't plant a single spy among these barbers with their Party pins...

They had to hike through the barbershop to arrive at the shelter, which was near the Adlon's mandarin wine cellars; the shelter was like a second hotel, with several rooms, each equipped with Louis Quatorze sofas and armchairs. Page boys in powder blue coats and hats had assembled like a little army to assist the guests. The youngest page was in his sixties; the oldest was eighty-five. All of them, like the Adlon's waiters, had come out of retirement to help cope with the war. Erik and the admiral had to find a safe corner where other guests couldn't intrude upon their conversation. The Adlon's electrical generators went dead, and Sabine moaned in the dark. The admiral didn't utter a single word to soothe her. A soft yellow light began to sputter as the page boys scurried for candles to fit into the candelabra. It fell unevenly on the admiral's face. He seemed to peer at Erik like a falcon out of one eye.

'*Männe*, you're going to America, and you're taking Emil. Both of you will leave next week.'

'Herr Admiral, I can't believe that you're reviving that silly adventure. All our agents in the last two landings were caught within a week. What is the use of these landings?'

'They have no use, *Männe*. Our contacts have all been compromised. But it doesn't matter. We have to get our little baron out of the country before the SD grabs him by the pants.'

The SD was Hitler's own secret service within the SS; it rivaled the Abwehr, and was much more ruthless. But it didn't have the Abwehr's expertise.

Erik had to measure that falcon's eye in the crooked light. 'It was Emil who provided the Jewish underground with uniforms and a truck.'

'He is the Jewish underground.'

'And yet you took him into the Abwehr.'

The admiral sat with Sabine and Kasper in his lap. 'And what should I have done with the little baron? Given him to the Gestapo? How could I have realized that he hadn't severed the umbilical cord with his uncle, that they moved Die Drei Krokodile to another location – their own minds.'

'Then Baron von Hecht is involved with all this?'

'*Gott*,' said the admiral. 'He's their Doctor Mabuse. He sits in his emperor's bed at the hospital and saves as many Jews as he can.'

The room began to rumble; the Mosquitoes must have been flying over the Tiergarten with their load of bombs. The candles flickered, and the sleeve of a doddering page boy caught fire. Erik had to leap up and smother that fire with the cape of his leather coat. The dachshunds seemed enthralled by the dying licks of flame.

Erik returned to the admiral with a scorched lining.

'*Alte*, the baron isn't safe in his bed. Should I carry him to America on my back?'

'We can't save the whole world. But we might save Emil.'

They could no longer talk spy to spy. Frau Adlon had come into the shelter with three dachshunds of her own. She sat down next to the admiral. She was built like a battle-ax but had once danced the tango with Pola Negri during the tea dances that she herself had started at the Adlon. Pola Negri couldn't survive the coming of talkies in America. Her Polish accent made her sound like an artillery captain. She exiled herself in a suite at the Adlon, made films at the Babelsberg studios – *Mazurka* and *Moskau-Shanghai* – and danced the tango with Frau Adlon in the Beethoven Salon, wearing a mustache and a Cossack cape. She had many lovers, including the Führer himself, some might say, but she wouldn't dance at the Adlon without her mustache.

Frau Adlon whispered to the waiters, who vanished into the wine cellars and returned with goblets of champagne. And then the Grand Mufti arrived with his contingent of Arab Gestapo agents, who installed him close to Caligari in a Louis Quatorze chair.

'Herr Admiral, you have an excellent boy. The *Engländers* have put a price on my head, and your Cesare frightened one of their assassins out of this hotel.'

'Assassins?' muttered Frau Adlon, with marks of hysteria between her eyebrows. 'We have no assassins here. The Adlon wouldn't allow it. We have our own detectives, our own index cards, like the Abwehr. Isn't that so, Herr Admiral?'

Caligari kissed her hand. '*Gnädige Frau*, I can guarantee you that your files are better than ours.'

Erik slipped away. He didn't care how many bombs fell over Berlin. He'd rather breathe the brittle air of a flak-filled night than sit in some cellar. But he couldn't escape. The barbers' salon was lit. And Hitler's own barber, Herr Winterdorf, was behind his chair in a white smock, whetting his razor on a long leather strop. He could have been a general in the Kaiserskorps. The barber was a very tall man with steel gray hair. He had served as an infantryman in the Great War, and had almost been blinded in a gas attack. Erik had read his file in the Abwehr's inner sanctum, called the 'Little Library' – shelf after shelf of index cards kept under lock and key at the Tirpitz embankment.

Three of the barber's four sons had been killed on the eastern front. His fourth son was feebleminded and had been tucked away on a farm, hidden from the Nazis' euthanasia fanatics. The Abwehr could have used this information against the barber, kept him on a string, but the admiral wouldn't allow a feebleminded boy to become a pawn in his rivalry with the SS.

Erik didn't have the same scruples. Herr Winterdorf had taken part in *Kristallnacht,* had raided Scheunenviertel, setting fire to synagogues, pulling on the beards of old men. He'd kept a Jewish maid at the hotel as his mistress before denouncing her. Erik dreamt of punishing the barber in his own chair. But on another night.

He sailed past Herr Winterdorf without offering the Hitler salute.

'Herr Cesare,' the barber said, 'where's the rush? The *Engländers'* wooden planes are still in the sky. And soon we will have to put cement in the Adlon's front windows or sit in a world of glass. But how will we live without light?'

'You survive in your cave, Herr Winterdorf.'

'But it is only a barbershop, not the lobby. And please call me Fritz... Come, I will give you a shave.'

175

Erik stared at the razor and the long leather strop that looked like the lone suspender of some lost German giant. He smiled and sat down in Fritz's gleaming black chair. It might turn into a merry evening if the barber meant to kill him. Erik saw his own sad face in the salon's wonderland of mirrors. He really was Cesare, a wanderer in Berlin. But he slid the dirk out of his sleeve.

'Close your eyes,' the barber whispered. '*Mensch*, I cannot shave you if you're not relaxed. I might cut your chin.'

The somnambulist closed his eyes. Fritz pumped on a treadle, and his black chair turned into a bed. Cesare lay on the leather upholstery, wondering if the barber had prepared a coffin for him. Suddenly, he had a hot towel on his face with the scent of lilacs. And the barber slid his fingers under the towel to massage Cesare's temples and his scalp.

'Herr Kapitän, you must warn the Jewish baron.'

Erik held his dirk close to the barber's groin. 'And why is that, Herr Fritz? Is the SD going to spank him for being the wealthiest man in Berlin?'

'The SD has nothing to do with this. I'm talking about the Leibstandarte commandos. They have been compromised. Fifty Jews disappear from their own fingers, on a truck that does not belong to them, with other Jews posing as officers in Leibstandarte uniforms. They're not fools. Who could have financed such an *Aktion*? Only a man who had once seduced Berlin with Die Drei Krokodile, only the baron. And who could have helped him? Only the Abwehr… but this is not a criticism, Herr Kapitän.'

'Then what is it?' Erik asked from under the hot white mask of a towel with monograms. But Fritz wouldn't answer; he stopped massaging Erik's scalp, plucked off the towel, smothered the somnambulist in shaving cream, stooped over the reclining chair, and plunged with his razor in one hand. Erik was like a captured bird; he couldn't even maneuver with his knife while the barber scraped his chin. The sound of it roared in Erik's ears.

'I am fond of the baron. He was always kind to me. He even wore the Party pin once upon a time... until he was obliged to give it back. He would permit no other barber to shave him. And when I had problems with my own finances, it was the baron who paid my bills. You must get him out of Berlin. The Leibstandarte SS mean to kill the baron and his daughter. But there will be no arrest, Herr Kapitän Cesare, no interrogation. They hope to set an example and burn them alive – in the forest. An auto-da-fé in front of the Leibstandarte high command.'

Erik tried to clamber out of the chair, but Fritz held him down with his free hand.

'Do you want to ruin my reputation? I can't let you out of my shop looking like a *wilder Mann*. The baron still has three more days.'

So Erik sat through the ritual of razor scrapes, perfumes, and talcum powder. And Fritz wouldn't even accept a gratuity.

'You don't have much of a future, Herr Kapitän. The Leibstandarte also have you on their lists. You should leave Berlin with the baron. They are a little frightened of you, yes. They have never had to confront a magician. But that won't stop them from trampling you to death.'

Erik climbed up the sixteen steps to the reception hall, which was deserted now and looked like a moonscape with palm trees and reddish marble pillars. He went through the revolving doors and out onto Unter den Linden with its row of Nazi banners planted in the ground. There wasn't even an air raid warden to shout him back inside the hotel. But Cesare did have his own silent serenade. Four Leibstandarte commandos appeared from under the Adlon's canopy and rushed him into a field car. They didn't attack him with their fists. They had truncheons that resembled rubber snakes. They threw him into the rear of the car, bounced him on their laps, and said, 'We were expecting you, Herr Magician,' before they knocked him senseless with their rubber snakes.

The *Krankenhaus*

18

T HEY WERE CAREFUL WITH THE magician. They didn't vanish with him into their barracks, where he couldn't have survived the night. The commandos would have plucked out his eyes, trampled on him until every bone in his body had become a relic. So they sneaked him into Gestapo headquarters on Prinz-Albrecht-Strasse, sat him down in the cellar, and it was the Leibstandarte's own intelligence chief, Colonel – SS Standartenführer – Joachim, who interrogated him. The Standartenführer wore a plum-colored leather coat and boots of the very same deep red. He had the long fingers of a fiddler. He had once played duets with that other fiddler, Reinhard Heydrich. Colonel Joachim swiped his light blond mustache with one long finger. He didn't look like a murderer. He had a kind of merriment in his eyes.

'Magician,' he said, offering Erik a Roth-Händle from a burnished silver case. 'Must we hurt you? Frau Valentiner has already scratched your face. Ah, her marks have a certain symmetry, no?'

'What is it you want, Joachim? And Frau Valentiner is none of your fucking business.'

'But that is what concerns us, dear Erik. *Your* fucking business. You shouldn't be sleeping with *Mischlinge,* particularly one who's married to an SS man. Standartenführer Valentiner is important to us.'

'Yes, he pulls the gold teeth out of cadavers in all the conquered countries.'

But it was Joachim and his Death's-Heads who were the real ghouls. They had massacred civilians in Poland and Moravia – princes and priests, Jewish merchants, kindergarten teachers, lawyers, and professors – murdered them wholesale, buried them without a trace.

'What is it you want from me, Joachim? *Schnell.* Why did you bring me here?'

'You shouldn't have interfered with the factory raid, pretending that the headquarters of Spartakus was the atelier of a mad photographer.'

'Fine, then take me to your barracks and beat me to death.'

'I have a much better plan. I want you to arrest Frau Valentiner and the Jewish baron.'

Erik was bewildered. Fritz had talked of an auto-da-fé in the forest.

'You're confusing me with the Gestapo, Joachim. I'm not a policeman.'

'Ah, but you carry a Gestapo card in your pocket. And sometimes you even wear our uniform.'

'But that's only to unsettle our enemies. I couldn't survive without a cover.'

The colonel sneered at him. 'You have no cover, Herr Magician. Shoemakers in Dresden know about your exploits. That's the only reason you're still alive. And don't think that Caligari's Brandenbergers can save you. They're locked inside their barracks at the moment. The Führer is sending them to the eastern front.'

Erik suddenly realized that he would have to build his own auto-da-fé.

'*Richtig,*' he said. 'I'll do it.'

'Do what, Herr Magician? You talk in riddles.'

'Arrest the Jew and his daughter – but not tonight.'

The colonel started to groan. 'But we'll lose the element of surprise. And you might warn them.'

'Joachim, I'm like a mouse in a mousetrap. And where can the baron go? The *Krankenhaus* on Iranische Strasse is his very last kingdom.'

'Cesare,' the colonel said, wiping the Gestapo's dust from his plum-colored coat. 'I am suspicious of such a king. Our baron has a taste for royalty. That could be a danger to us all.'

Erik smiled to himself: He remembered an article Colonel Joachim had written in *Das Schwarze Korps*, the weekly journal put out on pink paper by the SS. Joachim, who fancied himself a literary critic and might even have studied *Hamlet* at Heidelberg, mocked the young Danish prince, said that Hamlet was the *Dreck* and *Schweinerei* of Shakespeare's own diseased intellect. Hamlet was a feebleminded weakling with a flair for hysterical language – Hamlet could never have been a member of the Black Corps. And Erik wondered if the Black Corps' literary critic considered the baron some kind of demented Lear with one depraved daughter instead of three.

'Joachim, we will catch Berlin's Jewish Lear and his Cordelia in the *Krankenhaus*. And then you can write about it in *Das Schwarze Korps*.'

THE SAME COMMANDOS RETURNED HIM to the Adlon, but this time Erik sat up front while they passed around a bottle of liebfraumilch and sang 'Schöner Gigolo.' The gigolos began to disappear from Berlin tearooms after the Nazis seized power. Perhaps the craze lasted a little longer at Unter den Linden, because of Frau Hedda's own craze to dance the tango on Sunday afternoons. She took over the Beethoven Salon for herself, dressed as an Apache, and danced with perfect strangers... after Pola Negri vacated her suite and vanished from Berlin. But it astonished Erik that Leibstandarte commandos should have memorized a song about taxi dancers; he could imagine them beating up the very gigolos they serenaded in the song.

'Herr Cesare,' they said, 'we will help you catch the Jew.'

Colonel Joachim had ordered these commandos to spy on him; they would sit like spiders outside the hotel.

The main hall was packed with bellboys in their buttoned uniforms and pillbox hats; the red veins in the marble pillars seemed to dance in the light. It dazzled him – he had to save Lisalein and the baron.

He saw a curious angel float above the carpets on the central staircase in a stunning white robe. It was only a trick of light. The Grand Mufti of Jerusalem had come downstairs with his Arab bodyguards. He signaled to Erik, and the two of them sat in red chairs under the vaulted marble ceiling.

'I am mindful of Baron von Hecht. He donated millions of marks to the poor of Jerusalem. I might be able to help you smuggle the baron and his daughter out of Berlin.'

The Mufti's men had captured an ambulance and parked it outside the hotel.

'Excellency, if those bloodhounds at the SS ever find out...'

The Mufti laughed. His beard had gone gray; his mustache was all mottled, and his dark eyes were pierced with tiny bullets of light. He was a wanderer with a price on his head. He'd defied the *Engländers,* and now the Germans kept him in a golden cage. But he wasn't their magnificent myna bird.

'Herr Cesare, if they bury me in the Tiergarten, all of Arabia will revolt. And the Führer will be furious... No, they'll let me have one Jewish baron. But I would like to see the Germans and the *Engländers* out of the way.'

Erik found the ambulance, put on the white orderly's coat and cap that the Mufti's agents had left for him beside the steering wheel, and drove across the river Spree and the ragged roofs of Wedding in the midst of a sudden storm of trolley cars. The streets were strewn with broken glass and the debris of battered buildings. He left the ambulance right on Iranische Strasse and marched through the main entrance in his hospital hat, knowing that the SS commandos in their field car couldn't be far behind. Cows still lived on the lawn. Nurses and wounded soldiers from the Wehrmacht hospital on the grounds tended to the garden; the Gestapo jail was still embroiled in barbed wire. But the Jewish Hospital of Wedding could have come out of a fairy tale, not a torn Berlin; the Mosquitoes had left all seven pavilions untouched, except for a few missing tiles on the roofs.

Erik climbed up the stairs of the main pavilion to the baron's 'hotel,' which had no chains on the doors. The *Extrastation* was like an added wing of the Adlon. Frau Hedda had permitted the baron to borrow one of her Empire mirrors and Louis Quatorze chairs. The baron was in bed, smoking a Roth-Händle and wearing silk pajamas. The nurse beside him had a yellow star sewn on her blouse. Erik couldn't have mistaken her blond hair.

He was puzzled by her different movements and emanations, had always been. She was Mata Hari one day, and Rosa Luxemburg the next. He could never really *find* Lisa. No sooner did he catch the baron's daughter than she metamorphosed into something else. She seemed the mistress of her own fierce ballet, and he was always excluded, always locked out. She danced with Fanni at the White Mouse and defied the whole German apparatus, grabbing Jewish children away from the SS. And now she wore the costume of a nurse.

'Sister Lisa,' he said. She turned toward him with a savage swiftness and a snarl that puffed out her eyes and made her look like a she-wolf. He lost his footing under her attack. Stumbling, he had to hold on to the baron's bed.

She growled at him. 'Why are you here with your funny hat?'

'I have an ambulance downstairs. We have to leave the hospital right away.'

'And where did you get your ambulance?' she asked with that same snarl.

'The Grand Mufti of Jerusalem gave it to me – he admires the baron.'

Lisa leered at him just like a she-wolf. 'Admires him enough to send us all into Hell.'

'What does it matter? Hell won't keep me from saving you and the baron from destruction.'

'And who would dare destroy us?' the baron asked, his chest ruffling under his silk pajamas. 'I have a letter signed by the chief of all the *Sammellager*. We're safe.'

'Baron, the Leibstandarte are minutes away. They won't even bother arresting you. They mean to burn you alive.'

The she-wolf went to scratch his face, but Erik clutched both her wrists.

'It's a lie,' she said.

Erik shivered under his white coat.

'Couldn't you have told me about Spartakus? What do I care that you were all a bunch of Reds? We were both moving submariners, saving Jews.'

'Idiot,' she said, 'why do you think I asked Emil to invite you to dinner? To reminisce with my little lost protégé? *Vati* may be sentimental, but I am not. It was to groom you, Captain – groom you for your own death.'

His knees were shaking. It was her rancor that terrified him. He let go of her wrists.

'Half the men you murdered, Herr Magician – in Majorca, Paris, Madrid – half of them were Jews.'

'Yes, from some forgotten Red Brigade. But most of them I never touched. I had the Abwehr behind me. I paid them to disappear. They're sitting out the war on some Greek island.'

'It's still assassination,' she said. 'You tore them away from us. *Vati,* throw him out.'

'I can't,' the baron said. 'It's not in my constitution.'

'Then I'll leave you here with him.'

'Frau Valentiner,' Erik said, his eyes aiming like an ax between her shoulder blades, not to harm Lisalein, but to hook her to him before she disappeared again into another mask. 'Then our times together were only an *Aktion*?'

She roared at Erik, and her shoulders began to heave. 'Darling, how did you ever survive so long? Haven't you noticed? I cannot bear the smell of a man.'

But when Lisa saw the sadness on his face, she seemed to soften. She kissed him, sucked at his mouth as if to uproot him from the baron's little hotel, and even caressed his hospital hat.

'Don't worry, darling. I'll take the back stairs. Your commandos will never find me.'

And she shoved through the *Extrastation*'s inner and outer doors, engulfed by the crippling perfume of her own flesh.

'Captain,' the baron said, 'she's in love with you; I would bet my life on it. Or half in love. With Lisa, it comes to the same thing. She was always full of mischief.'

Erik looked out the baron's window and caught the commandos

trampling across the garden. The cows stared at them and started to bellow and moan.

'Baron, I wish we had more time to chat... but the Death's Heads are in the garden.'

The baron was defiant until he heard the lowing of the cows. That mournful noise diminished him. He tumbled into Erik's arms. He wanted to raid his own closet at the *Extrastation* and wear his best satin coat and alligator shoes, but the magician swooped him out of bed in his slippers and silk pajamas and hoisted him onto his back, so that the baron felt like some kind of lighthouse with human eyes.

Erik had to find a route to the ambulance, but he wondered now if the ambulance itself was a time bomb that the Mufti had set into motion. *Nein,* he muttered to himself. The ambulance wasn't a booby trap. The Mufti had to fight not to become a Nazi toy. His suite at the Adlon had become a miniature radio station. He gave interviews against the *Engländers* that were beamed across Arabia. He posed with Hitler at the Chancellery. He visited munitions factories, had even gone onto the roof of IG Farben and sat in the cradle of an ack-ack gun. Erik had seen him in the *Illustrirte,* with a quizzical look on his face, as if he mocked his role as performing monkey, but was still defiant in his very performance.

Erik couldn't play hide-and-seek with commandos on the hospital stairs. So he went down into the basement, with the baron riding on his back. One winding staircase brought him into that tunnel land, lit with tiny red bulbs. Chairs and sofas and hospital beds were strewn about, since the basement also served as a bunker. He thought of Herr Herman Melville, and wondered if he was inside the belly of the White Whale, or a monstrous caterpillar, because the tunnel had its own striations, its own limbs, and Erik was confused after five minutes, but then he stumbled upon a wooden sign that read SCHWESTERNHEIM, with an arrow that pointed along a particular limb. It was darker than the rest, and this tunnel belched a bluish smoke that started to burn Erik's nose.

It also had a low ceiling, and the baron had to duck his head so as not to bang into the iron cages that housed the red lights. He hadn't had such adventure since he was a little boy, playing on his father's grounds in the Grunewald. He grew up surrounded by barons. His father had served two Kaisers, with a hump on his back, had financed the Kaisers' wars and was given his own black charger, which he would ride in the Grunewald like a member of the cavalry.

His father had died before he was fifty, his heart exploding against the narrowing walls of his chest. And young Wilfrid inherited his father's vast holdings and the hump on his back. But that didn't prevent him from becoming an officer in the Kaiser's cavalry. He had two pillows stitched to his saddle, and his sword was tied to his right hand with thick leather thongs. But Lt. Wilfrid von Hecht never led a single charge during the Great War; there were few charges to lead against tanks and an army living in enormous holes in the ground. He was useless without his horse. But he still wandered in that no-man's-land with a pistol and the same sword, and he did earn an Iron Cross Second Class, but he loved his horse more than his own men.

None of his accomplishments – the banks, the department stores in Berlin – could ever make his heart race. It was only the toy horse he rode in the Grunewald, or that saddle he had in the horse patrol, with its seat as high as a castle, that could ever satisfy him… until now. Riding on the magician's back was like having his hobbyhorse *and* his high saddle. And it was better than a forest or a battlefield. Nothing was ever so dark or severe as this tunnel, with its whorish red lamps. And then half his joy was gone, and the wind went out of his chest as he saw the flickering shadows. Commandos had stolen up behind him and his hobbyhorse with their powerful flashlights. He heard them shout '*Scheisse*' in the dark as they banged into the tunnel's winding walls.

'Herr Cesare,' he said, 'we will never outrun such an army. You must abandon me. Please. I have no wind left. Run for your life.'

'Baron, you are my life. You sent me to the Jewish Gymnasium.'

'And gave you to Uncle Heinrich, fool that I am. Heinrich sentenced you to his barn.'

'But I loved the animals, Herr Baron. Their bodies were like furnaces in the winter – did you ever sleep near a cow? But I cannot run and talk.'

So Erik ran silently in that labyrinthine limb of the tunnel. And most of the baron's joy came back... until he thought of Lisalein. The baron had married an opera singer who had the quivering nostrils and broad shoulders of a Valkyrie. And she gave him a strapping blond daughter without the familial trademark – that hump of the von Hechts. He didn't want much more from his Valkyrie. He'd never been in love. He rewarded the opera singer with her own castle on the Rhine, her own opera house, and had her sign away all her rights to Lisalein. It was a monstrous act. He raised Lisalein in the Grunewald with a houseful of servants who waited on her every whim. But he couldn't wipe out that Valkyrie of a wife. Soon Lisa's shoulders were broader than his. Her nostrils flared. Her whispers were twice as resonant as his own shouts. She was willful, stubborn, and violent with the servants. No school or summer camp could govern Lisa. He sent her to Switzerland. Lisa's Swiss boarding school sent her back. He hired tutors, the finest young women and men, and Lisa seduced them all. She went off for a month with a former nanny, a woman uglier than a frog. At sixteen, Lisa wanted to resurrect Rosa Luxemburg, while the baron did everything in his power to destroy the Reds, who would have made of Berlin one vast commune.

Lisa married a Nazi, Josef Valentiner, who had managed the baron's empire even while he was a boy. She brought Reds into their villa on Herman-Göring-Strasse as house servants. She ran her own network two doors away from the gauleiter of Berlin. Herr Goebbels never knew that one of his nearest neighbors was Spartakus.

She wouldn't flee Germany, wouldn't go into exile. And the baron wouldn't leave without her. He'd financed entire boatloads of German Jews, but these boats wandered the ocean without a country that would have them. The baron bribed more and more officials, flung his reichsmarks wherever he could, but Berlin had become a tightening knot. Josef Valentiner grew suspicious of servants who sneered at him; he sacked one after the other, and Lisa had to move her Red Brigade into the *Schwesternheim*. It wasn't so difficult. All she had to do was wear a yellow star and pretend to be a nurse. She seduced the headmistress and slept with some of the sisters.

Yet it wasn't all about seduction and the baron's marks. In spite of their ambiguity as Jewish nurses in Nazi Berlin, and their own fear of the Gestapo and the SS, who could strip them of their licenses and hurl them onto a transport truck, these sisters still wanted to help. And so the *Extrastation* had become the ganglia and nerve center of Spartakus. The baron's own accountants kept track of all the submariners. His banks had been seized by the Reich, but some of the managers remained loyal to him and guarded his cash boxes. It was Lisa who put them all at risk. She decided to counterattack, to have her own lightning war against the Death's-Heads and their factory raid. The baron had to buy a transport truck and hire actors to play commandos with white gloves. And now the Death's-Heads were right behind him in the tunnel. But he could no longer see the flicker of their flashlights on the walls.

'Herr Cesare,' he said, 'we have arrived.'

The baron slid off Erik's back. His hump was much more apparent in silk pajamas. He groped along the wall and found a tiny knob. It was the only protuberance of a door that couldn't be seen in the tunnel's dim red light. He rattled the knob.

'Lisa, it's me and the magician – let us in.'

But he had to turn the knob himself. And Erik could see Lisalein huddled in some kind of closet. She looked at Erik with all the loneliness of a wounded animal.

And then the tunnel was bathed in light; Erik was blinded for a moment, with terrible spots in his eyes. But soon he could see the commandos crouching with their flashlights and machine pistols. And Colonel Joachim appeared in his plum-colored coat, with dust on his service cap, his face covered in grime. He was clutching a machine pistol, but he didn't point it at Erik.

'Herr Magician, I'm so happy you led us to the blond bitch.' Erik moved toward that elfin door, tried to seal in Lisalein, when Joachim hit him with the pistol butt. And a strange image flashed in front of Erik's eyes – he'd gone to paradise. But this paradise was a bordello with marble pillars and nurses who wore nothing but garter belts. They had no clients but themselves. They prowled under the pillars, in their garter belts, with magnificent strides. Erik wanted to watch them forever. But Joachim hit him again, and he hurtled into some kind of sleep.

Blue Moon

19

H E WOKE IN THE BARON'S own bed, wearing a hospital gown with a yellow star over his heart. He looked at himself in Frau Hedda's gilded mirror. He had a bandage over one eye and purple marks on his chin. He *was* Cesare the somnambulist, a haunted dreamer and magician. A nurse hovered over him, wearing her own yellow star.

'*Schwester,* you must help me into my clothes. I have to find Lisalein and Baron von Hecht.'

She turned away from him, and he discovered a tall man with a dueling scar on his right cheek. It was Commander Stolz, head of Aktion. Stolz was the real sorcerer; Cesare only had to play himself.

'Helmut,' he said, sitting up, with the bandage over his eye. A sharp pain shot across his spine, and he had to lie down again. 'I have to rescue Frau Valentiner. Joachim must be holding her and the baron in his favorite Gestapo cellar. We'll mount a raid on Prinz-Albrecht-Strasse. We won't need more than two Aktion commandos.'

'A brilliant strategy,' said the commander. 'We'll start a war between the Death's-Heads and the Abwehr. They'll drown us in our own *Kanal*.'

'Then I'll do it myself. But you'll have to wrap me in bandages, or I'll never be able to leave this hotel.'

'It's too late, damn you. Joachim didn't take them to Prinz-Albrecht-Strasse. He shot them in the forest at Sachsenhausen, burnt their bodies, and buried their bones in a communal grave. There are no relics – nothing. You won't be able to tell their bones from any of the others.'

'Joachim wouldn't dare,' said Erik, beginning to sob, his own tears blinding him. 'He's holding them somewhere. They'll stand in chains before the People's Court, wait in the executioner's shed, and walk to the guillotine. But we'll be there first.'

'*Mensch,* they're kaput.'

The commander took some items out of a little sack – shreds of the baron's silk pajamas and a crop of long blond hair, braided with a rubber band.

'They tore off the baron's pajamas… and Joachim cut her hair with his own razor before he shot her.'

'I'll kill him.'

'Erik, he did it as a favor to Frau Valentiner. He swore on his life that he would give you her hair. She braided it herself, in front of their machine pistols, smiling half the time.'

'He conspired with her. I'll kill him.'

And then a voice shot from behind Stolz's back.

'*Männe,* you'll do nothing but sit in bed.'

It was Uncle Willi in his admiral's uniform, but without his dachshunds. There were blotches on his face, but his blue eyes shone like bullets. He'd had to bargain half the night with the Death's-Heads. They wanted to drink Erik's blood. It was the Grand Mufti who rescued Erik, not the Abwehr. The Mufti went to Himmler, said that Herr Cesare was the best bodyguard he'd ever had in Berlin, and that he would not sing Nazi songs on the radio again if they harmed him. But even that wasn't enough. The admiral had to swear that he was sending Cesare across the

Atlantic, into America's bloodstream, and that the Abwehr would soon be able to broadcast near the needle on top of the Empire State Building.

'*Männe*, it's all been arranged. The Death's-Heads are throwing a farewell party at the Adlon, in one of the grand salons. They're glad to get rid of you.'

'*Alte*, you have it wrong. I'll get rid of them.'

'Silence,' said the admiral. 'I forbid you to speak. We have to live with their *Schweinerei*. We have no other choice. Do you think I don't mourn Lisa and the baron? I took her sailing when she was a little girl. She was much more of a mariner than my own daughters. She wasn't even frightened of the sharks. She fed them from the footropes, tiny pieces of cake. I swear to you, those sinister creatures fell in love with Lisa. They followed her with their pink eyes…'

A violent shiver snaked through the admiral's body. He sat down and drank from Erik's glass of water. '*Männe*, we will settle with Joachim, but not now. You will smile at the Death's-Heads, dance with their wives. If you don't, they'll never let Emil out of Berlin. And I want to save the little baron.'

The admiral stood up, stroked Erik's cheek as he might have done with a child, and walked out of the room with Commander Stolz.

THE ABWEHR'S OWN TAILORS had come to the *Krankenhaus* with a splendid tie and shoes; they'd woven his initials into a silk shirt; his suit had been smuggled out of Shantung years ago and sat in one of the Abwehr's closets. It was perfect for Erik's christening, his bon voyage. The tailors stood on tiny ladders that they themselves had brought, smoothed out the wrinkles in Erik's Shantung suit, while one of the sisters shaved him. He couldn't bear to look at himself in the mirror; he had the complexion of clay. The Abwehr's assassin had become a clay man.

An Abwehr chauffeur escorted him downstairs, a seaman second class. There were craters in the garden, holes that looked like gigantic pockmarks; the cows had disappeared. The seaman second class took him to the limousine parked on Iranische Strasse and dug a red rose into his lapel.

'It comes from one of our hothouses, Herr Kapitän. The admiral had it flown in from Spain, with his strawberries.'

Erik almost smiled. 'Uncle Willi can't live without his strawberries.'

'He does it for the dogs, sir. They love all that sweet pulp.'

They rode down from Wedding. It was an afternoon in April, with a chill that swept the air. Some of the trees were still winterish, without a leaf. Others had begun to bloom, with random pink and red blossoms that reminded him of a peacock's tail...

The Adlon's page boys and wartime guests stared at the clay man, as if someone were about to knight him. Erik ached so much that he could barely march from the main hall to the Rembrandt Room, Hitler's favorite salon. It was a world of Empire mirrors with damask on the walls, and chandeliers made of pure crystal. There were even faux Rembrandts planted in the salon, portraits of the painter himself in a floppy hat. But Erik dreamt of Goya's Saturn devouring his son. He had seen that painting on his last mission to Madrid. Saturn's black eyes were on fire. Erik clung to that image. He, too, wanted to devour – Saturn's skinny legs could have been his own.

There was wine and food on the center table; herring and salami that must have come out of the Leibstandarte's special rations; there was kuchen and meat pies, pigs' knuckles and the Adlon's best champagne. And Erik had to wander into a sea of faces. Frau

Hedda had come to welcome him with her dachshunds. There were also the same commandos who had knocked him senseless underneath the *Schwesternheim,* had stolen away with Lisa and the baron, shot them in the neck, set their corpses on fire, and buried them somewhere in Sachsenhausen forest. They rushed at Erik, like members of the same *Fussball* team, jostled him with affection.

'Good hunting, Kapitän. Bring us back Herr Roosevelt in his wheelchair.'

All of Berlin seemed to know about his secret mission. And he wanted nothing more than to devour these Death's-Heads. And then their chief executioner, Joachim, spun him around. Erik winced; suddenly, the clay man had bones of brittle glass.

'Dear Erik, you must forgive me. Would you have preferred a public trial? They did not suffer, and we had to get rid of them. I let them have their submariners. Why should my commandos care about men and women hiding in some hole? Jews were meant to grovel under the ground. But they shouldn't have interfered with the factory raids... Tell me that you forgive me, Herr Magician, or I might have bad dreams.'

Erik would have to smile and smile and be like a villain, as Hamlet had done. He would have to wear his antic face, or he'd never survive this little party and summon the strength to murder Joachim and his men.

'Forgive you,' he said, and pressed deeper into that maelstrom. He had to greet the Müller twins, Franz and Fränze, who had trained with him at the SS officers' school, and who skirted between the Abwehr and the Death's-Heads. They were sworn to Colonel Joachim, not to Uncle Willi. But he had gone on several missions with them; the Müller twins had even saved his life in Budapest, when two Soviet agents had nearly strangled him. They'd come from a family of acrobats, and had grown up in a caravan. Fränze could barely read or write. She'd joined the League of German Maidens but had been expelled after she broke the back of a farmer who had tried to fondle her.

Both twins were as dark as blackbirds; Franz was slow-witted compared to his sister. He had to count on his fingers. But he was six feet tall, and as lithe as anyone Erik had ever seen. The Müller twins moved like their own little family of acrobats; they seemed to spin all the while they walked. They would have joined their uncle's circus had there been no Hitler and no war. Fränze was much more ambitious than her brother. She had pleaded with Erik on their missions to help her with her own erratic penmanship. He was patient with Fränze, taught her as best he could to spell. She plucked off her clothes in the middle of a lesson, assuming he wanted to sleep with her. But he couldn't summon up the least desire for her herculean body and rough, masculine face. She never forgave Erik, and neither did Franz. They were much more aloof on their next missions. But now they were assigned to the same submarine as Erik. They would be crossing the Atlantic with him as Abwehr agents. He couldn't misread their mean little eyes. They were his Rosencrantz and Guildenstern, put there to cancel him in the middle of the voyage.

They didn't pretend. That's what he liked about the Müller twins. They would warn him in advance.

'Erik,' Fränze said, 'you might get seasick. I think you should hide in the submarine base. Don't come on board the *Milchkuh*.'

The admiral wasn't going to borrow an attack boat with torpedoes, or even a training vessel, but a *Milchkuh,* one of the old, haggard cows of the submarine fleet that carried no torpedoes or torpedo tubes, but one pathetic cannon, and were used as refueling boats. This milk cow would have no extra fuel, and wouldn't rendezvous with another submarine. It would stick to the surface as much as it could. And it would be Erik's iron coffin.

'Fränze,' he said. 'I've never been on board a milk cow. It will be my maiden voyage.'

Franz said nothing; he let his sister talk. They lived together, slept in the same bed, and if the Müller twins made love, it must have been like marvelous acrobats. But Franz did start to talk. The *Milchkuh* must have disturbed him. Suddenly, he didn't want to play an assassin. And Erik knew, even before the voyage, that it would be a fatal flaw. Franz might jump into the void with his eyes open.

'Kapitän,' he said, 'it's not Uncle Willi who's sending us to accompany you.'

'I know,' Cesare said.

'Then why did you volunteer for such a suicide mission?'

'I want to see America.'

'You are mistaken. You cannot get to America from a *Milchkuh*.'

'But we shouldn't discourage him,' Fränze said. 'Our Erik is a dreamer.'

She was the dangerous one, as supple and efficient as a dirk. Franz would be a blink behind Erik, planning out his moves. He would have to keep brother and sister apart on board the *Milchkuh*, wedge his way between them. First Franz, and then Fränze. He wasn't frightened of the Müller twins. And it unsettled them to see that bravado of Cesare the somnambulist, who would welcome the *Milchkuh* as his coffin, since he slept in a coffin every night.

And Erik did have an ally – the captain of the tub, Peter Kleist, the most celebrated submarine ace of the war. He sank more Allied tonnage and British corvettes than any other U-boat commander. But he fell into disgrace during the summer of '42. He'd been declared 'lost at sea' with all his crew, and then reappeared several months later, in his crumpled commander's cap, with the ribbons of his Knight's Cross wrapped around his neck, as if he'd stepped out of a fairy tale. He mentioned amnesia. The admirals didn't believe him. It was unthinkable that a captain should survive without his men. He'd walked onto a beach near Le Havre and was whisked to Berlin. The Kreigsmarine had to be careful with Kapitän Peter Kleist. The Führer himself had awarded this commander the Knight's Cross with Oak Leaves, Swords, and Diamonds. No other submarine ace had such a Knight's Cross. But the admirals assumed that the *Engländers* had turned him around and thrown him back to Herr Hitler. They would give him no other command, not even a *Milchkuh*. He sat in Berlin for six months, spent his afternoons in exile at the Adlon. Then they let him have a training ship at Kiel. But he was virtually a prisoner at the base. And now suddenly he had a new command, a milk cow to America. Kapitän Kleist hated the Nazis, hated the Death's-Heads, hated the Hitler salute. He wouldn't have conspired with Himmler or Colonel Joachim.

He was a short, burly man with blond hair; he'd lost a finger at sea, and his left earlobe had been ripped off by a harpoon. When he drank too much, he fell on his face. Erik had found him like that many a time in the Adlon bar and had carried him up the main staircase to the Abwehr suite. But Kleist had his own clarity even in an alcoholic haze. He adored *Moby-Dick*. And they would spend half the night talking about white whales.

He seemed glum at Erik's party. He talked like a gangster, even though he was descended from margraves, at least on his mother's side. He wasn't wearing his white commander's cap or his *Ritterkreuz*, on a ribbon around his neck. He was dressed in a worn leather jacket and his sea boots. He'd already gulped five glasses of champagne.

'Scat,' he said. 'The sharks have come out of the water with their medals and white gloves. I'll go with you to Portugal. We'll wear a disguise... I couldn't even pick my own first mate on this run. Colonel Joachim assembled the crew. Half of them aren't even sailors, but his own sweethearts from the SS. Uncle Willi must be getting senile.'

'He picked you to command the tub, didn't he?'

'*Mensch,* I haven't been to sea in a year. I'm a nursemaid to a bunch of cadets. We crash-dive in enormous vats of water... Where the hell is the admiral? Why hasn't he come to your party? He's given you a ticket to Herr Teufel.'

Kleist's hands were shaking. His eyes began to wander. Erik had to seize the champagne glass and sit Kleist down in one of Hedda Adlon's chairs. And then he saw a ghost with blond hair drinking champagne with the Death's-Heads. He couldn't have been crazy. His Lisalein had risen out of Sachsenhausen forest to send him off on a milk cow. He would wean her from Joachim and his men, dance with her on that table of salamis.

What did he care if her flesh wasn't so solid? He would be tender with her charred bones. But he listened to her laugh – and it wasn't Lisa's throaty roar. That *Greifer* Fanni Grünspan was hobnobbing with her new handlers. And now Erik understood the entire script: Colonel Joachim hadn't stumbled upon Spartakus, hadn't been able to unmask Lisa and the baron on his own. The *Greifer* had given them away.

Erik had one last mission before he said good-bye to Berlin. He would strangle Fanni here, in the Rembrandt Room, in front of all these men in their black uniforms, with their drunken red faces and silvered sleeves. And then he heard a strange tootling. The Adlon's own little orchestra had arrived in the Rembrandt Room and set up its stand next to the piano. The Adlon had once had the best dance music in Berlin – a pair of dueling orchestras that played at all the afternoon tea dances in the Beethoven Salon or the Rembrandt

Room. These dueling orchestras – the Martinets and the Bald Eagles – had become the sensation of Berlin. 'Afternoon Tea at the Adlon' had been broadcast throughout the Greater Reich. But there was a tiny problem. The Martinets and the Bald Eagles both had Jewish bandleaders and Jewish musicians. The hotel held on to them as long as it could, but the Adlon couldn't have 'Jewish Jazz' a few blocks from the Chancellery. And Frau Hedda couldn't seem to find Aryan musicians with the same heat. The broadcasts were dropped, and the afternoon teas disappeared with the dueling orchestras.

And now Erik was confronted with musicians who looked like refugees from a labor camp. They might have been retired schoolteachers. But he looked again. They had yellow stars sewn on their dinner jackets. He wondered if they were the resurrected Eagles or Martinets. There were five of them – a bass fiddler, a pianist, a trumpet, a clarinet, and a tenor sax.

Colonel Joachim shouted at him across the salon. 'Herr Magician, in your honor. Jewish Jazz. For your trip to America.'

The Jewish jazzmen stood there like phantoms in dinner jackets. They didn't look anyone in the eye. Joachim must have plucked them from the *Sammellager* or the Gestapo ward at the Jewish Hospital. They didn't even have to rehearse. They started to play 'Blue Moon.' And their soft, measured cry startled him. He'd heard nothing but tubas in the street, and the strains of marching music. Let them banish *Moby-Dick*, and set fire to all the books. But even as a subcadet in Kiel, abused and pissed upon, he'd lived by the sounds of Herman Hermann and his Martinets. He didn't know anything then about tea dances or gigolos at the Adlon, only the cry of Herman's horn and the countercry of his Martinets. And now he had five scarecrows to soften Herman Hermann's wail with 'Blue Moon.'

No one started to dance, not even Frau Hedda, who was feeding morsels of smoked fish to her dachshunds. Erik had to steal Fräulein Fanni away from Joachim and his men.

'Remember me?' he muttered, with one hand on the small of her back. He would play her like a counterbass, pluck music from her ribs before he broke her in half. She didn't resist. She moved to his broken rhythm; Erik still had legs of clay. His whole body hurt.

'Whore,' he said, 'you gave Lisa up to Joachim, didn't you? You tattled about Spartakus, led them right to the baron.'

'Darling, did I have a choice? That bitch was crazy. She fucked me every night, in the bomb shelter. That's why she moved to Iranische Strasse and put on a nurse's smock – to be near me. She bit my nipples to pieces. My cunt's still sore. She dove into me like a fisherman, with all five fingers.'

'Shut up, or I'll strangle you right on this floor.'

'But I might have an orgasm, and it will ruin your party... She shouldn't have provoked the Death's-Heads, stealing fifty Jews from them during their biggest operation in Berlin. It ruined the *Fabrikaktion*. I warned whoever I could. But Lisalein knew what would happen next, and still she provoked them. What could I do, darling? Joachim knows I rule the hospital. The sisters and the doctors are all afraid of the blond Lorelei. He put my mother and father on the next truck. He was going to set my face on fire.'

'I'll do worse than that,' Erik told her.

'Ah, but there's a difference. I might like whatever you did.'

She *was* the blond Lorelei. He couldn't even threaten her with his tricks. 'Blue Moon' was beginning to creep into his bones. And then the music stopped. The Grand Mufti had come into the salon in his white robe, with his Arab Gestapo agents behind him. They frightened the Jewish musicians and all the Death's Heads, who had never seen such ferocious men, with their beetle eyes and hawkish faces.

The Death's-Heads clicked their heels and shot out their hands in a Hitler salute. The Grand Mufti wouldn't acknowledge them. He stopped for no one but Frau Hedda. He smiled at her for an instant and then seized Erik by the arm.

'Walk with me, Cesare.'

And the Grand Mufti strode with Erik across the salon, while the wives of certain SS officers, their faces gleaming under the chandeliers, salaamed as if they were greeting a rajah in Berlin.

'Herr Magician, how often can you rise from the dead? They mean to kill you before you ever get to Kiel. I complained to the ministry, and I slowed them down. They'll let you board the submarine, but you won't leave it alive. Their two best assassins will be your babysitters.'

'Rosencrantz and Guildenstern... the Müller twins. I know them very well.'

The Mufti seemed to shiver under his white robe. 'I've used up all my capital in Berlin. And unfortunately, Admiral Canaris has even less than I do. Himmler's SS are picking away at the Abwehr's feathers, and soon none of you will fly.'

'Then I will have to fall into the sea like Icarus, Excellency.'

'Or drown in a submarine. Cesare, these vultures dream of nothing but your grave. But perhaps we are all vultures come to celebrate your drowning. No wonder the admiral has kept away. He cannot help you, or help himself. He must be hiding in his Fox's Lair.'

The Grand Mufti had come to warn Erik, but wouldn't preside at his wake. He left the salon with his bodyguards. But he'd misread the admiral, who appeared in his rumpled suit, with the little baron beside him. Emil wore some kind of military uniform that the

Abwehr's tailors must have stitched for him, borrowing from half a dozen ranks. Emil had an admiral's ceremonial dagger and the buttons and silver piping of a sea captain. Colonel Joachim wanted to arrest Emil, but he wouldn't ruin Erik's party. Emil would die on the *Milchkuh,* with the admiral's magician.

Joachim clapped his hands. 'This isn't a morgue. I want my Jewish Jazz!'

The five musicians were jolted out of their little dream. Their yellow stars swayed behind the bandstand. They went back to 'Blue Moon.' There was such lament in their sounds that Erik almost began to wail with them. But he would survive his mission to America.

The admiral himself had orchestrated this *Aktion.* And the admiral had not come here to mourn. He went about the salon with Emil, nibbling on salami and greeting the Death's-Heads, clutching each one by the hand. That gesture belied his rumpled suit, his growing distance from the Führer's ear – he no longer had monthly chats with Herr Hitler, and Goebbels had stopped calling him Caligari. His magic, it seems, was a little too close to the Jews. He could rescue rabbis in Warsaw but couldn't kidnap Pope Pius. And Canaris' shadow fell over Jewish Berlin.

He sat forever in his Fox's Lair, with his dachshunds, a spymaster who had sent his saboteurs into Poland, and had unwittingly helped turn Warsaw into a vast hunting ground for the Death's-Heads. He'd watched Colonel Joachim stand in his field car like a circus performer, on the shoulders of his men, and shoot at rabbis and high school teachers and Jewish children in the ruined streets of Warsaw. Joachim had been wearing goggles that day, like some colonel in the Afrika Korps. But it was no act of bravura or majesty. There was a horrific storm of dust and blood. The rubble seemed to rise up off the wreckage with a whisper and a will of its own;

it whipped strings of blood into the faces of the SS, blinded them, until they had to look for shelter in the dusty caverns of their field cars. It only maddened Joachim, made him retreat into his goggles and find more children to shoot. It was the admiral and his band of saboteurs who broke up that relentless slaughter. He marched in front of Joachim's telescopic sights and shooed the child away from the Death's-Heads, and onto another pile of rubble.

The admiral hadn't told Erik this story, but the myth had circulated in the halls of the Abwehr. Uncle Willi was always irritable when he had to spend too much time away from his dogs. But he was here now, in the lions' den of the Death's-Heads. He had a pasty look about him. He was a man who lived in closets. He wouldn't even visit Eva in her five-star asylum, though he thought about her constantly. He rode his Arabian mare in the Grunewald, slept on a military cot with his dachshunds, worried about their indigestion, and dreamt up missions against the *Engländers* and the Americans that would never happen. The Abwehr had come to a halt months ago. It lived within a whirlwind of activity, as deceptive as a matador's cape. The Abwehr plotted to murder that Asiatic monster, Stalin, to poison the cigar-sucking satyr, Winston Churchill, and blow up the wheelchair of that paralytic, Franklin Roosevelt. The plots grew more and more elaborate. They were Tolstoyan in length and attention to detail. But the field agents and *V-Männer* in these reports existed only in the mind and imagination of the Fox's Lair. And yet the admiral had come to the Adlon on a mission that mattered to him. He didn't have to speak to Erik, didn't have to hold his hand. He salaamed to Frau Hedda and talked in deadly earnest about the diet of her dachshunds. He smiled at the musicians and started to dance with the *gnädige Frau,* queen of the afternoon teas, who had danced with Pola Negri.

No one had suspected the admiral's suppleness, the lightness he had under his dour mien. *Gott,* he moved like a gigolo. He had mastered the strains of 'Blue Moon.' Frau Hedda already had a wildness in her eyes. Her huge, buxom body seemed in a trance. But all the while the admiral was signaling to Erik, signaling without a word.

It was no suicide mission. *Männe,* the admiral was saying with every beat of 'Blue Moon.' *You will not perish on a submarine. I am sending you to the mainland of America.* But Erik couldn't think of Atlantic crossings. He could see Saturn on the wall, being devoured by Berlin – and then Lisa lying in her own blood. He was already a clay man. And clay men were hard to kill.

WHILE HE DANCED, THE ADMIRAL dreamt of Rosa Luxemburg. He could still picture her bruised eyes, the blood on her fingers. He shouldn't have been part of the conspiracy. But he had to save Berlin. The Spartakus putsch would have overwhelmed a nation already crippled by war. The Kaiser had fled to Holland. The sailors at Kiel had flown their Red flags and turned half the town into a brothel. Some of these rebel sailors had rushed through Berlin in the first days of 1919 and behaved like burglars at the Chancellery, carrying desks and typewriters on their backs. Canaris was a young officer who had joined a volunteer naval brigade to thwart these sailors and their revolution. His brigade had helped capture the Spartakus leaders, Liebknecht and Luxemburg. She was the brave one, the mad one, who went around reviling the entire officer corps. There would be no officers in the Red Rose's new army and navy.

He never saw Liebknecht, never saw him once. Liebknecht had been dragged into a different car. His navy escort was supposed to deliver him to Moabit prison. But Liebknecht never got to Moabit. Liebknecht was shot in the neck on the way there – the Gestapo

Genickschuss. And Rosa Luxemburg sat next to Canaris in the second car. She'd already been mauled by members of the Freikorps at the Hotel Eden. She was barely alive. Canaris fed her water and wiped her brow. She clutched his hand, searched his pale blue eyes. But he couldn't rescue her. That foolish cavalry lieutenant, Vogel, was on the running board, his waxed mustache wavering in the wind. He had a pistol in his hand, like some desperado of the Wild West. He didn't deliver the *Genickschuss.* He shot Rosa in the head. But Canaris might as well have killed her. She died in his arms, as if Rosa's executioner had also become her very last lover.

He put a blanket over her and screamed at Vogel, who laughed. It wasn't the murder itself, you see. Rosa would never have gotten to Moabit. It was the look of pleasure in Vogel's eyes, his deep exultation. Canaris' face was splattered with blood. Vogel twirled his mustache. Canaris threw him off the running board.

He couldn't recall if it was his idea to drop her in the Landwehrkanal. Her corpse didn't rise for nearly six months. But every afternoon, while standing on his balcony at the Fox's Lair, with his dachshunds in his arms, Canaris kept waiting for the Red Rose to rise again, to mock him with her broken shape, in the muddy water of the *Kanal.*

She was a tiny woman, like his Eva. He could still hear her heart beat. And then the jazz musicians brought him out of his dream. Frau Hedda was in his arms, not Eva, not the Red Rose. And he looked at Cesare, his *Männe,* whom he'd stolen from a miserable barrack in Kiel. *Alte* should have left him where he'd found him, as a subcadet on the seawall.

Blue Moon, Blue Moon. He hid in Frau Hedda's remarkable bosom. He didn't want Cesare to see him cry.

THE NORTH ATLANTIC

Fränze

We should have fled Berlin and run back to the circus, my brother and
I. We loved the high wire. I had such confidence hanging from his arms
a hundred feet above the ground. I had thought of no other man, and no
other man had pursued me until Colonel Joachim, with his idiotic love
proposals. 'Fränze, I can always send your brother to the eastern front.'

'And what good would that do, my little colonel?'

I was always contemptuous of him, even as I obeyed his commands.
But he liked to play rough with his Fränze, because he had come from
a society of landlords and mayors, while Franz and I were the children
of circus people who couldn't bother sending us to school.

'Well, my beauty,' he said, his hand on his chin.

I wasn't beautiful at all. I had the shoulders and grip of a man. My
belly didn't ripple with curves. I had no belly, and I had no curves.

'Well, without Franz, I could have a taste of your cunt.'

I would have torn his eyes out, but I couldn't disappoint the Führer.
The army and the navy had been a league of barons until the Führer
came to Berlin. The Führer didn't mock us – the lowly ones would
replace the landlords and the barons in the new social order.

'Give me your answer, my beauty, and be quick.'

'Darling Joachim,' I said, blinking at him like a debutante, 'you
would have to fly to China on a broomstick before you'd ever taste my
cunt.'

He raged under his high collar. But there was nothing he could do.
Joachim needed us.

'Then make sure the magician gets a good whiff of you. I don't want him coming out of the Atlantic alive.'

'Jawohl,' I said, his little soldier again. And I marched out of the office he kept at Gestapo headquarters. He was always sneaking around from one office to the next. He was jealous of our closeness to Dr Caligari. But we weren't close to the admiral at all. Caligari's agents knew we were with the Death's-Heads. And Joachim hated Erik. Joachim wasn't brave enough to sleep in a coffin. He liked to trample women and children, and show off his insignias. But Erik could scare people without a death's-head pinned to his collar.

The magician would never have repeated Joachim's idiotic love proposal. He was too polite even to look into my eyes. He taught me how to scribble words on a page, how to wander through Wilhelm Shakespeare. He'd brush my hand while we were reading, his kneecap next to mine. I would feel a jolt, like an electrical wire twisting through my bowels. And copying from Joachim, I said, 'Herr Magician, would you like to taste my cunt?'

I could tell – he was returning to his coffin, without Fränze Müller, without me. He had such a sad look. There were no more lessons, no more talk about the demons in Hamlet's head. I loved the magician, and I wanted to crush his skull.

He should have laughed, taken me in his arms, called me a foolish girl, and I would have forgiven him. But now there was a wall of fire between us. And I was choking on that fire. I wouldn't stop choking until I tore his every limb. I had warned him at that ridiculous party, but he wouldn't listen. Only an imbecile – or an Abwehr magician – would come to a party celebrating his departure from this world. Yet even now, on the eve of going to Kiel, I wanted to lie down with Erik in his coffin and have him lick me until I was dead.

Franz and Fränze

20

THEY WERE PUT IN THE same shack where Erik had lived eight years ago as a subcadet, behind the old Warrant Officer's School on the Mühlenstrasse, near the seawall. Half the city lay in ruins. The cadets' own nightclub, Trocadero, had disappeared with much of the Kaiserstrasse. The old submarine pens and corrals couldn't survive the nightly raids. Kiel had no celebrated gun girls like Tilli the Toiler; it had no gun girls at all. But it did have a multitude of slave laborers from Moravia and the Ukraine, who lived like troglodytes in the ruins; some slept in bomb craters, while others crawled on their knees into little holes under the seawall. Erik and Emil fed them from their own meager ration of salami. The women kissed Erik's hand and offered to undress for him in the rubble. They were frightened of hunchbacks, but they might have undressed for Emil, too, had Erik demanded it. But he wouldn't accept their favors. He didn't have the slightest dream of their flesh. All he could imagine was Lisa's own searing flesh in Sachsenhausen forest.

He lived with other members of *Milchkuh* Number Nine in the same shack – a skeleton crew of forty men and Fränze – but these men wouldn't part with their salami and pieces of lemon cake. They weren't genuine sailors, the lords of a submarine. They had cropped skulls and wore Party pins. Some were mechanics and pipe fitters; there was even a radioman. They could have operated a tub like *Milchkuh* Number Nine. But they hadn't been put there to take orders from a drunken U-boat commander with the Knight's Cross. The Müller twins were their leader, and since Franz seldom talked, they listened only to Fränze.

'Shitheads,' she told them, 'you'll share your salami with those starving Ukrainians, or none of you will ever snore again.'

These louts were in love with Fränze and would have leapt off the seawall for her, but they were delirious when she went into the shower with them. She was like a long silver mermaid with black hair.

'Brothers,' she would say, 'soap my back.'

She laughed when they tried to cover their erections.

'Jesus, this isn't a nursery school. We're going to live together on a tub. Why are you hiding your little cocks?'

They grew murderous when Emil came into the showers with the magician. They couldn't bear to look at the hump on his back. But it was Fränze who hiked across the showerheads to Emil, who put her hands on that strange carbuncle – it was like a gray mountain that sometimes moved – and soaped him from his eyebrows to his ankles while she watched Erik.

'Cesare,' she rasped, 'you're next.'

He smiled, knowing that he'd never leave this shack alive without Fränze. His own dirk couldn't save him. Franz and the Forty Thieves, as he called this crew of cutthroats, would have smothered him with their pillows the minute he closed his eyes if Fränze hadn't held the string to his existence and deflected her brother and the Forty Thieves. He understood her tactical maneuvers: She would dance around the magician until the very last day, in the middle of some orgasm that would flare up with his death – just as the milk cow arrived off the coast of Maine.

Franz brooded while his sister soaped Erik's ears and ground her belly into his. He didn't break his silence – he leapt onto Erik. It was Fränze who got in the way and hissed at her twin.

'I'll abandon you, little brother. I'll leave you here with these smelly men and run back to Berlin. Joachim will train you to become a zookeeper. You'll have to wash a leopard's balls.'

Franz knelt in front of his sister. The anguished look on his face was unbearable to see. 'I am sorry, Fränze.'

'But you have wronged the magician. Apologize to him.'

The muscles on his back quivered like bolts.

'Herr Magician,' he said with a twisted smile. 'I should not have attacked. My little sister is in love with you, and she regrets that we will have to feed you and the hunchback to the sharks. But it will give me a great deal of pleasure to imagine you at the bottom of the Atlantic with sharks' blood in your eyes.'

Fränze was startled at first; Franz had never uttered three whole sentences in his life. But she still slapped his face, and he tottered, off guard, losing his magnificent balance and landing in the muck of the shower stalls.

'Franz,' she hissed, 'that's poison, not an apology.'

And she strode out of the stalls, that silver mermaid with mannish shoulders, while the Forty Thieves were bereft without Fränze's naked body, and her brother stared at Erik and Emil with murder in his eyes.

AND SO IT WENT WHILE THE *Milchkuh* was being provisioned and prepared for sea; it sat in dry dock for six weeks, with a broken propeller and rotting fins. And the tub's commander, its *Kapitän zur See,* didn't appear once at Erik's bivouac on the Mühlenstrasse. Perhaps he was frightened of his own crew and didn't want to face such cutthroats on dry land. A ship's captain had little purchase away from his own tub.

Fränze mocked him mercilessly. 'Where is the famous Peter Kleist, with that black-white-and-red ribbon round his neck? *Gott*, I'll strangle him with it if I ever see him again.'

'Fränze,' said one of the Forty Thieves. 'You're our *Kapitän*. We don't need Kleist.'

She wore a long coat of purple leather, with wings that could have covered half the Kiel Kanal; it must have been a gift from Colonel Joachim and the Leibstandarte commandos; she could gather five or six members of the crew in its folds. And she marched through Kiel like that, with the shore patrol saluting her, the town's last cadets scattering in her wake, and the Moravian laborers staring at her from the dunes of broken buildings. Erik could have remained in the shed with Emil, but Franz might have doubled back with some of the Nazi crew, and he would have had to fend them off with his dirk. The Abwehr had issued him a snub-nosed automatic, but he wouldn't carry it around with him. It sat in one of his drawers at the Dragonerstrasse. He wasn't going to shoot off a man's face.

And so he clung to Fränze, who was his savior in Kiel, and would become his assassin once they were out at sea. She didn't know how to behave in his presence. She tingled and blushed whenever he drew near; sometimes Fränze put her arm around Erik, as if they were comrades and conspirators, forgetting that her mission was to conspire against him. And if he brushed against her, she would bristle with confusion… and a curious delight.

She'd drag him off into the cellar of a bombed-out store, hiding Emil within the wings of her coat, to save him from being trampled by the Forty Thieves.

'Herr Magician, you could seduce me a thousand times and

you'll still have to die on board the *Milchkuh*. It's been preordained.'

He'd rub her face, not out of spite, but because he was touched by her brutal plainness, and she'd start to tremble.

'And what if you seduced me, Fräulein Fränze?'

She turned away from him, hugging Emil under her coat. And her whispers grew hoarse with her own wildness. 'You're the magician, not me. And I've never kissed a man other than Franz.'

He hated himself, but he had to weave an invisible cloak around Fränze, tie her to him with uncertain strings before he climbed onto the *Milchkuh*, or he'd never escape Franz and the Forty Thieves. He leaned against Fränze, who was exactly his height, and he brushed her cheek with his lips. Her skin had the feel of very soft leather, like the fuzz on a doe that had once strayed into his uncle's barn during a storm. The doe had panicked, and Erik began to ease its fright, slid the blade of his hand across its flank, like a warm knife.

'You're a torturer,' she whispered. And then she made a noise that was like the strangled mooing of a cow. It troubled the magician, because her chaotic cry was ferocious and tender. Her body stiffened all of a sudden and the mooing stopped.

'Franz's coming,' she said. 'He'll kill us both... and I hate to think what he'll do to Emil.'

She shoved Erik out of the cellar with one great sweep and catapulted Emil from under her coat as Franz and the Forty Thieves rounded the corner of Kaiserstrasse. Franz's dark eyes turned pink in the sunlight. He was clutching a pistol that looked like a blue toy. But he didn't even menace the magician. He was much too distracted. Something about the cellar must have terrorized him, not its darkness, but the fact that he had lost contact with Fränze for a few moments and couldn't seem to find her in Kiel.

She glided up to him on the wings of her coat, kissed him on the mouth in front of the whole crew, while her hand slid behind her and grazed Erik's kneecap. Franz was the one who broke away from the kiss, his forehead wrinkling with worry lines.

'Fränze, I thought the Reds had captured you.'

'Brother, there haven't been Red sailors in this harbor for twenty-five years.'

'There are always Red sailors,' he said.

She plucked his ears to reassure him and flew into the wind with the Forty Thieves. Kiel had become a graveyard with several submarines. The town didn't even have a commandant. The submarine bases had been moved to France and Norway, with their deep vaults to withstand the shock of nightly bombings and attacks. But the *Engländers* still bombed Kiel. And there was no one to resist Fränze. She raided a tiny canteen on Kaiserstrasse that served as a club for Ukrainians who were starving to death in Kiel.

Fränze was their avenging angel. She shouted at the civilian recruiters who had come from Hamburg to lure these large-boned Ukrainian women into prostitution rings that would service crippled warriors home from the front. They had a permit from the Gestapo in their hands, licenses from half a dozen ministries. They had two gray trucks parked in the street, with barbers inside who would disinfect the women and probe their scalps for lice, give them girdles to wear and lace underpants.

These recruiters waved their permit at Fränze.

'We're protected,' they said. 'One phone call, Fräulein, and the Gestapo will wage war on you.'

But Fränze leapt on the recruiters, tore up their licenses, and bit one of them on the cheek. 'Werewolf,' he moaned, and ran out of the canteen with the other recruiters. All the Ukrainian women kissed Fränze and flirted with the Forty Thieves. They even danced with Emil, fondling the bump on his back. Fränze danced with Franz, but she never took her eyes off the magician – Erik alone seemed to recognize the plight of these large-boned women. They would starve in Kiel, no matter how many rations of salami the crew members gave them. And what would happen after *Milchkuh* Number Nine left port? The women might have been better off in the gray trucks, as part of a portable brothel, wandering from town to town. At least they would be fed, and wouldn't have lice in their hair.

But he didn't even have time to ponder their fate. The recruiters returned with the shore patrol and a team of Gestapo agents in felt hats.

'A werewolf, she's a werewolf,' said the recruiters, pointing to Fränze, as they scampered behind the Gestapo agents, who had to be cautious around such a tall, brazen woman in the purple leather coat of a Leibstandarte commando.

'*Gnädige Fräulein,*' they said, 'you have destroyed official documents. You must give your filthy Ukrainian whores to these gentlemen. They have to be deloused. They have not bathed in a month's time. Their stench is unbearable. All of Kiel smells like a rat's den.'

'You must learn to live with it,' she said. 'Berlin will not like this interference.'

The Gestapo agents seemed agitated. Their quarters in Kiel had been bombed twice, and they'd inherited a mousy station near the submarine corrals. They were frightened to death of Berlin. They had spent the last six months rounding up laborers who had run away from the dry docks and precision-instrument factories. They had little appetite to sleep with these lice-infected women and decided to sell them to Hamburg as whores. And now there was talk of Berlin from this werewolf in a leather coat.

In their own hysteria they decided to beat her brains out with their leather truncheons. The Forty Thieves stood idle. Devoted as they were to Fränze, they were Party members and couldn't attack the Gestapo. It was Franz who leapt on these agents, and also the magician, after he hid Emil behind the bar. But they couldn't shield Fränze from all the truncheons.

Fränze wasn't afraid. She kept watching Erik with hungry eyes as he battled for her. The recruiters chortled while blood and spit began to fly. The Gestapo agents would have dragged Erik and the twins back to their cellar if the Ukrainian women hadn't intervened. They beat back the Gestapo with nothing but their hands. They squashed the felt hats, thwacked the recruiters, and drove the Gestapo out onto the Kaiserstrasse.

Fränze saw the blood behind Erik's ear and whispered, '*Liebchen*, run while you have the chance, run for your life. I cannot speak for Franz. But I will find no pleasure in killing you on the *Milchkuh*.'

The magician had spots in front of his eyes. The Gestapo had clubbed him into the canteen's sticky floor. He'd lost the power to calculate. But he wouldn't flee from Kiel. Fränze kept mooing in his ear. It sounded like a serenade, moistened with Fränze's own spit. He had nowhere to run, not the Black Forest, not Scheunenviertel, not the castles in Bavaria. He had to cross the ocean, dead or alive.

Milchkuh Number Nine

21

THEY PACKED THEIR WHITE WOOLEN sweaters, their leather pants and leather jackets, their sou'westers and sea boots. None of them were real navy men. Erik was a cadet who had been ripped out of training school, even though Admiral Canaris had awarded him the rank of *Kapitän zur See.* He was no sea captain. He was some sort of magician who seemed to resurrect the men he had to kill. Fränze and Franz had never once been on a tub, and the little baron was scared to death of ocean voyages. The Forty Thieves pretended to be sailors; some had even gone to submarine school. But their whole lives depended on the Party, and the Party had sent them here, to preside over the funeral of a rogue Abwehr agent. They might even have to hurl Kapitän Kleist into the Atlantic. But none of them, even Fränze, was capable of captaining a U-boat – sinking Kleist was also to sink themselves. But they might tie him to the periscope saddle with a gun to his head and have him conduct a periscope school.

They marched across Kiel, from their shed on the Mühlenstrasse to the submarine corrals. Not one sailor welcomed them; there was no pink champagne or a band with tubas and a drum. There wasn't another sea captain in sight; cadets were scarce, and the admirals had abandoned Kiel with its regatta. The Ukrainian women had all gone into the gray trucks, seduced by little pots of perfume and underpants made of synthetic silk. The Forty Thieves found nothing but their own tub in its berth; the captain was standing alone on the weather deck. They climbed the gangplank and hopped over the steel cables and onto the tub, a gray monster with fiendish fins.

Six red-and-white pennants flew from the periscope housing on the bridge; these pennants marked a captain's 'kills' – white for tankers and red for warships – but they were flown at the end of a voyage, when a tub that was part of a combat flotilla returned to its base. *Milchkuh* Number Nine didn't belong to Wolf Pack Neptune or Polar Bear, or any wolf pack at all. It had never had a single kill. And yet Kapitän Kleist flaunted sea lore with pennants on a submarine that didn't have a single torpedo. And he'd had a picture of the Devil painted on the conning tower, replete with red horns and a gruesome red mouth.

It was *Schweinerei,* according to the captain's Nazi crew, men who would have been worthless in a wolf pack, or any combat flotilla, but who could thrive on a *Milchkuh* that wasn't trying to hunt *Engländers*, only remain invisible on the high seas. But to paint a red devil on the conning tower, as if Herr Kapitän Kleist were reviving his own past as the war's most prominent submarine ace. He hadn't commanded a tub in over a year. He was drunk half the time, this captain who had lost his own tub and all his men in foreign waters and rose out of the sea months later. The Kriegsmarine could no longer trust Herr Kapitän Kleist and had banished him to a training ship in a huge bathtub near the submarine corrals. Yet here he was, a captain again, hoping to ferry Abwehr agents into American waters.

The Forty Thieves meant to shove Kapitän Kleist out of the way. But he stood on the weather deck in his dress uniform, with ceremonial scabbard and dagger, his black silk tie stained with mustard and his buttons having gone a bluish green with rust. He wore his Knight's Cross with Diamonds, its red-white-and-black ribbon knitted around his neck like a hangman's noose. He swayed on the deck, of course, swollen with schnapps, but the dagger and silver-and-black cross disheartened the Forty Thieves, intimidated them. They were shy around daggers and dress uniforms.

He didn't return their Hitler salute, but he was clutching a dented water bucket that often doubled as a lemonade pail.

'Youngsters,' he said, 'no one will bring an unauthorized weapon on board while I am captain – give over or get off my tub.'

Franz and the Forty Thieves growled among themselves, but they couldn't risk a mutiny in Kiel, before the *Milchkuh* left the harbor. They held on to their sailors' knives but threw their pistols and truncheons into the lemonade pail and crept down the nearest hatch into the belly of that worthless sea cow.

NOW ERIK UNDERSTOOD WHY THE captain had disappeared for ten days and never met with his crew on dry land, wouldn't even rehearse them or have any mock runs. He had been on the milk cow all this time. Kapitän Kleist couldn't depend on a crew of cutthroats. He was his own first mate, his own navigator, and chief engineer. He hopped across the narrow passageway that snaked across the length of the submarine, spilling bags of lemons and cartons of canned bread off hammocks, bumping into crew members, banging into the open doors of lockers while pots and pans flew all around him, as he hopped fore and aft, from the engine room to the conning tower, from the map chest to the radio shack, or else he was in the saddle of his periscope, or up on the bridge with his binoculars. They couldn't leave him stranded, have him strangle in the water while they submerged the submarine. They didn't know how to crash-dive, or dive at all. And the captain taught the cutthroats only what he wanted them to know. They could start or stop the diesels, pick up the soundings of another sub, sight an enemy ship on the horizon while they stood watch, but they couldn't master the periscope, outrun a Swordfish torpedo bomber, or return to Kiel on their own.

They were helpless without Herr Kapitän Kleist and hated him all the more. They watched him at the periscope, watched him crawl among the engines, with grease on him like a Jewish blackface singer – Al Jolson of the North Atlantic – and hoped to mimic his actions and moves, and thus become their own *Kapitän*. But they mastered only what he wanted them to master, not one whit more, and so they grew surly and mean. They grumbled whenever he ordered them to their stations and barked some command.

They saluted and said, '*Jawohl, mein Führer*,' and dreamt of murdering him in his sleep. They no longer cared whether they were stranded at sea, or if one of the *Engländers'* corsairs flew out of the fog and captured them. But the Kapitän always slept with one eye open behind the red curtain of his tiny closet. There was no real captain's quarters, only a bunk enclosed by a bulkhead and a flimsy wall, where he wrote at his tiny desk screwed into the bulkhead, and where Erik and Emil slept on boards that also served as the captain's table.

Erik and Emil wouldn't have survived long in their own separate bunks. Both of them ate at the captain's table, stood watch with Kleist, accompanied him to the tiny toilet, which was aft of the crew's quarters, showered right after him, though they had to preserve what water they had, and their showers were nothing but a trickle of cold water. They grew whiskers, like the *Kapitän*, dug into the same bag of prunes, sucked on lemons with him. Kleist was suspicious of the cooks, who happened to be Franz and Fränze, but Erik didn't believe that the twins would poison them.

So he gobbled Fränze's puddings and cakes, while Emil and the *Kapitän* looked at him agog.

'*Mensch,*' Erik rasped, 'she might split me from ear to ear, but she wouldn't poison us. It's beneath her dignity. Herr Kapitän, you commissioned her as a cook, and cook she will be.'

'Why are you so sure?' Kleist asked.

'Because I've gone on *Aktionen* with her and Franz. They both have a medieval sense of battle, even for Abwehr agents.'

'I thought they were with the Death's-Heads.'

'They're still loyal to Uncle Willi. If they decide to harm me on this tub, they'll drop their gauntlet.'

'What gauntlet?' the *Kapitän* growled.

'It could be anything – a cake with a candle in it, a torn scarf. But she could also change her mind and attack without notice, or send her Nazis after us.'

But Fränze was far too perverse to read or unravel in that stinking cave of a *Milchkuh,* where red and blue lights blinked, where cockroaches as long as fingers crawled out of the galley and climbed into Erik's pockets, where lice plagued everyone's eyebrows and eyelashes, where ringworm grew rampant and half the crew had to have their heads shaved, where bread, boots, and lemon rinds turned a moldy green, where the reek of men wafted across the tub like sour perfume.

Fränze had stopped bothering to wear clothes. She slept in the same hammock with Franz, probed the scalps of the Forty Thieves for the first signs of ringworm. She was the one who shaved their skulls. She also inspected their groins for crab lice. And she threatened to stop cooking for the whole tub unless Erik, Emil, and Kapitän Kleist stood in front of her magnifying glass with their pants down. She didn't bother much with Emil or the *Kapitän*, raising and lowering their cocks with one finger while she foraged with her glass in their little forest of hair.

'Perfect specimens,' she muttered, an unlit Roth-Händle in her mouth. 'No crabs.'

But she was overwhelmed by Erik's nakedness, and she lost most of her élan. The Roth-Händle fell from her mouth. She had set up shop in the crew's quarters, and now the men stared at her from their hammocks and bunks. She probed with her glass without ever touching Erik. The glass wavered in her hand.

'Herr Magician,' she finally said. 'You will need some treatment. I have found something suspicious near your balls.'

The Nazis began to laugh. 'Shave him, Fränze. Deprive the magician of his magic.'

But Franz wasn't laughing. He watched this drama of the wavering glass from his hammock, his hands behind his head, his eyes like condemning coals in the uneven light of the tub.

The crew cried, 'Shave the magician,' but Fränze didn't remove her razor from the milk cow's medical kit. She'd become both doctor and nurse on board the tub. She had a foul yellow salve that could kill the crabs; she had pills to stimulate the heart, potions that could put a dragon to sleep, vials of morphine to deal with the pain of an amputated limb, but she had nothing in her metal box to hypnotize the magician and make him fond of her. Even with her kit, she was no Caligari, who could turn Erik into Cesare. She might have been able to seduce a sleepwalker, rut with him once like a wild rabbit, before she had to break his neck.

So she lived on the morphine in her metal box; it eased the pain of loving a magician who couldn't love her back. But she would walk around in a fugue while her muscles twitched, or lie down with Franz and feel the magician next to her. She couldn't sleep.

She was an assassin, not a seducer, but she still had to plot how to spend more time with Erik on this tub.

'Herr Magician, I will have to treat you twice a day.'

And she wandered into another compartment, her buttocks like two perfect overlapping hearts, and her back a musical instrument made of skin and bone. She had her own strange musk that seemed to soften the sour perfume of so many unwashed bodies. Perhaps it was the morphine, or the smell of her longing. But the men seemed riveted to her, would follow her around as if they were dreamers caught in a web and Fränze was a wildflower with a masculine face on a submarine full of cockroaches and marauding lice, ringworm and rampant rot.

She had to trap Erik coming out of the toilet. Her own naked body, the litheness of her arms and legs, held little allure for him. Even Emil and the captain would glance at her buttocks and luxuriate in Fränze's trail of sweet smoke. Only the magician was immune to her musk.

She tried to be formal with him, to wear the mask of a medic.

'You must not miss your treatments, Herr Cesare, or you will be covered with vermin. The salve stings, but it will cure you in five days. You do not want any lice with you in America.'

'Fränze,' he said, Emil behind him. 'We were both at Bad Tölz with the SS. We learned to groom ourselves every morning like chimpanzees. I don't have any lice, do I, Fränze?'

'No,' she said. 'It was all a lie.'

Emil tried not to listen, but Fränze pretended he wasn't there. 'Magician, I told you to run for your life. This milk cow is nothing but a mousetrap.'

'But the mousetrap is going to America.'

She had to beg the magician. 'Couldn't you kiss me?'

'I kissed you once – in Kiel.'

She could smile at him without wearing a mask. The sound of his voice, his hot breath on the submarine, had burnt her terror away.

'But it's not like a kiss on the ocean,' she said.

And then she warbled in his ear, dizzy with the closeness of him.

'Lie down with me, Erik, live with me on this tub, and I'll let you have your America.'

'Beautiful! Franz will kill both of us in our hammock, and that will be the end of our *Milchkuh* marriage.'

'I don't care,' she said. 'They'll bury us at sea.'

It hurt him to look at the hunger in her eyes. She had never longed for a man until the magician had taught her to spell and to read the pages of a book. She couldn't even say if she desired Franz. They were twins who slept in the same bed. Their copulations were like a primitive form of exercise, as if Fränze were being fondled in front of a mirror. But she had no mirror for the magician. She could not find her own image in him. She was a different Fränze, wild with a tenderness she could not control. She wanted to touch his ears, hold his cock like a tiny bird. But she saw no recognition on his face, not the least desire, and her tenderness turned to cruelty.

'Herr Magician,' she cackled, 'if you can't lend me your cock, you and the hunchback won't breathe much longer.'

She shoved Emil aside, her body unfolding like a knife, and disappeared into the gloom of the submarine while pots and potato sacks fell in her wake.

Kapitän zur See

22

T HEY'D GONE FROM KIEL HARBOR to the Norwegian Sea and into the North Atlantic without much of a wrinkle. There were no enemy 'Q-ships,' gunboats disguised as freighters, no Lockheed Lightnings to swoop out of the sky with their forked tails, no Sunderland flying fish to strafe an unwary submarine. The captain couldn't read his instruments, stand on the bridge, sit in his saddle, attend to the diesels, *and* fight the Forty Thieves. He would have to arrive off the coast of Maine by luck alone, and dead reckoning.

But there were always alerts and alarms – a Q-ship suddenly coming out of the fog like a shark in masquerade, with its guns hidden behind a freighter's false hull, and the captain had to crash-dive with the help of a crew that stumbled to its battle stations. Kleist had to lock all the hatches, or the tub would have drowned in a well of seawater. He had to scream instructions from his saddle, have an incompetent radioman take soundings of other 'sharks' that might have been near.

All his crash dives were performed in pantomime, as if the *Milchkuh* lived in a world of slow motion. It was only a matter of time before some cruiser or flying fish startled the tub and sent it to oblivion at the bottom of the sea. He couldn't hide all day underwater and break the surface only after dark. He had to ride

227

with the waves while the sun was still out, or he'd never leave the North Atlantic. Even with such louts, he could cruise at eleven or twelve knots.

It wasn't the Atlantic he feared, or the *Engländers* – it was Fränze. She seemed to exist in a trance, warbling at Erik while she was in the galley, or when she strode naked from stem to stern. He had to plead with the magician.

'*Mensch,* will you make love to her, for God's sake? She'll kill us all.'

It wouldn't have been unnatural to Erik, or even a chore. He'd seduced the mistresses of enemy agents while he was on some *Aktion* for Uncle Willi. He'd slept with 'swallows,' who tried to seduce him. And he still dreamt of strangling Fanni Grünspan while they rutted somewhere. But he couldn't seem to climb into Fränze's hammock. He wasn't worried that Franz might split him from his ears to his navel while he was with Fränze, or that the Forty Thieves might dirk him to death. It was Fränze herself.

He couldn't have feigned some kind of passion with her, fooled her dark eyes. His mind was elsewhere, not on America. He couldn't imagine the hills and pastures of Maine, or the secretive life of Shoeless Joe Jackson. He could only imagine Lisa's burning bones in an unmarked forest grave. That's why he seemed so lugubrious on board the milk cow. Or perhaps he was born with a funeral face.

He couldn't tuck Lisa's limbs onto Fränze, pretend that Lisa was a lithe acrobat from Munich. And even if he could have accomplished such a trick, Fränze would have seen right through the magician, sensed that he was conjuring a Jewish princess from her very own heartache. And so he avoided her.

He'd ask the captain's permission to stand watch on the bridge. First he'd shove Emil up the ladder of the conning tower, and then he'd mount the stairs himself. That first rush of wind and air drove the stink of unwashed bodies out of his nostrils. The submarine's stench was enough to cripple a man; the tub had become one endless toilet. He clung to the rails of the bridge while the *Milchkuh* rocked and rose with the waves. He held the little baron next to his heart; sailors had been known to topple off the bridge and sink into the sea. He was always startled when the captain wore his white cap on the bridge, without worrying that the wind might blow it off his head. Erik would clutch the bill of his own blue cap while he was on the bridge.

Emil wore a sou'wester. Erik could barely see his chin.

The sky had a molten color, could have been made of hot lead. It wasn't a sky Erik had ever seen on land. He wasn't much of a *Kapitän zur See*. He was nauseous after five minutes on the bridge. But he sucked in the salty air. He scoured the horizon with his binoculars and didn't see a scratch. But he heard a strange squeal, and suddenly a dolphin shot out of the water and followed the lurches of the milk cow, mimicking its rise and fall. The dolphin could have been another submarine, but it was much smaller and sleeker, without the milk cow's metal gray. It seemed to have a spout in the middle of its head, or perhaps it could spit water at an incredible rate.

The dolphin wasn't an albino, but Erik called it Moby Dick. It did have a white streak across its flank. Its eyes revolved like a turret, and it flicked the tub's own debris with its tail. Erik let out a bitter laugh. The dolphin seemed more human, more playful and quick than half the men on the tub.

'Cesare,' said Emil, clutching Erik's thigh, 'talk to the monster. It might talk back.'

Erik danced on the roof of the conning tower, and the dolphin flew past his head. It's an omen, he thought, an omen of America. And then the dolphin disappeared.

'Cesare, do you think the dollars the admiral gave us are counterfeit? The Abwehr has the very best engravers. I would like to open a department store in America, bigger than Die Drei Krokodile.'

'But we'd have to find another Alexanderplatz. And I'm not sure America has its own Alex.'

'God forbid,' said Emil. 'I wouldn't want to go from Berlin… to Berlin.'

'But I miss Scheunenviertel. Not the way it is now – it's a haunted house, with the Death's-Heads and their trucks. But before the Death's-Heads went into the alleys and chased little children. There was a fiddlers' society right outside my window. I woke to its sounds, and fell asleep with a fiddle in my ears. Emil, it was paradise.'

The little baron started to sniffle, and the sentences spun out of him. 'All the fiddlers are gone… and Lisalein. Lisa and the baron are gone because of me. I have a demon in my head, a red devil, like the one on the captain's tower. I encouraged her to compete with the SS, to have her own truck, her own silver-and-black uniforms. I thought I was still in the store, that I had as many departments as Die Drei Krokodile. The Abwehr *is* a department store, and I stole from one department, and then another. Our tailors made the SS uniforms, and then I requisitioned a truck from one of our garages near the *Kanal*. I plotted behind Uncle Willi's back. I bribed whoever I had to bribe. But I should have figured what would happen to Lisa.'

'Stop crying,' the magician said. 'The salt will get into your eyes, and they'll sting like your own little red devil… Spartakus had no future in Berlin. Colonel Joachim would have stumbled upon Lisa and the baron sooner or later. And you struck a blow. You snatched fifty Jews away from the Death's-Heads in the heart of Berlin.'

The water turned black in front of their eyes. The wind tasted of darkness. Erik couldn't have spied a thing with his binoculars, except a kind of dread. Then he heard the dolphin whistle. And he could *feel* its silver streak.

THEY'D BEEN AT SEA A MONTH. The crew was getting surly. It attacked the captain in the control room, and he shot one of the Forty Thieves in the shoulder. He had to become Jesse James on his own tub, a man of the American West. It was Fränze who stepped in, shoved the Forty Thieves out of the control room. They were more involved in her naked limbs than in a mutiny. She had sensed that these louts couldn't run a *Milchkuh* on their own. They would have had to surrender to the nearest freighter.

She took over the tub; the captain still barked orders, but he was little more than a prisoner on a very long leash. She hadn't rationed the *Milchkuh*'s grub, and there was nothing to eat but rice and biscuits. All the lemons were gone. The roaches had multiplied, and Erik had to listen to their filthy shells crackle in his sleep. But sleep itself had become a miracle. He couldn't doze more than ten minutes at a time. He had his own headquarters in the wardroom, near the captain's red curtain. The entire tub had become infested, caught in a plague. His meager portion of rice was littered with black beetles and cockroach wings. The biscuits turned to paste in his hands. The water wasn't sweet.

He'd begun to hallucinate. Lisalein visited him in that shadow land between waking and dreaming. Her body wasn't ripped with fire, wasn't even bruised. She wore lipstick as rich as blood. They weren't at the Adlon, with Lisa crouching between one of the hotel's double doors. They weren't dancing at a Gestapo cabaret, or making love on the Dragonerstrasse, in that same apartment where

Erik had lived as a boy. They were on board the milk cow, and Lisa's naked body was covered with machine oil. It glistened under the tub's twitching lamps. Her hair wasn't long, with a curl over one eye, like a cabaret singer, or a Nazi vamp. It had been clipped short, like a slave laborer, and she had a hole in her neck where the Leibstandarte commandos had shot her in Sachsenhausen forest; blood had dried around that hole in the shape of a heart.

Lisa was wearing a mechanic's gloves. She must have been the captain of the engine room. But she seized Erik's hand with an oily glove and led him aft to the crew's quarters. Erik was astonished, because none of the Forty Thieves leered at him. It was an altogether different crew – sisters and patients and Gestapo guards from the Jewish Hospital on Iranische Strasse. They were lying down in their hammocks and bunks, smoking Roth-Händles, when it was forbidden to light a cigarette on board the *Milchkuh*. And Lisa, in her shiny cloak of machine oil, delivered Erik to her own hammock, which had silver hooks and was made of the finest satin.

Ah, he muttered to himself, it's just like the *Extrastation* at the Jewish Hospital. Satin sheets. Roth-Händles in bed. But when he climbed into the hammock with Lisa, it began to sway like a tub in a treacherous sea – the satin tore and the silver hooks shattered, and all he had in his hand was Lisa's oily glove.

He looked up and found Emil hanging from a hook in the wardroom. His neck had been broken, but the little baron's knuckles weren't even raw. He was dressed in his rain gear, as if he'd just come back from riding the waves on the captain's bridge. There was no look of alarm in his eyes. He must have died dreaming of that silver dolphin.

Romance

23

H E WAS NO LESS A prisoner than Kapitän Kleist, but he had to bury the little baron. So he put on his antic disposition, smiled at the Forty Thieves, who helped him carry Emil up the ladder, bundled in the captain's own silk flag. The entire crew had assembled on the upper deck in their leather jackets, with lice in their beards. Fränze stood naked on the windswept tub, shivering in her brother's arms. She wouldn't gloat. It didn't matter to her that she had masterminded Emil's death. She must have laced Erik's last meal with a sleeping potion. And the Forty Thieves fell upon Emil without a struggle. Otherwise, they would have had to murder the magician. Had she herself spun Emil's ears until his neck snapped? She was mourning now.

'We commend Emil von Hecht to the sea,' said the captain, as Erik held the little baron in his arms, folded inside the flag. 'May his soul rise out of the body's own corruption, rise out of the deep in the company of angels. Amen.'

It was Fränze who helped Erik slide the little baron overboard in his silk coffin, which bobbed a few times and then was sucked into the waves. The Forty Thieves sniffed at the salt in the air and began to knead their caps with their thick fingers while Erik read from Revelation.

Behold, I am coming soon, bringing my recompense, to repay every one for what he has done. I am the Alpha and the Omega, the first and the last, the beginning and the end.

'Alpha and Omega,' Fränze whispered, and went down the hatch, followed by Franz and the Forty Thieves.

'Erik,' the captain said, 'you can't fight them. You have no angels on your side. We're two mortals on a mad submarine.'

'But I never relied on angels,' Erik muttered, without his antic smile. 'I'm an Abwehr man. But you must tell me, Herr Kapitän, why the admiral picked you to command this tub, and why Colonel Joachim even allowed you on board. He knows how much you hate the Nazis. Tell the truth. What happened to your own tub? Why did your men drown and not you?'

'My men didn't drown,' he said. 'They're in a prison camp in Wales. I surrendered my own tub to the *Engländers*.'

Erik could barely believe such a tale. But the submarine service had always been free of Berlin and the claws of the SS. Kleist did have a couple of Nazis on board, including his first mate, but he strangled them in their sleep and stuffed each one in a torpedo tube. The rest of his crew remained loyal to the last man.

He wasn't looking for a cigar from Winston Churchill. He just wanted to pull his own tub out of the war. He was sick of destroying freighters and watching men drown in the sea. But the *Engländers* wouldn't even put him in the same camp with his crew. He was held under house arrest at a country manor, where women paraded without their clothes and he dined on pâté and pink champagne.

He thought he would go out of his mind. He was a submarine commander, not some little lord. A man in knickers appeared, punched Kleist in the face, and told him he could either get shot or become a spy. Other men in knickers arrived. They worked on him for three months. Then they grew tired. They had a combat team send Kleist back across the ocean and land him on a beach near Le Havre – in his white cap. The admirals in Berlin didn't know how to treat a captain who should have been dead but was suddenly washed ashore without his crew. Kleist had become an embarrassment. But these admirals had to protect the honor of the U-bootwaffe. They couldn't send one of their own sailors to the guillotine with a *Ritterkreuz* around his neck.

'And now we're stuck in the same pile of shit,' Erik said. 'Both of us are captains without a country.'

HE STILL HAD TO SOLVE the country of this submarine. Franz and the Forty Thieves watched the captain's every move, but they ignored the magician, let him wander wherever he liked. These louts didn't even slap the dirk out of his sleeve. Franz had seen the magician walk through a wall and disarm a whole room, yet the Forty Thieves hadn't bothered to wrap Erik up in a silk flag, like Emil.

He was a pet, after all, Fränze's pet, and she wanted him alive. Whatever immortality he had on the *Milchkuh* came from her. She hadn't broken Emil's neck out of anger or spite. It was her own crazy love call to Erik.

She couldn't entice him with her musk. She had to get his attention with a kill. She was waiting for the magician. And all he had to do was follow the lines of his own hallucination. He found her in the engine room. Her hair wasn't cropped, like Lisa's ghost. And Fränze didn't glisten with machine oil. But she had smeared her mouth with red paint.

There were no mechanics in the engine room. The twin diesels made a terrible racket, like raucous birds; the lights kept twinkling in time to the room's constant rattle. There was only a narrow path between the engines, and that's where Fränze stood with her slightly brutal face, her red lips on fire, her naked body like a magnificent knife.

He didn't try to fool her, or wear his antic mask.

'Fräulein, if we make love, it will only be a mission, and you'll never survive it.'

Her brutal features began to shift in the rattling light; her face softened into a submarine flower.

'Couldn't you call me *Liebchen*? We've been to school together, disposed of enemy agents. And we've kissed.'

'But Fränze, I deceived you with that kiss. I'm in love with someone else.'

Her hand reached out of all that rattle and clasped his.

'I know,' she said. 'You're in love with a corpse. Congratulations, my sweet prince... Lie down with me. I promise not to tell Lisalein.'

He wanted to shut his eyes and not remember the cockroaches and beetles that thrived in the hissing heat of the engine room. But he couldn't afford to shut his eyes. Franz might have been crouching behind one of the diesels, and the Forty Thieves could have been waiting in the next compartment with their dirks.

Fränze lay down in that cockroach country and eased Erik onto her, whispering in his ear. '*Liebchen,* let this be our last mission.'

He sucked on her mouth to keep her from talking. She writhed under him and ripped off his belt. He didn't hear the crunch of any beetles. He entered Fränze, her legs scissoring around him. And suddenly she started to cry.

'Am I hurting you, Fränze? Should I stop?'

She didn't answer. Erik was confused. How would he ever throttle her if she wasn't in the middle of her own rapture? But when he tried to pull out of Fränze, she clutched him around the waist and squeezed him with her legs in a python's grip. He had blood spots in his eyes. He couldn't breathe. He was like some muddled Jack the Ripper. She meant to suffocate him, squeeze the air out of his lungs so he could begin his own death rattle.

But then she started to purr and she gave up that python's grip. She licked his ear until he felt a storm inside his head.

'You mustn't stop, sweet Erik. I have kissed no one in my life but my brother. And he is not a magician.'

She didn't growl, like Lisalein. Her tenderness disturbed him. He was about to sob, when he recalled that the acrobat lying under him had broken Emil's neck. And he moved inside her with his own deadly rhythm. He made her writhe – like a magician. And when he put his hands on her windpipe, she smiled and moaned all the more. Her moans turned into a strange bark, but there was no agony in her eyes as her face turned blue.

He didn't have to feel the pulse in her neck. He stood up to buckle his belt, then lifted Fränze. There wasn't one beetle or cockroach underneath. The floor was smooth as silk. He carried her out of the engine room and into the next compartment, her long arms dangling. She'd kept all her litheness. And she was lighter than he could ever have imagined for such a large-boned girl.

He carried her into the crew's quarters. The Forty Thieves froze in their bunks, looked at him agog. Franz could have split his back open with a single blow. But Franz couldn't be found. And Erik placed her gently in her hammock. He had an eerie notion that Fränze might awake if he rocked the hammock once. *Gott,* he was waiting for her resurrection. He wanted her to lick his ear again.

America

24

THE FORTY THIEVES WOULDN'T BURY Fränze at sea. They kept her in the hammock. She didn't seem to rot around their rotting clothes. But after a week the magician ventured into their quarters, wrapped Fränze in her own hammock, tied it at both ends until it resembled a cloth sarcophagus, carried her up the ladder all by himself, and pitched her into the Atlantic.

Without Fränze, the Forty Thieves had lost control of the tub. They were frightened of Erik and took to kissing his hand. He was their little führer. Kleist was the one who sent them to their battle stations, but Erik was the real *Kapitän zur See*.

'We have captured them by the tail,' Kleist said. 'We should toss them overboard and let them live with the whales.'

Erik peered at Kleist from under his blue cap. 'No wonder the admirals in Berlin are wary of you. You're a captain who likes to get rid of his crew.'

And Erik searched the tub for traces of Franz. But Franz seemed to have vanished from this gray Leviathan. And then, during their fifth week at sea, Erik noticed a phantom crawl out of the map chest. This phantom was double-jointed and could fold himself into closets. He was terribly thin and must have been starving himself. Erik had to feed him some of the tub's wretched rice, filled with beetles and bugs. He was pondering what damage a phantom acrobat might do, but saw right away that Franz was helpless without his sister.

'Herr Magician, don't kill me, please. I'll be your slave. You can kiss me as much as you want.'

'Shut up. We have to prepare. We'll be landing soon.'

They'd arrived off the coast of Maine with a listless crew and the captain's dead reckoning. The milk cow had crept underwater into the mouth of Frenchman Bay. Kleist had to make a silent run, or the American naval base at Bar Harbor would have picked up their soundings and captured the tub. They proceeded past Ironbound Island and the Porcupines at periscope depth and approached their destination point – Crabtree Neck, a wooded peninsula that was part of the mainland.

But Kleist couldn't risk a landing. The weather was much too spectacular. The lighthouses along the peninsula lit the night sky like a series of flaming balls. Patrol boats would have spotted the tub's tower in five minutes. And so the milk cow had to sit blindly at the bottom of the sea and wait for a storm to brew.

Erik wasn't idle. He didn't have to memorize his call signals, since he meant to bury his *Afu* radio kit in the forest the first chance he had. He tried to help Franz pronounce some American lingo, but Franz had never heard of Mark Twain and Moby Dick, or Shoeless Joe Jackson and Filene's bargain basement. He could only sit and count his dollars. He never talked of Fränze, and Erik began to wonder when Franz's anger would break.

But Franz was frightened of America. He didn't want to leave the tub. His teeth chattered all the time. Erik had to calm him like a high-strung horse. He didn't have to think of too many details. Uncle Willi had created a 'legend' for him at the Abwehr. And the Abwehr's legends didn't stray too far into fiction. 'A legend should cling to a man,' Uncle Willi loved to declare. And so Erik

239

Holdermann of Berlin would become Eric Holder of Boston, Massachusetts, with a driver's license, a Social Security card, a draft card, and a bankbook with the seal of the First National Bank of Boston. The cards and licenses were magnificent forgeries, dated with authentic stamps. Uncle Willi had been building this legend for years, so that Erik already had a shadow self in North America, with a bank account that was quite real.

All Erik had to do was land on the beach at Crabtree Neck and dive right into his shadow self. This shadow would soon be his second skin. Uncle Willi had never intended him to hit the mainland as a secret agent. The admiral couldn't save himself, but he could cure his own magician of the Third Reich.

ERIK AND FRANZ SHED THEIR uniforms and wore shirts and trousers with American labels. They had Camels and Lucky Strikes in their waterproof pockets. They had combs, shoelaces, American dollars, and American mints. And when the wind started to rip and the fog obscured that 'pharaoh's eye' of the lighthouses, the diesels started to roar, the propellers churned, and *Milchkuh* Number Nine broke the surface of Frenchman Bay, off Crabtree Neck. Erik and Franz stood on the weather deck in rainwear from Martha's Vineyard.

Some of the Forty Thieves began to sniffle in front of Erik.

'*Auf Wiedersehen, mein kleine Führer.*'

The captain whispered in Erik's ear the moment Franz climbed into the rubber boat that would carry them to Crabtree Neck.

'Erik, kill him as soon as we submerge. Bash in his skull with the oar. Otherwise, it will be too late.'

But the magician wasn't in a murderous mood. He sat with Franz in the rubber boat, with his cards and radio kit, and the two secret agents rowed into the fog. Franz was facing him, but Erik could see nothing but one nostril, which quivered all the time.

'Herr Magician, will you let me live?'

'Shut up. Our voices carry like gunshots in this water.'

Franz fell back into silence, and Erik listened to the rhythmic pattern of Franz's oars. Both blades struck the water with a startling swoosh. And then Franz's music stopped.

'Keep rowing,' the magician said, 'or I will get rid of you. Who knows how long the fog will last? And we can't be caught in this boat.'

That swoosh began again. Franz was no more than three feet away in this rubber boat, yet it wasn't only the fog that obscured Franz. The acrobat was wearing a much more diabolic mask.

'Herr Cesare, I saw you fuck my sister.'

The magician kept rowing. He was waiting for the suck of Franz's oars to stop. And then he would attack with his own oar.

'I was right there, in the engine room, in an open closet, above your ass and balls. My poor sister had lost track of me, but I could have broken your head with my own hand.'

Erik had to keep him talking, in spite of the echo that could have carried across the water to a lighthouse, or ricocheted off the side of a patrol boat.

'Why didn't you when you had the chance?'

Erik's ears pricked at the unbroken pattern of Franz's oars.

'I couldn't. I was frightened by Fränze's face – her noises, like a crazy cow. She was never a cow with me. I couldn't make her moan and scream.'

And then the swooshing stopped. Erik stood up and swung the blade of his oar like a baseball bat. But he was as unlucky as Shoeless Joe. The blade struck nothing but patches of fog. The rubber boat washed onto the beach, and Franz disappeared into the forest. Erik couldn't chase after him. There would have been too much of a racket. And sailors from the base at Bar Harbor would search the whole of Crabtree Neck. The FBI might come from Boston on a seaplane. And Erik would have disgraced Uncle Willi minutes after he arrived in America.

No, he'd have to carry the rubber boat into the woods with his *Afu*, bury what had to be buried, and move on before the manhunt began. He knew that Franz would be captured. It was only a matter of time. The acrobat couldn't hide his own frenzy, and he'd left most of his dollars in a briefcase. But Eric Holder of Boston had learned the art of invisibility. He didn't kiss the ground like Robinson Crusoe. He couldn't even catch sight of the trees in all that mist. He was one more captain without a country.

He didn't even have that illusion very long. Eric hadn't climbed a hundred feet from the ragged shoreline when the whole of Crabtree Neck seemed to light up like some gigantic movie set that broke right through the mist; every tree was strung with lanterns, and sailors in white spats crept out from between the lanterns, rifles in their hands; they leered at him with red faces, shoved him right into the shore, until Eric stood with one foot on land and one in the sea, like some strange amphibious creature. The glare from the lanterns blinded him, burnt into his eyes. These American sailors had no mercy. Their brilliant white spats flew around him as they kicked at Eric and drubbed him with their rifle butts. A ferocious sailor nibbled on his ear.

'Cesare, welcome to the United States.'

BERLIN USA

From the desk of Admiral Wilhelm Canaris
72-76 Tirpitz-Ufer
Berlin

Our food stores have dwindled at the Abwehr. I can no longer help beggars on the street. I've become the beggar. Yesterday an old man near the Kanal wanted to share his crumbs with me. I hadn't deceived him. He saw my admiral's uniform. And he must have thought that even admirals were starving in Berlin. I did not want to disillusion him, or disturb his dignity. So we ate together like a pair of tramps. I produced an apple from my pocket and sliced it with my dirk. 'It's delicious,' he said. We watched the barges from our perch along the embankment. Their hulls were hollowed out, and they did not have much coal to carry. They could have been skeletons on a skeleton river. Coal was as scarce as sugar, even under Berlin's blazing sun. There would be no reserves for winter, nothing at all. Come December, we would have to feed our little stove in the Fox's Lair with whatever debris we could find.

My new friend wore a Party pin. It bewildered me. I wondered what rules he had broken. The Party wasn't in the habit of creating beggars. It looked out for its own. And here was this frail old man with his offering of crumbs. He believed in Hitler, but not in all the bloodshed. The Party had given him a sinecure: it was his job to mark the front doors of Jewish families in Scheunenviertel and Wedding with yellow stars. He was paid a pretty penny, he said. He used a very fat crayon. But he ran out of doors to mark. So he began marking doors at

245

random. The Party took away his sinecure. There was talk of expelling him, but both his sons had died in the Ukraine, and his daughter, an army nurse, had been raped by the Russians. She was discovered wandering about the battlefield. A Soviet army doctor had rescued her, a Soviet Jew. He'd risked his own life for a Nazi nurse. And it plagued this old man. He would dream about the doors he had marked. In his dreams, it was his own daughter who was always behind the doors. He could no longer sleep.

'Herr Admiral, it is not guilt. I would have used my crayon forever if I'd had the chance. Helga is not a Jewess in my dreams. But she stands behind the doors, as mad as the moon.'

I didn't know what to do with this old man. I wanted to shield him, take him into the Fox's Lair, but I couldn't even shield myself. The Tirpitz-Ufer was overrun with Nazi apes. Soon I would have SS informers sitting in my lap. Suddenly, the old man had a mysterious smile.

'Herr Admiral, are you also burdened with dreadful dreams?'

Was he some mountebank planted near the Kanal? Night after night I dreamt of Erik bathing in blood. What could it mean? The Americans had taken him in. I had assurances, coded messages from my contacts. And still my Erik bathed in blood.

I said good-bye to this strange old man and went back inside the Fox's Lair. I couldn't work or play with my dogs. I'd gone to Switzerland, you see. I'd met with those gangsters from the American Secret Service a fortnight ago. I sat with the gangsters in the heart of Geneva. They were all in mufti, but I wouldn't sneak into a Swiss hotel without my uniform. The gangsters had offered me one of their own chalets, with a stunning view of the Old Town, but I insisted on the Métropole – it was the local Den of Iniquity, where all the secret agents met, much worse than Istanbul, with a spy on every street corner. But I was less visible than the gangsters were, even in my uniform. They fidgeted too *much, played with their cuffs. Finally, they talked about Cesare.*

Yes, they said. He had landed in America with his brains intact. No harm had come to him. Erik had his own cottage, they said. In the countryside. And now they wanted me to kidnap Göring. They thought I could snap my fingers and stop the war. They had very precise plans. They would level Munich once Germany surrendered, level Kiel. And I would become viceroy of this wasteland. So they said. I was no more to them than some eccentric fool who did magic tricks. They were startled when I wouldn't use the interpreter they had brought along. They didn't know I had almost married an American girl, that I had learnt their language from American pirates in half a dozen ports.

'Gentlemen,' I said, 'I won't be viceroy of the fuckland you intend to build on German bones and German soil. And if you harm my Cesare, I will break up all your networks in France, Turkey, Spain, and Yugoslavia. You won't have a single spy.'

They were in much more of a bargaining mood after that. I was Admiral Canaris, not the future viceroy. They didn't chortle in my face. They smoked in silence, never asked about Hitler's camps. I could have given them the blueprint of every camp. But that wasn't on their agenda. We didn't speak of the Jews. I was like that old man near the Kanal, *drawing yellow stars on every other door in my sleep. His madness was also mine. We were all brutes, but I didn't need lessons in morality from these American pirates with their Phi Beta Kappa keys. I'd already damned myself. Perhaps I was the viceroy of this fuckland we had all become.*

They wanted to know if Himmler or Göring was second in command.

'There is no second in command,' I said. 'Blondi is much closer to Hitler than Hermann Göring.'

I'd confused them. They whispered among themselves, rubbed their Phi Beta Kappa keys.

'Admiral, for God's sake, who is Blondi?'

'Hitler's dog,' I said.

They all laughed. But I still had visions of Erik bathed in blood.

Ghosts

25

HE REMEMBERED HOW COLONEL JOACHIM had described America in that SS rag of his, *Das Schwarze Korps*. 'It's the land where Superman lives with his kike friends. It does not have one blue mountain. It has Jewish bedbugs and dung beetles.' But Eric Holder, lately of Boston and Berlin, would have liked to ask his captors the difference between a Christian beetle and a Jewish one.

He rode across the country with a hood over his eyes. They'd tied up his hands. He could have been some trained falcon, a falcon that couldn't fly. From time to time, a sailor sitting with him in the back of their sedan would raise the hood above his chin and allow Eric to suck on a cigarette. It wasn't half as good as a Roth-Händle. And in spite of Eric's own erudition, and all his scrupulous study, he couldn't make out a word of the sailors' slang.

They spoke in a nervous clutter of half sentences. It was a sailor's jazz, and he couldn't find the lilt. So he barked at them in German.

'*Schwanz, ich bin der Teufel.*'

And they laughed at Eric, poked him in the ribs. 'Don't talk Deutsch, sonny boy. We're Americans here.'

He couldn't really smoke with the rough hairs of a hood over his eyes and mouth. His captors offered him nothing but a lump of peanut brittle that they shoved under his hood. They drove for hours and hours, and they ended up at a navy brig – a hospital prison yard that must have been near the water, since he could smell the salt in the sea.

Finally, the bastards had taken off his hood. It was the most desolate landscape Eric had ever seen – a concrete desert with barbed wire and buildings that belonged on the moon. These buildings were as heartless as the bunkers in Berlin that housed the air raid shelters and the ack-ack batteries; they had no real windows, nothing but little glassed-in holes. And for a moment, Eric thought he saw Tilli the Toiler on the roof of a navy bunker. She smiled at him.

He was stripped, hosed down by some maniac, and given convict's clothes to wear: navy blue pajamas without a single pocket, sandals and no socks. He had to live in a cell that was narrower than a lion's cage at the Berlin Zoo. He had a desk screwed into the wall, a monk's bed, a sink, and what the sailors called 'a tin can,' a stainless-steel commode that rocked and swayed every time Eric sat down on the seat.

But he didn't understand his status here. Was he a secret prisoner of war? His cell wasn't locked. Eric could wander wherever he wanted, but he had nowhere to wander in this gray world. He met American admirals in the passageways. He met priests and women dressed like prostitutes. And he realized that this navy brig was a kind of Fox's Lair, or crazy school for spies. Nurses would come into his cage and comb his hair. He couldn't tell if these *Schwestern* were male or female. They had big biceps and big breasts – 'pectorals,' the nurses called them, 'pecs.' Once a nurse tiptoed into his cell in the middle of the night and whispered like a snake, 'Cesare, be a good boy and give us a *Kuss.*'

He tossed this nurse out of his cell. Others came back and beat him with rubber sticks. They tried to dig their tongues into Eric's ear. He battled with them for half an hour. It was like being a subcadet in Kiel all over again. After six or seven assaults, these nurses with enormous biceps were much more careful with Eric; soon he learned their American lingo, their own *jive*. And he began to curse like any sailor at this hideout in Norfolk, Virginia, a town he had never seen. Was it like Kiel, with its harbor and seawall? He could no longer smell the sea from this dank tomb where he now lived.

After he'd been there a month, he found a note on his bed. He recognized the stationery of the Abwehr, and the admiral's own personal seal: two couched lions with a serpent in the middle. His hands shivered as he tore the envelope.

Tirpitz-Ufer, July 1943

Männe, *I wanted to say good-bye and wish you the finest years of your life in America. You must forget me and your comrades at the* Fuchsbau *the minute you read this note. Please burn it, dear Erik. Eva sends her love. She says you are the nicest spy she ever met. I had to put her in another institution far from Berlin and the Russian dogs, who will one day soon be sitting in our lap. I would die if those dogs ever raped my little girl. I should have put her on the* Milchkuh *with you and Emil. I am sorry I could not save Emil. But I couldn't overload the* Milchkuh *with Abwehr agents. I remember the day I met you on the seawall at Kiel. How ferocious you were,* Männe, *but still concerned with the safety of one old man being attacked by young wolves. I was frightened that you had no fear. I had to kidnap you, bring you to Berlin. You must forgive your* Alte *for training you as his Cesare. But I am a selfish old fool who loves you as much as my Eva and*

my dachshunds. Do not think ill of me, Mr Eric Holder of the
United States. I hope you have found a lovely house somewhere
in the woods.

I kiss you on your cheek.
Uncle Willi

Eric couldn't stop crying. And he wouldn't destroy the note from
Uncle Willi, which had become far more wondrous than any house
in the woods. He could survive in this little gray world with his note
and his pocketless pajamas. He did not need America. And then a
navy captain in shoulder boards and summer whites pranced into
his cell and leaned against a wall. Eric recognized the *Schmiss* on
the captain's cheek, but it wasn't a dueling scar. Eric had wounded
this man himself, made him bleed like a pig at the Adlon. It was the
American Berliner, Werner Wolfe, who had tried to assassinate the
Grand Mufti of Jerusalem for British intelligence. But he'd grown
fatter in a year, had lost all his leanness; he had the ripened look of
a well-fed man, and not Eric's sunken, sallow cheeks. He started to
babble in a Berliner's raucous accent.

Eric had to correct him. 'Stop talking Deutsch. Your mother
pees with her dick in her hand.'

The navy captain started to laugh. 'Cesare, you've been learning
from my own lads… You shouldn't be here. It's the admiral's fault.
Canaris couldn't make up his mind. He kept hopping over to
Switzerland to meet with us. We had lovely chats about a negotiated
peace, but he wouldn't step away from the war. I had to find a code
name for him. Guess what it was?'

'Wolfie, I don't have that deep an imagination.'

'Hamlet – we called him Hamlet behind his back.'

Eric laughed bitterly to himself. *Hamlet*. He conjured up

an image of Uncle Willi meeting with American and British spymasters, his collar wrinkled, crumbs in the crevices of his pants, and all alone without his dachshunds. What bargain could this weary gray-haired Hamlet have reached with the American sharks? Eric always knew in his gut that such brutal spymasters wouldn't tolerate a Berlin somnambulist on their soil.

'Wolfie, what the fuck do you want from me? Why am I a prisoner in this navy asylum? Your nurses are almost as fickle as the transvestites at the White Mouse.'

'Ah,' said Captain Wolfe, who plucked a split of champagne from inside his tunic, uncorked it with his thumb, and found a pair of flutes in another pocket. 'Prisoner, what kind of prisoner? You're free to walk out of here. But how long would you last? With your phony cards and your phony dollars. We looked at the gelt the Abwehr gave you. It's all counterfeit – the shittiest stuff. You would have been picked up within days. A German officer without his uniform. They'd hang you as a spy. We did you a fucking favor.'

'Where's Franz?'

'Ah, that's another story,' said Captain Wolfe, pouring the champagne. 'Little Franzie is incommunicado at the moment. He'll never survive without his sister. Shame on you. Ah, let's have a toast.'

'What are we celebrating?'

'Your success… as a secret agent.'

Eric didn't touch the champagne.

'It's simple,' Wolfe said. 'We're sending you back to Germany.'

Eric should have strangled Wolfie when he'd had the chance, finished him off inside the Adlon, had him leave Berlin as a corpse.

'You tricked the admiral, sang him a song about America…'

The captain poured himself another glass. 'The landscape

shifted. We thought we had the Müller twins. And now all we have is you. The admiral's a dreamer. What did he expect? It would have taken a hundred commandos just to keep you alive. And suppose you were caught? All our intel would have been compromised. The president would shut us down. And for one little admiral with pee all over his pants?'

Eric pounced on Captain Wolfe, ripped off his shoulder boards, but Wolfe waved off the security guards, who would have clubbed Eric into the stainless-steel commode. Then he picked up the flutes and pranced out of the cell, but Eric wouldn't let the fucker go scot-free. He grabbed the tails of Captain Wolfe's tunic.

'Will I be shipped back in my coffin, the better to break into Goebbels' villa and strangle him in bed?'

'No. That dwarf will soon be on our side.'

Eric gave Wolfe's tails another pull. 'Then what the fuck can Cesare the somnambulist do?'

'Be our eyes and ears. We'll build you up into the greatest hero the Nazis ever had. We'll invent manhunts, chases across the Rockies. You'll have your photo in *Berliner Illustrirte*.'

'I'll agree to nothing unless I can bring the admiral out.'

Werner started to laugh *and* groan. 'That's impossible. He'd never abandon his agents… and his mad daughter. You're going back to Berlin. There's no other option. Now get your fucking hands off my coat.'

And he was gone, like some phantom with a pair of flutes. And Eric was suddenly stricken with an unbearable bout of loneliness. He missed the admiral, and the streets of Scheunenviertel, and the lovely sweat on Lisalein, and even Fränze's naked ballet on board the submarine. He couldn't seem to get her out of his mind – her silent love cries while he strangled her. She would remain attached to Eric for the rest of his life.

He wandered into the commissary. He could have swiped anything off the shelves. But this madhouse had its own blue-and-gold scrip, and Eric preferred to pay for his candy bars and his Camels, which had at least a hint of the Roth-Händle's flavor.

And while navigating through the aisles of the commissary, he caught a glimpse of a ghost near the ice-cream freezer. It was Fränze, come floating out of Atlantic waters. She wasn't naked in this madhouse. Her dark hair shone in the fluorescent light. She wore brutal red lipstick and very high heels. It was the same uniform Fränze often used when she went out on a kill. But Eric didn't care. The sight of Fränze soothed him. Suddenly, he wasn't in a house of strangers. He rushed toward her, but he tripped over a crate that had been left in the aisle, and nearly tumbled into a cornucopia of candy bars. He shouldn't have taken his eyes off the ghost. Fränze was no longer by the freezer. He searched every one of the commissary's little islands, but the ghost was gone.

IT WASN'T FRÄNZE'S GHOST HE had seen near the freezer, but Franz in drag, dressed as his sister. That was Franz's way of keeping her alive. Wolfie's men had found him wandering like a madman in the woods of Maine. The nurses were all in love with Franz, who reminded them of Linda Darnell. He would strut through the halls in his high heels and then vanish for a week.

So Eric looked everywhere for Franz. He drifted deeper into this prison and chanced upon a pavilion called Berlin USA: an enormous rat's maze that was a replica of Berlin – with dollhouses that served as the Chancellery, the admiral's *Fuchsbau* on the Landwehrkanal, the zoo with its empty cages, Prinz-Albrecht-Strasse, the Adlon Hotel, and Alexanderplatz, with toy trolleys and toy men. He felt like some kind of Gulliver in the land of the small.

But there was a difference between both Berlins. American flags flew in the windows, and the toy sailors on the trolleys had white spats. There were no bomb craters, no air raid wardens made of sticks, no gun girls. This couldn't have been the battle plan of some monstrous siege; the town was already occupied with American sailors.

Eric grew forlorn in this fake Berlin – it couldn't conjure up Uncle Willi or the children of Scheunenviertel – it was like a Nazi town shorn of Nazis. He had no interest in exploring this asylum. He returned to his own little lion's cage. The nurses no longer plagued him. Admirals stopped looking into his cell. He was Cesare the somnambulist, a relic from Alt-Berlin.

Eric woke in the middle of the night and discovered Linda Darnell staring at him through thick eyelashes. He wasn't frightened of Fränze's ghost. The *Milchkuh* had been far more real to him than this madhouse. He felt a terrible pity for Franz.

'Cesare, would you like to give me a *Kuss*? But you'll have to pay with your life.'

Franz had broken off a spoon handle and sharpened it into a dirk. Eric still wouldn't defend himself. His only weapon was the lulling music of his voice.

'*Dreckshund*, I'm all you have.'

'Don't talk Deutsch,' said Franz. All of a sudden, he started to cry. He was lonely for Fränze. He'd never spent a day without his sister. Fränze made all the plans, Fränze groomed him, told him what shirt or sweater to wear. She fondled him, kissed him to sleep. He never had to say a word. She wrote all the letters, was in charge of their accounts. She doled out pocket change to him as she might have done to a little boy. *Her little boy.*

Cesare was the admiral's magician, while Fränze and Franz were circus folk. Cesare didn't speak sentences, but snakebites. Yet Franz was more connected to Fränze's murderer than to the cowboys in this hidden hospital.

'Magician, let's get married. I could be your navy wife.'

Eric was still too forlorn to laugh. *Married to Linda Darnell.* He sat down on his commode, the one comfortable seat he had in this cage, and the acrobat curled up near his feet.

Mackie Messer

26

WOLFIE WOKE HIM IN THE morning. He'd come with half a dozen nurses, who drove Franz out of the cage with their truncheons.

'Cut it out, Cap,' Franz said. 'We're getting married.'

The captain barked at Franz. 'There are no fucking brides in my house.'

'Wolfie, leave him alone,' Eric barked back. 'Franz is my fiancée.'

'He's demented,' the captain said. 'And you and I have business to discuss. There's been a change of plans. We're sending you to Bohemia.'

'Wonderful. And what am I going to find? Hangman Heydrich's ghost?'

'No. Mackie Messer.'

There was only one Mack the Knife – Bernhard Beck, the greatest cabaret star Berlin had ever had. He'd appeared in the original production of *The Threepenny Opera,* and when he sang 'The Ballad of Mack the Knife' in 1928, half of Berlin fell into a colossal fever. Beck lived at the Adlon, had become the uncrowned prince of the Babelsberg studios… until Herr Hitler took over the Chancellery. And still Beck stayed on in Berlin, held court every morning in the Rembrandt Room. But his followers dwindled one by one. Berlin's very last cabarets closed. And Babelsberg no longer had much interest in Jewish cabaret. Beck was an enormous rolypoly man who fluttered about with all the insouciance of an elephant on ice skates. Goebbels came to him at the Adlon with his entire entourage: the Nazis might permit him to prosper if he agreed to act in a propaganda film for the Reich. Beck refused. He was hurled out of the Adlon and into the street. But he had hundreds of fans who defied the Nazis and fed him. Smuggled out of Germany, he performed in Paris and Amsterdam, where he remained Mackie Messer. But he was captured in 1943 in one of the Dutch Gestapo's dragnets and delivered to Theresienstadt, where Goebbels now convinced him to act in a propaganda film, *The Cabaret King Comes to Bohemia*. He would have been sent to Auschwitz had he refused Goebbels again. But Eric couldn't understand why naval intelligence should have been concerned with Mack the Knife.

'Wolfie, are you eager to have Beck perform for Herr Franklin and Frau Eleanor in the White House?'

'That's part of the deal. And Louis B. Mayer wants him for a musical.'

Eric was deeply suspicious. 'MGM will allow him to sing in Deutsch?'

'They'll dub his voice,' said Captain Wolfe.

A rage began to build under Eric's eyes. What was Beck without his *Berliner* rendering of Mack the Knife? Mayer might as well have cut out his tongue and left him to wail like a lunatic. But Wolfe must have sensed Eric's chagrin.

'It has nothing to do with MGM or Frau Eleanor,' he said. 'It's the beauty of it. We kidnap the king of cabaret right out of a concentration camp.'

'And what about all the other Jewish souls? Do we leave them to rot until they're shipped to Auschwitz?'

'Jesus, we can't capture a concentration camp. But we can make a lot of noise.'

Tactics, it was all tactics with Wolfie. Sound without substance. And never the toll of human misery.

'Lend me twenty sailors and I'll free the whole camp.'

'It can't be done,' said Captain Wolfe. 'And I'm not authorized to give you twenty of my boys. I have to scrape for every recruit. And hide them in an insane asylum. But you're another story. The Abwehr spy who escapes his American captors –'

'And Berlin USA. You like to build cities in a madhouse, don't you?'

'It keeps us focused, points us to the end of the game… Berlin as our prize, but not as a river of ruins. That's what will happen if the Russkies get there first.'

'And you want Berlin as one big cabaret, with Bernhard Beck singing "Mack the Knife." Well, leave me out of your new American empire.'

'I can't… Besides, you have a special reason for visiting Theresienstadt – Lisalein.'

Eric's rage spilled over and he lunged at Wolfe, but his head began to spin, and he fell into the captain's arms. The nurses fed him water. They sat him down on the commode, like some trained seal, while Wolfe stood over him.

'Somebody tricked you, kiddo. She's still alive.'

'I'll bite your fucking head off, spit your blood into my sink.'

Wolfe handed him a photo of Lisa with white hair; there were marks on her face, and one of her eyes was much darker than the other. It was no illusion, no trick shot from the Abwehr's archives, no double hired by naval intelligence, no Lisa look-alike. She could have been the residue of her own firestorm. But no one could have imitated that stark defiance, that wanton smile of a woman who outlasted her own auto-da-fé.

He didn't ask Wolfe any of the details. The captain would only have lied, or created a legend for Lisa. And Eric would have had to whirl around in some elaborate fiction, another Berlin USA.

'Cesare,' the fat captain whispered, 'will you go to Theresienstadt for us?'

'Yes.'

'Will you bring out Mackie Messer and not start a revolution at the camp?'

'Yes.'

And Eric closed his eyes and fell into a dark sleep. He dreamt of Lisa with her white hair, weaving across Theresienstadt Castle in a shawl that looked like a burial gown. But she hadn't wandered out of any coffin. And with her was Mackie Messer. They could have been man and wife. He wasn't jealous. Beck was still a star, even among the camp guards, who collected pieces of his velvet jacket as a souvenir. But he wouldn't sing for any living soul at this castle. He walked in silence with Lisalein.

PARADISE

January 3, 1944

From the desk of Admiral Wilhelm Canaris
72-76 Tirpitz-Ufer
Berlin

The Fox's Lair has no fox. All my networks have been compromised or dismantled. Commander Stolz, the very best battler we ever had at the Abwehr, was plucked out of my office and accused of being a Soviet spy. The Führer cannot forget that he had once been Rosa Luxemburg's bodyguard. And who will protect him now? Not his Uncle Willi. I have my own Gestapo babysitters. Gott, they follow me into the toilet. My dachshunds are frightened of their grim faces. Poor Sabine hasn't moved her bowels since last Sunday. But I do not allow these swine to interfere with my itinerary. I ride with them in their own car to Prinz-Albrecht-Strasse. Berlin has become our necropolis, a city with mountains of rubble. The Engländers *bomb day and night. Himmler is in a panic. That's the only reason I'm still alive. He thinks I can help him broker a deal with the Allies. The SS would prefer to fight the Russians behind American tanks. But there are no American tanks in Berlin.*

I enter Gestapo headquarters with my babysitters. I'm led downstairs to Stolz's quarters in the dungeon. He's a special guest. They can't afford to knock him senseless while I'm still chief of the Abwehr.

My babysitters come into Stolz's cellar suite, reserved for enemies of the Reich who might still be of some use. There's blood on Stolz's suspenders. He smiles at me – the swine have pulled out all his teeth. They've broken his knuckles with their little Nazi nutcracker. But Stolz will never bend to their will. I can't even call the Führer. I no

265

*longer exist at the Wilhelmstrasse. They see my own invisible hand
behind every plot against Hitler. I'm not with the plotters. I simply
allow them to assemble in their own little closets.*

*Stolz signals to me that he does not want any doctor to look at
his hands. But we don't have to whisper. The babysitters have little
curiosity.*

*I've brought Stolz a basket of oranges, smuggled out of Africa by the
last agents on my roster. He knows I cannot help him, and he doesn't
talk about himself.*

'Uncle Willi, why the hell is Cesare in Berlin?'

*I start to groan. It is the saddest moment of my life, sadder than
having my Eva sit in an asylum.*

'It wasn't my doing. Himmler struck some monstrous deal with
the American spymasters. They smuggled him across the Atlantic
on a neutral freighter. Himmler let him land in Normandy like a
beached whale. He gets a hero's welcome. They swear he went on a
spree, butchering FBI men like some German Goliath. It was all made
up.'

'His picture was in the Illustrirte... but how did they lure him
back?'

'Lisa,' I say. 'The Americans must have told him she's in Paradise.'

*What a diabolic name for a concentration camp. But that was how
the Nazis advertised Theresienstadt – a little paradise for Jews away
from Germany, with their own orchestra, their own workshops, their
own Fussball field, in a fortified Bohemian town. But this paradise
was mingled with filth and disease, a castle with cockroaches on the
way to Auschwitz.*

'Uncle Willi, it's my fault. We shouldn't have staged her death.'

'And how else would we have gotten him onto that damn Milchkuh?
He'd have followed Lisa into whatever hell she was in.'

'And now the Dreckshunde have given him the Knight's Cross, and *he'll strangle on the ribbon around his neck… We must prevent him from going to Paradise.'*

'How?' I ask. 'And with what?'

'Your own magic, Herr Dr Caligari.'

I start to cry. Dr Caligari can't even help himself.

'If I was such a magician, Helmut, wouldn't I free you from Gestapo-land?'

Suddenly, he smiles, even with the broken knuckles and the blood on his suspenders. 'Alte, *none of us are magicians without your Cesare.'*

He will not mention Rosa Luxemburg, though he is dying to talk about her – he is as haunted by her as I am, even if he doesn't stand on the balcony every afternoon and wait for Luxemburg to rise again from the Landwehrkanal. I was not her lover. I only held her hand as she was riding to her own death.

I'll never see the commander again. Himmler will hide him somewhere well beyond my reach. And so I kiss Helmut on the cheek, and then I hop out of the dungeon, with my babysitters right behind.

They escort me to the Adlon. How symmetrical it is that the SS should celebrate Cesare's return in the Rembrandt Room, where they sent him off with their kiss of death. But I knew he would survive that coffin of a Milchkuh, or perhaps I'm an old fool who believes in blind faith.

The salon is swollen with SS colonels and Gestapo commandants, together with Party hacks. These Hunde *stare at me, bewildered that the Reich's invisible admiral has dared come into their domain. The menu is different today. The banquet tables are filled with vegetarian delights in honor of Herr Hitler – potato dumplings, nuts and yellow rice, custards and egg soufflés prepared by the Führer's three-hundred-pound Bavarian chef, since the Adlon's own kitchen has been reduced to a kind of genteel beggary.*

The whole salon is waiting, and I cannot get close to Eric Holder *of Boston, Massachusetts, who is my Erik again, with his* Ritterkreuz. *He is surrounded by the Leibstandarte SS. These Death's-Heads have him in their sway. Perhaps he is angry at his* Alte *for having tricked him over Lisalein. He won't acknowledge my glance, but he sees my babysitters, and doesn't want to put me in any danger. He must sense the travesty of the whole thing, and I want to shout –* Männe, *go back to America!*

And then it's too late. The Führer has arrived with his Nazi barber, Fritz, who wears his decoration from the Great War, his Iron Cross. A silence descends upon the salon. There are no sighs, no hiccoughs, no gasps of breath. This is the power Herr Hitler has – he could cut the air right out of your lungs. I have seen him snarl, with spittle flying from his tongue. I have seen him harangue his generals for an hour. But he is calm today, one hand curled inside his sleeve. Himmler has bamboozled him again, woven one of his errant songs around our gullible Führer, who believes that Erik was on the rampage, slaughtering American souls. And there is a gaiety in Hitler's step, a kind of trick dance; for the moment, Erik can assuage all the military blunders, the mad scheme of conquering a world that is chaotic and far more cruel than the Nazis themselves, with their love of banners and parades and blond beer.

But the Führer takes his trembling hand out of his sleeve and waves it, like the maestro of Berlin. There's a gleam in his eyes, in spite of the dark pouches. Fritz the barber bows and touches his lips to the colored ribbons around Erik's neck.

And finally Erik glances at his admiral, not with anger, but with his own silent song – Alte, *welcome to the asylum!*

Babelsberg on the River Ohře

27

IT WAS A VAST CONSPIRACY. That's what bothered Erik the most. It was as if the Abwehr and the studios at Babelsberg had plotted to build a ghetto town that was totally picturesque – a postcard village with a central square inhabited by shadows. It had a café with somber faces, a restaurant where meals were never served. It had novelty shops without novelties, bakeries without bread. The town itself was a fortress, Castle Theresienstadt, run by the SS. Even the Wehrmacht couldn't wander in. No general or diplomat ever stopped here on the way to Prague.

Across the river Ohře was another castle, known as the Little Fortress; the most notorious prison in Bohemia, it was where Czech army officers, black marketeers, and resistance fighters were beaten to death by the Gestapo and the SS. But Babelsberg didn't reach across the river. No attempt was ever made to prettify the Little Fortress – it was a house of murder, unadorned.

But its lack of niceties didn't trouble Erik. The Little Fortress had no return tickets. It's where you went to die. It wasn't touched by Paradise. It couldn't break your heart. But the main castle on the other side of the river, with its rough red walls and battlements, was a maddening enterprise. It had been built as a fort in the northwest of Bohemia at the end of the eighteenth century. Because it couldn't flourish in its own isolation, this red castle became a prison, then a small, unpretentious village of seven thousand souls. But in 1941, after Reinhard Heydrich was appointed Protector of Bohemia, he decided to toss out the seven thousand and turn Castle Theresienstadt into a phantasmagorical town, a paradise for German and Czech Jews, a walled ghetto where Jews themselves would volunteer to live – novelists, poets, dancers, musicians, retired millionaires. It was one more of Heydrich's brilliant, diabolic schemes, like *Nacht und Nebel*. It would show the world that Hitler was magnanimous to the Jews, and that he had deigned to give them a city where they might prosper on their own.

It was a fool's trap. But there were many volunteers at first, and then the stories spread: Theresienstadt was a closed castle. The only means to graduate from Hitler's Paradise was to climb aboard the cattle car to Auschwitz. Jewish conductors might have their own chorale at the castle, but then they were gassed together with their chorale. And the Nazis made a colossal blunder. They hurled several hundred Jews from Denmark into Theresienstadt in 1943. These were the only Danish Jews the SS could find. The vast majority of Jews had been hidden by the Danes themselves. But the unlucky ones, who landed in Theresienstadt, complained to their king about the appalling conditions at the castle – the bedbugs, the lice, the lack of winter clothes. The Nazis couldn't comprehend that Danish Jews had the rights of ordinary human beings. The Danes insisted that the Red Cross come to inspect the castle.

It threw the SS into a panic. With their sense of superiority at stake, they couldn't contradict the Red Cross. And so they prepared for the visit. In order to end the brutal overcrowding, they sent more and more inmates to Auschwitz. They refurbished the barracks, and had the castle's Jews live like campers, fifty in a compartment, rather than a hundred. And they found a Jewish hero, a Jewish star. They plucked Bernhard Beck out of Amsterdam with all the other

Jews, coddled him a bit, brought in an entire crew from Babelsberg, and had Beck star in their own fairy tale, *The Cabaret King Comes to Bohemia.*

It was a masterpiece of cunning and guile. Beck reenacted his rise from Berlin's Jewish ghetto to Mackie Messer, and then they veered the tale in their own direction. They pretended that Bernhard was still at the Adlon in '43, still performing Mack the Knife, and had decided to leave his adoring fans in Berlin and move to Paradise, where he falls in love with a blind Jewess and has his own wondrous cabaret.

Goebbels took a chance and had *Cabaret King* shown in Berlin. There was a furor over the film; audiences flocked to it, rode right out of the rubble to watch their beloved Beck prance about and sing 'The Ballad of Mack the Knife.' A tenor with the sweetest tones, he had remained their idol through all the years of Nazi rule, reminding them of the lost art of cabaret. Audiences wept the moment Mackie Messer appeared on screen, that rolypoly man, as large and round as Hitler's own Bavarian chef. They wept after he abandoned his suite at the Adlon and traded Berlin for Bohemia. But they were in awe of this town their Führer had built for the Jews, with its own river, its own castle, its painting studios, its *Fussball* fields on the ramparts, its symphony hall in an attic, and its milk cows (borrowed from some pasture). Castle Theresienstadt wasn't bombed by the *Engländers*, had no ashes and rubble. Mack the Knife seemed to thrive in his new home. He was surrounded by Jewish jazz musicians, and had his own cabaret in the SS clubhouse. His German guardians felt privileged to hear him sing.

The film enriched the Reich, and declared to the world that the Nazis could support a Jewish star. And Erik's mission was to kidnap the Reich's movie star from Theresienstadt. He couldn't do it alone. The Americans had their own man within the walls.

But Erik wasn't even curious about this mastermind. He'd come to rescue Lisa, and he had to find her first.

But he was another one of Goebbels' propaganda pieces, no less fraudulent than *Cabaret King*, even if his name wasn't lit up in half-bombed Berlin movie palaces. How could he have massacred a whole slew of Canadian Royal Mounties, or FBI men and small-town sheriffs he had never met? There couldn't have been a mad chase across the Rockies, or a manhunt in Manhattan. The nearest he ever got to Manhattan was an unlocked cage at an espionage school in Norfolk that masked itself as an asylum. He'd seen no more of the continent than a sandbar in Maine. America had become for him an elaborate game of blindman's bluff, with a Knight's Cross as his reward... and five minutes with the Führer.

He'd been gone nine months, and it might as well have been half a century. He could not recognize *his* Berlin. Women roamed the streets with their life's belongings toppling out of baby carriages. The Nazi banners were now rags in the wind. His apartment on the Dragonerstrasse had been looted; it seemed as if some madman or host of starving children had sucked the paint and plaster from the walls. The furniture was gone, with his mother's heirlooms and the paraphernalia of a secret agent. The Gestapo had stopped patrolling the streets in their black sedans; there was nothing to patrol, and no one to arrest. Even the Adlon had little of its old allure. The large windows on the ground floor had been covered with bricks to protect the hotel from shattering glass. The Adlon was like a bunker now, Berlin's bunker hotel.

And yet his picture had been in the *Illustrirte*. Children saluted him from their little forts in the rubble; old men fondled the sleeves of the SS uniform he now had to wear. The wives of generals looked at him with wild-eyed lust. They didn't really desire him, but had bolted their own madness and hysteria onto his myth. The Führer had been no less hysterical, hopping around Erik in the Rembrandt Room, asking him whether the Royal Mounties had blue eyes.

Erik should have plucked out the Führer's own pale eyes, but he couldn't. The Führer was like a bemused child with a suddenly found toy to take his mind off a winter campaign where Russian snipers dressed in white could fire at will in the brutal glare that leapt off the snow and destroy cadre after cadre in a matter of minutes. And so the Führer had danced in front of Himmler's fabricated hero, while Erik stared at the murderers who surrounded Admiral Canaris and were slowly squeezing the life out of him. The admiral was a glorified prisoner, and had Erik tried to get near him at the Adlon, just to clasp his hand, blows would have rained down on the admiral's head, and Erik would have been whisked away without a bite of lemon custard. The ribbons around his neck were nothing but a noose.

He was flown to Prague; he saw no spires, no walls, not one glimpse of the city. A command car plucked him right out of the airport and onto a military road. He was caught in a dream of tanks and field cars, but it was maddening, because cows moved along the same road. There were no towns, no fields of winter corn, just ridges of snow stained with oil, like bird droppings. And then Paradise appeared, with its red walls, and it filled Erik with a curious longing, but not for an ersatz city that was a disguised killing field. Perhaps this town in Bohemia that Hitler gave the Jews was more complicated and various than the Nazis could ever have imagined.

They stopped at a sentry box – the sentry gawked at Erik – and passed through an enormous armored gate in the red wall and onto a bumpy road. Along that road was the strangest sight Erik had ever seen. A decrepit hearse with smashed lanterns was filled with loaves of bread that wobbled like living things. But this hearse had no dray horses. It was dragged along by men who were hitched to the hearse. They had weary, skeletal faces. They wore black jackets like undertakers, with Jewish stars emblazoned over their hearts.

This load of bread must have been a nightmare; the wheels sagged and the wagon swayed. But the men didn't moan or complain. They were having a heated argument about Plato.

'Plato's shadows are not yours or mine.'

'What are they, then?'

'Dancers on a wall. Images of delight. Like a puppet show.'

'I won't listen to you, Albert. You mock the whole myth of the cave. They are the shadows we have become and will always be.'

Erik was enthralled. He wanted to hitch himself to the same wagon. Perhaps he'd really come to Paradise. But he'd startled these philosopher–wagon men. Suddenly, they crept out of their own absorption and noticed Erik and his uniform. They released their leather straps, saluted Erik, curtsied several times, and started to tremble.

'Please don't punish us,' the lead wagon man whimpered. 'We meant no disrespect. We would have taken another road, *mein Herr*, if…'

Erik had wounded these wagon men somehow.

'You mustn't be frightened of me. I'm only a guest at the castle. Here, let me help you with your burden.'

The wagon men were horrified.

'*Mein Herr*, they'll put us on the next transport if they catch us together.'

An SS guard arrived and struck the lead wagon man with a baton.

'*Stinkjude*, how dare you insult a German officer.'

Erik knocked the baton out of the guard's hand.

'He didn't insult me. They were talking about Plato, and I listened.'

This guard gawked at Erik, as the sentry had done. He recognized the ghost warrior who had come out of America alive.

'Herr Kapitän Holdermann, these settlers are not allowed to look at a German officer. They have no language, not –'

'Enough,' Erik told him. He helped the wagon men hitch themselves to the hearse again and said good-bye. He'd rather talk with 'settlers,' as the Jews of Paradise were called, than the contingent of guards that arrived out of nowhere. He was given a metal cup of schnapps to fortify himself against the wind that swept across the plains of Theresienstadt.

He soon discovered that the castle wasn't a castle at all, but resembled the Jewish Hospital of Berlin with its great outer wall and seven pavilions, though Theresienstadt's pavilions were a deepening maze, with courtyards that went nowhere in a world of barracks, hidden spires, and walls within walls. He was led into the first pavilion and up a flight of serpentine stairs, with a sign over the landing that read SETTLERS FORBIDDEN HERE UNDER PENALTY OF DEATH. He went through an alcove and into a grand salon, where he was introduced to the castle's commandant – it was Colonel Joachim of the SS, who had taken over Theresienstadt several months ago.

There was a tic in the milieu of his blond mustache, like a tiny creature crawling under the skin. Erik realized in an instant that Joachim was Werner Wolfe's own man in Paradise, and America was his escape route. Wolfie had been plotting with the SS, and Joachim must have been his liaison with Heinrich Himmler.

'Herr Magician,' Joachim said, glancing at the *Ritterkreuz,* 'how are you?'

'Phone the Führer. And find out. If I'd known you were at

Theresienstadt, I would have asked him for the privilege of breaking your neck.'

Joachim cupped a hand over his mustache. He couldn't control the tic. But he still managed to smile. 'You should be more careful with a commandant. I could have you shot. Cesare, we both know why you're here. Mackie Messer. But he's been getting jumpy. I'm not sure he wants to leave Theresienstadt. This is the site of his biggest success. The cabaret king in Paradise. I'd like you to steal Mackie once the Red Cross comes to inspect the camp. Mackie is our jewel. He'll perform for the Red Cross commissioners. And then you can have him.'

The commandant seemed bewitched, and Erik didn't understand why. All the commissioners in the world couldn't close a concentration camp. There had to be another reason.

'Colonel, since when are SS commandos frightened of the Red Cross?'

Joachim wouldn't even look at Erik. 'It's not the Red Cross. It's Berlin – the Führer is obsessed with the visit. He wants to be remembered as the father of this ghost town. That's why he tolerates a Jewish Mack the Knife. But he won't tolerate him very long.'

Erik wasn't concerned about a cabaret king's swan song in front of the Red Cross.

'Mackie's your problem child, not mine. Now take me to Lisalein.'

And still there was that throbbing mustache. 'She's been sick,' he said. 'The baroness isn't allowed to see a soul.'

'Take me to Lisalein… or I'll have to plow through all your men.'

The Burning Tree of Sachsenhausen

28

S HE WAS ON THE TOP floor of the first pavilion, in a tiny hospital ward that must have been a kind of *Extrastation* for SS officers and prominent Jews at Theresienstadt. It had six or seven cots, with its own male nurse, who looked like a domesticated bulldog and was called 'Little Sister'; only one of the cots was occupied – by Lisalein. She had burn marks on the side of her face and different-colored eyes. One was green and the other was shot through with blood. Her blond hair was streaked with white, like the witch of Paradise. She could have been a hundred, but then he recalled that Lisa wasn't much older than himself. It was hard to describe his own confusion of pity, anger, and delight – anger that he hadn't known she was still alive, and delight that his own heartbeat could have been hers – that's how near he was to Lisalein.

The witch of Paradise wasn't even startled to see him.

'Darling,' she said, as if she were continuing a conversation she'd had with him yesterday, 'did you come without champagne?'

Erik snarled at the SS guard outside the door. 'Champagne, you son of a bitch. And two cups.'

'Three,' Lisa said. 'Little Sister has to have a taste of whatever I drink... You look divine in your uniform. And it's nice of you to bring me a present – your *Ritterkreuz*.'

Erik removed the *Ritterkreuz* and wrapped its ribbon around Lisa's neck.

'Does that make me a heroine of the Reich?' she asked, but there were tears in her eyes, and it tormented Erik to see them. He started to shiver, and she clutched his hand.

'I missed you,' she said. 'I had no one I liked enough to battle with. Joachim doesn't count. He's a snake.'

'I'll drag him up here and we'll drink the champagne from his skull… I'm taking you out of this hole.'

'I can't leave, darling. The settlers depend on me. I negotiate for them. I play strip poker with the guards. But I'm not such a catch.'

'Play strip poker with me,' he said.

'It wouldn't be fair. I'd always win. And you'd never find out what's under my hospital gown.'

'Ah,' he said, 'where's the baron? He always wanted to see Theresienstadt for himself.'

The champagne arrived – it was Czech champagne, as yellow as a dachshund's pee and twice as bitter. But Erik didn't make a fuss. He filled a cup for Little Sister, the male nurse, and then he drank with Lisalein, who kept rubbing the ribbon and the cross.

'Father isn't here,' she whispered into his dark eyes, and then she told him why. There was little enchantment in her tale. It was all about bargaining with the Leibstandarte SS, just before Erik crossed the Atlantic on his *Milchkuh*. Berlin was in the business of Jews, she said. The roundups and the factory raids had only whetted the SS's appetite. The Leibstandarte's coffers were filled with Jewish gold and Jewish *Geld*. But the People's Court would have sent Lisa and her *Vati* to the guillotine had Colonel Joachim not staged their deaths at Sachsenhausen forest. Commander Stolz was the go-between. He had to pay Joachim the last of the baron's fortune from Die Drei Krokodile, a few hundred thousand reichsmarks.

Joachim had promised to send Lisa and the baron into Switzerland, but he never did. He held them in the Leibstandarte's barracks outside Berlin. But it wasn't some dungeon in the dark, like in *The Count of Monte Cristo*. Lisa lived in the officers' quarters with her father, in the colonel's own apartment. They had dinner with Joachim, fed on goose fat and wine from Medoc. Lisa was his prisoner, and she also wasn't. He lit the candles, served the wine. Sometimes his mustache trembled. He was aching to sleep with her, but he didn't want to ask. He could have ripped off her clothes, threatened to kill the baron. But his pride was shot. He was a murderer looking for romance.

She should have twisted his earlobes and taken him into his own bed. What would it have cost her? But she liked to watch him suffer. And then he pounced like a jackal.

First he broke her kneecaps; then he took her and the baron back to Sachsenhausen forest, had them undress, and with his own hands he rubbed lard on her body, lathering between her legs, and he set Lisa on fire, wanting to fry her like a duck in a pan. She cackled like a wild woman, spat in his face, and dreamt she was a burning tree.

'I'll finish him,' Erik shouted, 'one finger at a time.'

Lisa stroked the throbbing pulse under Erik's eye. 'Darling, what good would it do? They'd only bring in another commandant, far worse than Joachim. And all the settlers would suffer.'

'Settlers,' he hissed. 'They'll never recover from this little camp… I can't bear to imagine you as a burning tree.'

'Shh,' she told him. And she went on with her tale.

Commander Stolz appeared in the nick of time with his own commandos. He'd been shadowing Joachim for a month. But Lisa didn't remember much. She woke up at the Jewish Hospital, in her father's old bed at the *Extrastation*. The baron hadn't survived Joachim's little funeral pyre. He died of a heart attack on the way to

Iranische Strasse. And Lisa lay in the grip of some powerful fever, her skin like the hot crust of a mountain ready to erupt. But she wasn't free of Colonel Joachim.

He would show up at her bedside, clutching a fistful of flowers.

'He begged me to run away with him and whatever he had left of my father's millions. He sang about country streams in Switzerland, about caverns that rained gold. I assured him I'd seen such a cavern in the Grunewald, and promised I would rip his heart out as soon as I got well… I'm a girl who breaks her promises.'

'But the *Schwanz* didn't run away.'

'No, darling. But he got out of Berlin. He licked Himmler's boots and was assigned to Paradise. I still couldn't get free of him. He had me flown to Prague on Himmler's private plane. He cries and grovels whenever he visits my room. I hurl my shoes at him. It's a big act. I don't even hate him enough to care. He has to feed the settlers, fatten them up, if he wants to remain in my good graces. Now fewer of them will starve to death. So you mustn't disturb the equilibrium we have in Paradise. But why haven't you kissed me?'

Erik was bewildered. He could only imagine her as a burning tree.

'Come under the covers,' she said. 'I promise not to break. And Little Sister won't snitch on us.'

Erik slid down onto her narrow cot as gently as he could. He did believe her bones would break. He kissed her clotted eye. 'Darling,' she said, and fell asleep in his arms while Erik wondered about this ghost town behind ghetto walls. The Führer slaughtered Jews and waited for the Red Cross to redeem his monstrous lie that he had fathered a Jewish Paradise in Bohemia. Was it Werner Wolfe who had sent Erik here, or was it the Führer himself, who wanted him to fall right into Theresienstadt, as another piece of decoration for the Red Cross?

False Kronen

29

FINALLY HE VENTURED BEYOND THE first pavilion, into the settlement itself, this maze where the Jews of Theresienstadt lived, sometimes in little houses, or monstrous barracks, sometimes in shelves built right into the main wall, sometimes in huts that were part of a dead end, sometimes in dormitories within a pavilion. They didn't wear the little gray caps and rumpled black-and-gray flannel of concentration camps. The Nazis wanted to give them the illusion of never-never land, their own resettlement town, a new Zion on the right bank of the river Ohře.

The fog crept over the battlements, and Erik stumbled like a blind man. He had to wander about until the sun burnt the fog away. The settlers he saw bowed to him and then scattered. He had to make them aware that he, too, was a settler, even if he wore the *Totenkopf* of the SS. But they had already heard of the strange magician who had helped hide submariners in Berlin. Children showed him the paintings they had done. Little girls defied their keepers and held the magician's hand. Artists invited him into the little studios they had concocted between two barren walls. Widows flirted with him. Other settlers were feverish when he offered them cigarettes – they were forbidden to smoke in their very own Paradise.

He smoked with them. After a while, they trusted him enough

to laugh. There were philosophers, playwrights, and novelists, all half-starved. They were astonished when he told them he'd gone to the Jewish Gymnasium, but within one afternoon he even found a classmate, a woebegone young man without a tooth in his head. And all of a sudden Erik had become part of some select society, as an unmoored secret agent who could enter into this labyrinth of Jews.

They had jazz clubs of their own, but these starving musicians had little wind to spare and couldn't huff and puff into their clarinets; their music came in hysterical gasps; their instruments had missing keys. It wasn't Jewish Jazz, but some kind of bitter and brutal lament, the lament of Paradise on a swollen river. The staccato bleats nearly drove Erik insane, but he listened. He wouldn't flee from these wounded clarinets.

The children had their own schools, taught by the settlers themselves, even though the SS outlawed every school in Theresienstadt. Children were supposed to work from the age of fourteen; one of the far pavilions housed a factory where coffins were made, and the children stood along a crooked assembly line as nailers and polishers. These young coffin makers were quite adept and could produce twenty or thirty in a day – coffins with the finest shellac. But none of the settlers was ever buried in them. If they died of starvation or neglect, they were carried to the crematorium outside the walls in a horseless hearse.

The SS had no supervisors at the coffin factory; thus, the children would accomplish their quotas by noon and then run off to the outlawed schools, held in some dark corner where the Nazis had never been. These Nazis seldom ventured beyond their own clubhouse or pavilions; they had Czech hirelings and fifty Jewish informers, who received extra rations but were as blind as the Nazis themselves.

Still, the looming visit by the Red Cross had changed the complexion of the camp. The SS had to mingle with the Jews, had to entice the camp's carpenters to construct a fake farmhouse stocked with stolen animals – a cow, a rooster, a rabbit; they turned Theresienstadt into a huge Monopoly board, with their own false money – kronen with a Jewish star and a picture of Moses emblazoned on them, kronen that could be bartered nowhere, except that the SS never understood the ingenuity of the settlers, who had their own system of trade. These worthless kronen could buy black-market shoelaces, the special favor of fixing a child's toy or relining an overcoat with real lamb's wool, private clarinet lessons on the same wounded clarinets, or even sexual favors. And such piss-poor paper, with which the SS hoped to hoodwink the Red Cross, began to explode in value day after day, so that Theresienstadt had a whole army of usurers after a while, and the biggest usurer of them all was Bernhard Beck.

The king of cabaret used his piles of kronen to lord it over the settlers. Bernhard had grown brutally fat at Theresienstadt, fatter than he'd ever been; he stuffed his mouth with black-market chocolate and marzipan from the commandant himself. Joachim was in league with Mackie Messer, who would hold Paradise in line when the Red Cross appeared in their mythical white trucks; each afternoon, children climbed the battlements to search the countryside for these trucks and the salvation the trucks would bring. But Bernhard knew better. The Red Cross would fall right into the Nazis' ruse. It would see kronen with Jewish stars and a café in the town square. And Mackie Messer would squeeze every Jewish heart.

He'd already done so. He'd made his devilish masterpiece last fall, *The Cabaret King Comes to Bohemia*, where he wheedled stunning performances out of the settlers. Bernhard had bribed them, seduced them, until Theresienstadt took on a surreal tone, and spectator after spectator in a multitude of movie houses inside Hitler's Europe believed that this somber camp was Paradise. Now Red Cross commissioners were coming to see for themselves. Mackie Messer would be their guide.

This man-mountain wore sable around his throat; he had sweaters and coats, suspenders of an SS captain, kid gloves that couldn't contain his monstrous fingers. He carried a cudgel, and with him were his Czech bodyguards, louts who lived off their master's droppings. They surrounded Erik in a deserted courtyard and began to menace him.

'Magician,' Bernhard shouted in a very weak voice. 'I know why you're here. I have my own grapevine, and it's much better than yours. You'll never kidnap me, not while I breathe.'

'Maestro,' Erik said. 'Louis B. Mayer wants you at MGM. What the hell is Theresienstadt compared to Hollywood?'

But the maestro swerved under his enormous weight. He was performing his own little cabaret.

'Are you deaf? I lost it all. I can't sing a note. My voice starts to crack.'

Erik tried to convince this maniac. 'MGM will give you another voice. It's done all the time.'

A great sadness settled onto that swollen mask of a face, with its piggish eyes and tiny mouth.

'Magician, I'm disappointed in you. What would I be with another man's voice? I prefer Paradise.'

And Erik was ashamed of himself. There was only one Mack the Knife.

'Besides,' said this new prince of shylocks, 'the commandant would never let me go. I'm his meal ticket.'

'But you're wrong. Joachim works for the Americans now.'

'Perhaps,' said Bernhard Beck, an obscene quiver erupting on his tiny mouth. 'Perhaps not.'

And he fell upon Erik with his bodyguards and the perverse grace of his own bearish body. Erik had realized something was amiss with that quivering mouth. He darted around the fat man's cudgel, but the Czech bodyguards still wrestled him to the ground.

He had to stare at those piggish eyes, a mountain looming over him.

'Magician, you might not survive your first trip to Paradise.'

Bernhard snorted as he was about to attack, but then he started to squeal and cover his shoulders with his kid gloves. Someone stood behind him, thwacking him with a cane.

'*Schwester*,' he squealed, 'I meant no harm. I was introducing myself to the magician, honest to God.'

Erik could barely believe it. His Lisa had climbed out of her hospital bed. She was limping, and had to hold on to Bernhard as she struck him with her cane. Behind her was a whole cadre of settlers, men and women who tossed loose pieces of battlement – lumps of stone and brick – at the Czech bodyguards.

'*Schwester* Lisa,' Bernhard groaned as his bodyguards scattered. 'I'll behave, honest to God.'

'Mackie,' she said, tossing a fistful of kronen at him. 'Take your lucre and leave us alone.'

He kissed her hands, scooped up the kronen in a bearish ballet, and ran after the bodyguards. Theresienstadt was another *Wunderland*, like the *Fuchsbau* above the Landwehrkanal. And Lisa was in the midst of some resurrection he still couldn't understand; she kept rising out of Sachsenhausen forest like a forlorn bird. But she wasn't forlorn as she stooped with the help of her cane and stroked Erik's hair.

'*Schwester* Lisa,' said one of the settlers, 'are you all right?'

'Yes, yes, I'm fine… Now you must let me be with my man.'

Wunderland, Erik muttered before he shut his eyes and fell into his own forlorn sleep.

Lisa

30

S HE'D ARRIVED IN PARADISE NEAR the end of '43, on an ambulance from Prague, arrived with Joachim, the new commandant. He couldn't make up his mind whether to hurl Lisa off the battlements or have her survive. The fool was in love with a shadow – that's all she was. He nursed Lisa himself, read fairy tales to her with a fury in his eye. He had his own adjutant pretend to be a male nurse. Little Sister was in love with her, too. They had a sack of gold hidden somewhere, and they dreamt of another life, in Switzerland, Canada, or New Zealand, or at a 'nursery school' in Virginia, run by naval intelligence. And while they plotted, the commandant began to moan. The Führer had pinned medals on his tunic, and here he was flirting with the Allies like a whore with a pot of gold.

They fed her porridge, and considered how they could earn more money from the camp itself. The Red Cross was coming, and Joachim had to be on his guard. But he kept reducing the rations for these settlers, and pocketed whatever he could. And they schemed in front of Lisa, as if she were some damaged child who had no relation to the Jews of Theresienstadt. She snored, pretended to sleep, and plotted against the plotters.

She could win Little Sister over with a couple of winks. And whenever she had the strength, she wrapped herself in a military cloak and hobbled down the stairs with her cane. She didn't even have to introduce herself to these Jewish ghosts. She was the baroness who had started a rebellion against the Gestapo, who had saved countless children and young girls.

What did they really know about her? She was the one who had been the somnambulist in Nazi Berlin, maneuvering with her eyes closed, wearing a nurse's uniform at the Jewish Hospital, hiding her little quota of submariners, most often replicas of herself, fierce young women of the mercantile class, blond and beautiful, with willowy legs. She could not remember having saved a single man, young or old, handsome or not. And when she visited the submariners in their attic rooms, bringing them food and sometimes cosmetics, didn't she fondle one or two, fall on them behind a fake wall until those submariners were like addicts who waited for her kisses?

They were as naïve and frightened as children, with Lisalein as their savior – and their Nosferatu. She might as well have sucked the blood out of them. She had selected the brightest ones, the beautiful ones, with whom she could discuss Franz Kafka and Thomas Mann, while she made their nipples as taut as delectable knives...

But she wouldn't prey upon the beautiful girls in Paradise, wouldn't be their Nosferatu. She hid behind her officer's cloak, and could protect such girls, since she had some kind of curious relationship with the commandant. She became their *Schwester* Lisa. She taught in the settlers' clandestine schools, stole food from the commandant, allowed the camp's artists to sketch her, and was the only one who could fight back against Bernhard Beck. He had grown into a gangster at Theresienstadt. He ate like a wolf, swallowed up the rations of twenty men, while children starved. But the Berlin Jews were still in awe of him. They couldn't forget how he'd swagger in front of the Nazis on Unter den Linden, with a golden toothpick peering from a corner of his mouth, and scribble

Mack the Kike whenever the Nazis begged him for his autograph.

But all his defiance was gone, replaced by a relentless greed. Mack the Kike lived only to feed himself and collect his kronen. But who the hell was she to talk? She had always been a predator who devoured men and women with the same cold fury. Seduction had been for Lisa a series of stratagems, a manual of war. And that's why she had held on to that boy with the big eyes at the Jewish orphanage in Berlin, years and years ago, when she herself was just a girl. Erik was as wild as she was in his own timid way, and she had wanted to kiss him the moment she saw those German Gypsy eyes, take him into a corner and bite his head off.

And here she was with him at the end of the world, within the battlements at Theresienstadt, after Mack the Kike and his henchmen had roughed him up, and she still wanted to bite his head off, but she hid that from him. When Joachim had greased her like a capon in Sachsenhausen forest and set her hair on fire – while half of her was sizzling, and she wished her own death – all she could see in front of her eyes was the magician's mournful face.

He had his own quarters in the first pavilion, given to him by the commandant, but he carried her up the steps to that little hospital ward in the attic. She dismissed Joachim's adjutant, the male nurse, and she lay down with Erik on her own rumpled bed. They didn't even bother to undress. They fumbled with each other in their clothes, like vagabonds. And when he tried to unbutton her, she clutched at his hands.

'I haven't washed,' she said. 'You'll have to ravish me with my clothes on.'

And Erik wore that same mournful face. He didn't know what to do. He wouldn't tie her arms to the bed, as he had done at the Adlon and on the Dragonerstrasse, to inflict his own pain on her, to wound her the way she had once wounded him. He moved in her with a kind of soft dream. He did not want to wake. And he whimpered in his dream with Lisa, worried she wouldn't be there.

She wasn't beside him when he woke. He panicked until he saw her shoes near the bed and heard the faucets running. Lisa was taking a bath somewhere within the battlements. But the sound of running water reverberated across the pavilion's many walls, and Erik couldn't even tell where it was coming from.

He wandered in and out of alcoves, expecting some Mad Hatter to leap at him from a wall. He went down a staircase to an alcove between two floors and discovered a bathroom with its own little flight of stairs. Lisa was inside. She had turned the faucets off, but was humming a childish tune she must have picked up from her nanny in the Grunewald. It was about a wild boar and a girl with golden hair. The boar devours the girl but is driven to madness by the memory of her hair and leaps off a ravine.

Erik was riveted to Lisa's lament. He opened the door. Lisa was drying herself with an enormous towel. But she hadn't folded herself into the towel yet. The sunlight streamed onto her from a dormer window until she was ablaze. She wasn't a witch. All that burning light had come from the bluish marks on her body – she was scarred from her shoulders to her thighs.

She caught him looking at her. She didn't bury herself in the towel, or scream at Erik. She stood there.

It wasn't pity he felt. The markings on her limbs were beautiful. He longed to kiss every scar. The Nazis didn't know how to destroy Lisalein. They were like children bent on mischief, but the more damage they did, the grayer these *Dreckshunde* grew. Joachim could break her bones. But he couldn't catch her. And what about Erik? Would he catch Lisalein before Paradise shrank within its own walls?

Erik sang out his love. But he sounded like one of the wounded

290

clarinets of Theresienstadt. So he shut his mouth. And he made love to Lisalein on her enormous towel, under the battlements, his uniform piled like a little mountain of laundry, with his boots on top. He kissed as many of her scars as he could, while Lisa examined his own markings, all the punctures and scratches of an Abwehr man. She'd never seen him naked in such streaming light. It astounded her.

'Erik,' she whispered, 'it's like an illustrated map of war.'

'I was careless,' he said.

'A careless man wouldn't have come to Bohemia to visit his fiancée – this is a charnel house. Even the Nazis are corpses here.'

'But the settlers tell me how you fight off every guard to feed the children.'

'No one *settles* at Theresienstadt. We're dead souls in transit. Except for Mackie Messer. Greed keeps him alive.'

'And what if I'm greedy for you?'

'Then you'll rouse the dead Lisa with your kisses… and she'll start to cry. It's much too painful to be alive.'

'And if I devote myself to you, kiss every blue bump on your body?'

'Ah,' she said, 'I might change my mind.'

And she snuggled next to one of his knife wounds, the light burning a halo into her hair.

The Baroness of Theresienstadt

31

DEAD LISA WAS MORE AND more alive. She had to wake the ghetto before the Red Cross got here and the ghetto ran out of time. The Red Cross would lull the Jews into believing that each man, woman, and child was safe within the walls. Hitler had become their dark angel. That's what infuriated Lisa. They had joined the conspiracy of their own ruin; they were wanderers in a land of wind and lice, trying to persevere until the Red Cross waved a magic wand. The most gullible of them all were the *Prominenten* – scientists, opera singers, millionaires, and members of the Jewish royal caste.

Such *Prominenten* looked with great scorn at the Jews in their crowded barracks, considered themselves a breed apart, and wondered why they were at Theresienstadt. The SS had promised to send them to the island of Madagascar, where they would have their very own colony of *Prominenten* like themselves, without lice-laden Jews. All they had to do was sing the camp's praises to the Red Cross, tra-la-la!

Madagascar was another myth. There was no such resettlement colony. In fact, she'd learned from the commandant himself that it was a code name for Auschwitz. One night, all these notables would be put on a train to Madagascar. And so Lisa pitied them, even with their haughtiness. They had no one but Lisa to look after them, to barter on the black market for an extra blanket, to find the cough medicine that Countess X needed, or to delouse another countess's lice-laden shawl.

The shrewdest among them had found work in the ghetto, had ventured out of their tiny asylum, had wrapped bandages, or helped children learn to draw, or read books to the dying. The others just vegetated in their vast illusions, sat in clothes that would never have been washed without Lisa's care, convinced that the Kaiser's former guardsmen would free them from this city of Jews. Yet they also had a kind of cruel comprehension of the camp. They weren't utterly ignorant of what went on outside the walls of their little crumbling 'palace' that had once been a poorhouse.

'Baroness, have you gone riding with the commandant?'

They meant to wound her with that remark, to imply that she was Joachim's whore, that she might have been stuck here with them had it not been for the commandant. But she didn't answer with any malice.

'It's difficult for me to mount even the gentlest mare. And I have little time to ride.'

'What a pity,' said Countess X, pursing her lips. 'I hear he calls his own white Arabian "Lisalein." Surely that should give you some influence.'

'None at all,' said Lisa, relishing her own little lie. 'But he's determined to ride me one way or another.'

All the countesses began to titter, and Lisa decided to make one last appeal.

'Comrades, you must confide in the commissioners when they come. They will listen to you. You must reveal the fault lines in Hitler's Paradise, every lie.'

'And ruin our chances with the Red Cross,' hissed Countess Y. There was such venom on their faces that Lisa left this poorhouse of a palace. She still had to think of their soiled clothes, and whom she would have to bribe to put the countesses' 'trousseaus' high up on the laundry list, or nothing would get washed for another three months.

Bribery and fear were the language of Theresienstadt, and both were often intertwined. The SS lived in their own strange hierarchy. They had their compounds, their clubs. But they couldn't repair a toilet or bake a loaf of bread. The chief baker was the real king of Theresienstadt. Husbands threw their wives at the baker for an extra portion of bread. Children clung to him. He had his little army of sycophants. He didn't sleep in any barrack. He kept three rooms on the top floor of the old garrison bakery near the ramparts. He had his own transportation – not a motorbike, like the SS, or a white Arabian, like the commandant, or even a hearse pulled by old men, but a dogcart with a team of German shepherds, given to him by the SS garrison at the Little Fortress.

The SS were beholden to him. He supplied the commandant and his men with a tub of ersatz tapioca pudding that was much tastier than any pudding they might have happened upon in the depleted shops of Prague. He wanted to show them what the chief of all the cooks at Theresienstadt was worth.

He was waiting with his dogcart the moment Lisa left the countesses. He feared Lisa much more than he ever did the commandant, who wouldn't have dared put *his* baker on a transport to Poland. But the baroness was much more fickle. She was always demanding little cakes from him, not for herself, but for orphans and the living dead in the tuberculosis ward. If he failed her, she might whisper in the commandant's ear, and God knows what she might say. He could land in a cattle car going east, and all the pudding in the world wouldn't save him.

No wonder half the women in their little Paradise called her

Frau Kommandant. Who could describe the madness that went on between her and Colonel Joachim? So the chief of all the cooks was careful with her.

'Baroness,' he said, after clucking at his dogs, 'where might I take you, please?'

'To Hell,' she told him.

'Ah,' he said, because he had a touch of fickleness in him, too. 'Then we might as well close our eyes and just stand still.'

'What have you to complain about? You won't find another heaven like Theresienstadt. You were a grubby baker's assistant before you came here – you worm, why have you put the whole children's barracks on such short rations? And your bakers steal bread from the mouths of old men.'

Suddenly, he was shivering, and the dogs could sense his apprehension; they began to howl and bark at the wind.

'Who has slandered me, Baroness, who? I don't steal from children or the old.'

'Then why do I see them almost delirious with hunger, while your lackeys deliver bread everywhere in their hearses?'

'I'll punish every crime,' he muttered. 'Whoever's been hoarding, I'll break his neck.'

And Lisa climbed aboard the cart with the help of her cane. 'The *Blindenheim*,' she shouted into the wind; the dogs kept barking, and the dust swirled all around them on the unpaved roads of Paradise until Lisa was in her own blinding storm. She preferred it that way. She wouldn't have to look inside the barracks and see six or seven thousand souls crammed into a space where several hundred soldiers had once lived – half-starved men or women packed like pale sardines from the rafters to the cellars down below. But it was wicked of her to consider sardines in a camp where men would have killed for one or two precious tins from Portugal. *Sardines, sardines.*

The dust storm lifted and she could see the town's Jewish carpenters dismantling the old numbered signs of the ghetto's nameless streets and putting up the new street signs – Lange Strasse, Rathausgasse, Turmgasse – of the Nazi's fictional health spa for Jewish heroes and rich retirees, and then there was that ultimate lie, as the SS rechristened the ghetto with still larger signs that read THERESIENBAD, as if they had created a new Marienbad in the dusty sun.

There were no miraculous springs, no luxurious hotels, no five-star meals; this health spa was nothing but a *cvokárna,* as the Czech inmates called Theresienstadt in ghetto slang, a nuthouse where the real lunatics were the SS, and the Jews had to battle with all their might to preserve the least sense of sanity.

She caught a squad of old men wandering in the street. The old men had been scavenging garbage barrels for potato peels and lost their way. She had them hold on to the dogcart and led them back to their barrack. But she could hear their stomachs growl, and she had the baker stop at his own compound and give them each a slice of bread.

'Baroness,' the baker rasped, 'you spoil these old men. They put on a big act in front of you, and they know you'll feed them. It's just cabaret.'

'Yes,' she said. 'And will it also be cabaret when I ask the elders to revoke your license, and you become another beggar at Theresienstadt?'

The baker kept quiet. He drove the baroness to the little ragged fort on Badhausgasse where the blind lived and then disappeared into his own swirl of dust. She'd come to visit the blind women who worked in the mica factory. It was a grueling but delicate ordeal. Mica was one of the Nazis' 'war' minerals used as an electrical insulator at Hermann Göring's aircraft factories. But it came in flat sheets that had to be cut into the thinnest-possible portions. This cutting needed a woman's fine hands. Any man, even a surgeon, couldn't manipulate the mica worker's blunt knife; he'd press too hard, and the sheet would shatter. And so a small band of women were locked inside the cutting room with their knives. But the mica sheets gave off such a wicked glare that the women's eyes would begin to bleed after a few hours. Thus, the SS scoured the barracks for blind women who wouldn't suffer from migraines while they were at the bench.

But even blind women weren't immune to the glare. Their eyes also bled. So Lisa had come to visit the *Blindenheim*'s three blind mica workers. She had a lotion for the blind women that the doctors had given her. She also fed them pudding from the commandant's own supply. And she read to them. These women weren't as snobbish as the countesses, though they were far more valuable to the camp's economy, and, for the moment at least, were safe from the transports. Colonel Joachim would never have allowed them onto a cattle car.

And the blind women loved to clutch Lisa's hands while she read to them from a strange Czech author who wrote in a macabre and brutally simple German about a hunger artist, a man who lived in a cage and starved himself for spectators.

'Baroness,' the blind women said, 'he should have joined us at this camp.' But it was a cruel joke, since the author's own sister, Ottilie Kafka, had once been a settler here; she'd left on a transport of ragged, frightened, barefoot boys from Bialystock with fifty other nurses, and none of them ever came back, neither the nurses nor the barefoot boys.

The blind women hadn't meant to be cruel, and when they recalled Ottilie, who had been so gentle with them, they began to cry. Ottilie had disappeared before Lisa's time at the camp. But she couldn't stop thinking of Kafka's sad tale about Gregor Samsa and his sister, Grete. Gregor could have been at Theresienstadt. He lived in a world of bedbugs, like the settlers, who were overrun with bugs once the lights went out. One morning, Gregor himself is transformed into a monstrous bug. It's Grete who feeds him and cleans his room. It's Grete who keeps him alive, and it's Grete who finally abandons him.

Lisa had always seen herself as another Grete, who had abandoned everyone – a father who had loved her a little too much, blond submariners who had depended on her every whim – until she was a monstrous creature with her own carapace. She, too, had landed in a world of bedbugs. And she belonged here…

Ännchen and the *Frau Kommandant*

32

LISA LEFT THE *BLINDENHEIM* AND limped along Parkstrasse, ablaze with a bed of roses planted by Jewish gardeners to beguile the Red Cross. Every maneuver was done with the Red Cross in mind, every twist, every turn.

She arrived at Magdeburg Barracks, the camp's own administration building. The entire ghetto was run from this building. It was where the council of elders convened and where the tailors had their workshop. These men made and repaired uniforms for the Gestapo and the SS; they stitched with a kind of golden thread. There was a wild, irrational demand for their services. They had twenty apprentices and helpers in their workshop. And such was the brutal irony of ghetto life that their former bosses, the dethroned manufacturers of Hamburg and Berlin, couldn't have survived without attaching themselves to these tailors, the new princes of Theresienstadt.

Bankers and other millionaires had become beggars at the camp. The cleverest ones had joined the administration as clerks, while the rest were 'mules' who swept the streets or were hitched to hearses – the trolley cars of this ghetto – carting corpses and loaves of bread, dirty laundry, barrels of potatoes, or exhausted and starving widows who wanted to attend lectures at the other end of town.

Magdeburg was also the headquarters of the camp's Jewish police force, hooligans from Prague or young Berliners in jackboots and ridiculous top hats tied with yellow ribbons. They carried cudgels, like the SS, and went after 'rat packs' of children who stole from the living and the dead. Their own mothers had taught these children to steal. They had the force of logic behind them. If the SS stole from the Jews, why shouldn't the Jews steal from themselves?

Yet the council of elders couldn't tolerate such open plunder, and the little thieves were cudgeled and kept in jail until they went before the children's tribunal, which was held in an ornate room of the barracks that served as a courthouse. The children stood before a judge, often one of the elders, while another elder recited a litany of charges, prepared by some clerk. Lisa loved to attend such 'recitals,' since they exposed all the contradictions of the camp. Children, wild or not, had become the saviors of most families, since they were far more clever and adept at stealing food than adults. Men, women, and children all lived in separate barracks. But it was the children who often kept their fathers alive, smuggling food into the barracks, or meeting their mothers near the ramparts.

The tribunal was full today. The elders had to clear the streets before the young thieves poisoned the atmosphere and ruined things for the Red Cross. Lisa counted thirty children in the prisoners' dock as she entered the tribunal, all of them looking bewildered and worn. There was a murmur among the elders and the clerks of the court. She had become an avenging angel with that limp of hers, and they were wary of the *Frau Kommandant*. The elders and their clerks had to prepare the list of all those who were to be sent east on the transports – a thousand names for each transport, often more. It was a shattering task, trying to save some and offering up others to the SS. They had their 'exemptions,' and so did the commandant, who didn't want to lose his tailor or his stable boys.

The transport quotas came down from Berlin, and the commandant had to comply. But the *Frau Kommandant* complicated things. She would protect *every* child on a transport. The elders worked like dogs with the ghetto police, trying to console those who were selected – often a husband would volunteer to accompany his wife to Madagascar – and carrying the torches that lit the way to the little railroad outside the gate.

And what would they find? The baroness sitting in a cattle car with a child, volunteering herself as a nurse. The young SS officers grew hysterical. They couldn't strike Lisa with a pistol butt, or drag her from the transport. And they couldn't allow her to go with the child. They were the ones who understood what *Madagascar* meant – it was the land of no return.

So they had to wake the commandant, who was always in a foul mood in the middle of the night. The commandant himself had checked off this child, who was a bit slow in the head. He arrived in his pajamas and boots, his military tunic slung over his shoulders. He'd rant and cuff an elder on the ear until he recognized Lisa. Then he'd turn pale; his blond mustache would twitch, while the child was crossed off the transport list.

And now the elders sat with their seltzer siphons at the tribunal and worried what to do about the baroness; these siphons were a mark of their prestige. Not a single tailor had his own supply of seltzer. And the siphons infuriated Lisa, because they should have gone to patients at one of the ghetto hospitals. But what infuriated her more was the sight of Ännchen in the dock; she was a retarded girl of twelve, the very child Lisa had saved from the cattle car. She lived in the 'lepers' ward' of the children's barracks, with orphans and illegitimate boys and girls – *mamzers* in ghetto argot. The children had their own sense of hierarchy; they protected one another, never stole from old men or women lost in the street, kept their own mothers and fathers alive, sang in the children's choir if they had a good voice, acted in children's plays, had their own soccer league at the camp, and often found other ways to thrive, but they wouldn't allow orphans and *mamzers* in their rooms no matter what the elders preached to them.

It was Lisa who protected such unfortunates, took them on little pilgrimages inside the ghetto, let them ride with her on her own palomino, Nicodemus, whom she kept in the commandant's stalls. She couldn't canter on the dusty trails of the ghetto. Her body hurt too much; every movement in the saddle was a little shock that traveled up and down her spine, until she feared she would break like some unsprung jack-in-the-box. And she might knock down some poor grandmother in that infernal dust. Yet the children loved to ride with her, especially Ännchen.

Lisa kept her out of the camp's insane asylum, looked after her, screamed at any boy or girl who ventured near the 'lepers' ward' with mischief in mind. And when Lisa saw her in the dock, frightened, her head whipping back and forth as if it belonged to some rag doll, she shoved past a camp policeman in his silly hat, grabbed Ännchen's hand, and pulled her right out of the dock, even if her own body was trembling.

She whispered to one of the clerks, a Munich millionaire who was now a scrivener. '*Junge,* Ännchen belongs to me. I want her name wiped out of the docket. And if the elders aren't careful, I'll create my own storm and blow their little court down. Am I clear?'

'Yes, *Frau Kommandant.*'

The elders planned to cleanse the town of troublemakers, dwarfs, and little thieves while the Red Cross was in Theresienstadt. Constables in top hats would keep the old, the unsightly, and the insane in their barracks so that the ghetto could become a vacation ground for one morning and afternoon. *Theresienbad.* But Lisa wouldn't participate in such trickery. The elders didn't know what to do with the *Frau Kommandant*.

They whispered among themselves, and the judge leapt out of his chair. 'All charges dropped. We will have a one-day amnesty in honor of the baroness.'

But Lisa didn't listen to all their clatter. She led Ännchen out of Magdeburg Barracks. The girl was as tall as Lisa; her hair looked like prettified straw, but she had the bluest eyes Lisa had ever seen. That's why the SS plotted to get rid of her, to put her on a transport. She looked even more Aryan than they did, and they didn't like this maddening mirror of themselves.

Ännchen's head continued to whip back and forth, and suddenly the whipping stopped. She started to neigh, and her nostrils flared. Ännchen had her own magisterial motions and sounds. And Lisa could read her language. Ännchen wanted to go to the stables.

She bit at the wind like a horse biting fleas, and she swept Lisa along – for a moment Lisa's limp was gone. The dust flew around them, and Lisa could recognize companies of women waiting in line in a courtyard kitchen for their meager, miserable noon meal. They fared much better than the men at the camp, sometimes carrying their husbands on their backs while they stood in line. Some men retreated into poetry and arranged readings, but these camp poets were mainly poseurs. The genuine poets kept their lines inside their heads. At least that's what Lisa suspected.

All the women, even the few collaborators among them, worshipped the *Frau Kommandant*. They would have joined her in any revolt. And when they saw Lisa come out of a dust storm with the half-witted child, they curtsied like women at some royal court and kissed her hand. But Lisa had to fly with the wind. Ännchen had grown impatient.

The old riding school and its stables had been built right into the fortress's inner wall near Seestrasse. The Jewish stable boys seemed excited when they saw the *Frau Kommandant*. But the SS had taught them to be superstitious, and they'd convinced themselves that Ännchen had the evil eye and could turn them into a pile of salt. And so they covered their own eyes with the skirts of their leather aprons.

Lisa heard a roar from inside the stables. It was Joachim. He walked out of a dark swirl of dust and into the sunlight. He was wearing jodhpurs with his plum-colored boots and a silk riding blouse, with a white scarf around his neck.

Ännchen hid behind Lisa's legs. She liked this commandant and also hated him. He smelled funny, with that mingling of sweat and bittersweet perfume, like a bar of black chocolate. But Lisa knew how to deal with this madman of a colonel who loved her so much that he had to burn her alive.

'Joachim,' she said, 'if you aren't nice, I'll never visit again. And I should warn you. I go wherever Ännchen goes.'

He bowed to this little girl, who wasn't so little, and offered her some sponge cake from Prague. 'Princess Ann,' he said, 'it's my pleasure.'

Ännchen devoured the cake in one bite. Her head began to whip again. She wanted to see the palomino with his spotted legs and white mane. And so the commandant led Nicodemus out of his stall. And Ännchen uttered the single word she had ever cared to master.

'*Nico*,' she said. Nicodemus was fond of the girl. He began to rub against her with his nose and nibble on her sleeve. He was a curious creature. He had the words U.S. CAVALRY stamped on his hindquarters. What was an American cavalry horse doing in Bohemia? Nicodemus must have belonged to the old garrison. Perhaps a Czech soldier had branded him as some kind of a joke.

He wasn't much of a charger and might have been blind in one eye. The commandant wanted to have Nico shot, but Lisa appropriated him a week after she arrived in Theresienstadt.

He'd saddled Nicodemus half an hour ago. He could sense that Lisa would come with the half-wit – no, it was the palomino who sensed it, who could catch the 'flavor' of his mistress from the ghetto's far wall. Nicodemus had beat against the earthen floor of the stable with one hoof until Joachim listened. The commandant would bide his time. He still planned to turn the palomino into glue.

He helped Lisa onto the horse, stood her cane against a stall, then hoisted Ännchen onto the saddle, cinching her to Lisa with a leather belt.

'Joachim,' she said, 'are you going to stuff us after we die and put us in your museum?'

'What museum?' he asked.

'The memorial that Himmler is planning for the Jews. But we'll all have to vanish before he starts.'

It was another one of the Nazis' macabre schemes. They were collecting while they killed – Jewish pianos, Jewish clothing, Jewish books. The center of the whole project would be Prague, but every town in the Greater Reich would have its own Jewish museum. Abandoned synagogues would be selected, or some cultural center that had been caught in a pogrom. Joachim himself was in charge of the Theresienstadt museum. It would be housed in the Magdeburg Barracks, where future German tourists could wander through halls that had once accommodated the council of elders.

'Joachim,' she said from her perch in the saddle, 'would you like me to run away with you?'

She was forever teasing him, mocking him.

'And what would I have to do, Baroness? Free every Yid in Theresienstadt?'

She smiled at him with a morsel of tenderness, and he was almost grateful. He would have done anything for this blond bitch whose scalp had gone all white. He would have broken her kneecaps again, torn out the roots of her hair, and cradled her in his arms for the rest of his life.

'Well,' he said, 'should I free the Yids?'

'No, darling. That would only give the Czech Gestapo an excuse to murder every single one. But you could lock up all the elders so they can't steal seltzer from the clinics or punish children who have committed no real crime. And you could stop creating a false Paradise for the Red Cross – let the commissioners see our wonderful camp with their own eyes.'

Lisa listened to his raucous laugh. He was a moment away from strangling her.

'Baroness, the Red Cross would still believe in the fable of Theresienstadt. It's useless for you to intervene. Come, admit your defeat and spend one night with me here, among the horses. We'll have our own little manger, far from the Red Cross.'

Lisa's own laugh was now as raucous as his. 'It would be a catastrophe, darling. If you touched me once, I might break... Joachim, you shouldn't have brought Erik to Theresienstadt.'

'I had nothing to do with it,' he pleaded. 'It was U.S. naval intelligence. They want to kidnap Bernhard Beck for their own reasons. It will boost American morale. I'm just the conduit.'

'Stop it,' she said. 'It was your idea. And the Americans were insane enough to buy into your scheme. Do you intend to stamp "U.S. Cavalry" on Bernhard's buttocks?'

'Yes. I would love to brand his hide.'

'You think that holding Erik in your hands will give you some power over me, that you can bargain with his life – Joachim, take another look. I'm already one of your museum pieces. So is Erik.'

And she rode off into the dust with her palomino. Ännchen let out a whooping cry that had its own raw melody. And the commandant had nothing but his prize Arabian mare in the stalls, Lisalein, a strong-blooded horse who tolerated his love and might even have loved him back. But he would get nothing from the baroness. He'd risked his whole career. He'd come to this fortress, far from Berlin, because it was the one place where he might protect a Jewish half-breed. He still meant to vanish with her, woo her right out of the war. He'd even tolerate the idiot girl with the straw hair. He'd adopt Ännchen. They might live near Basel, where his family had a farm. And when he saw her rocking on Nicodemus, in and out of that constant curtain of dust, he realized that Hitler's *Endziel,* his quest to destroy all the Jews and turn their bones and dust into the relics of a ridiculous museum, was only another mirage, another curtain of dust.

THE *FRAU KOMMANDANT* CAME OUT of that curtain as she rode along her 'bridle path' near the battlements. She didn't have the same aura as the commandant. Whenever he rode his Arabian, an SS bugler would give three long bleats on his horn: It was the signal that all streets and lanes had to be cleared of settlers and their traffic of hearses and other carts. The commandant and his white mare could make time stand still; settlers either rushed into the barracks or stood like stone until that bugle sounded again.

But there was no bugler for Nicodemus. The palomino hobbled along, foam in his mouth. He never responded to Lisa's reins. But it didn't really matter to Ännchen, who was high above the ground, as if she had her own moving ladder. She stared at the Catholic church, with its steeple, at the red roofs of the barracks, at the lone circus tent, which swayed in the wind; it had once been filled with benches and bottles of ink dust, but it was now a great hollow, like a tunnel with soft billowing walls. But there was still ink dust all over the place, and Nicodemus started to whinny and sneeze. She held on to his ears. Nico didn't mind. Ännchen was tied to the beautiful baroness with scars on her cheek. Everyone shivered around the baroness. But the baroness never barked at Ännchen. She smelled like tapioca and wet leaves. She smelled like the river and whitewash on a wall. Ännchen could hear her heart beat. Nico went round and round the ramparts. And then all her joy was gone as Nico stopped in front of her barrack. It didn't matter how much she wailed. Nico wouldn't move. The beautiful baroness untied the belt that bound them, and Ännchen slid down from the saddle.

'Darling, you mustn't cry,' the baroness said. 'I'll take you riding again. But I have to lie down.'

Then the baroness allowed her head to drop on Nico's whitey-white mane, and the two of them left the girl standing there and went back into the dust.

On the Battlements

33

THE FIRST TIME ERIK SAW the commandant's Arabian, he dreamt of Motte, Admiral Canaris' white mare. He wondered if the admiral and his mare might be safer at Theresienstadt. This Paradise Ghetto had battlements and walls. It even had a strange new sheriff, who wore the *Ritterkreuz* until he lent it to Lisa.

She kept it discreetly under her commandant's cloak, but the ribbons stuck out of her collar whenever she taught school. What subjects could she teach in a concentration camp that posed as a settlement town? She'd heard stories of how Rosa Luxemburg had gone into the ghetto schools of Scheunenviertel with her very own song. It was about teaching Berlin's poor to read. Lisa had memorized this song, and she sang it to the children.

And away we'll go on the wings of a word.
We are the kind ones even at our cruelest,
We kill the hunter so that you won't have to weep.

Erik worked with the older children, who begged him for tales about America. But he had no American tales. He relied on what he alone could tell, his maneuvers as an Abwehr agent. He didn't reveal one secret, since last year's missions belonged to the dust of ancient history. But the children – boys and girls – were enthralled by his tales of museums, hotels, and department stores, where women dressed as men, where clerks carried bombs in bottles of perfume, where mannequins had messages on their tongues, written in indelible ink...

'Bravo, bravo,' Erik heard from the back of this clandestine classroom. The commandant stood there, clapping his hands. He was all alone, without one Czech bodyguard. The children seemed terrified. Joachim had never bothered to infiltrate their hideouts, their secret dens.

'Children, children,' he said. 'I would like to borrow your professor.'

Erik had to control his rage, or he would have deepened the children's terror, thrown them into a panic. He smiled at them, tousled their hair as he walked from desk to desk, but his mouth was twitching as he exited this hut, hidden behind a pavilion.

He marched with Joachim along a narrow path.

'I'll kill you if you ever come into my classroom again.'

Joachim started to laugh. 'Quite the dedicated teacher... but you shouldn't give our secrets away. Haven't you heard? The Abwehr is now a branch of the SS.'

The commandant talked about Canaris' last days at the *Fuchsbau*, when the SS trampled through his offices on the *Kanal*, frightened his dachshunds, and broke into his safe. 'What wonderful material we found. You're mentioned repeatedly, Herr Kapitän, in the most heroic terms. The Führer cried when he read your dossier.'

The admiral was under an elaborate form of house arrest. He could still ride Motte in the Grunewald, but his Jewish tailors were gone, and his forgers now toiled for the SS. They were the ones who had dreamt up the idea of Jewish currency at Theresienstadt. They struck every coin, printed kronen in different colors and denominations, while the admiral sat in his wrinkled uniform, with old messages in his pockets, bread crumbs swimming in his trouser cuffs. He missed his Cesare 'to the point of madness,' the commandant said. 'He laments that you were thrown out of America. But that's our good fortune.'

'Joachim, you won't survive this little hike. I'll set your ears on fire.'

'What a pity, that. I'm the savior of Theresienstadt. Without me, the camp would close and all the Jews will be sent on a picnic to Auschwitz, including your lovely children... You ought to make certain I don't fall off a parapet. It would be fatal – to everyone.'

'What do you and your *Hunde* want from me?'

Joachim laughed and leapt up onto the battlements and balanced himself on the crumbling walkway.

'You'll wear your *Ritterkreuz* when the Red Cross comes. You'll be our Pied Piper, the great hero who's returned from American soil. And you'll show the Red Cross the model town that our beloved Führer built for the Jewish people.'

'And perpetuate your lies... These settlers will all be gassed, sooner or later.'

Joachim began to purr like a demented cat. 'Come on up, Cesare. Join me. It's quite a view.'

Erik climbed onto the battlements. He could make out the Little Fortress through the mist. The river had begun to boil. The trees resembled raw red giants.

'There's a world of difference between sooner and later. The Third Reich might collapse. It's an excellent gamble. One day we'll find Patton's tanks in our front yard. It's only a matter of time.'

The red giants seemed to move in the mist.

'And if I tattle on you to the Red Cross? If I show them what a farce your resettlement camp is?'

'Cesare,' Joachim said, doing his own little dance on the

battlements, 'the Danes and the Swedes can't help you. They're only functionaries, even with their famous white trucks. They have no machine guns. King Christian will cry to the Danish parliament, and the Führer will have a fit if we throw the Red Cross out on its ass. Perhaps he'll punish me. But he'll get over his lament. Will you? I'll murder the baroness, as much as I love her. And if you don't decide right this minute, I'll pick fifty of your precious children and have them cremated, ten at a time.'

Erik had a sudden bout of vertigo. He could feel himself topple over the battlement, but his fall never seemed to end. He had no magic in this camp, no means out of this dilemma. He was in harness again, an Abwehr agent on his very last mission. He couldn't save the settlers, couldn't save Lisalein, but he could let their hearts beat a little longer. He was like one of the clarinetists at Theresienstadt, tinkering with a broken toy… and that special jazz peculiar to Paradise. Tinkerers didn't have much of a choice.

Café Kavalir

34

LISA WOULD HAVE NO PART in the charade. She wanted the settlers, children and adults alike, to scream their heads off at the Red Cross. But she was overruled by the council of elders. Such royal men didn't want to see their Paradise ruined.

'*Meine Herren*' – she had to shout, since they were a little deaf – 'the Red Cross will go away in their white trucks and think the SS have built a spa for us, a retirement colony and a kindergarten, with a Jewish bank and its dream money, a Jewish police force that doesn't even have the right to police itself.'

And that's when Bernhard Beck began to swagger like a rhinoceros and shove the elders out of the way. He was wearing a cummerbund and one gold earring, as Theresienstadt's cabaret king.

'And what is the alternative, *Liebchen*? If we squeal, the Danes will scribble a few notes in their reports. And they'll dismiss us as the camp's lunatics.'

Lisa rose up on the handle of her cane to rip at Bernard's fat cheek with her fingernails. 'That's for you, darling. You've become a banker with your fortune of kronen. You'd love to swindle the Red Cross.'

Bernhard began to blubber like a child; he was performing for the settlers in his cummerbund. 'She's crazy. She's the commandant's concubine.'

He was waiting for Erik to tap him on the head so he could gather sympathy from the elders. But Erik wouldn't knock his brains out here, in front of the elders.

Bernhard's whole body began to sway. 'The Red Cross doesn't give a fart about us. Its monitors are already in Hitler's pockets.'

'All the more reason to lash out at them, to make them see who we are,' Lisa yelled. 'We should revolt on the morning they arrive.'

'Revolt with what?' asked one of the elders. 'We have no rifles. The SS will slaughter our children.'

They were sitting in the Café Kavalir on the south side of Marktplatz. The café was named after the Kavalir Barracks, where the old, the mad, and the infirm were stored; it was Theresienstadt's own little insane asylum. There were children and young couples at the camp, but most of the settlers were in their seventies. The Nazis had promised them a health spa in Bohemia, where they could have their own bathhouses and villas; they'd paid thousands of reichsmarks for the privilege of reserving a spot at *Theresienbad*. Some had arrived with their chauffeurs and limousines, and were stripped of everything once they entered the gates. They lost their fortunes and their limousines in one stroke. Many had been millionaires; now they were paupers who had to live in a barrack. Half of them became zombies within a week and were locked inside the Kavalir Barracks. The other half managed not to lose their minds.

Several of these former bankers and business tycoons now sat among the elders in their own new asylum, the Café Kavalir. The commandant of Prague had opened his storerooms to help 'beautify' Theresienstadt and stock it with the normal supplies and goods of a Czech town. And so the Café Kavalir had the ersatz coffee and lumpy little cakes that could be found in the canteen at the SS clubhouse across Marktplatz. It had folding chairs and tables that had been manufactured in the settlers' own workshops at Theresienstadt. It had an SS battle flag above the counter and a blackened mirror that turned everyone, Nazi or Jew, into a humpbacked demon.

It was a mirror that appealed to Lisalein, who never tired of staring into it and staring right back at her own torn reflection.

'Rifles aren't everything,' she said. 'We need to draw out these Danish diplomats with their Red Cross armbands. They have to see who and what we really are – settlers in Hell.'

'No,' said Bernhard Beck, caressing the marks on his cheek. 'No, no, no.'

The elders sought out their Abwehr magician, who sat with them, drinking the same bitter coffee.

'Kapitän, tell us what to do.'

Erik also stared into that blackened mirror and smiled at his own humpbacked demon. He'd come to kidnap Bernhard Beck and free Lisalein from this infernal camp, but he couldn't even accomplish that. Lisa wasn't wrong. They had to signal *something* to the Red Cross, to reveal the rotten underbelly of this camp, and disown all the cosmetics – the fanciful kindergarten next to the town square, the schools that were suddenly legalized and encouraged, the brand-new clarinets presented to the camp's musicians…

And what would it serve? If he wasn't careful, those Nazi butchers would rend the population in two and close the camp, as Joachim had said. And that lunatic might even set the children on fire, as he had done to Lisalein.

'We have no choice,' Erik told the elders. 'We must fight for time… We'll help them build their little crèche, we'll perform for the Red Cross, and hope these Danish bureaucrats can see for themselves the little wounds in the web that the Nazis have woven around Theresienstadt.'

They would have to be more accomplished actors than the SS. And yet he could tell from Lisa's ravaged, raging eyes that he'd already lost her. He couldn't go along with her gamble. He understood the ferocious points of the Nazis' play. They had prettified Paradise, shrunk the population by sending some of the Czech settlers to the 'Family Camp' at Auschwitz, where these former settlers could write postcards to their friends and relatives at Theresienstadt about their excellent accommodations, while Erik knew in his gut that everyone in that Family Camp would be murdered a week after the Red Cross landed in Bohemia and left. And still he had to stay quiet.

He sat there with his SS coffee and SS kuchen, and looked out upon the manicured lawns of Marktplatz and the music pavilion that these murderers had built. The town was cluttered with madmen; they couldn't all be warehoused in the Kavalir Barracks. The old women kept their wits, but the ancient millionaires wandered about, mumbling to themselves, and dropped in the narrow streets like flies; children carted them in wheelbarrows to the little morgue outside the walls. This traffic was constant, but the child thieves were cautious around the SS and seldom stole a pocket watch or a pair of shoelaces. It was the SS guards inside the crematorium who kept all the plunder. A single shoelace was worth ten kronen in the camp's crazy currency.

But it was peaceful this afternoon. Erik didn't have to grimace at the squeak of one hearse or wheelbarrow. He could hear a few notes of Brahms from the music pavilion. Having been plucked out of the Jewish Gymnasium at twelve, he'd never mastered the witchcraft of music. He couldn't even carry the simplest tune. But he listened to the Brahms – it was a violin concerto. That much he could tell. The camp's principal orchestra had once played in Prague. Its musicians would have been coveted by every orchestra in Greater Germany

316

had they not been Jewish. The Fat One, Hermann Göring, had tried to steal them away for his own ensemble at Carinhall. But he couldn't sneak them past Himmler's wall of fanatics.

The music wafted into the Café Kavalir. It had its own terrifying enchantment. And for a moment Theresienstadt could have been the Jewish Marienbad. The chess players lingered over a move, prisoners of Brahms. But Lisa wasn't caught in that spell. She paid for the coffee with her kronen. Erik followed her outside the café. She hobbled across the town square to Hauptstrasse, and then wandered up to the very edge of the fortress's inner wall to the Kavalir Barracks, where the feeble and the insane lived and slept, and where several camp artists had their studios in the attic.

He didn't have to help Lisa climb the steps; she maneuvered with her cane. The artists, some of whom belonged in the same mad barrack, murmured the moment they saw her. *'Frau Kommandant,'* they said. She undressed in front of their easels, smoking one of the camp's own rotten cigarettes, smuggled in from Prague. The scars on her body resembled fish scales with a silver glow in the attic light. She never looked at Erik once.

The artists were tenacious. Their hands trembled as they accomplished sketch after sketch of Lisalein with their pathetic sticks of charcoal, which kept breaking, and soon they had to draw her with their own blackened fingers. The barracks' deranged population of old men kept climbing the stairs with their doctors – Theresienstadt was the one institution in the world that had as many doctor prisoners as patients. Some of these doctors were also insane. But one old man disturbed Erik; he had the angelic smile and slightly humped back of Baron von Hecht.

Did ghosts dance on the attic boards? But it wasn't the baron. It was a former surgeon at the Charité Hospital in Berlin. His mouth was thick with foam. He demanded Erik's autograph.

'I collect the signatures of somnambulists,' said this wily surgeon. 'Will you help me, *mein Herr*?'

'Anything,' Erik said. 'What can I do, Herr Professor Doctor?'

'Strangle me... You are the famous strangler, are you not?'

'That was a lifetime ago,' said Erik, and he handed the surgeon back to his own keeper, a much less distinguished doctor, who had never practiced at the Charité.

Later he walked Lisa home to her little attic ward in the first pavilion. She was silent through the whole journey. But she didn't banish Erik from her hospital bed. The furor of their meeting with the elders seemed to have worn off. She was as tender with him as she had ever been, hugged him all night, lay in his arms. He felt like a child, a bit of a fool, who could never crack Lisa's mystery.

He was alone under the blankets when he woke up. Little Sister, the commandant's own bull-necked adjutant, sat near the door with a brutal grin. *He'll kill me one day,* Erik mused, *or I'll have to kill him.* Erik could feel the clutch of silk around his neck. Lisa had returned the *Ritterkreuz*. It sat over his heart like a miniature molten torpedo. Erik wondered if it could leak its own blood onto him.

The Theresienstädter Ensemble

35

T HE ROUTE HAD BEEN PLOTTED weeks in advance; walls were whitewashed, streets and sidewalks scrubbed with soap. The crematorium was closed, the Kavalir Barracks put under lock and key. There were no stragglers or wandering old men. A playhouse with glass walls was constructed by camp carpenters for the children of Theresienstadt, with its own showers and swimming pool. The elders were given top hats to wear. The kitchen workers wore white gloves. A jazz band waited all morning in the music pavilion, the Theresienstadt Swingers, with their borrowed clarinets. Two soccer teams pretended to struggle in front of the pretty house where the SS soldiers and guards lived. In their blazing red-and-blue uniforms, it was hard to tell that the team members were all skin and bones...

It was a sunny morning in June. The fog over Theresienstadt had already lifted. The mountains on the far side of the fortress were wrapped in a slight blue haze. The grasshoppers leapt like lions in the little green patches at the edge of the old seawall near the western barracks. The cicadas chirped in Brunenpark. Children stood on the battlements, making binoculars out of their half-closed fists, and searched the landscape for the Red Cross's telltale white trucks; in their own wild imagination, the trucks meant freedom to them – the same impossible myth had spread from barrack to barrack, that the white trucks would be coming to empty out the entire ghetto and carry the settlers to another Paradise, another Jewish Marienbad, without the SS.

There were no white trucks. A motorcade of black Mercedes limousines passed under the main gate near the railroad tracks, without a single field car or Gestapo bodyguard, just a few SS men on motorbikes. No one wore a uniform among the Red Cross cortege, not even the Czech propaganda minister, or a colonel from the Reich's foreign ministry; with them were five professor doctors, one from the Danish health ministry, two from the Danish Red Cross, one from the German Red Cross, and one from the International Red Cross in Geneva. The five of them looked like brothers out of the very same brood, with thick lips, red noses, and meticulous blue eyes; they all had monocles screwed into their cheeks.

Joachim met them all at the gate; he was also in mufti. There were no Hitler salutes, no clicking of heels. Erik was the only one in uniform, since he had nothing else to wear. His cuffs were frayed; the *Ritterkreuz* dangled from its ribbons. Bernhard Beck had the same costume as he did at the Café Kavalir – his cummerbund and gold earring. He also had a top hat. The five professor doctors fawned over him. He was the hero of *The Cabaret King Comes to Bohemia*. Their whole image of Theresienstadt, this Jewish Paradise in the flatlands outside of Prague, had been nurtured by that film. It was still playing in Copenhagen. And they begged Bernhard to sing 'The Ballad of Mack the Knife.'

He twirled his entire body in front of the five professor doctors, as if he were balancing some invisible object on his cummerbund, and winked at these bureaucrats.

'*Meine Herren,* I've lost my voice. It's terrible, I know. I can't entertain you. But I have prepared a skit with the Theresienstädter Ensemble.'

'Ah, you have your own troupe,' said the Czech propaganda minister.

'Yes, some of the performers are from Berlin.'

'Marvelous,' said the same minister. 'Then we will have Jewish cabaret at Theresienstadt.'

'And Jewish Jazz,' said Colonel Joachim. 'They are rehearsing while we speak.'

'What a delight!' said one of the Danes.

Erik wanted to rip all their eyes out. The whole visit would be another propaganda film, *The Red Cross Comes to Bohemia*. He should have listened to Lisalein and led a revolt. Perhaps it was better, even for the children, to disappear all at once than to burn slowly in Joachim's fire. These *Herren* with all their fancy titles were little better than Nazis in disguise – no, they were simply sons of bitches who had closed their eyes.

But there was a little flea in the ointment of their lives, and they had to maneuver with a bit of caution. The Allies had landed in Normandy, and God knows when Patton would appear out of the mist with his tanks. And so these ministers and bureaucrats crunched their monocles with an air of objectivity, as the elders in their top hats began to lead them along the prescribed route. They passed Kleiner Park, where children were playing on the slides that ghetto carpenters had installed a week ago. These children rushed up to the commandant. 'Uncle Joachim, Uncle Joachim, no more sardines. We've had sardines every day.'

It was a bitter joke. Who had rehearsed them, who had manufactured such a lie? Was it the elders or that maestro, Bernhard Beck? These children had never tasted a sardine at Theresienstadt. Sardines arrived in mysterious packets from Portugal, packets that only the commandant or a ghetto prince could afford.

The delegation marched up Lange Strasse, passing under the

new street signs. The camp had never had legitimate streets – just block numbers and barrack numbers – until last month.

The Danish settlers had been plucked from their barracks and hurled into a little yellow chalet on Rathausgasse, with bunks and lamps and bedspreads. They'd been warned to smile and curtsy to the Red Cross delegation, and they did. These same settlers asked the delegation to thank their own king for his concern about their welfare.

'King Christian is a good king,' they recited, as if glancing at little memory cards. 'You must tell him we are happy here. And he should thank the Führer for building us our own town. We want for nothing at Theresienstadt.'

'Indeed,' said one of the ministers, 'an admirable Jewish town, as far as the eye can see.'

Erik grew more and more morose by the middle of the morning. He felt like Saturn, ready to devour all the sons of man, particularly these sons, with their Red Cross insignias and armbands, and he wanted to pull up the earth of Theresienstadt, swallow the barracks whole, swallow the stones, and bricks, and grass. But he didn't stray from the cortege. These monocle-men had heard of Cesare, the Abwehr magician who went on a rampage in America, slaughtered a hundred state troopers and federal agents – the numbers multiplied with each retelling of the tale. Soon he would be the conqueror of half the nation.

'Herr Cesare,' these fools muttered on their march across the little plain of Theresienstadt, 'isn't it a miracle? A retirement colony away from the war… where Jewish pensioners can contemplate at their leisure, right under the battlements.'

'Miracle,' Erik muttered, and moved to the rear of the little caravan.

They arrived at Marktplatz, where the Jewish jazzmen had

assembled on the platform of the music pavilion. They still didn't have enough breath to tootle on their clarinets with much skill. Their fingers flew all over the keys, but little was accomplished; it was like a chorale of goats bleating into a tin pail.

'Ah,' said the ministers, 'Jewish Jazz.'

'Isn't the Führer generous with his Jews,' remarked the Czech prime minister. 'He allows them their own degenerate music. He won't even judge these conniving children.'

But it wasn't Jewish Jazz. It was raucous, chaotic chatter with its own desperate fury. The tin that resounded off the bandbox touched Erik's heart. It was much closer to the desolation of the camp than the children's ballet performed in an old movie house on Hauptstrasse that had become a concert hall for the Red Cross. The ballet was replete with dancing elves, blond princesses, and little soldiers in black uniforms – a perfect fairy tale for diplomats.

They had a long, dreamy lunch at the 'restaurant' inside Magdeburg Barracks – a storage room had been converted into a dining hall. There were festoons of twisted flowers on the walls and pictures of some imaginary Zion, with a fortress and mountains. The delegation mingled with settlers in the dining hall, drank champagne presented by the Czech propaganda minister – it was the usual piss, and Erik closed his eyes and swallowed that yellow poison.

Joachim kept nudging him. 'Make a toast.'

The Nazis must have been hiding Lisalein, holding her prisoner while the Red Cross was in Theresienstadt, and they might break her bones, but Erik still couldn't toast these monocle-men. It was Bernhard in his cummerbund who rescued him.

Mack the Knife rose up with all his bulk, held out his glass, and said, *Meine Herren,* what a splendid day to have you here, to witness for yourselves and the world what the Führer has done for us.' He started to cry into the blue napkin that he brought to every meal. 'I was starving in Amsterdam. What do the Dutch know about Berlin cabaret? It was Herr Goebbels who begged me to come back to the homeland. "Bernhard," he said, "you will make a film for the Führer, celebrating Theresienstadt. You won't have to wear a costume. You'll play yourself – the Jewish king comes to Bohemia to be near his own people, who are under the protection of the Führer's elite troops. Let the *Engländers* spread their lies. But Winston Churchill never gave a town to the Jews!"'

The diplomats clapped and stamped their feet and licked their champagne like avaricious cats. And in the midst of this furor, Erik whispered in Bernhard's ear, 'Mackie, you make me sick.'

Bernhard whispered right back. 'Cesare, I just saved your stinking life.'

The settlers drank in silence. They realized soon enough that the Red Cross had come with a cotillion of clowns. Nothing could save them now. They had kept their promise. They didn't stop performing for the diplomats. They'd taught the children to sing and dance and do their entrechats. But the whitewashed walls would disappear once the Red Cross left Theresienstadt. The new kindergarten would be crushed. The Danish settlers would be swept back into their old barracks.

The railroad runs to Auschwitz would begin again. Children would have to suck the earth outside their barracks or starve to death. The bazaar on Neue Gasse would stop selling jewelry and clothes. The Café Kavalir would lose its tables and chairs, until one day it would be a room without warmth or light; the chess pieces would be buried in piles of dust. Circus tents would reappear in Marktplatz; children and old men would have to labor in the little factories under the tents, collecting ink dust and old rusty nails. These collectors would suffer from coughing fits and spasms after a month, as the ink dust landed in their lungs, and the Nazis would have to scamper for fresh recruits.

The settlers drank that Czech champagne and were relieved once the cotillion of clowns vanished from the dining hall and left them in peace. But the commandant's helpmates didn't allow them to sit for very long. They had to follow the cotillion to the café, where that gangster, Bernhard Beck, would be performing with the Theresienstädter Ensemble. They distrusted him, but at least Bernhard was *their* gangster, even if he collaborated with the SS and had bundles of kronen in every pocket. The Berliners among them had grown up with cabaret. And the others knew about the myth of Mackie Messer. They had photos of him at the Adlon. The gangster had once performed with Charlie Chaplin. He'd been engaged to Paulette Goddard for a week. Dietrich had adored him. No one could resist the king of cabaret.

The Café Kavalir had never held more than a few hundred souls. But it was packed with a thousand today; it felt as if half the camp had come to hear Mackie sing in that miserable broken voice of his. There were settlers outside, cluttering the sidewalks like a band of ghetto mice. Erik couldn't even count the faces in the café windows. They looked worn and grim from his perch inside the Kavalir; they could have been spectral creatures, citizens of the night. And then a sudden path ripped right through the Kavalir, and a deep murmur, as the commandant elbowed his way to the platform where Bernhard stood alone. With him was Lisalein. The settlers gaped at her.

'The baroness, the baroness.'

She wore a black sheath under the commandant's cape, with a doll's powder on her cheeks, her lipstick like a raw red wound. She must have made some pact with the commandant, a promise that she wouldn't scream at the diplomats. He wanted her there to watch a command performance by the Theresienstädter Ensemble for these royals of the Red Cross. But the ensemble was Bernard himself. He had no fellow actors or cohorts.

He stood on a tiny platform like some circus animal destined for a balancing act. But Bernard had no balloons on his nose. His cummerbund was his only costume. He made no introductory remarks. He didn't even thank the commandant. He launched right into his act – it was his own special cabaret, without music or words. The maestro would sing with his haunted face.

Erik started to shiver. He sensed that something was wrong. But he couldn't shout, *Mackie, stop... before it's too late.* Who would have listened? No one at Theresienstadt would have dared interrupt the maestro, not even the Nazis themselves. Erik would have been dragged out of the café by his hair, would have been scalped. So he watched Bernhard Beck.

If the maestro couldn't sing, he could still hum. He was his very own violin, but with wicked strings. He was humming a kind of madcap syncopated Brahms, while the expressions on his face shifted like some diabolic engine – first he was the Führer, in the midst of a speech, ogling Nazis, Jews, and diplomats in the café with that signature scowl of his, a plaintive look that could chill a man's bones; Bernhard's swollen body began to shrink. Hunkering down, he'd reduced himself to Hitler's height, which only increased the menace. Erik saw a woman swoon; others turned away, or held a hand over their eyes, and muttered, 'The Führer has come to Theresienstadt.'

The diplomats didn't know what to think, so they nervously clapped their hands, while the Berlin Jews whispered, '*Wunderbar*,' and the maestro wiped away the Führer with one twist of his jowls and suddenly had a long, lugubrious face; he sucked in half of himself, grew tall and thin, until the crowd began to laugh and cry. 'Herr Cesare,' they moaned.

Again the diplomats started to clap. Even Joachim laughed. Then Bernhard barreled out again, and he was Winston Churchill, lumbering along the tiny platform, pretending to bite into a fat cigar. The maestro was warming up; these were only curtain raisers at the Kavalir. Now he went into a whole skit. It was obvious from the subtle maneuvers of his body that the maestro was acting out the Red Cross's royal visit to Theresienstadt. He squatted with an imaginary helmet over his eyes and clutched invisible handlebars; the maestro was an SS man on a motorbike, part of the Red Cross cortege. The image struck an immediate nerve, since the SS went nowhere in Theresienstadt without their motorbikes. Then Bernhard imitated all the monocle-men with their smug, owlish looks as they strutted about the camp, or lapped up their champagne.

The diplomats were no longer amused. But they were trapped inside the Kavalir, caught in that crush of people. And that's when Erik saw the hint of a smile on Lisa's powdered face. Bernhard hadn't plotted alone. He must have made peace with the baroness. She was his unsung partner in the Theresienstädter Ensemble. She'd staged that flare-up among the elders, had scratched Bernhard's cheek as the very first scene of their little sketch.

But Erik had misunderstood Bernhard's genius. He hadn't come here to mock the diplomats and reveal the travesty of their visit. He was after something else. And now he loomed over the entire audience, his body like a menacing snake. That swollen creature could only have been the Jews themselves, these settlers in Paradise, who would swallow up the SS, with all their barracks, moats, and battlements, and disgorge them into that tiny sea outside the walls.

It wasn't a fanciful wish. Perhaps it was only a cabaret king who could understand that as multiple and protean as he might have been, he was still only a prisoner of his audience, their faint reflection. Theresienstadt was a Nazi cabaret. And it took an illusionist like Erik to comprehend its lines and lineaments. He'd never really won on his missions to Paris or Madrid; he'd entwined himself with other actors, and he was as much of a ghost as his victims. The SS could murder everyone in this camp, children and demented millionaires, and they themselves would fade into the reflections of those they had killed.

Of course the commandant believed none of this. He clapped the loudest when Bernhard's skit was done, but there was no human connection in his eyes, not even anger. The SS emptied half the café and shoved settlers from the sidewalks so that the diplomats could march to their black limousines. Then Joachim returned to the Kavalir with his own cadre of SS. He had that same mad disconnection in his eyes. There were no roundups or arrests. He moved from elder to elder and crushed the top hats on their heads. And while Joachim was in the midst of his own whirlwind, the maestro startled the café; like some capricious, wanton child, he burst into song. His voice hadn't really betrayed him. He was Bernhard Beck of old Berlin, back at the Tingel-Tangel Club, where he first began. His eyes lit and bulged with the witchcraft of cabaret. He was no longer in the commandant's kindergarten. He hopped off the platform and began to strut, his body winding like an unbreakable machine, while he reached into his pockets and flung all the kronen he'd collected at Joachim's lackeys.

I'm Mack the Kike, my dears,
I run this camp ragged
And should a man complain
I sing out an old song
Send him to Paradise
And should a man complain
Send him to Paradise

The commandant seized Bernhard's fist with its kronen, then he seized Bernhard, slapped him, and beat on his brains with a rifle butt. And when Erik tried to intervene, the SS created a wall around their commandant. He still would have rushed them if Lisa hadn't held his hand.

'Darling,' she whispered, a deep melancholy on her scarred face, 'you mustn't meddle.'

And while the café watched, the commandant kicked and kicked Bernhard. The cabaret king never moaned or cried, but his fingers twitched inside their velvet gloves; his cummerbund heaved, and then he lay still.

Pola Negri

36

No one knew if the cabaret king was alive or dead. He hadn't been carted to the crematorium in one of the hearses. He simply disappeared from Theresienstadt. The elders assumed he had been whisked across the aqueduct to the Little Fortress and would never be seen again. The baroness was as much of a mystery. She no longer appeared on the streets of Paradise, no longer visited the 'lepers' ward,' no longer sat on her palomino, with one of her half-wits tied to the saddle.

Lisa couldn't get out of her hospital bed; her bones seemed about to shatter; her skin resembled slices of bark. Little Sister would bring her food, with messages from the commandant and flowers from his private garden. She tore up the messages and swallowed each flower like some cannibal. And when Joachim's adjutant came near to button her nightdress, she'd attack him with her fork.

'Little Sister, I'll stab your eye if you come one inch closer.'

He started to sniffle, but he wouldn't invade her private territory. And she'd fall into a dream with her head between her knees. Not about Theresienstadt, or even about Erik or a missing cabaret king, but about her childhood in the Grunewald, her life as a lizard. Lisa was fourteen. She couldn't bear being cooped up in a villa all the time, surrounded by other villas and trees. So she went to afternoon teas at the Adlon, accompanied by her chauffeur, Karl-Oskar, who was a bit of a snob, because his last employer was a bankrupt archduke. He liked to spit disgusting words in her ear, but if she rubbed up against him for five minutes in the baron's Mercedes, Karl-Oskar would leave her alone.

It was 1930, and the Adlon was flooded with Jews and half-Jewish princesses, like herself. It must have been during the winter, because she wore wool stockings and a winter cape. She couldn't have cared a pin about the teas or afternoon tangos in the Rembrandt Room. She liked to stroll in the Adlon's wondrous reception hall, with light streaming on the pink and yellow marble pillars from some invisible window.

Lecherous old men would leer at her. She didn't mind. She would curtsy to them and their mistresses, who had their own suites at the Adlon. There were also young sea captains and commanders and young tycoons, who sent messages to Karl-Oskar, asking for a rendezvous with 'the little courtesan in the cape,' as they liked to call her. But she scoffed at them, which only made them shiver with delight.

And then Karl-Oskar arrived with another note – from Pola Negri, who was in exile after her first talkies. American audiences had tittered at her Polish accent and her interminable kisses on the screen. She was no jazz baby. She could swoon in bed, but her legs were too short to do wild kicks on top of a black piano. Lisa had seen none of Negri's films, but she'd read about her in the *Illustrirte*. And she liked the curious pinch of her handwriting: *Come to me at once. Pola*.

Karl-Oskar escorted Lisa up to Negri's suite, which was in the less fashionable side of the hotel, where piano teachers lived with retired opera singers. There wasn't even a view of Pariser Platz. Negri was wearing a silver bandeau. She was rather plump for a movie star, and Lisa stood next to her like a colossus, rising above Negri's frizzled hair and painted eyelashes.

'Child,' she said, 'you're a criminal.'

And Lisa wanted to laugh. She was already in love with this tiny woman, who seemed so preposterous, so out of place as a vamp. Without her bandeau, she could have been a pretty charwoman on one of the Adlon's lesser floors.

'And why do you call me a criminal, Fräulein?'

'I am Pola, please… I have watched you strut around the hotel, and I didn't even have the courage to introduce myself. You gave me palpitations – a child with the ferocious stance of a leopard or a lion.'

Lisa dismissed Karl-Oskar, sent him downstairs with two hundred marks, while the plump little vamp began to shiver. 'I'm afraid of you, child.'

'As you should be.'

Lisa closed her eyes and flung off her cape. And Negri kissed her everywhere, sobbing and shivering, and playing upon her body as if Lisa were nothing more than a flute with folds of flesh.

Lisa had to bribe Karl-Oskar, who didn't want money, but sexual favors. So she had to tolerate a few minutes of his fumbling, either on the backseat of the Mercedes or in a darkened alcove of the Adlon.

'Are you finished, Karl-Oskar? I couldn't feel a thing.'

'You shouldn't say such awful words,' the chauffeur grumbled. 'I might tell your father where you go every other afternoon.'

'I wish you would, Karl. And while you're at it, tell him who drives me there and begs me for disgusting little treats.'

It was Lisa's first love affair, and she kept a journal, without mentioning Negri by name. But it didn't last. The actress left for England, and scribbled a note. *Auf Wiedersehen, my adorable leopard. Good-bye, good-bye, good-bye.*

And when she returned to the Adlon several years later, she was even less of a movie star. Most of her allure was gone. Her cheeks were puffed out, but it wasn't that. Her eyes weren't in focus, and it seemed as if she no longer cared about the irregular music of Lisa's body. The actress had turned into a trampoline artist who trained in bed. Lisa never saw her again. But the tale had its own unusual twist. After she was brought back from Sachsenhausen forest with burns all over her body, and her father was dead and buried, it was a Gestapo officer who gave her the death certificate while she was convalescing at the Jewish Hospital. She looked under his visor. It was Karl-Oskar, a little sadder perhaps, but with the same lascivious face. He'd demanded a Jewish headstone in the Jewish cemetery at Weissensee. He'd had a service sung, even though it must have been dangerous for him.

'Your father was very kind to me, Frau Lisa. It was the least I could do.'

He clicked his heels and kissed her hand.

'But I wasn't so kind to you, Karl. I teased you all the time.'

'They were the happiest moments in my life,' he said, starting to cry. 'But I am so ashamed. I took advantage of a little girl.'

'Dear Karl, I wasn't so little. I was as tall as I am now. And I'm the one who took advantage of you.'

Kark-Oskar patted his eyes with the fingers of his glove. 'No, no, *gnädige Frau*, but at least we were conspirators.'

He clicked his heels again and walked out of the *Extrastation*, and she lay back in her enormous crib with high rails that kept her from spilling onto the hospital floor. And now she was in another kind of crib, without rails, in another *Extrastation*, a privileged ward that belonged to the SS. She was the only patient in this hospital. She kept a knife and fork under her blanket, and if the commandant sneaked upstairs on the toes of his splendid boots, she would blind him in a minute.

She heard a noise. She gripped her knife. It *was* the commandant. His blouse was filthy, and his plum-colored boots were covered with dust and straw. He hadn't shaved.

'I'll kill you,' she said.

He cackled at her. 'Kill me? Why? I've brought you a friend.'

Ännchen lingered behind the commandant. She was frightened of the knife in Lisa's hand and her face of white bark. She began to blubber. 'Nico,' she said over and over again, and imitated the broken strides of Lisa's half-blind horse. It tore at Lisa to see that stricken child.

'Joachim,' she whispered. 'Take her away. I look like death.'

'Ah,' the commandant said. 'But she can't survive without Nicodemus. And if you aren't nice to me, I'll turn that horse into glue.'

'Take her away. *Please.*'

Joachim shouted for his adjutant. 'You heard milady. Deliver the girl to her barrack. Make sure she isn't harmed.'

Little Sister arrived, utterly out of breath, his uniform unbuttoned. But when he tried to grab Ännchen's hand, she lurched away, ran up to Lisa, and touched that white bark. Then she started to laugh and led Little Sister out of the *Extrastation* in the attic, hobbling like Nicodemus.

Lisa was still clutching the knife. The commandant leaned a little closer to her.

'You shouldn't have conspired with Bernhard Beck. He betrayed us. He was supposed to deliver pure entertainment to the Red Cross.'

'It was pure entertainment,' Lisa said. She was coughing now. She turned away and spat dark phlegm into a little jar.

'I'll send for one of the Jew doctors,' the commandant said. 'He should have a look at your lungs.'

'I don't need a doctor...'

The commandant leaned closer still. 'Baroness, I was impetuous, I admit. But we paid Bernhard to perform. He was the richest man in Theresienstadt. And he made fools of us in front of the Red Cross. I had to punish him.'

'You should have punished me.'

A smile broke under the commandant's blond mustache. 'I did. Do you think I would have kicked him to pieces if you hadn't been there?'

'Idiot,' she told him. 'Bernhard welcomed your boots. It was part of his cabaret.'

The commandant began to brood. 'He could have gone to America with the magician. That was part of the deal. I would have let him out of here.'

How could she penetrate the skull of this murderer with the blond mustache? Bernhard Beck was a woeful man. He could not bear to see his own face in the mirror. He despised himself for having turned Theresienstadt into the Reich's own fairy tale. He should never, never have made that film. It was the only time in his life that the cabaret king had ever betrayed his art. And yet he allowed the cameras into the camp, he performed in front of his own crew, charmed all the men and women from the Ministry of Public Enlightenment and Propaganda, and ended up blaming Theresienstadt, blaming himself. And so he'd become a kind of werewolf, preying on the settlers, feeding off them while he fed on his own thickened flesh. It was Joachim who rescued him from his torment; each kick was a masterpiece, the final measure of Bernhard's show. But he was still one more victim of Paradise...

'Joachim, where did you hide his body?'

'I don't hide bodies. He'll be buried in Berlin as a Yid who martyred himself for the Reich.'

'Then Bernhard will laugh at you from his grave.'

She started to rise from her crib. She didn't need to blind the commandant, or puncture his throat. He was tucked away in his own hell. But she grew dizzy and almost dropped her knife.

'Darling,' she said, 'I hope we sit together through eternity.'

'Where?' he asked, delighted with the idea.

'At your favorite Jewish museum. You will be the central artifact, with your magnificent boots, and perhaps the reins of your horse. If we vanish, darling, so will you. Now get out of my sight.'

'But I'll take you to Berlin, to the Charité. I'll have the best doctors…'

'If you come here again, I'll cut off your prick and hang it with all your other black pennants.'

He stood there, bewildered in his dusty boots. And then he disappeared from the attic.

She must have slept for half an hour. Her tongue was made of lead. Her ears were ringing. She heard blond girls weeping in a closet. She was soothing them, stroking them, arousing the fever in their blood. And then the girls were gone. A pair of boots scraped against the floorboards. She gripped her knife. But it wasn't Joachim. It was her mournful magician.

'Erik, I'm going mad. I can't stop thinking of Berlin. We were all Hitler's helpmates… I chose my submariners. I never saved the youngest children.'

Erik couldn't bear to look at the agony in her eyes.

'Lisa, they couldn't have survived alone in a little closet. They would have whimpered all night… and the Gestapo would have arrested the families who took them in.'

'I saved only the prettiest girls, all blondes – and I made love to them, Erik. I turned some of them into my own whores… I should have carried a whip.'

'Stop it. You did save young children.'

'Never,' she said, with the glare of a chicken hawk.

Erik took the knife out of her hand. 'You stole young children from the SS during the factory raid – fifty of them.'

'That doesn't count,' she said. 'That was bravura. I used them as pawns... the way I use Joachim when he isn't trampling on settlers at the Café Kavalir. Can't you see? I loved you and hated you in your SS uniform. It was the perfect punishment.'

He kissed her crazed eyes, rocked her in his arms. It was his fault. He had played the SS man with Lisa in Berlin, had wanted to bruise her with his silver buttons.

'We have to run,' he said. 'Joachim will skin us alive.'

But Lisa couldn't run. She closed her eyes, slept with her knees against his chest, like someone who had been born out of his sinews and bones. And then she felt herself fall; she landed inside a barrack with poor little Ännchen, who was suddenly a giantess. Lisa didn't recognize a single millionaire or blind woman from the mica factory, or elders and human horses with their hearses. This barrack didn't have one broken toilet or wounded wall. She could have been inside the gallery of an extravagant whorehouse; both men and women were on display – she knew them all; there was Pola Negri in her silver bandeau, and her own father, wearing lipstick and behaving like a whore. But the moment she went up to him, he ran behind a pillar.

'I'm so ashamed,' he said, 'so ashamed.'

But she couldn't even touch his face. Then she saw Bernard Beck smoking a cigarette.

'Mackie,' she whispered, 'are you with the living, or have you crossed over the bridge?'

He, too, was wearing lipstick. 'It makes no difference, darling.'

Ännchen's shoulders began to heave, but she didn't have to whimper. Her voice was clear and crisp. 'I'm frightened, Fräulein Lisa.'

'But we're among friends.'

Ännchen held on to Lisa's hand like a brutal vise. Lisa was all out of breath. Then Pola went up to Lisa and the girl. She had a terrible lust in her eye. She'd grown fat in this bordello.

'Stay with us,' she whispered. But Lisa ran and ran with Ännchen, her fingers crushed in the girl's grip. The barrack had no exits, and she grew weaker and weaker with every step.

Dancing with the Dead

37

SHE WAS UTTERLY MAD IN the morning. Her hawk's glare had returned. Erik couldn't even hold her gaze. He'd sat beside her crib all night.

'*Mensch*,' she said, 'put on your Nazi uniform.'

Erik didn't know how to answer. 'It's falling apart,' he finally said. 'It's a hobo's paradise.'

'Put it on.'

His hands trembled; he buttoned himself into his blouse and dreaded what he saw in the mirror over her bed. His uniform looked like a rotting glove.

'My little magician,' she cooed, 'did you bring your Montblanc? Are you wearing it inside your pants?'

He started to cry like the orphan he had always been. He couldn't lie down with her in that uniform, but he did.

'*Mensch*,' she growled, 'how much will you pay Little Lisa? Do you think you can fuck for free?'

Her cheeks started to quiver, but when he tried to stop the quivering, she slapped his hand away.

'You mustn't touch… What can you pay?'

He was caught in some riddle he couldn't survive. 'In blood or money?' he asked.

She snickered and sat up in bed.

'I don't want your filthy lucre, or your blood. I want your fountain pen.'

He'd lost it at sea, on his voyage to America. He'd carried that Montblanc everywhere, on all his missions, but had misplaced it on board the *Milchkuh* while battling Fränze and her Nazi sailors.

'*Schwester* Lisa,' he said, but she put her hand over his mouth. 'Shhh.'

She never spoke another word. She was as mute as Ännchen, who only warbled in Lisa's dreams. The dead came to visit her. She sat with them at the Café Kavalir. She wasn't uncomfortable around them. They whispered her name. But she couldn't whisper back. There was every sort of freak at Theresienstadt – a Jewish SS man, a Jewish monk, a Jewish nun, who fell afoul of Hitler's racial laws. But they weren't with the dead. They had to wander among the living, scrounge for food, like other settlers. Lisa could hear them wail. She herself was too fatigued to cry. It hurt Lisa to have sounds inside her head. Her skull vibrated like a timpani drum. Her skin had begun to peel. She couldn't drift downstairs to the toilet, like a somnambulist. She had to piss into a pan. The water she passed was blue. She remembered what Rosa Luxemburg had recited to the children of Scheunenviertel: *We kill the hunter so that you won't have to weep.*

Both her eyes were shot with blood. She saw the magician's face, saw him grieve for her. The timpani drum was rattling again with words she'd never announce. She loved him as much as she could ever love a man. He'd followed her right to Theresienstadt. He'd have found her in a sand dune, under an empty well, or inside an attic near Paradise's southern gate…

Erik couldn't even feed her compote from the commandant's own kitchen. She ate nothing at all. Her students weren't allowed inside the pavilion, but Erik sneaked them upstairs to the attic.

They sang to Lisa, showed her their compositions and drawings, but her eyes couldn't seem to focus on the colors or words.

'Baroness,' the children cried, 'we cannot continue our classes without you. You must get better… promise.'

Her skin turned to paper. Erik groomed her, combed her white hair, washed the crust from her eyelids, wet her mouth with a sponge. He was only a secret agent who had willed death on other people. He wanted to move her bed as close as he could to the attic window so she might have a look at the mountains, but she died in transit, midway to the window, with the sunlight on her paper skin.

He carried her out of the attic, her arms dangling at his knees. He had no destination. There was a Jewish cemetery outside the walls, not far from the little delousing station, which was each settler's introduction to Theresienstadt. But Erik wasn't in the mood to bury Lisa or deliver her to the chapel on Südstrasse.

He didn't have much of a journey. The commandant met him on the stairs with his bull-necked adjutant. Both of them were horrified.

'Herr Cesare,' Joachim said, 'I let you have her while she was alive. You will give her to me now.'

He was in his nightshirt and his stockings; his nails had torn through the wool.

'Fool,' he rasped, his shoulders starting to shake. '*I* brought you here, not the Americans. It was my gift to the baroness. She couldn't survive without a glimpse of your gloomy face. So I bargained with those idiots at Norfolk. I gave them some meaningless numbers about the SS in Bohemia, numbers I pulled out of my hat. And I told them all about Mackie Messer. Their admirals knew nothing of Berlin cabaret, or of Beck. But I was counting on Werner Wolfe. "*Wunderbar,*" he said. He was convinced that Mackie would be a star in the United States.'

'Then why, why did you beat the life out of Beck?'

'On a whim,' he said, looking at Lisa's dangling arms while he scratched himself with a toenail. 'It was more than a whim. It was to hurt her, to break her heart, she and her Theresienstädter Ensemble. The admirals at Norfolk will never miss Beck... Now hand her over to me.'

Erik couldn't maneuver on the attic stairs. He tried to lurch past Joachim and his adjutant, but he couldn't hold on to Lisa and attack with his elbows. Little Sister wept into his handkerchief and struck Erik twice with the buckle of his belt. Erik tottered on the stairs, then tumbled past Little Sister and Joachim, tumbled headlong down a winding flight, the banister rails digging into his back, and landed on the bottom stair with plenty of splinters in his scalp and Lisa still in his arms.

The Magician

38

H E DIDN'T KNOW WHY, BUT he went straight to the Magdeburg Barracks like a true somnambulist and had the tailors sew a yellow star onto his SS tunic. They weren't eager to do so. They realized with every stitch that Joachim would blame them. Goyim weren't allowed to parade in yellow stars. Only the king of Denmark had that privilege. And that's because he'd tried to embarrass the SS and also save *his* Jews from the transport trucks. But Erik Holdermann was a German warrior, wearing the uniform of the Death's-Heads. Still, they couldn't refuse this mournful man. They saw the distress in his dark eyes. And they let him escape with a yellow star.

There was pandemonium within five minutes. The SS guards circled around Erik on their motorbikes. Then Little Sister arrived, his countenance raw with rage.

'Herr Magician, this is not how to mourn the baroness. You slander her, I think. You are not a settler, and you are not a Jew.'

There was already an SS man at Theresienstadt who had to wear a star, with Jewish grandparents hiding in his ancestral tree. At first, this SS man was scorned by the settlers. But after a month or so, they took him in. He'd been reared a Catholic, and he remained a Catholic at Theresienstandt. That was the strange democracy of the camp, where Catholics and Lutherans had their own 'synagogue.'

343

But no one had asked Erik to wear a star. He wasn't masquerading as the king of Denmark. Nor was he trying to be a martyr. It comforted Erik, made him feel that Lisa resided in him somewhere.

And Little Sister shouldn't have pounced on him with a cudgel. Erik cracked his windpipe with the flat of his hand. Joachim's adjutant writhed on the ground, his windpipe rattling as he choked to death. The SS guards leapt at Erik with their motorbikes. He swatted them away with his fist; one of the motorbikes landed in a tree. They had never battled anyone who could dance like a dervish with a yellow star. Finally, they were clever enough to hop off their bikes. It took a dozen of them to subdue Erik with their chains and their whips, while half the camp watched from the pavilions and the roofs of their barracks. It was much more satisfying than the show they had put on for the Red Cross, or the time they acted in Bernard Beck's propaganda film. It was the film that had troubled them the most – laughing into the camera like skeletons with leaping, animated bones. They never recovered from that ordeal. They didn't have a Nazi director to urge them on. It was Mackie Messer with his megaphone. He paid them in kronen. They couldn't destroy the bills. Paper was as scarce as sardines.

And now they had a magician who could send motorbikes into a tree. The Czech Jews saw this magician as a man of clay, a golem who had walked out of some dusty attic in Prague and would massacre all the Nazis in Theresienstadt. But they sat like dumb children and couldn't even help while the guards dragged their golem across the ghetto, wrapped in chains.

THESE MURDERERS COULD HAVE HID Erik in one of the underground cells of the Little Fortress, a river away, where none of the settlers would have noticed him, not even from the battlements, but the commandant wanted to make a spectacle of the Abwehr's own somnambulist. And so they threw him into the cellar of the commandant's pavilion, with common thieves and black-market men who forgot to share their profits with the SS. He lived among the cockroaches; lice crawled along his eyebrows. There wasn't a spark of heat from the stones. He had gruel in the morning and gruel at night.

One of the commandant's lackeys would parade him a little after dawn with a rope around his neck. His mind would drift. Suddenly, he was wandering in Scheunenviertel, a motherless child with the raw-boned Jewish prostitutes fanning their summer skirts in that tepid, stillborn air as they manufactured their own breeze.

'Little boy, would you like to peek inside my bloomers? It will cost you a pfennig.'

He remembered – his loins stirred. He blushed. His heart beat like a disconsolate drum as he dreamt of that secret hill under their bloomers.

But the same whores who had taunted him with the cruel mystery of female flesh also sneaked Erik into the Jewish orphanage on the Rosenstrasse. And so he had a little nation of godmothers who couldn't even rescue themselves. How many had been beaten to death by SS officers who didn't find a single one pretty enough or blond enough to save?

Joachim visited him every day, sometimes in his nightshirt, sometimes in his riding boots, sometimes in his bare feet. He always brought a delicacy with him – strudel from a secret shop in Prague – and a pot of coffee made with real chicory.

'Magician, they drink this stuff in New Orleans… Why haven't you tried to strangle me?'

'You'd like it too much, you perverted prick.'

Joachim chortled to himself. He loved Erik's insolence. No one else had been insolent with him in this crumbling fortress town, apart from Lisa herself.

'We're preparing your death warrant, you know. It's not so easy to kill a man with a *Ritterkreuz*. It requires a special stamp. But we have the forgers now, your old chums at the Abwehr. We could stand you under the scaffold in the Little Fortress. But it wouldn't be dignified. You'll get the guillotine. It's coming from Bavaria. There are expenses involved. And you haven't much in the way of kin – just a renegade uncle who was run over by the Gestapo last month in Munich. So we'll charge your execution to the admiral. Canaris will pay dearly for your loss.'

And now Erik did leap off his cot, but he tripped over his chains, and Joachim started to laugh.

'Some magician you are... No one can save you. The admiral hasn't one string left to pull. He's persona non grata at the Chancellery... But it's strange. I envy you. I have Lisa's ashes, but I never had her love.'

'*Schwanz*, it's a powerful aphrodisiac when you set someone on fire after breaking her kneecaps.'

Joachim ripped his strudel in half and shared it with Erik. 'See, you've grown talkative. Now we can have a genuine engagement, a tête-à-tête... Erik, I only did it out of pique. Even while she was burning she spat in my face. But whom will I talk with about Lisa when you're gone? I'll be lonelier than ever. Just say you never loved her, and I'll let you live.'

Joachim had the look of an eager little boy, one who was waiting to tear the wings off a fly. And Erik realized that he could have fueled Joachim's obsession day after day, long after the guillotine arrived, could have played some forlorn Scheherazade, feeding lies rather than fanciful tales to this mad commandant.

'Joachim, come closer, please.'

The same eagerness shone in the commandant's eyes. His cheeks were on fire in this damp cave. He was all flushed with a sudden joy. Erik didn't even bother to strangle him as the commandant crept close. He whispered, his lips grazing the commandant's ear.

'Joachim, I love her more than I ever did.'

The commandant dug his knuckles into his eyes, like a man blinding himself. But he wasn't blind.

'Ingrate, we could have spent a lifetime with her ashes. I exiled myself to this little land of lice to be with Lisa. She couldn't be happy without her Jews – now they'll be your own silent chorus when I chop off your head. But the executioner will never go near you if we don't get rid of your lice.'

The guillotine didn't arrive from one day to the next. Erik wanted to scribble a note to the admiral, but the commandant would have had it delivered to the SS in Berlin. And the Death's-Heads at Himmler's palace on Prinz-Albrecht-Strasse would block out half his sentences with their grease pencils. Erik's note would sound like gibberish. Better nothing, nothing at all.

The lice were all over him. A barber arrived from the delousing station and shaved Erik's armpits, scalp, and groin, but no one bothered with his uniform. And yet when he was paraded across the camp at the end of a rope, like some mangy camel, the children never mocked him. They picked the lice off Erik with their own hands, gave him whatever crusts they had.

And then one morning, the guillotine did come through the gate. A guillotine had never been used at Theresienstadt; there was a great furor among the guards. Erik recognized that little caravan on his morning march. It was the same traveling guillotine he remembered from before the war, when he'd followed the caravan from Kiel to Berlin. And the executioners were the same – Hansel and Gretel, former kindergarten teachers who had joined the SS. But they weren't as blond as they had once been. They wore goggles now and little caps, and their uniforms were almost as worn as Erik's. They had also recognized him, and their blue eyes moistened with grief the moment they guessed why they had come to Theresienstadt. How weary they must have been, how disconsolate, rushing from execution to execution in a time of war. They must have wished for their kindergarten again while they were with the caravan. The executions had multiplied year after year; they were lopping off the heads of lawyers who had written anonymous notes, charwomen who had hoarded bags of coal, assorted lunatics, and children who had scribbled the Führer's mustache on a wall.

These executioners weren't permitted to chat with Erik, or even share a cigarette with him. They had lunch in the SS canteen while Erik was stripped naked and given a fresh uniform to wear; even the ribbons of his *Ritterkreuz* had been laundered. Then he was marched out to the long yard in front of the Kavalir Barracks, where the guillotine had been installed. The commandant was waiting with an SS chaplain, who wouldn't even look at Erik. With them were Hansel and Gretel. Joachim read out some rigmarole about Erik's crimes against the Reich, and Erik had to sign the paper. Some of the mad millionaires from the Kavalir Barracks stood near the door with their keepers. They wrung their hands and cried.

The commandant shouted at them, and they all ran back into the building. But there were children on the roofs of other barracks, children on the ramparts, holding white banners and flags they must have made out of material from the secondhand shop on Neue Gasse. They were mourning Erik while he was still alive, and the flags must have been like funeral shrouds.

Joachim started to dance about in his boots. 'Magician, look, you have your audience of Jews. Would you like to say a few words? It's the last audience you'll ever have.'

Erik walked toward the guillotine with Hansel and Gretel, who whispered in his ear.

'We were so proud of your exploits, Kapitän Erik. And we were the ones who brought you to Berlin. But don't worry. We oiled the machine. It slides like butter. You won't feel a thing.'

They didn't tie his hands or give him a hood to wear. Erik gazed at the children on the ramparts, who were as fierce as an SS commandant. The children held him with their eyes, as if they could lift him out of the guillotine's cradle, right into Paradise. He could *feel* the glint of the blade in the sun, hear it rattle, and suddenly he was back in Berlin. He saw nothing but rubble and Nazi flags on the Linden. He crossed the Palace Bridge with its stone angels and gods, and marched into Mitte. The *Kanal* was gray and grim; he saw the jagged edge of an angel's wing bobbing in the Spree, as if one of the statues had crumbled off the bridge and into the brackish water.

He walked on the bitter, brutal plains of Alexanderplatz; the streetcar tracks were all awry, like twisted rails from some lost carnival. The only traffic he could find were stray dogs and women wheeling baby carriages piled with belongings – chairs, vanity tables, fur coats – until the carriages grew into tottering towers, under all the little rutted stones of the Alex.

Everything seemed desolate and strange in Alt-Berlin. He ventured into Scheunenviertel but lost his way. Erik couldn't even find the Dragonerstrasse, or the old fire-torn synagogues, or that street off the Alex where the Jewish prostitutes had plied their trade. He saw rubble, abandoned buildings, but not one child.

Scheisse, he thought to himself. *Scheunenviertel still belongs to the Jews.*

The bakeries were gone, the clothing shops, the stalls, the poets' societies and fiddlers' unions, all that bittersweet commotion and melody of strife. And in their place was a kind of morgue. But he did catch a faint tootling from a cellar somewhere.

My God, he muttered. *Jewish Jazz.*

He found that cellar near the Rosenthaler Strasse – it was a nightclub without a name, in Alt-Berlin. There was no one to guard the door. He went down the stairs and plunged into the dark. And his heart beat with a crazy delight. He'd come home. All the whores from Alexanderplatz were inside, with their summer blouses and silver earrings. There were a few clarinetists and a fiddler. The whores didn't need clients. They danced among themselves.

'Have you seen my Lisa?' he asked like a little boy.

They kissed him and pointed to a woman in the corner with cropped hair and scars on her legs. She wasn't even startled to see him. He must have conjured her out of a magician's dying dream – conjured her and a nameless nightclub in Alt-Berlin. She was wrapped in a white shroud of summer silk and wasn't wearing any shoes. He had his own barefoot baroness in Berlin.

'Darling,' she said, 'why have you kept me waiting?'

'I had to cross a crumbling bridge. The streets made no sense. It was like following an underground river that went nowhere.'

'Nowhere but to me.'

He took her in his arms, danced to the subtle screams of Jewish Jazz, her body caught in the clarinetists' cry, and it didn't matter to Erik what material she was made of – ashes or solid bone. Hansel and Gretel would have to wait. He was never going to leave this club.